D1737272

HAND-ME-DOWNS
THE SECRETS

To Lynda

BY *Joy Shannon Balmer*
-2007-

JOY SHANNON BALMER

Copyright © 2007 by Joy Shannon Blamer

All rights reserved. No part of this book shall be reproduced or transmitted in any form or by any means, electronic, mechanical, magnetic, photographic including photocopying, recording or by any information storage and retrieval system, without prior written permission of the publisher. No patent liability is assumed with respect to the use of the information contained herein. Although every precaution has been taken in the preparation of this book, the publisher and author assume no responsibility for errors or omissions. Neither is any liability assumed for damages resulting from the use of the information contained herein.

This is a work of fiction. Names, characters, places, and incidents either are the product of the author's imagination or are used fictitiously. Any resemblance to actual events or locales or persons, living or dead, is entirely coincidental.

ISBN 0-7414-4194-2

Published by:

INFINITY
PUBLISHING.COM

1094 New DeHaven Street, Suite 100
West Conshohocken, PA 19428-2713
Info@buybooksontheweb.com
www.buybooksontheweb.com
Toll-free (877) BUY BOOK
Local Phone (610) 941-9999
Fax (610) 941-9959

Printed in the United States of America

Printed on Recycled Paper

Published July 2007

Hand-Me-Downs, the Secrets

Every family closeknit or distant
has its share of hand-me-downs.
Heirlooms, some . . . names and dates
engraved in silver,
pedigrees recorded in photo albums and
Bibles,
in diaries and letters,
on certificates of marriage,
death and military service,
and on tombstones.
Others invisible—rumors, legends, skeletons,
genetic scars chiseled into family memory.
For every child there is an inheritance,
received at coming of age or
inscribed on the newborn soul,
suspended barely under
the surface of awareness.
Each child accepts into its innocence
all of its heritage,
polishes, catalogs,
puts it away behind glass,
paints it with the colors
of its own dreams and delusions,
and dutifully passes it on
to its own children.
Every so often,
an heirloom is dropped
or broken or burned.
Or a child,
from wisdom or from pain,
by fortune or by chance,
refuses to give birth to heirs.

from *Essays for Living*, by B. J. McIntosh

PROLOGUE

Monday afternoon
July 20, 1964
Nortonville, Kentucky

Rita Rossi thumbs two nickels into the middle coin slot and dials the Macon number. A Volkswagen van pulls up to the lone DX gas pump in front of the grocery store, and a boy about Rita's age scrambles out, leaving the engine running.

She can barely make out the yellow-on-black of the van's dust-covered California plates.

"It figures," she mutters. "With that hair, he couldn't be from around here. Geez!"

Three more boys pour out of the van and swarm around the white Mustang parked on the sparse patch of dead grass near the phone booth. Rita feels their grubby hands caressing the convertible's hood, its doors, as surely as if they were touching her own skin.

A honeysuckle voice interrupts the ringing of the phone, all but drowned out by the van: "Deposit one dollar and ten cents for the first three minutes, please."

Rita tries to shove the door of the phone booth closed, but it is dirt-welded into a permanent V-fold. From her collection of coins on the small wooden shelf, she jams in the three quarters, the dimes, and a nickel.

"Rita, is that you? Lord, you've not got in a wreck, have you?"

"Betty? Betty?" Rita presses her palm tighter against her free ear. It makes her voice sound like she's yelling into a bucket. "Look, Kid, I'm coming back."

The van's engine suddenly cuts off, and in the instant silence Rita's voice bounces off the grimy walls. She glares at the boys and they laugh, pushing, shoving one another, waving. The voice in her ear asks, "You're not givin' up so soon, are you? You knew it might take a while to find Emma."

The boys from the van go on into the store.

"But I did, Betty! Not just Emma. I found my grandmother! But she—she yelled at me like a crazy woman!" Rita digs in her purse for a tissue. "One thing, anyway. She gave me this little baby picture of my grandfather. Listen, I gotta go. I'll tell you everything tonight, okay?"

"Wait! What about Emma, then?"

"She's gone. Moved to North Carolina. And crazy too, probably. Even dead, I don't know. I don't even care. Listen, I gotta go. Bye now." She replaces the receiver before Betty can say another word and heads over to the Mustang, fishing the keys from her jeans pocket.

Just as a chorus of male voices bursts through the screen door of the store, Rita shoves the convertible's gearshift into reverse.

Another day she probably would have flirted with the boys, maybe the one who looks a little like Paul McCartney. And she would have laughed at their embarrassed faces when they discovered she's from California, too.

&

Three, four miles south of Nashville the highway curves around through a stand of tall sycamores. The concrete is grayed and cooled, shaded from the dogdays heat. Rita slows the Mustang, pulls off into a wide gravel area where three mailboxes stand guard over a private road that plunges into deep woods.

She unsnaps the front pocket of her purse, pulls out the wrinkled photograph, touches the face in the oval, resists turning it over to check one more time for writing on the other side. She tucks it into the clip on the sunvisor, and studies the baby's face. So familiar . . .

"Oh, geez, it's me! It's my little birthday party face, the picture on Mom's dresser!" The baby grandfather face blurs in front of her teary eyes. "Oh, geez," she whispers. Oh, geez. She wipes her eyes with the back of her hand.

"So, Kid, it's not just you I'm looking for, is it?"

She backs the Mustang into the crunch of the gravel, studies her map for a moment, then pulls out onto the road back to Nashville to catch Highway 40 east to North Carolina.

2

PART ONE

*925 Clarence Darrow dies, a week
after losing the Scopes Trial banning
the teaching of evolution in Tennessee
schools. . . . . . Time Magazine, weekly
news magazine, debuts. . . . . Massive
white-robed Ku Klux Klan march in
Washington D.C. . . . . . Teaching of
evolution prohibited in all Texas schools*

Sunday afternoon
November 9, 1925
Odessa, Texas

Yesterday Daniel Carmody buried his daughter, and today he has
a new son. But today he can deal with one truth only: he must hold
tightly to the threads of his own reasoning, because his wife Gerty is
undeniably coming undone.

"Get it away from me!" Gerty's hoarse, cold orders blast from the
open door of the bedroom and thud against the walls of the cottage.
"No more, I told you! I don't want no more babies!"

Daniel shivers, even though the cookstove in the tiny kitchenette warms both rooms. He is embarrassed at his own rudeness, ignoring the doctor's presence not ten feet away. But none of the words that scream through his mind are polite or sensible enough to say out loud without sounding downright foolish. He wishes the doctor's missus would heed Gerty's demands, if only to give them all a few moments of peace.

With the rumpled sleeve of his day-old shirt, he wipes across the window of the back door and peers out through the smudge at the muddy pond covering most of the patch of yard. The outhouse fades far into the background, shadowed under gathering thunderclouds on this pale Sunday afternoon.

"Let me alone! Get it away from me!"

Gerty's shriek rakes harsh against the place behind Daniel's eyes. He combs his fingers through his disheveled brown hair and kneads the back of his aching neck. He blinks hard, squints, runs his hand over the smooth window glass. For a moment, he could have sworn there were cracks in the window. The back fence appeared warped, distorted.

"He's a beautiful baby, Mrs. Carmody," the doctor's wife pleads. "Just look at him here, so nice and healthy! And you such a little thing, too. But we need to start him to nursing, to start making your milk come in."

The baby's fussing turns to a hungry whimper. Gerty's voice scrapes against Daniel like a rasp. "Daddy! Make them let me alone! Daddy!"

Acid etches Daniel's stomach. He swallows hard to hold back its burning and the shame that brings it on. If Gerty keeps this up, her daddy'll be hearing her all the way to Kentucky.

He is relieved to see that the doctor's back is turned, that he's preoccupied with wiping a clear precise circle on the window glass with his white handkerchief.

"It looks like it might—" The doctor flinches as a burst of white-cold lightning finishes his sentence, turning the room for an instant to stark blacks and silvers. Daniel sucks in a quick breath at the needle of pain in his left temple. Both men search the ceiling as though they expect the thunder to smash through rooftop. Daniel squeezes his eyes shut and leans his head on the glass, grateful for the chill, damp pressure against his face.

"That certainly was a close one," the doctor says.

The doctor's detached kindness has Daniel's salvation these past two days. And the wife is trying to help, too, but he wishes they'd all disappear, that he himself could disappear. Today it would take a considerable effort to think, even if he wanted to.

"I don't want it! Take it out of here!" Gerty's voice rises to a high-pitched screech. In spite of his professional mask, even the doctor's discomfort is obvious. Daniel wishes they would vanish, the doctor, his wife—and yes, even Gerty.

"Go away! Get it away from me!"

Especially Gerty. Mother Mary, just let him be.

"Now, Mrs. Carmody." The voice of the doctor's wife has taken on a whine that fills the cottage with grit. "I know it's been hard, you being so young. I feel real bad about your little girl. But your little boy and this baby are still here, and that sweet husband of yours is heart-broke out yonder."

Daniel winces and slumps into a chair by the wooden kitchen table. "Sorry," he mumbles, not sure for what. He forces himself to look up, hopes the doctor is not looking back at him. The doctor rearranges the folds of his overcoat draped over the back of the faded green living room chair. After a quick nod toward Daniel, a discreet glance at his pocket watch, the doctor turns to the window again.

"Well, we'll see, Missy." The doctor's wife pauses at the bedroom door. "You're going to have to feed this baby sooner or later." She shuts the door firmly behind her and brings the baby out into the front room where the men wait.

Daniel scrambles to his feet, bumping the table, rattling the dirty saucers and cups.

"Would you warm up a cup of that water we boiled," she asks him. "And add a spoonful of sugar, if you will." The doctor's wife tucks the wailing baby into the crook of one elbow while she pulls a clean folded handkerchief from her dress pocket.

Puzzled, Daniel stares, blinks at the cloth she offers him.

She pushes it into his hand. "I didn't see any bottles anywhere. We'll get him to suck some sugar water from the hanky, dear. He will do fine on that for a day . . . or two if he has to." Her frown is obviously aimed at the bedroom door.

Daniel goes to the stove, half listens to the voices behind him.

"I did my best, but I'm afraid I lost my patience with her. It's just not natural for a mother to refuse—"

"No, dear," the doctor interrupts, "but Mrs. Carmody's *life* has not been at all natural this week. She's not herself. I'm sure she'll see it better by morning."

Daniel pours the warm water into a clean cup, turns just in time to hear the woman's whisper, "Well, I think the girl's not quite right in her head!" She paces in small bouncy circles, jiggles the crying baby, whose mouth bobs against the ample front of her dress. She shifts him to her shoulder, offers him her finger to suck, eases herself down onto the couch.

Daniel sets the cup on the arm of the couch next to her, holds out the dripping handkerchief, not sure what to do with it. He will pretend that he didn't hear her remark. To admit it would only force him to acknowledge that he agrees with her. There is something very wrong with Gerty, and this horrible week has clearly changed it for the worse.

"I need to get back to my office," the doctor says, "but my wife will be glad to come back this evening after supper and help out, won't you, dear?" His wife nods, smiles. "She can bring some goat's milk and show you how to feed the little one here if she—if Mrs. Carmody is still not up to it."

Daniel remembers the covered dishes of food left by neighbors after the funeral, tries to remember if he has eaten today, himself.

The doctor's wife dips the handkerchief again and again into the sugary water. The baby quiets down, sucks greedily, complains in breathy squeaks when it is taken away for a few seconds.

"Thank you, Sir," Daniel says, "but I'll not want to be owing you any more. I've held aside the money for the new baby but I didn't plan on the . . . the other."

"Oh, there's no charge for my helping," she says, smiling at the baby now apparently content to suck his fist. "I'm not doctoring, just helping out."

"We'll need to finish up the birth certificate here," the doctor says. "I don't suppose . . . " The nod of his gray head indicates the closed bedroom door, behind which Gerty has apparently worn herself out and gone to sleep.

"No." Daniel wants nothing that will waken Gerty and start her off again. He rubs his throbbing forehead and a yawn escapes before he can hold it back. "Sorry."

"It's quite all right, Son. We've all had a long night here, and I doubt if you've slept much lately yourself." With a gentle touch on Daniel's shoulder, the doctor aims him toward the kitchen table.

The doctor sits down, screws the top off his fountain pen and waits. Daniel rubs his eyes to force a few more minutes of attention from them, then looks again at the closed bedroom door. What if it makes Gerty mad? She can be so hard to live with when she's mad. But no, he's been thinking on it all day. He'll do it anyway. He points to the certificate. Keeping his voice low, he says, "Put down for the name, Liam. L-i-a-m."

"I've never heard that name before." The wife's voice comes too brightly into the dimness of the room. She wraps the satisfied baby snugly in a small blanket. Daniel tries to pull a polite response from his mind for her.

The doctor fills in the clumsy moment. "I assume it's a family name, isn't it? Beulah, Mr. Carmody's from Ireland."

Her voice stabs at Daniel's drifting focus. "Is that right? Isn't that nice." She settles the baby into the cradle, fusses with the blanket.

"It's . . . it's for my grandfa'r, uh, grandfather," Daniel says in her general direction. Then back to the doctor: "And for the second name, put Listowel, L-i-s-t-o-w-e-l."

The doctor adds the name, frowns at it and shows it to Daniel. "It's . . . unusual," the doctor says. Daniel nods.

The doctor signs his name, adds the date. "Now then," he says as he stands and collects his pen and the certificate. He pulls a second paper, this one folded, from his shirt pocket. Before Daniel can look, the doctor's big hand reaches over to cover his. "Just put it away in some safe place for now."

As the doctor and his wife put on their coats to leave, Daniel allows himself a polite glance from the doctor's kind face to the wife's pitying smile, to the baby now settled into the cradle . . . the wooden cradle taken down from the attic early this morning. The cradle that he made last year for Odessa.

The paper in his hand demands his attention. He doesn't want to look, but he can't help himself. *Certificate of Death. Odessa Gertrude Carmody, November 7, 1925. Odessa, Texas.* He crumbles onto the couch, covers his face with his hands. His shoulders shake as he tries to keep control. "She was just walking last week, and was never sick before. I don't know what I did wrong! I couldn't wake her up!"

Floral cologne invades his breath. A hand pats his arm, paws at his sleeve. He pulls back from the smothering closeness. "There, there, dear," she says, "it wasn't anything you could help. The Lord wanted the little angel home, so He called her—"

"Beulah, let's leave Mr. Carmody to his privacy."

She stands and smoothes her coat, picks up her purse, pauses to stoop by the cradle and tuck the blanket one more needless time. "He'll sleep a while, and maybe Mrs. Carmody will feel better, then. I'm sure she will. And you try to get a little nap your own self, dear."

Gerty's loud, even snores rumble through the tiny house. She sleeps, exhausted from her night's labor. Daniel takes the dishpan from its hook on the back wall, pumps water into it and sets it on the stove. He gathers the dirty cups and saucers from the table and piles them into the pan. The clink of glass against glass, the sharp edges of sound stab like shardpricks into his eyes.

She'd have a fit if he told her she snores. He yawns, then squinting hard, he peers out the kitchen door window again. The dark thunderclouds have dissolved into slate, and the rain pours steadily. There'll be no work in the morning, not in this mud. It's strange, so much rain so late in the season. He feels around behind the curtain of the one small shelf that serves as a pantry, pulls out an old bottle of cheap whiskey, holds it up to the dim light from the window. Not much, only a swallow or two left, and when this is gone, there's no more to be bought since the dry law passed. But it will help. He puts the bottle to his lips, but he catches sight of the cradle beyond it, over by the couch. He studies the bottle, sets it back on the shelf.

He stretches his lean body onto the couch, props his head with the jacket left there from last night, and lets the welcome fatigue settle in around his shoulders.

Bobby Ray! He should go next door and check on the boy. Stella will be wondering about them. So good of the neighbors, Stella and Claude, to take the boy yesterday when they all got back from the funeral and found Gerty pacing, her pains close together. And poor Bobby Ray— forlorn, bewildered, at the cemetery. Almost three years old, and never away from Gerty for a whole day or night or from his sister since her birth. In just a minute, he'll go . . . in a minute.

Gerty? His body jerks awake again. He pulls himself up from the couch and pads in his stocking feet to the bedroom door, opens it and peeks in. "Gerty?" She moans, turns toward him, but she doesn't open her eyes. He leans on the doorframe and studies his wife's face. Dark hair that usually bounces in ringlets to her shoulders now hangs limp, sweat-dried, across her face, the face that still looks like the fifteen-year-old he married.

How surprised he was at twenty-five years old, that this impetuous girl so different from himself had picked him out to notice. She had reminded him of Ma, just a little. Before he realized he was going to do it, he kissed her. For a moment he stepped into a picture of Ma and Daddy laughing with the children at their childgames, while smiling, pinching, patting each other in their own playful desire. Even the little ones knew they would soon hear muffled laughter and then moaning from behind the grown-up bedroom door.

As Daniel grew up in Chicago the neighborhood girls flirted, then backed away from him insulted when he misread them. Even the ones who were paid showed their contempt for a man's needs, laughing at their power over him.

But Gerty apparently liked his awkward kiss. She giggled and offered her lips again, and one more time, and her hands touched him in ways that he had thought nice girls didn't know. Daniel's heart, so starved for childhood memories now fading, leapt at the possibility of bringing them real again into his own life. Even before he was sure he had actually asked, Gerty agreed to marry him.

Where has it all gone in four years? He's grown older . . . so much older . . . but Gerty stays the same. When she laughs, the picture of the young girl is there, but now her face reminds him more of a child . . . Bobby Ray . . . Odessa. He has taken on more fatherhood than he expected, while the child inside him still yearns for his own Ma.

Now Gerty's kisses and her grasping hands turn him cold. His needs are trifling to her, after all. Her own appetite is obviously the only one she seeks to satisfy. He gives in to her only when his body's response is more urgent than that of his heart. He goes back to the couch, finds a comfortable position for his body, but his meandering thoughts refuse to settle into sleep.

After the babies came, Gerty doted on the wee ones the best that she was able, he knows. First Bobby Ray, then her favorite, Odessa.

Ma always said a woman in a family way wasn't to go to wakes or funerals. He remembered her saying that, and he made Gerty stay home. Aunt Fiola didn't listen and went to Grandfa'r's wake. Her baby was born dead, just like Ma said. The doctor said it might help Gerty accept the death if she were allowed to go, but in the end he agreed it might bring on her labor.

Then, at home by herself, Gerty's pains started anyway. But the new boy, at least, is alive.

"Wha—" Daniel jolts upright, certain there's been a sound this time. The baby stirs in the cradle, sneezes. The new one—he's named the new one for his own Grandfa'r long dead, but he's not yet even touched the boy, not so much as looked at him, welcomed him. Once again he forces his body from its rest, reaches into the cradle, grunts as pain pushes against the left side of his head. He gathers the yawning baby close to his chest, his wee son Liam, disregarded on his first day of life.

Daniel glances around the room, as though eyes are watching him, then feels foolish for doing so. With babies there are always women, clucking, possessing. Always an Aunt Fiola . . . *now don't you be touching that baby, Danny!*

He wraps his arms around the baby, warm, soft in its innocence and trust, and carries him back to the couch, lies on his side holding the baby in the circle of his arm.

Ma . . . pretty Moira with grinning eyes . . . such a long time ago. Daniel should have stayed. He shouldn't have gone to America when Uncle Seamus sent for him. If he'd stayed, Ma wouldn't have died. He is sure of it. At seven years old, it was an adventure to the moon, going to America. They'd sent him off to a good life, but they didn't know Uncle Seamus. Cruel memory pushes into Daniel's throat with a bitter burning. He wants to crush it down, to never, ever let it come up. But he has to. He deserves to. If he had not left Ireland, Ma and Daddy and the little ones wouldn't have died. He's certain of it.

Odessa. He lets his mind wander to the edge again, ready to pull back when the pain gets too close. Odessa, with Ma's eyes, her pretty little face. A year-long year-short shining reminder of Ma, sent to haunt him.

Gerty had insisted on the name Odessa for the baby, after the little town where the wee girl's life began and where it has ended. He teased that it was a good thing they hadn't settled in Lubbock, a joke that made Gerty giggle, then. Now it thumps hard at the bottom of Daniel's stomach.

A year Odessa stayed, and for a year he looked at her with a mixture of haunting and delight. His mind-picture blurs from Ma to Odessa . . . then to nothing. Gone. Both images are gone, with no picture to keep except in his memory and that already fading. The baby stirs at his side and he studies for the first time the round sleeping face. Warm tears rush to his eyes. No, not gone at all, for in this new face, too, he sees again a promise of Ma. The tears break to the surface, and he holds Liam closer to his chest. How long will she stay with him this time? This time he must have a photograph, an image to carry with him even after the face is gone.

Weariness claims his body at last and he goes to sleep, holding baby Liam safe in the crook of his arm.

At dawn the next day

Gerty lies facing the wall in the early morning stillness. Her body aches. Her mind refuses to return to exhausted sleep, yet dares not come fully awake.

She hides her face from the muted morning light that turns the window to a pale gray square. The rain falls steadily onto the roof; her hazy mind hears rivers gathering, cascading to the ground . . . *shall we gather at the river . . . in Jesus' name . . .*

The sharp cramp in her belly is foreign, not registering any purpose to her. She rolls to her side, pulls her knees to her chest. Her face seeks a hiding place; her thoughts fight to hold onto their fogginess where no reality can intrude . . . *shall we gather at the river . . . I don't want to get saved, Mama . . . I don't want it . . . I baptize you in Jesus' name.*

"Gerty?" Daniel's voice comes nearer, from the place where the strange woman's voice prodded earlier *you must you have to you must.* She draws her face farther into the cocoon of her quilt.

"Gerty." Daniel pulls her shoulder toward him, forces the light of day onto her face.

Her body, its pain, its demands, speak louder than the larger truths she holds one level under the surface. Her breasts, hard and sore, leak their first sticky liquid. Her belly cramps under flabby hanging skin.

She needs to pee—but no, she must've already peed, for she feels the sticky wetness between her thighs. Maybe it's the curse. Where has it been for so long?

She opens her eyes, sees Daniel's face close to hers. She squeezes them tight again, against her woman shame. "Go away," she tells him. "I've got to use the pot."

He tugs at the quilt that she holds to her face, over her tight-squeezed eyes. "Here. Let me help."

"No! I need—get the washpan." After he leaves, she falls back on the pillow in relief. The open door lets in the warmth from the kitchen and the sound of water pumping into the teakettle. But still, she wishes he'd closed it. He brings the washpan, sets it on the seat of the cane-bottom chair beside the bed, hangs a towel over the back, and pads out.

She reaches an arm out into the chilly room, pulls it back into the warmth of the quilt—Mama's quilt, her hasty wedding present.

Oh, Mama, I want you! She looks up, half expects to see Mama, but it's Daniel again, holding a coffee cup, its handle facing her.

"It's how you like it, I'm thinking. Milk, three spoons of sugar?"

She reaches for the coffee with one hand, pulling the quilt tight against her chest with the other.

"Oh, and I forgot. Here's a washrag." He drops the cloth into the washpan. It sinks still folded into the steaming water. He tiptoes out again, pulling the door closed behind him this time.

Later the same morning

Daniel pours himself another cup of coffee and reads the telegram again. The rain blows hard against the front windowpanes, and he nearly misses the soft knock at the door. A peek through the fogged pane, then he motions for Stella to come in, pushes the door closed after her.

Through the glass he can see the rivulets running down the front slope, carrying off the Texas dirt that by November should be traveling as dust in the dry winter wind.

Stella pulls off her wet coat and spreads it over the back of the chair. "I thought I'd dash on over for a second and see how y'all are."

"Stella, I'd be grateful if—" Daniel starts, but he sees he's lost her attention. She kneels beside the cradle, caressing a newborn hand with the tips of her fingers.

Without looking up, she says, "I figured y'all must be all right when I saw the doctor leave yesterday evenin'."

"Gerty's bad off," Daniel says. "The baby's fine, but she's—"

"Gerty?" Stella struggles to her feet, her eyes filled with concern. At Daniel's shushing, her voice drops to a whisper. "Is she—"

"She won't tend the baby, hasn't even asked for him. I've been feeding him like they showed me, but . . . " He rubs his temples, tries to recover the elusive thought.

"One of your headaches?" she whispers.

He nods. "She's cleaning herself up. Maybe if you could help her? She won't let me."

At the bedroom door Stella knocks softly. "Gerty? It's me, Hon. Can I come in?"

Back to Daniel, she says, "Why don't you go on over and have some breakfast with Claude? I just took biscuits out of the oven, and I made plenty of gravy and lots of good strong coffee. You go ahead. Ruby and Bobby Ray were just wakin' up, and the baby's—my baby— is back to sleep. Bobby Ray's been askin' for his mama." She dismisses him with a wave of her hand. "You go on now."

Daniel hesitates, glances at the cradle. She waves him on again. "Now don't you worry. When he wakes up," she says, patting the front of her blouse, "good ol' Aunt Stella can take care of him."

With an obedient nod, Daniel grabs his creased jacket from the couch and steps out onto the porch, waits for an opening in the waterfall that pours from the eaves. He reaches one hand into the cascade and pulls the icy water onto his face, the shock clearing his headache for an instant. He drapes the jacket over his head, darts through the curtain of water out into the downpour, zigzagging to miss the ponds in his sprint to his neighbor's front step.

Noon the same day

Daniel has not yet noticed the rinsed, sun-dried sparkle of the noon sky. His mind is still overcast; his head throbs, but the coffee helps some. He pours two glasses of milk, sets one in front of Bobby Ray, then dishes up two plates of whatever it is that he found in a deep brown dish in the icebox. It smells good—rice, mixed with vegetables, small chunks of meat, he's not sure what. He forks out a bite and tastes it. Mutton, he thinks.

Bobby Ray tastes the milk, but shakes his head at the food, his dark uncombed curls bobbing on his forehead. "Bobby Way want Mama." His pout looks just like Gerty's.

"You sit here and eat your dinner, Son, and I'll see if Mama's sleeping." Daniel gathers the plate, the glass, a fork and a dishtowel. He considers balancing the plate on the full milk glass, but he thinks better of it and leaves the glass for another trip.

"Mama is sleepy, huh?" Bobby Ray asks, his forehead wrinkled into a frown. Then a solemn light of remembering comes to his face. "Dessa is sleepy, Daddy."

Daniel stops at the bedroom door, searches his mind for a simple response, but nothing comes except a hard swallow. He waits, stares unseeing at the plate in his hand before opening the door a crack.

"Gerty?" He takes in a deep breath and steps into the room. He must help her through this, somehow. He must do his best, the priest told him, but he has no idea how to start. He wishes he could ask Father Moreno to talk to Gerty, but he knows she won't hear of it. She had a fit over his calling the little Catholic church in town, but it was the only thing he knew to do.

"Gerty, sit up here and eat some of this, uh . . . this. It'll do you good. Gerty? I know you're awake. Now sit up here and eat."

"I don't want it," she says, her voice still sluggish with sleep, but she sits up, reaches for the plate.

Daniel squats at the side of the bed, smoothes the quilt. "Gerty, I'm real sorry about the funeral, but Ma always said . . . " The panic in her eyes stops him. She looks like a hound puppy swatted on the nose once and ducking the next swat. He didn't mean to plunge in like that. Now look how he's upset her. He tries again, slower this time. "Gerty, Father Moreno is concerned about you, and he told me—"

Gerty grabs the fork and shovels food into her mouth. As she chews and swallows, her face brightens. "Oh, this is real good. Get me some more, Daniel."

"We got a telegram . . . " But before he can bring out the yellow envelope, he hears the scuff of footsteps behind him. Step by careful step, Bobby Ray comes in carrying the big milk glass, pride glistening in his eyes concentrated on the milk. With only a yard of linoleum to cover, with giggles of triumph overtaking him, he dashes the few feet remaining, tripping over Daniel's foot.

Catching an overall strap, Daniel holds the boy upright. But the milk glass thuds against the side of the bed and bounces, flinging milk in a semicircle and leaving the quilt soaked and dripping before it comes to rest empty on the floor.

"Look at what you went and done!" Gerty yells.

Bobby Ray's bottom lip trembles. He tries to pull loose from his father's grip.

"Now don't you start squallin', you hear me?" Gerty reaches out for the boy's hand, but Daniel stands up, gathering the boy in his arms.

"Gerty, he was just wanting to help." Bobby Ray hides his face in the front of Daniel's shirt and hiccups back his crying.

Then a mewing sound comes from the front room, grabbing the attention of both father and son. Bobby Ray wiggles out of Daniel's grasp, points with pudgy finger to the front room, tugs at Daniel's shirt sleeve. "Daddy come see da baby! Come see, hurry!"

Daniel follows the boy. Gerty's sweet, icy voice hits him full in back of his head. "No, Bobby Ray, Sweetie. The baby is dead. Do you hear me? It's dead. The baby is dead."

Daniel can't bear to turn and look at her. With two long strides he is out of the door, slamming it behind them. He drops his son onto the couch, then stands with his fist jammed against his lips, trying to still the burning in his gut.

Bobby Ray slides off the couch and goes over to the cradle. "See, Daddy!" He points, pulls himself up taller. "My baby." Then a puzzle, a doubt, clouds the sparkle in his eyes. He put his hands behind him, and peeks back to the bedroom door. "Her is my baby Daddy, huh?"

"Yes, Son," Daniel says, his whisper belying the tightness in his throat. He stoops to lift the baby from the cradle, sits so the baby is at eye level with Bobby Ray. "He's your new baby brother, Liam."

"Lim," says Bobby Ray, nodding, his soft face solemn and tender. "Daddy? Go get Dessa, come see my baby . . . Lim."

The bedroom door opens and Gerty stands in the doorway with her empty plate in one hand. With the other she clutches the quilt around herself, its milk-soaked border dragging the floor. "I want some more," she says.

With the baby in one arm, Daniel pulls Bobby Ray by the hand and whispers, "Come on, Son, let's go see Aunt Stella."

Stella meets Daniel at the door, takes the baby from him, motions him on in. Her husband Claude pours himself a cup of coffee over at the cookstove.

"Claude, Honey, why don't you bring Daniel a cup of that good hot coffee. I'm sure he could use it." Stella herds Bobby Ray over to the quilt pallet where her own one-year-old Ruby plays near the front window.

Claude brings a cup over, offers it to Daniel, mumbles something. Daniel accepts it, mumbles something back to him. Neither of the two men looks at the other. Stella catches a pleading glance from her husband, yearns to jump into the clumsy void between them.

Claude makes an awkward effort. "So, Dan, that's your new boy there? Gee, uh, like I said before, I'm sorry about . . . " He reaches out clumsily and touches Daniel's shoulder. They both pull back after only a second. Daniel nods, says nothing, slumps onto the couch.

Stella's heart softens for her sweet husband—strong, muscular Claude, who talked with her long into the night about their concerns for Daniel and his family. But now, in the personal closeness of it, he stands childlike. *Men have no idea how to handle things,* Stella thinks.

The baby responds to her nearness. His open mouth presses the front of her cardigan, turns quickly impatient when the gray wool does not satisfy him. His cry brings on her body's familiar response: her breasts tingle with fullness and pressure. There will be plenty for this baby, too, along with her own. "If y'all will mind the big ones a few minutes, I'll take care of this one," she says, stopping at the door of the bedroom where month-old Claude Jr. sleeps.

"Uh, Hon, wait," Claude says, and he hurries over to her. "I need to get over to the worksite and, uh, check to see if everything's okay, you know with the mud and all." He glances back at Daniel. "I mean, if you can handle . . . " He nods in the direction of the children on the pallet.

She reaches to caress his cheek, to assure him that she understands. Later he'll apologize, and it'll be all right. Before he opens the door, Claude turns to Daniel, then in obvious relief that Daniel is not looking after him, he blows his wife a kiss and hurries out.

Stella studies Daniel, his eyes closed, his head leaning back against the wall. She can always tell when he has one of his headaches. There is a deep crease between his eyebrows, and his eyes fight to stay open.

The front room of Claude and Stella's home looks exactly like Daniel and Gerty's—the faded linoleum with roses arranged in circles, the warm cookstove in the kitchenette off to one corner, the identical lumpy couch where Daniel slouches, rubs his eyes and his forehead as though he is trying to erase them. She hopes he can leave behind for a few minutes the dreadful strain that fills his own house, the tenseness that always cuts her own visits shorter than she intends.

After she nurses Daniel's baby and changes his diaper, she tiptoes from the bedroom, tries not to startle Daniel from his dozing, but when she picks up his empty coffee cup from the arm of the couch, he is instantly awake.

"I squeezed him into the crib with Claude Jr.," she whispers. "They're both so sound asleep, I'm sure they neither one will notice." She takes Daniel's cup over to the cookstove to refill it and brings back a red apple cookie jar. She offers him a peanut butter cookie before she sits in the rocking chair.

"I guess Gerty's still not . . . " She nods toward the bedroom and the sleeping babies. The apple cookie jar in Stella's lap brings Bobby Ray scrambling to her side, and Ruby toddles after him.

Daniel shakes his head, as if he can't find words.

"How long do they last?" she asks.

His shrouded eyes peer back at her. Poor thing. She can almost imagine a fog in front of his face. "Oh, I mean the headaches. Is it still the same one from yesterday?"

He is still for a moment, then he nods. His focus apparently lands on what was hanging in the back of his mind. He pulls the creased yellow envelope from his pocket. "This came last night from Gerty's folks. They're wanting her and Bobby Ray to come back for a visit, after . . . well, I wired them yesterday about . . . about the . . . funeral. They don't even know about this new one yet. I don't know if Gerty told them when it was due." He runs his hand through his uncombed hair. "Her ma wants to come and take her and Bobby Ray back on the train, but I'm thinking I should drive them there myself and leave them for the rest of the winter."

Stella, chewing tiny bites of a cookie, has no answer, but then Daniel hasn't asked for one.

Bobby Ray and Ruby squeal in the sunstream from the window. They chomp into their cookies, and as crumbs dribble down the fronts of their overalls, they laugh at their own silliness.

Daniel sets his coffee cup on the floor, rubs his temples with both hands. "I don't know what to do. I never met her daddy . . . " He shrugs and leaves the rest of the thought unspoken, whatever it was.

Stella rocks quietly for a moment. "You know I'd be glad to help. I've always tried to keep an eye on Gerty. I would've anyway even if you hadn't asked me to." Stella tries to smile for his sake. She's not looking for an acknowledgment. The gratitude in his eyes tells her what she already knows. "But I confess," she says, "I just don't know if it would be everything she needs anymore. She might need more than that now." Stella taps a fingernail on the cookie jar. "When I was over there yesterday, you know? I told her how beautiful the baby is, and you know what she said? She said I had no right to go to the funeral and see her baby when you wouldn't let her go. She thought I was talkin' about Odessa . . . then . . . "

A lump lodges in the back of her throat, but she goes on anyway, hoping her voice won't betray her. "Then not two minutes later, she picks up that bonnet of Odessa's . . . you know that little white one with the pink flowers, and she says, 'She'll need to have this when it quits rainin'."

Stella's voice lowers almost to a whisper. "It sent a chill down my back. I was thinkin' on it all night. Now, this may have pushed her over into a place I don't know what to do with."

She wipes her tears with the tips of her fingers. "I know it's hard for her. I can't accept it myself. I keep expectin' to see that little girl. She was such a sweet little thing, and so smart. I always wondered if she looked like your family. Bobby Ray looks so like Gerty."

The haunted look in Daniel's eyes startles her, and the sudden movement of her hand sends the cookie jar crashing to the floor. She drops to her knees, scurrying to gather the shiny red shards of pottery, as if by grabbing them all up at once she can somehow put the moment back together.

Bobby Ray and Ruby, frantic at the noise and the mess of the cookie jar and the scattered cookies, pucker up to cry. A yelp of one baby, followed by the second one, comes from the bedroom—two baby strangers no doubt surprised at discovering each other's presence. As the clamor of four wailing children fills the two rooms, Stella looks wide-eyed at Daniel, her own tears washing down her cheeks.

Then she giggles.

Still on the floor, she sits back on her heels with both hands over her mouth, staring at the crying children. Her shoulders shake with smothered laughter-crying, and the laughter wins out. The emotions that she's pushed down all day and all night come rushing to her throat in a warped, confused jumble and her hands can't hold them back any longer.

Daniel looks startled at first, then a grin tickles at his lips and a held-in laugh snorts through his nose. He collapses back onto the couch and looks ceilingward, his arms tight against his heaving chest.

She tries to avoid looking at him, but each time their glances meet for an instant, the laughter bursts out again.

Bobby Ray looks frantically around the room. Ruby scrambles to get to her feet, plops back down onto the quilt.

Finally Stella manages to push herself up from the floor. Biting her lips hard together, she runs to retrieve the babies.

When she comes back with a baby in each arm, Daniel's face is turned away from the children, his hand pressed hard over his mouth, his shoulders shaking, a laugh still showing in his eyes.

She gently puts his dark-haired son into his arms and sits back into the rocker with blond Claude Jr., not daring to look Daniel in the eye. Their laughter empties from the room as quickly as it started and with no more logical reason. Daniel lets out a long noisy sigh and sags further back on the couch. The babies settle into familiar arms and yawn as though nothing has happened.

On the pallet Bobby Ray lays his head on the stuffed bear toy, sticks his thumb in his mouth. Ruby finds a stray cookie crumb on the quilt and studies it.

Stella wipes her wet face with a corner of Claude Jr.'s blanket. "Lordy, sometimes when you've done all the cryin' you can do, you just have to do somethin' different."

Daniel sits with his eyes closed, but his face looks curiously at ease, as though maybe the headache has let up some.

Stella feels the soft tears pressing themselves up into her eyes again. "By the way, Daniel, considering how well I know your new son already, isn't it time you introduced us? What is his name to be?"

Daniel holds his baby to his shoulder, copies Stella's rocking chair motion. "Liam. For . . . it's for my grandfather. I probably shouldn't have done it. Gerty more than likely won't like it, but . . . " He shrugs again.

"Well, I like it. And for your grandfather, I mean, that's nice."

Both babies settle back to sleep, and Daniel lays his son on the couch next to him. He glances at Stella but they both look quickly away.

Stella watches Daniel's awkward tenderness as he pats his son, tucks the long tail of the nightgown around his feet. A softness covers the room like a blanket, the warmth and the serenity of it welcome, but the intimacy of it uncomfortable. She'd like to hold the moment in her heart forever, but she can't bear it for another second.

"Do you reckon that's what y'all will be doin', then? Goin' back to Kentucky?"

It appears that he hasn't heard her, but then he yawns a simple nod. She suspects he has just this minute made up his mind what he will do. As he stands up and stretches his arms, the headache lines come back to his face.

"Well, then," she says, "y'all will have a lot to do, so you go on ahead and leave these babies with me."

"Oh, I can't ask you to—"

"Daniel, *you're* not askin'. *I'm* askin'." She bends to press her lips to the top of her baby's head, doesn't look back up at Daniel.

"I at least want a chance to tell these two a proper goodbye, you know? In case they don't come back?"

She doesn't seek his eyes—she can't—but she watches him stoop to ruffle Bobby Ray's hair before he ducks out into the cold afternoon, closing the door behind him.

If only she could keep him here in the serenity of her home—hers and Claude's—and protect him from whatever waits in his own house.

About three weeks later
Mahala, Kentucky

Daniel's boot kicks up a shiny piece of something from the ground. He bends to pick it up, turns it first to one side and then the other. Only his eyes study the glass, searching absently for something more than the glass of an old beer bottle. His mind has roamed back to Texas.

His father-in-law, Will Tucker, heaves the hundred-pound sack of corn meal into the back of the model-T truck, then climbs up and over the tailgate to adjust the load. He takes off his hat and fans his hair, then puts it back on. "Did you find you a pitcher of your Daddy?"

"Huh?" Daniel stares down at the piece of broken glass, then up at Will. "What did you say?"

Will chuckles, sits on the pile of burlap bags. "My daddy used to tell it that this old feller was out in the woods and he run across a broke-off piece of lookin' glass. He sees himself in it, and he says 'Why, lordamercy, I found me a pitcher of my daddy!' He takes it home and hides it under his bedstead, and ever' now and then he takes it out when he thinks nobody's around. One time his old woman sees him, and when he's gone, she goes and gets it out, and she says, 'So this is the ugly old hag he's been runnin' around with!'"

Daniel looks at the piece of glass, frowns, knows he's missed something. "Sorry, I wasn't—"

"Y'see, they'd neither one of 'em ever seen a lookin' glass before that . . . " Will waves it off, stands and rubs his back. "Never mind, Son. You got a lot goin' round in that head of yours."

Daniel tosses the piece of glass up under the store's porch, picks up two buckets, sorghum molasses and honey, and hands them up to Will. He goes back for the calico-print chicken feed sack that looks out of place with the burlap bags already stacked in the truck bed.

Will says. "Hilda's been waitin' for another feedsack like that one. She fancies it'll make up into a pretty shirtwaist, but reckon one wasn't enough." He pulls the sack up into the truck, piles it onto the others. "Leastwise I think I picked out the right one."

Daniel buttons his coat tight against the rising wind. "Gerty's never showed much interest in sewing."

"Her mama's pretty much spoilt Gerty all her life for doin' much of anything." Will grins and wipes sweat from his forehead on his coat sleeve. "But I reckon you got that figured out by now. At least she's gonna learn a lot more cookin'. Looks like Hilda's plannin' on bakin' from here on to Christmas."

They continue to load the supplies onto the truck, with an eye on the snowclouds crowding in. "I was meaning to ask you about something," Daniel remembers. "Is there a place to have a photograph taken around here? And would it be costing an earl's fortune, do you think?"

"Lookin' to get a pitcher of your Daddy?" Will grins, shrugs. "Not in Mahala, Son. We can ask Hilda. She might know about one, maybe over in Owensboro."

"Oh, no, never mind." Daniel interrupts. "I was just thinking of . . . it's nothing." Maybe it's a foolish idea, wanting a picture of the baby. Not anything to bother these folks about. Daniel looks off down the street and frowns. "I need to get back to Texas. My neighbor, Claude—he's the one who got me the job on the rigs with him—he's my foreman, and he said he'd see to it I got my job back if I'm gone just two, three weeks. They're hoping for another one of their wells to come in soon, and he'll need all the help he can get. And he'd rather hire me back than a stranger."

"I was kinda hopin' we could talk you out of goin' back at all."

"But I'm needing to get on back and finish what I started. I was planning on a year or two to save up for a piece of land, but then with Gerty I needed to rent a house, and then the babies, and I got behind buying the Ford. I'll be sending you money, and I'll be back for Gerty if she's . . . as soon as she's up to it."

Will leans an elbow on the cab of the truck. "Now, Dan'l, that's somethin' I can help with, if you'll let me. You know, havin' just the two girls and no sons of my own, my place will be left to Emma and Gerty and their kids, and I ain't farmed any of it since the sawmill finally caught on good. I'd be tickled to give you Gerty's now, and you and me can start a house on it as soon as the ground thaws out enough come spring to dig a foundation."

Now that you're in America, Danny, you're to be like my own son. Daniel shakes his head to push the memory of Uncle Seamus's voice from his mind, then he feels foolish for doing it.

He can feel Will's eyes studying him. "Uh, thank you, Sir, but I can't. I have to make it on my own. It's something I have to—I'm needing to do."

Will cups his gnarled hand on his son-in-law's shoulder. "Son, you're married into this family now, and what's ours *is* your own. Ain't it that way with your family too?"

Daniel steps back from this unaccustomed closeness of the older man. He picks up the last sack, carries it to the truck, tucks it in near the tailgate.

"My family didn't own any land," he says. "Oh, they may have, way back, but the English took most of it and left barely enough for the family to survive. When the potatoes rotted, they lost what was left of even that. We heard that story often enough when I was a boy."

Will points to the crank at the front of the truck and climbs behind the steering wheel. Daniel gives the crank a quick turn and as the engine sparks, he hurries around to jump into the cab.

"Come on, let me take you over and show you somethin'," Will says. As Daniel brushes the first wet clumps of snow from his coat, Will apparently changes his mind. "Well, no, we'd best get on home with this stuff, but tomorrow I'll take you over the hill yonder, the other side of the sawmill. I thought of buildin' Hilda and me a house over there someday, but she says what's the sense in movin' another half a mile more from town and from Emma's place, if I don't aim to farm it anyhow. They's enough land over there, not real big, just thirty-some-odd acres, with a good spring. It'd grow you all the p'taters you're wantin' and a lot more besides. And I ain't never heard of 'em rottin' around these parts."

Daniel stares at him. "Are you telling me your land goes all the way from your place to the sawmill and past?"

" 'Bout eighty acres, in my family since my great-granddaddy. The men in the family all farmed it 'til I come along and fancied myself a lumber man. Well, the sawmill, that was my daddy's idea—he started clearin' the loggin' road back yonder. Then he up and left, and my mama took us all back to Virginy. That's where I grew up and where I found Hilda and married her."

Daniel leans back and closes his eyes as the truck bumps off the highway and bounces its load along the half-mile of gravel that leads to the Tucker place. He's hoping the tightness in his neck is not a sign that a headache is coming on. There's no time for that. There's too much to do, too many decisions to make.

" 'Course if you don't want to farm," Will goes on, "I can use me a good hand at the mill. Gerty, she can keep a good big garden up." Will is silent for a moment.

Is Will waiting for an answer, right now? Daniel wonders. He is relieved when Will goes on. "It'd be good for her. Her mama always did. She never made Gerty help much with it but Gerty, she can learn. I'm satisfied she can."

The truck pulls up near the front porch of the weathered clapboard house. A wisp of smoke curls from the chimney into the slate of the sky. Will jumps out of the truck and pokes his head back inside the window of the cab. "And you think on this, Son." His voice drops low and husky. "I don't have a son to leave the sawmill to, neither."

Listen to your old uncle, Danny, and someday everything you see here will be yours. Daniel wants to trust this obviously good man, so unlike Uncle Seamus, who promised him much, took away more, and then in the end willed everything to other boys more willing to do his bidding. Fourteen-year-old Daniel was left with nothing but the permanent scars on his back and the gold pocket watch he snatched before he set out on his own, as far away from Chicago as he could run.

Many times he came close to pawning the watch, but he always found another way to manage, one more time. The symbol of Uncle Seamus became more a symbol of Daniel's courage and his ability to make it on his own. The watch now rests at the bottom of the small wooden box that holds the paltry few treasures he keeps to himself.

He wants to give in and stay, and he will, he knows it. There's no reason but stubborn pride to refuse. But deep inside him stirs the beginning of a fear he can't name, something with fingers reaching out to wrap itself around his very lifebreath if he gives in. Texas pulls him back, back to where he could forget by himself, at least for a short while.

Late the same afternoon

Gerty sits on a quilt pallet by the big stone fireplace, stacking empty wooden thread spools for Bobby Ray. She makes him wait until all the

spools are stacked, then lets him knock them over. When the spools
scatter, they both squeal.

In the old rocker pulled up by the hearth, Mama holds baby Liam
to her shoulder and pats a loud burp from him. "Well, Lordy, I wager
you feel better after that one!" she says.

Bobby Ray imitates the *bur-r-r-u-p* sound, chuckles at himself.

"It's a shame you never had milk for this 'un," Mama says. "This
canned milk don't set real good, with him so little."

Gerty adds her own imitation of the belch, and Bobby Ray cocks
his head, peers up at her, frowns.

"Well, at least you've still got your girlish figure," Mama goes on.
"I used to be slight like you, too, and your daddy said if I'd nursed
another'n I'd be so flat I'd poke out the back. He said it's a good thing
I put on some weight, so at least there's somethin' up here!"

"Oh, Mama!" Gerty can't imagine Daddy talking like that. She
pulls her fingers down through her long hair, dark like Mama says
hers was at Gerty's age but curlier, more like Daddy's used to be. The
sky is darkening and snowflakes begin to drift into the corners of the
window sill. "Look, Mama!" Gerty says. "Make us snowcream, Mama,
please? please?"

"They said over the radio it's fixin' to snow a good one tonight,
but it'll be late before they's enough. Did y'all have any snow in Texas,
for Bobby Ray to have snowcream?"

Gerty points Bobby Ray's face toward the window. "Look at the
snow, Sweetie! Mama's gonna make us snowcream."

"Well, I hope your daddy and Daniel get on back here in time to
bring in a load of wood while it's still light." Mama holds Liam across
her lap andwraps a crocheted shawl snug around him. "They're goin'
to be hungry when they get here."

Gerty says, "It's just like we're playin'-like with our dollbabies,
Mama, just like me and Wanda Fay used to."

"Well, now, Gerty, I don't reckon it's near the same."

"You never told me what it was like, havin' babies, Mama," Gerty
says. Her tone is accusing.

"Gerty, I never had a chance to tell you much of anything. You
run off with Daniel before we even knew you was sweet on him. And
I wasn't even thinkin' of you marryin' at all . . . I mean, I didn't even
know if you should've. But if you did, then I'd at least have liked
a nice little church weddin' for you, after Emma waited 'til the war
and then run off and . . . " She sniffs and makes a face. "Shewee, this

boy's messed his britches. The didees I wrung out and hung by the cookstove ought to be dry."

While Mama's in the kitchen, Gerty busies herself with stacking the spools. Bobby Ray yawns, puts his head down on the quilt, promptly goes to sleep in his bottom-up position.

When Mama comes back, Gerty says, "Well, I didn't know I was sweet on him neither. Wanda Fay and Myrt, they dared me to get him to kiss me, and I did, and then I did it again a time or two just 'cause I wanted to and it made me feel fluttery all over, and I got to wantin' him to touch me some more." She giggles. "And then I put his hand up on my titty, and I could feel that thing of his gettin' hard up against me and— "

"Gerty! My Lord, I'm not wantin' to hear all this foolishness! It's not proper to tell all that to your mama!"

Gerty quiets down, wonders what's wrong.

"And then," she starts again, "and then he said he was leavin' to work in Texas, and what if we got married, and I thought how Wanda Fay sure would be jealous 'cause she wanted him."

"Well, you worried us sick, you not but fifteen and not . . . well, your daddy's not forgive you yet. But you're a married woman and a mama now, and I'll not have you thinkin' these babies are playpretties you can just put down when you're tired of 'em."

Mama eases herself to her knees, lays Liam on the pallet and unpins his diaper, sticking the pins into the broad front of her print dress. "You're blessed to have got you such a good man, Gerty. You be good to him, you hear me?"

Gerty pouts at her mother's rebuke. "Oh, but Mama, he's so hateful to me. I told you he wouldn't let me go to the funeral."

"Now, Honey, it bein' so close to your time, he was tryin' to be good to you, seems to me like." Mama swaddles the baby snugly in the shawl, braces herself on the side of the rocker to stand up. "If I'd been there, I'd've done the same thing."

"And Mama, he . . . he didn't get the preacher from our church. He went and got the preacher from that church where the Mexicans go. When I told him it hurt my feelin's that he didn't get a preacher from my church, he said he didn't know I even *had* a church." Gerty scoots closer to the fireplace and pulls her favorite yellow sweater tighter around her.

Mama chuckles. The pink-orange of the embers that reflect on Mama's face make it look rounder, smoother. "Well now," she says,

"I about had to take you by the hair of your head to get you to go to meetin' myself. And when you did, y'all girls did a whole lot more gigglin' than prayin'. I can't feature you goin' to preachin' in Texas, with nobody watchin'." Mama turns her backside to the warmth of the fire. As the flames get lower, she backs closer. "Here," she says, "you take this baby, and I'll see if they's a stick or two of wood left."

Gerty can barely see her mother's face in the dimming firelight. Mama hands the baby to her, and in the same motion Gerty puts him down on the quilt.

"Daniel didn't go neither," Gerty says. "I didn't even know *he* had a church. He said somethin' foolish. He said, well, his church holds onto you even if you don't hold onto it." She picks at a loose thread on her sweater. "That didn't make no sense to me."

Mama takes the last big half-log from the woodbox, and tosses it onto the grate, pokes at the coals until the wood begins to catch fire around the edges. Gerty backs away as sparks brighten the room. Mama pulls a long splinter off a piece of kindling, holds one end in the flames until it catches and uses it to light the coal oil lamp on the mantel.

"Daniel's doin' the best he can, Gerty. You're lucky to have got him." Mama grunts as she stoops to pick the baby up from the quilt. She steps over sleeping Bobby Ray, and sits back in the rocker.

Gerty twists her face into a pout. "Well, you don't know how it was, losin' my sweet little dollbaby and then here's this squallin' boy of his, and—" *What's the matter with Mama?*

Mama draws back, lips and shoulders stiff and straight, then she slumps back into her rocking, silent for a long time. She says, "Gerty, you're not the only one to ever lose a baby. Ever'body loses at least one, seems like."

With a splinter of kindling, Gerty pokes at the embers, watches them spark.

Mama goes on, "I lost two babies before Emma. Named them both Emma, too, for my mama. The first one was born dead, and the other one lived nine days. She wasn't big enough, born a month and a half before time. And then after Emma—the third Emma—I lost two more babies before you. One was too soon to know if it was a boy or girl, and the other was a boy, named him Will, lived three days. Then when I labored nearly two days and two nights with you, and you and me both like to have died, the doctor told your daddy he wasn't to try for no more."

Gerty creeps over to the edge of the pallet to a spot beside the rocker at Mama's feet, and she looks for a long time at her mama's face, soft in the firelight. *Why, Mama looks old. How did Mama's face get so old?*

Mama wipes her cheeks with her apron. "I never told you about it. There wasn't any need. They's all buried over in Virginia, before we come back here after my mama and daddy had gone. I thank the Lord to have you and Emma, but I still think about my other babies, near ever' day. Even the little ones I never seen."

The afternoon deepens into early evening, with the eerie hush that happens only when snow is falling. Gerty stares into the embers for a long time, the rocking chair's *squeak squeak squeak* the only sound in the darkening room.

"But, Honey," Mama says, "I do know it was hard on you, with her more'n a year old. I wish y'all had got a picture made of her."

When Baby Liam stirs, she shifts him to her other arm. "Now this one, he looks like his daddy. Bobby Ray has your features, but this one's got a granddaddy and grandma somewhere that don't look a thing like Will and me."

"He's homely."

"Gerty!"

"Well, he is! And that silly name. I never heard of a name Lee-um." Gerty turns and peeks at her mother. "Daniel snuck and did it while he was off with the doctor by himself."

Mama stops rocking and Gerty can feel the straight-on stare on the back of her neck. She finds a wrinkle in the quilt that needs to be smoothed out.

"Gerty, men don't generally speak their feelin's, but don't you go forgettin' he's hurtin' from losin' that baby girl, too. He's a good man, like your daddy. He keeps to himself. Your daddy, he never would talk about it after we lost our babies, but he never was the same."

Gerty fidgets, searches her mind for an answer, any answer, thinks of something. "And Daniel hit me one time. He did it . . . because . . . because he didn't like his supper and . . . and he slapped me."

She turns away from her mother's gaze and goes on, "He's always hittin' me . . . and . . . and—"

The front door bursts open and Daddy staggers in, the hundred-pound flour sack on his shoulder. He holds the door open with his foot. Daniel follows with a burlap sack under each arm, then he kicks the door shut with a thud. The men stomp snow from their boots and carry their loads through to the kitchen.

Bobby Ray sits up, rubbing his sleepy eyes, "Daddy?"

Liam stirs, sucks his lip, and settles back to sleep against his grandmother's bosom.

Back from the kitchen, Daniel nods to his mother-in-law, sitting in the rocker with the baby. "Ma'am."

"You done yourself proud with these two boys, Daniel."

Daniel blushes. He digs a small sack from his coat pocket and drops it into Gerty's lap. "I brought you some horehound sticks, you and Bobby Ray."

Gerty tosses her curls and gives her husband a smile, giggles, hides the little sack in her sweater pocket. "Now Mama, you're just givin' Daniel the big head," she says.

Will rubs his hands together in front of the fire. "Come on," he says to Daniel. "We might as well get that stuff off the truck and into the smokehouse for tonight. The 'coons will be into it by mornin' if the snow lets up. And we need to load up this empty woodbox here before we shuck our coats. That stew on the stove smells awful good."

Mama carries the baby over to the bed, puts him down on the far side near the wall with a long bolster pillow beside him. "As soon as y'all bring me some wood, I'll put in some biscuits to go with it."

Gerty sneaks a piece of horehound candy from her pocket and pops it into her mouth. She answers Daddy's stern look with the smile she knows he likes, the one that shows her dimples. And like always, Daddy grins back and winks at her.

Will and Daniel push out into the wind and pull the heavy door behind them. On the porch, Will grabs Daniel's shoulder, points back toward the door. "Now you think on all of this, Son. I'd hold onto this if I was you. If you leave them boys of yours here and go back to Texas, I'm satisfied that when it comes time, neither one of us'll be able to pry 'em away from that grandma in yonder with a crowbar. She'd be tickled if you left 'em here for her to take over." The playful look on Will's face turns wistful. "And I 'spect Gerty wouldn't fight it none at all," he says.

Daniel cannot meet Will's look. He's ashamed of how tempting it is to unload the burden that weighs on him, to leave his children in Will and Hilda's capable hands and flee to Texas. The moments of relief even as he considers it are delicious and scarce. But no, he must not—cannot allow himself more.

He'll stay. He has to. Once before, he left his duty behind to find a better life for himself, and look what happened.

. . . . . 1926 . . . . . 1st transatlantic telephone
cable . . . . . First flight over North Pole
by Admiral Bird . . . . New heavyweight
champion John Tunney beats Jack Dempsey
1927 . . . . . Lindbergh lands in Paris after
first transatlantic solo flight . . . . .
Fifteen millionth Model T rolls off the line
After retooling, first Model A . . . . .
Babe Ruth makes record
60th home run in season . . . . 1928 . . .
Walt Disney introduces new character,
Mickey Mouse . . . . .

Two and a half years later
June 20, 1928
Mahala, Kentucky

Well, Mama can treat Gerty like the Queen of France if she wants to, Emma thinks, but she's not about to. You'd think her little sister was the only one in the family who ever gave birth. "Mama, there's not any need to pet her just because she's had another baby. She's actin' just like a big baby herself."

"Hush, Emma. Give me that towel and help clean her up. I'm goin' to take this baby out to the kitchen by the stove so his daddy can see him."

Gerty falls back against the wet pillow, panting, her stringy hair soaked with sweat. "Didn't I tell y'all? I knew it was a boy—a big one, didn't I tell you? I didn't want no girl."

"Lord yes, Gerty, you been tellin' us for months. Now, roll on over. You're too heavy for me to pick up. Hold that rag to you a minute, and I'll get another one. Move your hind end, so I can get this quilt out from under you and put down a clean one."

"Now, Emma, I want him called Will." Gerty rolls over onto her side, to the edge of the big feather bed. "You go and tell the doctor, and don't you let Daniel tell him different."

Emma pulls the soiled quilt out and tucks a clean one under Gerty. "Don't worry. Daniel acts like he's tickled to name the baby for Daddy. Mama's out there cleanin' your Little Will up. Roll back this way and let me fix this." She ought to offer to wash Gerty's hair, but she just doesn't feel like—

"Mama!" Gerty screams out. Her body goes rigid. She pulls her knees up hard and clings to the bedpost.

"Hold still, Gerty. Now you quit actin' like such a baby."

Mama rushes back into the bedroom. Gerty lies back, panting. "Mama, it was real bad, just like before!"

Mama pushes back Gerty's hair, wipes her face with a damp towel. "Now, now, Gerty, it's all right. Now hold—"

"No!" Gerty screams out again, this time digging her fingernails into Mama's arm.

"Now, Gerty, put your knees down," Mama says. "Now let go of me. Gerty! Let go!" Gerty screams again, holds on tighter. Emma grabs her hand and tries to pull the fingers away, leaving red scratches on Mama's arm.

"Grab ahold of her feet, Emma."

"Oh, Mama, she's just bein'—"

"Emma!"

Emma pulls one of Gerty's legs out straight, and before she can pull the nightgown down, Gerty pulls her knees up again, and the dark crown of a baby's head pushes its way out. As Gerty screams out again, a perfect miniature face appears, then the tiny body slips out onto the quilt between Gerty's thighs.

"Oh my Lord, Mama," Emma says, "it's another one!"

Gerty slumps back on the bed, at last letting go of Mama's arm. Emma stares, but Mama shoves her aside and reaches over to touch the baby, much smaller than its twin. The doll eyes open, and a kitteny cry comes from the mouth.

Gerty raises her head to look, then grunts as a bloody mass pushes out next to the baby. With a moan she sinks back onto the pillow.

"Reach me the scissors and the string and another clean towel," Mama says. "And go tell Daniel to get Dr. Jessup back here."

Emma squeezes her face up as Mama ties off the cord, cuts it.

"Go on! Scoot! And don't go scarin' Daniel. They'll be all right."

Mama wraps the baby in the towel. "Oh, and tell him we've got us a Little Hilda to go with our Little Will."

Later the same day

"Just a minute, Liam. Let's wait for Granddaddy." Daniel holds his two-and-a-half-year-old son tight as the boy squirms to get down. "You can't be getting down. We're going right back, and you'll be in Will—in your Grandfa'r—Granddaddy's way."

" 'Ossy!" Liam struggles to get down from Daniel's restraining arms. Will heaves the last of the new planks onto the pile and turns with a grin. "Now let's get on back to the house to see them new babies." He slaps Daniel on the shoulder and takes Liam from him, hoisting the boy onto his shoulders.

"Come on, Bobby Ray," Daniel yells over toward the sawdust pile. "Get down from there and come on!" The men start off down the road, leaving Bobby Ray still jumping in the sawdust. "Now Dan'l, you're awful sober for just havin' yourself two new younguns! Gerty's all right, ain't she?"

"I don't know if she is, to tell the truth. She's made such a fuss about not having a girl, and now I don't know how she'll be taking to this new one."

"Why, Son, I'd 'spect she'd be tickled to have a girl. Womenfolk always take to girls, with all them prissy little things they put on 'em."

Daniel keeps his frown, turns to call to Bobby Ray, "Bobby Ray, get down off the sawdust!" Bobby Ray jumps up onto the pile one more time. "Bobby Ray!" Will barks, and Bobby Ray clambers down from the pile and scrambles to catch up with the men.

Will gallops ahead, Liam bouncing on his shoulders, shrieking and squealing, hanging onto his granddaddy's gray hair.

"Dummy," Bobby Ray mutters, trudging along behind Daniel.

"What?" Daniel stops in the road and faces the boy. "What did I hear you say?"

"Liam, he's a dummy."

Daniel squats down on the dusty road and looks his son in the eye. "What a thing to say about your brother." Bobby Ray turns to run away, but Daniel grabs his arm. "Where did you get that?"

Bobby Ray sticks his stubborn little chin out. "Mama said."

Daniel stares down at the road. "Your Mama said that?" He takes in a deep breath and blows it out hard.

Bobby Ray jerks his arm free from Daniel's grasp, yanking him over onto his knees. He runs on down the road toward home.

Will turns back to where Daniel squats in the dust. "Somethin' the matter?" he asks.

Daniel gets up, dusts off his pantlegs. "It's nothing."

Liam pulls at Will's hair, jockeys on his shoulders. "'ossy! 'ossy!"

"I was thinkin'," says Will, "we'd best get on with puttin' up that barn for y'all, so's you can get a milkcow b'fore these two new 'uns is weaned. I hear milk is up to 15 cents a quart."

" 'oss," Liam reminds his granddaddy " 'ossy!"

"Speakin' of that, did you hear about this high-falutin' feller and his wife that come down from *Dee*troit? They was drivin' their big ol' Packard down this very road, when right over yonder this young buck, fifteen, sixteen year old, come runnin' out of the shumake, lookin' all about him ever' which way and near run into the car. This old gent says, 'Now, what in the world are you runnin' from, boy?' He's thinkin' maybe they's bears in them woods, and he's gettin' scared. But the boy runs off hollerin', 'I'm chasin' after my maw! That hateful old woman's tryin' to wean me!' "

" 'ossy!" comes Liam's single-minded urging.

Will stops and waits for Daniel, scratches his head. "Liam, I reckon we better let your daddy alone. He's got a lot on his mind. Let's go see that new brother and sister."

Will trots off down the road with Liam laughing and bouncing on his shoulders.

Daniel walks along behind. It's nothing. He picks up a rock from the dirt road and slams it into the blackberry briars, sending three crows squawking out into the sun.

Nothing.

July 1928
Mahala, Kentucky

"What's the matter with *this* one, Gerty," Emma says, "is that just like *that* one, she's hungry. Her name is Hildy Mae. She's three weeks old and I don't reckon you've called her by it once." Emma is sitting across the wide kitchen table from Gerty, jiggling the fussing girl on her lap. Gerty nurses Little Will, with six-year-old Bobby Ray next to her, watching.

"I was only teasin' about namin' her for me," Mama says from over at the cookstove where she warms canned milk in a pan. "But Daniel was so sweet, he swore he would've done it anyhow. Has he got Liam with him?"

"You know he does, Mama," Emma says.

Mama fills the bottle, pulls the rubber nipple over the top and sprinkles a drop of milk on her wrist. "Here, Bobby Ray, you come get this and give it to your Aunt Emma."

Bobby Ray goes over for the bottle, delivers it to Emma, and puts himself right back as close to his mother as he can get.

"What do you think about this new brother and sister, Bobby Ray?" Emma asks, but the boy ducks behind Gerty.

Mama sets the dishpan over on the washstand to cool down a little. "Your daddy and Daniel built you a real nice big kitchen, Gerty. Let's us all come down here and put up our t'maters this time."

Gerty pouts. "Mama, you like Daniel better'n me."

Emma settles the baby into the crook of her arm and looks hard across the table at her sister. "The way you act it'd be easy to."

"Emma! Shame on you!" Mama wipes the last dish and hangs up the dishtowel. "Gerty's gettin' over a hard birth. You be nice to her."

"It's not any wonder it was hard," Gerty says, "with the *two* of 'em." Her complaint is obviously aimed across the table at the girl baby.

"Gerty," Emma says, "you took a whole day laborin' 'cause Little Will was not so little at all. And it didn't help any that you got so big and heavy yourself. This little girl slipped out easy. I saw her."

"Now, Emma, I told you, let Gerty alone. She's doin' the best she can do."

"Mama, you're all the time taking up for Gerty. Well, I'll not have her blamin' this baby."

Mama carries the dishpan over to the screendoor, backs into it and holds it open with her backside while she tosses the dishwater out into the yard. She wipes the pan dry and hangs it on its peg behind the stove. "Emma, she don't mean nothin' by it. Now you let her alone."

Gerty leans back and yawns, popping her nipple right out of the baby's mouth. Her elbow bumps Bobby Ray. "Sweetie, are you waitin' for a titty too?" She laughs, lays the baby down on the table and pulls her blouse open, showing both her full breasts. "Come on, Sweetie, you can have one, too." She pulls him over against her, buries his face in her breast.

Emma shivers at the look on Gerty's face. It's not *decent*. "Gerty, quit that," she says. "Bobby Ray's . . . it's not proper. Now you cover yourself up."

"Bobby Ray's seen my titties before, ain't you, Sweetie? He likes my titties." She holds one breast with both hands and giggles. "Look how big my titties are gettin', Mama."

Mama wipes her hands on her apron and comes over, yanks the front of Gerty's dress closed and snatches the baby from the table. "Gerty, I told you about this before. The Bible says a woman ought to be proper."

Gerty gets up, stretches her whole body into her noisy yawn. Her hands wander down the unbuttoned front of her dress and one slips inside, massaging, squeezing her breast. "Bobby Ray, Sweetie, you come on in and lay down with me."

"Now Gerty, he's gettin' way too big to need to lay down in the daytime." Mama nudges Bobby Ray toward the door. "You run on out and play, Son. Gerty, you stop babyin' that boy. He's too big." Bobby Ray dawdles at the screendoor.

"But Mama, I want him to lay down with me."

"Go on," Mama says to Bobby Ray and he scampers on out the door and into the yard. "Now, you go get yourself a nap, Gerty."

Emma watches until Gerty has gone off into the front room. She shifts Hildy to her other arm and sits feeding her for a quiet minute or two, rocking.

"Mama, doesn't it worry you at all how Gerty acts with these children?"

"Now Emma, don't start in. Gerty can't help it, with havin' all these babies this close, and with her losin' the other girl. She's never got over that." Hilda tucks the blanket snugly about the baby.

"I'll wager this one looks like Bobby Ray did. And he'll be just as big. Look at Bobby Ray out yonder, six years old but he's bigger than your Wayne, and Wayne more'n two years older. This baby is another Tucker. He'll grow up to be as big as Will—Big Will."

She holds the baby to her shoulder, pats and rubs his back until he burps. "Seems funny, callin' your daddy *Big* Will. He's real proud, your daddy is."

"Mama, listen to me! If you could've, and if my J.D. had come home from the war, you and me both would have been tickled to have had a dozen babies apiece and a year apart, and we'd have loved 'em all the same. And your losin' babies didn't make you act like that to me or Gerty."

Hildy cries. Emma's bouncing her too hard, talking too loud. She drops her voice. "Mama, Gerty's hateful to Liam, and she ruins Bobby Ray so much you'd reckon he's the only one she's got. Why do you reckon Daniel all the time takes Liam with him?"

Emma looks at the front room door. Something deep inside her shivers. She hugs the baby close to her, too tightly; little Hildy lets out a squeaky grunt.

"I know we always had to be careful with Gerty," Emma goes on, "her bein' backward and—"

"Don't you *ever* use that word on Gerty! It would break your daddy's heart to hear you talkin' such."

Little Will's startled face twists up to cry, so Mama paces, carrying him with a bouncy step.

"Well, Daddy can keep on lookin' past it if he wants to, but you know better. And you know I always watched out for her, but she's gettin' worse, and I'll not have her takin' it out on these babies. If she doesn't want this little girl, I'll take her myself."

"Now, you quit it. Whoever heard of a mama not wantin' her baby girl? In no time at all she'll be dressin' this one in little bonnets and dresses, and—"

"Mama, yesterday she looked at this baby—I'd wager that's the first time she ever looked her in the face—and said 'She's a ugly little thing, ain't she?' And more'n once she's said the same kind of thing to Liam, right to his face."

Mama winces but doesn't offer an answer. She turns her face to the window. "I did get her to nurse this time."

"Well, she can't nurse but one of them at a time, so somebody else is always havin' to look after the other one. And you notice which one the *other* one always is."

Emma lays Hildy on the table, rewraps the shawl, reaches for the empty bottle. "I'm goin' on home now, Mama, and I'll just carry her on with me, so you won't have them both to take care of. And I doubt if Gerty will miss this baby any at all."

From the screendoor, she says, "Wayne's over helpin' his granddaddy and Daniel at the mill. I'll come back after I get his dinner and feed my chickens."

Mama nods, sways from one foot to the other with Little Will and gazes out at the garden.

. . . . . 1928 . . . . . Herbert Hoover
wins presidential election over
Catholic Al Smith
—1ˢᵗ time since Civil War, Republicans
take some southern states 1929

. . . . .

Lindbergh baby's body found!
Outraged public demands that
kidnapping be made
a federal crime with death penalty . . .

Almost a year later
June, 1929
Mahala, Kentucky

Daniel leans his straight-back chair up against the oak and yawns in the midday heat. Something cold to drink would taste good right now, but not good enough to pry him from the chair to go get it just yet.

Little Will sits on the pallet spread in the shade close to Daniel's chair, satisfied to play on the quilt.

Hildy, just this week trying out her twiggy legs, is the one to keep an eye on. She wobbles over to Daniel, stumbles against his knee and hangs onto his leg with both arms. He helps her steady herself, then she reaches up to him, waiting, unsmiling, imploring. When she looks at him that way, he has the eerie feeling that she can see right down to some ragged spot in his soul that has never healed. He pulls her up onto his lap, holds her tightly to his chest, stares past her dark head to the woods out beyond the tomato patch. For the few moments that Hildy sits very still he can feel her soft pulse against his chest.

Big Will drags a cane-bottom chair over to join Daniel in the cool shade. "Mighty fine family you got here, Dan'l. Bobby Ray'll be as tall as you in another year or two."

Hildy wiggles out of Daniel's grasp, staggers over to the quilt.

"Where's Liam at?" Big Will asks.

Daniel frowns and looks around. Yes, where is the boy?

Big Will brought over some planks and sawhorses from the saw-mill this morning and set them up for a table. The women spread an oilcloth, and they bring bowls and plates of food out from the kitchen.

Maybe they ought to put a permanent table out here in the shade, Daniel thinks. Daniel and Big Will built a big kitchen like Gerty asked for, with a good-sized window to look out at the children playing. But as far as Daniel can tell, Gerty spends most of her time in the front porch swing, where this afternoon Bobby Ray and his cousin Wayne are swinging high, banging into the rail behind it. The hooks will likely need resetting after this. Daniel has put up new hooks for it twice now, since Gerty put on so much weight.

They did a good job on the house, he and Big Will, with the room for all the children, a smokehouse for salted and cured pork and this spring, the barn. Daniel enjoys working with wood. He's glad he took Big Will up on the job at the sawmill.

It's good to take an afternoon once in a while, just to do nothing. At least he looks for it to be good and plans to do nothing. But before the day's half over, an uneasiness always comes over him, pulling him back to work.

Hilda brought toys for the twins' birthday, but the sock doll can wait for sleepier times. Hildy, up on all-fours like a grasshopper, will be running off again if he doesn't watch her.

Daniel allows his mind to drift back to the time that is harder and harder to keep in focus. "I had baby twin sisters," he says to no one in particular, unless Big Will wants to listen. "They were like two wee peas together. Daddy'd take one up and the other one would cry. Then he'd put that one down and take up the other one. Ma laughed at him trying to figure out how to—"

"Well, least you don't have no problem tellin' these two apart with him twicet her size. She's about the size of a chigger. What does he do, eat his dinner and hers both?"

Odd, but Daniel can't picture the babies, the sisters. Their names —he can't even remember their names!

Hildy has escaped. Daniel starts to get up, but he settles back when he sees that she has made it all the way over to the table, where Emma holds her up to see the cake.

"Look here, Hildy! Look what Mammaw made this morning, Hon, for you and Little Will." Emma laughs across the table at her mother. "Lord, Mama, there's more food here than we all could eat today if we had to—no wait, Hon!"

Before Emma can catch her, Hildy has grabbed a fistful of the birthday cake. Her hand is a mess of sticky seven-minute icing and furry coconut.

"Gerty, get me the rag over yonder, will you?"

Gerty bustles over with the dishrag, throws it down on the table, grabs Hildy's clean hand and slaps her arm hard. The girl turns her tight-squeezed face away, but she makes no sound.

"Gerty, you didn't have to go and do that," Emma says. "She was just doin' what any baby would do."

"She's all the time messin' in somethin'. She's nothin' but a little pig." Gerty stomps back around to the other side of the table.

Daniel tries to turn his attention away. Gerty won't listen to him if he complains to her. Sometimes it seems like she does this to spite him. He hopes Hilda will say something, but she's fussing with the plates of chicken and sliced tomatoes. He leans down and picks up an acorn, looks absently around for its cap, picks up an odd one.

Big Will laughs. "Feisty little thing, ain't she?" Daniel fiddles with the acorn cap, idly twisting it this way and that, as though it will somehow fit the acorn if he can find just the right angle.

Emma brings Hildy back to the quilt under the big oak tree. Her seven-year-old Wayne follows from the table, dodges around to the side where his mother holds Hildy on her hip. He gently touches the baby's arm near the red fingerwelts. She stares at him for a moment, then flashes him a shy smile, hides her face in Emma's sleeve.

Emma says, "Now you two men just look at your boy there." Little Will has crawled off the quilt and sits pulling at an acorn still hanging onto its twig, his bare knees and his diaper matted with dirt and leaves. "It's a good thing he's not walkin' yet," Emma says, "or he'd be down at the spring catchin' crawdads by now."

"Sorry." All this activity around Daniel pulls at him, demands too much from him, exhausts him. He wishes he could creep away into his own mind and close off the door for anybody to follow.

Emma motions to Wayne to sit down on the quilt and sits Hildy down between his outstretched legs. She brushes the dirt off Little Will and plops him back onto the quilt. "Look at the playpretties Mammaw brought you!" When Hildy squirms to get up, Wayne helps her to her feet. She staggers over to take the doll. Little Will ignores the ball and grabs for the doll, too, and Hildy gives it up.

He shakes it by the arm, startled the first time the doll whaps him in the face. But when Hildy squeals, patting her hands, laughing, he tries to do it again. Wayne giggles and scoots closer, rolls the ball to Little Will. Still hanging onto the doll, Little Will smacks the ball and it rolls off the quilt. Hildy teeters after it.

Gerty huffs over to the pallet. "Now, here, you don't want that old dollbaby, Little Will." She snatches the doll from him and shoves it into Hildy's belly hard, pushing her with a thump to the ground. Little Will howls, and Hildy whimpers in Wayne's direction. He creeps closer to her, puts his arm around her shoulders. Gerty grabs the doll from Hildy, hands it to her brother and stomps away muttering, "Selfish little brat."

Big Will shakes his head at Daniel, chuckling. He gets up, drags his chair after him. "Dan'l, that fried chicken looks mighty good. Little Will, you come on here to Granddaddy."

Emma picks up Hildy, and to Daniel she whispers, "I'll keep her with me." With her free arm, she hugs Wayne to her.

Daniel means to speak to Emma, to let her know how much he appreciates this, but can only manage a nod. Hildy's little arms cling to Emma's neck. He can't picture her ever doing that with Gerty.

"Y'all come on to the table now," Hilda calls out.

Daniel takes his time, shoves his chair away from the tree and gets up. He stretches and lets his glance wander over past the garden. Down the hill the saplings line the cleared garden patch. The woods, the trees, the briars, stand ready to take back the land the minute he stops fighting them off.

Gerty drags chairs from the kitchen up to the table. "Bobby Ray, you come on now!" she hollers, looking around. "Now where did he run off to? Daniel, go get us two more chairs from in the house."

Wayne sits next to his mother, holds Hildy while Emma dishes up a small pile of potato salad, then pulls Hildy up onto her lap. "Is Liam asleep, Gerty? I've not seen him for a while."

Daniel waits on the kitchen steps, listens for Gerty's answer.

Gerty waddles around the table, putting plates down, a smug, self-satisfied look on her face. "I had to whup him, and I sent him to bed when he wouldn't quit his squallin'."

Daniel stares down at the steps for a minute, then goes on into the house.

On this stifling day the curtains are all pulled closed in the room where the children sleep. In the dimness, Daniel can barely make out the beds along the one wall.

He squats next to the cot in the corner, where four-year-old Liam lies curled up, facing the wall. "Liam?"

Liam rolls over and in one move is up from the bed, wrapping his arms around Daniel's neck and sobbing against his shoulder.

Daniel sits back onto the floor, pulls Liam down into his lap and rocks him. "It's all right, Son," Daniel promises, but he knows it's a lie. Nothing is all right, and he feels helpless to make it all right.

In the faint light of the room he can see harsh red marks on the boy's legs where a tree limb switch has left its raw stripes. Daniel's boy-memory crowds to the front, counting the marks—muffled at first, but louder, louder, the *swish swish* of the limb . . . his body jerks with each blow . . . *count . . . keep the mind busy . . . Uncle Seamus . . . bigger, bigger . . . his hands grow huge . . . Danny, you belong to me now. You will do as I say!* Danny's body shrinking, shrinking into a corner as Uncle Seamus fills the room.

Sweat drenches Daniel's face, and he knows he must have cried out. He tries to slow his breath, the hammering in his chest. The smothering closeness of the room squeezes him like a vice.

"Daddy?" Liam peers up at him in the near darkness.

Daniel gets to his feet, pulling the boy up, carries him through the front room door, out past the smokehouse and down the hill.

Down by the creek he sets Liam on a big flat rock, pulls a loose stone out from the wall that encloses the spring. He reaches into the hole for the canning jar half filled with homemade corn whiskey, washes the mud off the jar in the running creek and unscrews the lid. He gulps down several swallows of the fiery liquid, waits until he can feel the warmth spreading, numbing his body and his memory.

Only now does he take a long look at his son, sitting on the rock in the cool bright shade, his face puffed and red, his eyes squinting at the light. Daniel takes the dipper from the hook by the spring, fills it with cool water, pours a few drops of whiskey into it and holds the dipper for the boy to drink. Liam sips and makes a face then, looking Daniel straight in the eye, he obediently gulps down the rest.

Daniel meets the boy's gaze for only a second before his shame allows no more. He fills the dipper again, pours in some more of the whiskey. Then he kneels next to his boy, lifts his lean bare foot and props it on his own thigh, trickles the cool water over the fiery red welts on Liam's legs.

Emma feeds potato salad to Hildy, who sits with her mouth open like a baby sparrow. "Here, Hon, look here at Aunt Emma."

With each bite, Emma has to pull Hildy's attention back to the spoon. The little girls eyes never lose sight of Gerty's large form, working around the table, handing out forks and knives. As Gerty's huge shadow crosses Emma's lap, Hildy cowers down, hides her face and refuses the next bite.

"You might as well not try and feed her that," Gerty says. "She won't eat it. She won't eat nothin' unless I slap her and make her. Here, Daddy," she says across the table to Big Will, who holds Little Will on his lap, "take this here plate and—oh, watch out!"

The big bowl of pinto beans and stewed tomatoes spills over Big Will and the boy. Big Will struggles to keep his chair upright. Little Will stares wide-eyed, still hanging onto the edge of the bowl with both chubby hands. Beans, tomatoes and juice drip down the front of him, speckling his face, beading his eyelashes.

"Look, Mama," Gerty says, laughing. "He couldn't wait to get at them good beans of yours."

Hilda rescues Little Will from the mess, takes him down to the end of the table and sits him next to the waterbucket. He grabs the top of the bucket and tries to pull himself up. She manages to get his shirt off, pours a dipperful of water over it, then tries to hold the squirming boy still while she wipes him clean with the wet shirt.

When Big Will reaches over and takes a piece of chicken, Hildy turns toward the movement, her mouth still open.

"Here, Emma," Big Will says, "give that little chigger a chicken leg. That's what she's wantin'." He holds out the drumstick. Hildy grabs it with both her hands, venturing to suck on the end of it. Gerty sits down in the chair across from Emma. Emma narrows her eyes at her sister, daring her to say anything about the chicken.

Big Will finishes off another chicken leg himself and reaches for one more. "Where's Daniel gone to, anyhow?"

"I was wonderin' that too," Emma says, restless, self-conscious at having said it. She looks around, but it doesn't seem like anybody noticed. Her attention shifts to the boys, scuffling at the far end of the table, where Wayne has joined his cousin, closer to the cake.

"Wayne!" Emma yells. "Y'all boys quit foolin' around down there. Take you a piece of cake and get away from the table. And y'all leave a piece for Liam."

Gerty stretches her flabby arms up over her head and yawns. "Oh, don't mess with that. He won't eat it." Emma glares at her sister and decides words would just be wasted on her.

"Well," Mama says from the end of the table, too loud. "We'd best finish up and get this food out of the flies. Y'all boys take your

plates on around to the porch swing and we'll clear the rest off.
Go on, now, shoo!" Big Will snatches up the last chicken wing and
gets up, follows Bobby Ray out of the way of the women's work.
Wayne hangs back, comes around the table and sits on the edge of the
chair next to Emma.

"Don't you want to go with them, Wayne?"

"Bobby Ray's talkin' hateful. I get kinda tired of it."

Emma gives him a little pat on the cheek and half a smile. She
pries the drumstick from Hildy's hands and wipes them with the
dish towel, hands her to Wayne. Then she gathers Little Will and
heads up to the shady pallet under the tree, Wayne following along,
carrying Hildy. Maybe Gerty will help Mama if nobody else does.

Mama gathers up an armload of dishes. Gerty stretches to scoop
the last scraps from the potato salad bowl onto her plate.

On the pallet under the oak Wayne sits between the twins and
tries to interest them in their toys. Hildy is on her feet again.

"Here, Hildy," Wayne says, handing the ball to her. "Throw it
to me." Instead, Hildy merely drops the ball in front of Little Will.
He laughs, and she tries to pick it up again.

Emma watches and can't help smiling. Too bad Wayne never had
brothers and sisters. He's so good with little ones.

"Hildy!" Gerty yells from over at the table. The little girl lowers
her head to her shoulders like a turtle and looks straight ahead. Gerty's
voice rises to a shriek. "Get away from him!" Emma gathers Hildy
over onto her lap, hugs her close to her, but the girl stiffens. "What's
the matter, Hon?" She pulls up Hildy's shirt, uncovering a yellowing
purple bruise on her back. "Gerty, what is this place on Hildy?"

"Oh, quit makin' such a fuss over her," Gerty yells. "It just makes
her worse."

"Mama," Wayne says, "If Aunt Gerty doesn't want Hildy, you
reckon we could have her?"

> . . . . . *1929* . . . . . *Stock market crashes;*
> *some fear depression but Hoover*
> *disagrees* . . . . . *Bank of the U.S. closes 60*
> *branches* . . . . . *1930* . . . . . *U.S. census:*
> *U.S. population reaches 122,775,000* . . . . .
> *Nobel Prize for Medicine for discovery of*
> *human blood groups* . . . . .

About three years later
Summer 1932
Mahala, Kentucky

Daniel straightens up from his weed chopping, looks around him in the field of yard-high corn. Six-year-old Liam's dark head bobs along bodyless on the lake of green, a dozen rows away. "Look, Daddy! The corn's near as big as me!"

"That it is, Son. It's catching up on you." Daniel takes off his hat and wipes his forehead with his sleeve, fans his face with the hat. He shields his eyes from the midday sun, looks over the acre of new tassels that barely move in the hot, still day.

Beyond the cornfield the deep green oak trees cover the low hills in pools of thick gray shadow. A worn path snakes up and across the grassy hillside kept close-cropped by the two milkcows hiding out from the sun in the dark shade.

The twang of the bandsaw from the mill on the other side of the hill tugs at Daniel. He should go over and see what it is that has Will working on a Sunday.

Early each morning Daniel travels the path to the sawmill just over the rise. And late each afternoon he gathers the cows on his way back and leads them to the barn for milking. After sending one of the kids into the house with the milk bucket, he stays out in the fields until past dark, past the hour when the mosquitoes drive everybody else inside, before he finally goes inside and eats whatever was left from the family's supper.

He plants and hoes and weeds; each season he pushes himself to plant more, to harvest more, striving for something he cannot name, and he doesn't try. The preserving and the giving away of the food he leaves to others. His mind does not connect his own efforts with the rows of canning jars filled with tomatoes, squash, pickles. With times getting harder and harder, neighbors thank him for what he shares with them.

Will teases him, to be sure . . . *you bit off 'way more than you can swaller now, Boy!* But Daniel doesn't mind. It's Will's way. Only with Will is Daniel mindful of where he stands, and behind the teasing he can see the pleasure in his father-in-law's eyes at his hard work at the mill and in the fields.

Over the other direction on the next rise, Gerty, a yellow dot of Sunday church dress, sits in the porch swing overseeing Bobby Ray

and the Renshaw boy. The boys chase around in the field across the
road, their shouts like far-distant crows quarreling over the cornfield.

He wishes she'd leave the boy alone. He's ten years old, for God's
sake, and nearly as tall as Daniel.

A wave of breeze comes up, ripples across the field in one big
whisper, dies at the end of the rows. Off to the west a thundercloud
heaps itself up on the horizon. Good. The corn needs the rain.

Daniel fingers an ear of corn not four inches long, wonders
if the yellow kernels lined up in rows under their green husks are
any bigger than last week. He jerks his hand back, seeing Will's grin,
hearing Will's voice in his head: *Now Dan'l! That corn'll grow by itself.
You're worryin' it to death!*

Will could be right. He might have overdone it this year, with all
this corn, hill after hill of tomatoes and squash up near the house, and
potatoes . . . the potatoes. He grins, embarrassed, even out here in the
field with nobody watching him.

Over near the far edge of the corn, Liam's head floats above the
tasseled stalks. Now they sprout an arm, pointing up to the oaks where
Will trots toward them down the path.

"Here comes Granddaddy!" Liam calls over.

Daniel chuckles. He's coming over here to get on me about the
potatoes. He won't even take Sunday off! *Are you aimin' to feed the
whole county, Boy? With all them p'taters under there, the whole field is
gonna raise up four foot.* Will would certainly tease him ten times more
if he knew that Daniel daily fights off the urge to pull a vine up to see
if potatoes are indeed forming on its roots.

Liam dodges between the cornrows to meet his grandfather
at the edge of the field. Daniel drops his hoe and heads unhurried
in their direction. "Hey, Dan'l! I knew I'd find you out here! If you
don't let up on this farmin' you won't have time to help me out at the
mill." Daniel grins, stops and waits for Will and Liam to meet him.
Will catches Liam up in his arms, lifts him to his wide shoulders. He
bounces the boy, laughing and squealing, through the corn and dumps
him off next to Daniel.

"You think maybe he's getting too big for that, Will? Don't you
notice he's taller than this corn?" Daniel winks at Liam, who laughs up
at his grandfather and stretches at least an inch taller.

"I'm pretty near seven years old, Granddaddy!"

"Well, y'all will need him to be full grown by the time all them
p'taters come in!" Will slaps Daniel on the shoulder, peers squint-eyed

off beyond the house to the potato field, shading his eyes with his hand. "It's lookin' right good," he says, "an' I swear, the ground's rose up two foot already!"

Gerty moves from the swing over to the porch railing. She yells something over to them before she back goes into the house, but Daniel can't distinguish her words from the shouts of the boys out in the dirt road.

"You hungry, Will? Go on over to the house. Gerty's probably got dinner waiting. Looks like the Renshaw boy tagged along home with her from church to play with Bobby Ray."

"Ah, naw, I come to see you, and I've got to get on back. Hilda says the preacher was askin' this mornin' about them new benches I promised awhile back we'd build for the Sunday school. She and Emma's got the twins, takin' 'em to pick strawberries." He grins at Liam. "I reckon your daddy clean forgot to plant five or six acres of strawberries."

Will goes on, "I'd forgot all about them benches, so I was thinkin' I ought to go on over and work on 'em a while right now, leastwise cut up the planks. Could use your help after you're done lookin' after your plantation here."

Daniel nods. "I'll get this boy on down to the house for some dinner, and I'll be on over in a while."

"Can I come too, Daddy?"

"So you're wantin' to learn the sawmill business, are you, Son?" Big Will asks.

Liam laughs, leans against Daniel. "Naw, I want to be a farmer just like Daddy."

Will rumples the boy's hair with both hands, then he heads up towards the sawmill, his husky laugh whooping down the rows and rows of corn.

Liam sets out in the same direction, and Daniel turns back toward the spot where he left his hoe.

After he chops at the almost-clean row for a while, he stretches his cramped arms.

The air is heavy and heat lines shimmer over the distant fields. The afternoon quiet of the countryside is broken only by the noises of the boys. Even the crows have drawn themselves into the cool of the trees for the day's hottest hours.

Daniel searches for Liam, spies him up on the hill, waves him on down. He leans on the hoe and waits for the boy to make his way down through the corn, holding up two fistfuls of something. "I got three June bugs, Daddy! One for me and one for Little Will and one for Chigger. Can we tie 'em up?" When he reaches Daniel, he opens his fists and the three iridescent green beetles crawl out. One takes wing before Liam can catch it. Another one drops to the dirt and lands on its back, running in an upside-down frenzy before it flips over and flies away.

"It's all right, Son. The twins are up at Mammaw's anyway, but we'll find you some twine for that one. Let's go on down and get you some dinner. We'll be getting a storm in a while." They start on toward the house. The storm cloud off in the distance is building fast.

"Daddy, how come Granddaddy laughed at me?"

Daniel looks down at Liam, frowning, puzzled.

"How come he laughed at me wantin' to be a farmer like you?"

"Oh, no, Son, he was laughing about my farming, not at you. You know how Granddaddy likes to kid me about that."

"Mama says I'm just like you, but she don't laugh." Liam stops, opens his hand and lets the last June bug fly away, wipes his hand on his overall pants.

"How come you let him go?"

"He was wigglin' and scratchin' my hand. And I was feelin' sorry for him." They pick their way on down toward the house.

"Daddy, who is my name for? Little Will's is for Granddaddy, and Chigger's for Mammaw, but who am I for?"

"Don't you remember? I told you a long time ago. Liam is for *my* granddaddy."

"Yeah. I just like to hear it again, I reckon. So I don't forget it."

"Well, I want you to be sure to remember. And your other name is for the place where I was born, where my family—your family— lived, in Ireland. Don't forget. Even when I'm not here to tell you."

Liam stops right where he is at the edge of the cornfield, his eyes wide. "Are you goin' someplace? Can't I go with you?"

Daniel takes his hand, pulling him on. "I didn't mean today. Just sometime."

As they near the house, a familiar feeling comes over Daniel, the tightness in the back of his neck. When he comes in from the fields, the contentment that had settled on him like a blanket rises and disappears, taking with it his reminiscences of Ireland.

When the memories come the next time he chops and digs, they're fainter, as though something behind him was being erased, and the new that takes its place is different, distorted, pale. And growing underneath is the knowing that he has no right to any contentment in the fields, no matter how much he craves it or how little time it lasts.

Out beyond the smokehouse, the boys' voices are louder, taking on a mean sound as their playing turns to bickering. The Renshaw boy chases Bobby Ray across the road toward the house. Bobby Ray stumbles up to the front porch steps, yelling "I never!"

"Did too, did too," comes back from the boy. "You're a goddam crybaby, Bobby Ray!"

Gerty storms out onto the porch. Daniel holds Liam back, but there's no need to. Liam hangs onto Daniel's leg, showing no sign of wanting to go another step farther into the middle of the squabble. Daniel steers him back behind the smokehouse, where they both squat on the ground. Dinner can wait a while longer until things settle down. The sky is thickening up, and the sluggish air lays heavy on the fields around him.

"Bobby Ray," Gerty's voice whines from the porch. "Sweetie, you come on in the house with Mama." Then her voice goes stern and loud. "And you get yourself on home, Sonny Renshaw! I'll not have you takin' the Lord's name, and of a Sunday too!"

"Aw, Mama, let me alone!" Bobby Ray whines.

The Renshaw boy backs away toward the road, but he doesn't stop his taunts. "Go on, Baby Ray, listen to Mama. Y'all go on in now and be good, you hear me?"

Daniel can picture Bobby Ray standing between Gerty and the boy, biting his mouth down hard and holding his fists tight, glaring at Gerty.

Gerty's footsteps stomp back into the house, then her voice comes loud but sticky sweet from inside: "Bobby Ray, did you hear me, Sweetie? You come on in here now. Mama's got your dinner all ready and gettin' cold."

The mocking comes from out at the road, "Did you hear me, get in there, Mama's little sweetie baby!"

"Bobby Ray! You come on in here and don't you listen to him and he'll let you alone." More stomping feet. The screendoor bangs.

Daniel and Liam squat in a narrow strip of shade by the smokehouse, waiting for the boy to leave, but the voice still comes from out at the road, "Mama's baby, crybaby!"

"Daddy," Liam asks. "How come Bobby Ray is all the time so hateful to me?"

"I guess because he's bigger than you, just like Sonny Renshaw's bigger than him." This is not the right answer; Daniel knows it. But he knows if he digs deep enough to find it, he's sure to reach places inside that he can't bear to touch. He rubs the back of his neck, as the pressure reaches its tentacles up toward his temples. Another headache coming on. Odd how they come so often on Sunday, after a good day in his fields.

Liam goes on, "And how come Mama just likes Bobby Ray, not Chiggar and Little and me?"

The voice out front gets louder and bolder. The boy is up in the yard again. "Hey, Mama's baby, come on out. Come on, I dare you!"

Daniel pulls up a weed growing out from under the smokehouse and into the sun. He pinches the leaves off one by one and drops them to the ground. The truth is, he can't give his son the answers he's still struggling to find for himself.

It sounds like the Renshaw boy is right up at the porch steps. "Hey, Mama's little baby, ya hear me? Come on out here, Sweet—" The sound of a gunshot cracks the air between Daniel and the front door of the house.

Daniel looks instinctively to the thundercloud, then down at Liam. The air hangs still for an eternal instant, its very color changed. In the ghostly stillness, Daniel and Liam get to their feet, looking, listening, not sure for what. Then without a word between them, they bolt from behind the smokehouse, up the rise toward the porch, but Daniel stops so short that Liam bumps into him.

Up near the porch the Renshaw boy sprawls flat on the ground, as if somebody pushed him backwards hard. A dark stain spreads across the front of his blue chambray shirt. The air reeks with sulfury smell of gunpowder.

"Liam, run over to the mill and get your Granddaddy!" Liam stares, but Daniel pushes him on. "Go on! Hurry!" Daniel takes the porch steps in two jumps, jerks open the screendoor—the screendoor with a clean hole through the lower left corner—and faces Gerty's empty stare.

Bobby Ray is pulling on the barrel of the .22 held tight in Gerty's grip. "She—she—" he says, with his voice tight and whiny. He backs off when Daniel charges into the room and grabs the gun from her hands. With three, four long strides, he is back out on the porch.

On the ground at the bottom of the steps, the Renshaw boy's face blurs in front of Daniel's eyes. His empty stomach heaves and nausea spreads out and up. He squeezes his eyes shut, trying to force some steady vision from them. He eases himself down to the middle step, tries to steady his head, to slow the pumping of blood that pounds in his ears. Acid burns its way up to his mouth.

Will's truck plows up into the space between the house and the road. Still hanging onto the .22, Daniel pulls himself to his feet, grabs the railing as his stomach heaves again.

Will jumps out of the truck and thunders up to the porch. "I told that boy to never point that gun at anybody!" he says.

The gun. Daniel looks dumbly at the gun, just now realizing he's holding it, not sure how it got there. His mind tries to make sense of Will's words. The gun goes suddenly heavy, and Daniel drops it on the bottom step.

Will kneels beside the boy, rips open the front of his shirt. The boy moans, his eyes open, and he struggles to get up. Daniel sucks in a quick breath. *Mother of God, I thought he was dead.*

"You hold still, Son," Will says to the boy. Still trying to hold him down, he turns to Daniel. "Doc's on his way, him and Russ. I don't reckon it's too bad. Here. Help me get him over in the shade."

Daniel picks up the boy's feet, drops one. He bends to pick it up again, and the pain in his head presses his left temple. He wills his body to move faster, but it is much too slow, its clumsiness a shame to him. Almost in spite of Daniel's help, Will carries the boy to the patch of hard bare dirt under the oak.

Will says, "Now get me some water and let's get him cleaned up." Daniel brings the waterbucket from the back porch over to where Will waits, cajoling the boy to hold still. Will wets his big handkerchief in the bucket and wipes the boy's shoulder wound, gently rolls him onto his right side.

Gerty comes out onto the porch and sits in the swing, with a vacant stare out at the hubbub in the yard. "Will," Daniel starts, but he can't bring himself to speak above a whisper. "I don't believe it was . . . him." He glances up to the porch, where Gerty pushes the swing back and forth, back and forth.

Will hasn't looked up from the boy but Daniel can feel a change, a tensing up. Something tells him not to go on; he can't stop himself. "Will, *she's* the one who had the gun."

Without moving closer, Big Will's thunderous face looms larger in Daniel's vision and he can feel the old man's measured breaths. The calm words that come from Will's mouth do not fit the brittle tautness in the air. "Liam said he couldn't tell who shot the gun. It came from in the house."

"I . . . I'm sorry, Will, I'm . . . " He's what? Wrong about Gerty? But he saw the gun in Gerty's hands. Didn't he?

The sheriff's car races in from the road, stopping inches from Will's truck, and Dr. Jessup's model-T tears in beside it. The doctor bounds from his car and sprints over to the boy on the ground, the sheriff right behind him.

Will stands away a few feet, his face a darkening cloud, his glare bearing down on Daniel. Daniel shrinks back, almost sure that Will means to hit him right here in front of everybody.

Will crowds behind Dr. Jessup and the sheriff as they crouch over the boy. "It's my own damn fault," Will says, his apologetic words belying the fierceness of his face. "I'd a never give it to Bobby Ray if I thought he wasn't old enough to use it right. Emma kept sayin' he wasn't old enough for it. I shoulda listened to her. I told him to never point it at nobody." He paces behind the busy doctor, who ignores him, but the sheriff turns to acknowledge him with a nod.

Daniel can't believe what he's hearing and seeing. Didn't Will hear? "No, Will . . . " Daniel starts, but Will's words step up in sound and intensity, expand to fill all the empty space, leaving no room for interference.

"I told that boy not to aim it at anybody! I swear he'll never get it back 'til he's got some sense in him."

The sheriff turns back to the boy on the ground, and Will comes over to where Daniel stands rooted.

Daniel puzzles at the older man's rigid face that does not match the repentant words he continues to direct at the sheriff. "I swear, Russ, he won't never get it back. I never should've give it to him."

The doctor finishes up with the boy and stands up. "I reckon he'll be all right. It looks a whole lot nastier than it is. Looks like it glanced off of his shoulder bone. I'll take him on back with me."

The boy stirs, whimpers, and the doctor eases him to his feet.

The sheriff strides over to where Will and Daniel wait. The doctor calls after him, "You want me to see to the boy's folks, Russ?"

"No. I will," the sheriff yells back, but he stands with his feet wide apart, arms folded over his chest, looking from Will to Daniel and back. He takes a quick sideways glance up at the porch, where Bobby Ray has slipped out the screendoor and is leaning on the post at the far end of the porch from Gerty.

"What happened here? Daniel?"

Will puts a hand on Daniel's shoulder, his firm, insistent grip hushing any words Daniel might summon.

"Now look, Russ," Will drops his voice low and confidential, pulls Daniel by the shoulders into a tighter circle with the sheriff. "Like I said, my grandson, he wasn't old enough for a .22 for his birthday after all. But you know—Russ, you know how boys'll fool around. I can't b'lieve he did it a'purpose."

The sheriff pulls back and beckons to Bobby Ray, who starts down from the porch, hesitating on each step.

"Russ, listen," Will says, scratching the back of his gray head. "Seems like to me we don't need to . . . I reckon we can just put this down as an accident, can't we? You can bet he'll get what's comin' to him. I'll see to that myself."

Bobby Ray comes up and stands a few feet away, his eyes full of fear and confusion. He starts to say something, but stops short at the hard look from his grandfather.

The sheriff takes a long squint-eyed look at Bobby Ray's dirty tear-streaked face, then barely moving his head, he glances up at Gerty, on the porch, then back at Will.

"Gerty!" Will's voice booms past Bobby Ray, and the boy's body jerks like a trapped animal. "Gerty, you go on back in the house now, you hear me? Go on!"

Gerty struggles out of the swing and goes inside. "It's too hot out here," Will explains. "She can't stand the heat."

The sheriff stares back at him, his eyes narrowed with questions and suspicion, his mouth puckered. Another glance at the porch, the empty swing still swaying.

Will goes on, "And ever'body knows that Renshaw kid's a bully, Russ. Why, he'd drive St. Peter himself to shoot him."

No! No, Will! Daniel shakes his head, but the words won't budge from his throat.

From back beyond the house the first flashes of heat lightning jar the western side of the dulling afternoon. Muffled thunder follows, rolling far back into the hills. A chill rushes from Daniel's stomach to his neck and shoulders, and he's shaking, cold.

Finally the sheriff takes in a deep breath, walks over and picks up the .22. "All right, Will. If that's the way you're aimin' to leave it." He shoves the gun in Will's direction. "And you're givin' me your word that this will stay out of the wrong hands from now on?"

Daniel can't understand how Will can keep meeting the sheriff's stare straight on, without so much as a blink of an eye. The sheriff takes a long look at Bobby Ray, starts to leave. One more time, he glances back over his shoulder at the porch, shakes his head and heads on out to his car.

Bobby Ray's face abruptly meets the truth of the situation head on. He comes alive, stammering toward the sheriff's back. "What? But I didn't do—"

"Bobby Ray!" Will's measured, teeth-gritted voice forces Bobby Ray to visibly shrink, as if a huge thumb pressed him to the ground. "We are not talkin' about this any more, you hear me?"

"But Granddaddy," Bobby Ray says, his voice rising to a whine. "You don't—"

"Bobby Ray! You hear me?"

Bobby Ray's face twists up, too full to cry. His eyes meet his father's for an eternal second. Daniel must look away—away from the betrayal, the loathing in his son's eyes. Bobby Ray backs away a few steps, stumbles, then turns and runs off toward the barn.

Gerty twists a handful of her apron and peers out again from behind the front window curtain.

Daddy and the sheriff talk out by the truck, but she can't make out any words. The doctor leaves with Sonny Renshaw. Daniel just stands there hunch-shouldered, wadding his old hat in front of him with both hands. And where's Bobby Ray run off too? His dinner is getting cold.

She busies herself with the broom, jabbing it into the corner by the door, but the crack of light between the window curtains keeps drawing her back.

Daniel starts up toward the house, and Daddy's just standing there watching him go. Why isn't Daddy coming in? She doesn't want Daniel. Daniel will be hateful to her without Daddy here.

Gerty shoves the broom into the corner and hurries back into the kitchen. The dinner dumplings sit lukewarm at the back of the stove. The fire has gone out, and it won't be time to start supper for hours yet, but she pulls up a burner lid and stuffs kindling into the hole.

The stifling heavy air of the room soaks into her limp yellow dress. She should've changed it after church. It's too hot, but she likes the fancy feeling of wearing it. Maybe she should go to church more regular, then she could dress up more. That would be nice.

Daniel comes in by himself, tracking dust from his boots. He goes straight for the table and leans on it with both arms, his chest heaving. She watches him sideways. Isn't Daddy coming in?

"Gerty, what in the *hell* were you thinking about?" Daniel's fist slams down hard on the table, bouncing the covered plate of dinner biscuits. "We're lucky that boy's not dead!" The word bounces through the kitchen. *dead dead dead.* She holds her head high and rigid, her lips tight. He's got no right to holler at her this way. "That boy was callin' Bobby Ray a crybaby and Bobby Ray was cryin' and—"

"Gerty, Bobby Ray *is* a crybaby! That boy was just yelling the truth! You don't go and shoot somebody for that!"

She flinches at the anger in Daniel's eyes. "I scared him away just like them hateful old crows. Just like when I scared the crows away."

"Gerty, you could've killed him!"

Daniel's got no right to this meanness. She'll tell Daddy.

Daniel lowers himself onto the chair and presses his head tight between his hands. There's a shuffle of boots on the porch. Daddy comes in, and Gerty runs to him, her face wet with sudden tears. "Make him stop, Daddy! Make Daniel stop!"

"Gerty, I want you to listen to me." With hands on her shoulders, Daddy holds her at arm's length, peers into her face. "I want you to go on out and get in my truck, and I'll come out directly and take you on up home to see Mama. Go on."

Gerty looks at the door, scared. "The sheriff and them have left. You go on out and wait for me."

She smiles the dimply smile that Daddy likes.

"Go on, Gerty," he says a little more gently. "Go on and get in the truck." He points to the door, and she obeys.

Will sags into a chair and leans his elbows onto the big oak table, digs into his hair with both hands. All the bluster and swagger that Will showed to the sheriff are gone, and now a broken old man sits at the table, pulling at his own hair.

Daniel says the only thing he can think of saying. "Would you be wanting some coffee, Will?" Will doesn't respond. Daniel shrugs. No, it's not coffee that Will is needing.

Daniel rubs his temples hard. It helps the pain. He feels dizzy. The room fractures into slivers of bright light. Words crowd to the front of his mind, fighting to get out, then disappear before he can line them up in the right order.

He picks up the stirring spoon from the stove and studies the dried gravy on both sides of it. He lifts the lid of the pot, fishes out a chunk of lukewarm dumpling, bites into it. His empty stomach lurches with the urgent demand for attention that has been denied it all day. He gulps the rest of the dumpling, and it forces its way past the choke in his throat, hitting his stomach with a thud.

Embarrassed by his lapse of good manners, he says, "Will, this fire's out but I can get it going if you . . . " But Will's face tells him that the old man is hurting for something far different than food.

Will huffs out a breath and looks hard at Daniel. Daniel can meet his look for only a second. He can't let on that he sees the old man's shame, the tears that glisten hard and cold in his eyes.

Will hits the table hard with his fist, and the biscuit plate rattles closer to the edge. "Dammit, they're all wrong! Hilda spoilt her all her life. I knew that wasn't right, but I never said, 'cause she was hurt by nearly losin' her, knowin' she couldn't have no more, and . . . and Gerty's spoilt, but she's smart. When she was little, I carried her with me and I taught her. She just don't remember things exactly right."

The heat building up in the room squeezes Daniel's head tighter. He wants to back up against the door, to run out into the cornfield. As thunder rumbles, closer this time, he thinks how good the rain would feel on his face.

Will sags into the chair, speaks low and strained. "Russ says he'll put it down as an accident. Won't nobody question it. And it won't be the first time a boy got his gun took away from him in this county."

Daniel squeezes his eyes shut, but he can still see Bobby Ray's eyes, black with hatred. "But Will, how can the boy live with —"

"Aw, they won't do nothin' to a kid." He waves the thought away like a fly in his face. "I knew they wouldn't."

"But people might be hard on him, thinking he—"

"They'll forget about it inside a month."

Daniel searches Will's face, but he knows the old man's mind is made up and there's no sense in arguing with him.

Will turns his big hands over, as if he has just discovered the red-brown dried blood at the edges of his fingernails. He goes over to the washstand, pours a dipperful of water, then another into the washpan. He scrubs his hands, wipes them on his overalls, all the while looking like his thoughts are far away, set in stone.

"Will, isn't there something we can do for her? Is there some-where we could get her some help?"

"You talkin' about a doctor? I'm not lettin' some fool doctor send my little girl up to the asylum! They's nothin' wrong with her except she's spoilt rotten. I'll allow that. She's spoilt! But I'll not have folks thinkin' she's . . . she's . . . " *crazy crazy crazy* . . . the unspoken word hangs heavy in the room. Will straightens himself tall, jams on his hat and heads for the door. "It would kill her mama, and I'll not allow it." Daniel leans on the cold cookstove, not even following Will out onto the porch. He drags himself to the table and slumps into a chair, shame rising from somewhere deep in the pit of his stomach. He didn't think of how Hilda would feel. How could he not have been thinking of Hilda?

As the first rain spurts onto the roof, the first movement of air through the kitchen window brings with it the sudden smell of wet-dry summer dust. Daniel stares at the plate of biscuits and bites his bottom lip hard. Then with one furious sweep he slams the biscuit plate from the table. It crashes into the castiron stove, shards and biscuits flying. He lays his throbbing head on his arm and lets go the sobs that have been dammed up in his chest for too long.

Bobby Ray pulls the screendoor open and lets it hit against his backside as he stands in the doorway. He stoops to pick up a biscuit that lays near his feet, among the shatters of the blue plate.

Daddy sits at the table, his head down on his arms, shoulders shaking, choking out sounds like a bellowing cow.

Disgust and anger thrust up to Bobby Ray's throat, and he hurls the biscuit at Daddy. Daddy is on his feet, and before Bobby Ray can run for the porch steps, Daddy catches him and yanks him around to face him, drops to his knees in front of him.

Bobby Ray pulls away and waits for a blow from this stranger of a father abruptly here, with nothing or nobody between them. But Daddy pulls him tight against him—too tight, too close.

"Son, I'm . . . I'm sorry," he croaks into Bobby Ray's chest.

Bobby Ray's rigid body struggles at this closeness he has ached for as long as he can remember, but now with it pushed on him, he can't bear it, and he tries to free himself.

"Get away from me!" he spits out. "You knew what she done and you never told 'em different!" He backs up to the door. "You never did nothin' about it!"

"I'm sorry. I tried . . . " He stops and just shrugs, doesn't move to follow. "It's no use . . . I can't—"

"What if it was Liam they was tryin' to blame? You never did care nothin' about me, just Liam!"

Daddy's voice whines like a hog, with some of the words coming out as pitiful squeals. "That's not so, Son! He . . . she didn't want him. He needed me . . . "

Bobby Ray backs off, his teeth and jaw so tight that his whole body shakes. "You never stand up for me! You let her swallow me up and you never cared a damn what she did to me! You're supposed to be strong and stand up to her. I hate her! And I hate you . . . I hate you more!"

Bobby Ray jerks away and scrambles down the porch steps, out across the potato field toward the woods path that leads to his hiding place. The first blow of the rainstorm hits him full in the face. The skin of mud on the bare dirt between the potato vines sticks to his bare feet, pulls at him, slows his running.

He slips and his hands grab into the mud; he gets up and keeps on running, slipping. He flings the mud from his hands, but he can't fling away the hateful darkness that stains deep and humiliating into his soul.

. . . . . 1932 . . . .
. Franklin Delano Roosevelt
elected in landslide over Hoover . . . . .
. . . . . Unemployment up to 13 million . . . . .
Act of Congress makes the
Star Spangled Banner the U.S. national anthem
. . . . . 1933 . . . . . FDR: "nothing to fear
but fear itself"
. . . . FDR establishes the Tennessee Valley
Authority, the Civilian Conservation Corps, the
NIRA . . . . . 21st amendment repeals prohibition
of sale of liquor. Public rejoices:
"FDR gave us back our beer!" . . . . .
1934 . . . . FDR establishes Securities Exchange
Commission and Federal
Housing Administration

Dupont announces
a new polymer to be called
"nylon" . . . . . 1935 . . . . .
FDR establishes Works Progress
Administration,
Rural Electrification Administration,
and Social Security . . . . .
Beloved American philosopher
Will Rogers dies
According to Will, "Everything is
funny—as long as it happens
to somebody else."
. . . . King Edward VIII of England
abdicates the throne in favor of his
younger brother. who will take the
name of George VI . . . . .
1936 . . . . . Hitler offended by
Jesse Owens'
competition in Summer Olympics in
Munich,
infuriated when Owens wins
4 gold medals . . . . .
FDR elected over Alf Landon for
unprecedented third term . . . . .
1937 . . . . .
Gone With the Wind wins Pulitzer
Prize after selling
one million copies in
first six months

PART TWO

Five years later
May, 1937
Mahala, Kentucky

Wayne tries to drag a heavy 2x12 toward the truck. "Come on, Bobby Ray. Get over here and help me with this plank. Uncle Daniel said we're supposed to have all this stuff stacked by the time they get back here. I can't pack it by myself."

At seventeen, Wayne is a wiry banty rooster who makes up for in energy and pluck what he lacks in size and strength. He's no match for Bobby Ray. Nobody'd guess Bobby Ray younger by more than two years. Wayne looks like the slight young soldier face in the picture that sits on his mama Emma's chest of drawers, the only picture they have of J.D. Hartley.

Bobby Ray looks more like Big Will Tucker every day.

"*Uncle Daniel*, he ain't the boss here." Bobby Ray leans against the shed wall, smoking a cigarette and taking his time about it.

"Well, he's your daddy. And him and Granddaddy aim to deliver this stuff to old man Pyle soon as they get back here. I don't know about you, but I'm not wantin' my tail whupped when they show up back here."

"Ain't nobody whuppin' my tail. Nobody around here's near big enough." Bobby Ray drops his cigarette butt and stomps it into the ground. He stands with his thumbs hooked into his overall straps, still making no move to pick up the other end of the 2x12.

"Well, Granddaddy could," Wayne says. "Now get hold of this plank, will you?" He turns around, switching his hands to behind his back so as to carry the 2x12 face forward, if Bobby Ray ever makes up his mind to pick up the other end. "Yeah, I reckon you got a ways to go to be bigger'n Granddaddy. " He looks back over his shoulder at Bobby Ray. "Or maybe they'll get your Mama to. Now if *she* ever gets her hands on you, I reckon she's big enough to whup all of—"

Pain tears into the side of Wayne's head as something hard and jagged gouges into the round of the bone above his left eye. The 2x12 thunders onto the ground, bouncing in the dust. Wayne staggers sideways, bumps into a sawhorse. He tries to grab hold of it to steady himself, but falls over to the dirt on the other side, landing hard on one elbow. "You—you son of a bitch!" Wayne yells into the fury hovering somewhere above him, around him. He can barely open his eyes for the blinding spot of pain, but he tries to get back to his feet to protect himself from whatever is coming next.

"What's the matter with you!" His vision dizzies, and he drops back onto his knees, grabs onto the sawhorse. The hulk of Bobby Ray comes at him, a piece of 2x4 pulled back high over his shoulder. Wayne dives back to the ground, rolling, crawling backwards. The wood smashes onto the sawhorse, clatters to the ground. He makes it to the worktable and crawls under to the other side, as pressure from the swelling wound spreads the pain through his whole head. Salty, sticky blood streaks his face, dripping in dark blobs on the dirt under him. He scrambles up onto his feet.

As Bobby Ray comes at him around the end of the table, Wayne grabs a hammer from the bench, backs up to the side of the shed. "Get away from me! You crazy fool! You like to have killed me! Get back!" He can hear the rage in Bobby Ray's breathing, forcing the air hard in and out. Bobby Ray's smothering form bullies its way into Wayne's face and easily removes the hammer from his grasp.

Wayne covers his head with his arms, tries to press himself into the wall . . . *I'm gonna puke* . . . everything slows to a crawl as his whole body screams out, waiting for the blow. The sound cracks and splinters into his left ear and the echo bounces through his skull . . . *I can't feel it . . . why can't I feel it? Am I dead?* But he can still feel his feet on the hard dirt, his back flattened to the ungiving rough wood of the wall, his arms pressed against his face, blood soaking into his shirt sleeve. Footsteps pound away from him on the hard ground, and then everything is quiet, except for the *thud thud thud* of his own pulse inside his head.

When he dares, he peeks under his arm still tight across his face, then lowers the arm. Sunlight stabs his eyes. With his good eye, the one that's not fast swelling shut, he can see the lumber yard, empty, silent.

He sucks in a sharp breath—he's been holding it, not realizing it. The movement of it brushes his hair against a hard cold thing next to his face. The hammer is stuck by its claws into the wall not two inches from his ear.

Bobby Ray meant to miss him, he's pretty sure of it. Wayne knows his cousin too well. Last summer Bobby Ray threw his pocket knife into a boy's foot in a fast game of mumbledy-peg. When the mother screamed that he'd done on purpose, Bobby Ray said, swaggering away without even looking behind him, "If I'd a done it a'purpose, I wouldn't of hit him in the foot." Maybe she didn't believe him, but Wayne did.

He waits until he's pretty sure Bobby Ray's not coming back, reaches up for the hammer and hangs onto it to hold himself steady for a second or two. The whole side of his head, the part that's not already seeping out of the gash, tries to break through the tight skin.

With the last bit of feverish strength he can muster, he wrenches the hammer from the wall. He slides down to sitting on the ground, the butt of his overall pants the only protection from the wood. He hangs onto the hammer as the weight of it races him to the ground and clunks into the dust beside him.

Nausea spreads out all over him. His head fills with orange-black prickly lights as the black sucks in all the light around him and the day disappears. The next thing he knows, he's flat out on the ground, looking up at faces looming over him.

"Well, Son," The voice tells him the bulk above him is Granddaddy. "I don't reckon you done this to yourself with this hammer." Granddaddy's relieved face turns serious. "What happened here? Where's Bobby Ray? And I sure as hell hope they ain't no connection 'tween the two."

Wayne tries to get himself up, but the jolt of pain changes his mind. He eases himself back down onto the shirt that somebody has pillowed under his head. "I swear, I don't know why he did this to me." He tries to keep the tears back. "He's got a temper, but I've never seen him like that." He shudders at the sight of the hammer in Granddaddy's hand. "He's a fool idiot," Wayne says.

For a minute it's hard to remember that Uncle Daniel is kin to Bobby Ray at all. "I'm sorry, Uncle Daniel, but it's the truth. He went crazy!" Uncle Daniel looks ashamed, not agreeing but not standing up for Bobby Ray either.

"Well," Granddaddy says, straightening himself up from squatting on the ground, "You quit talkin' and we'll get the doctor, Son. Me and your Uncle Dan'l, we'll take care of it." And to Uncle Daniel he says, his voice lower, "You walk him over to Doc Jessup's and I'll go after our other one myself. He's got way too big for his britches this time."

Soon afterward

Bobby Ray stomps into the house and slams the door. "What's the matter, Sweetie?" Mama waddles over to him, her nearly three hundred pounds hanging on her bones like a enormous featherbed. She reaches for the cowlick that hangs into his face, but he yanks his head out of the way of her touch.

"Let me alone!" He backs out the kitchen door, right into Liam coming up the steps with his arms full of kindling.

Liam cowers back down the steps, but his foot misses the middle step and twists under him, dumping him hard on the ground, sending sticks flying out all over the steps.

Bobby Ray yells at him, "What's the matter, Snotnose? That little bitty armload of wood too heavy for you?"

"I—I couldn't get more." Liam scrambles to pick up all the scattered sticks. "There wasn't nobody to load me up."

Bobby Ray looks behind him at the screendoor. He knows it. He can feel it. Mama has followed him to the door, and there she stands behind him like an echo of his own words, like a shadow hanging over and around him, her face twisted up into a sneer aimed at Liam. "Dammit, let me be, Mama!" Bobby Ray yells back at her as he jumps off the side of the porch and heads off out to the barn. Just before he ducks behind the barn door, he turns back and yells in the direction of the house. "Do you hear me, Mama? Get away from me! Let me alone!"

He paces the haystrewn floor of the barn, rakes his hands through his sweat-soaked hair, wishes he had a cigarette.

You crazy fool, you could have killed me! He swats the thought out of the air like a mosquito, but it won't leave . . . *you like to have killed me!* Even in the muggy hay-smelling heat of the barn, he shivers at the picture of what he's done. *You like to have killed me!*

He pulls at his hair with both hands, as if to make a thousand openings for the blame to escape his head. His terror leaps out in every direction, but there's no fence, no wall to hold it in. He could have killed Wayne! He came so close to killing Wayne with that hammer! *Somebody help me!*

"Bobby Ray!"

The force of his own breath sucking in nearly knocks Bobby Ray backwards. He slumps down to his knees, all the fury gone out of him. His shoulders let go of the burdensome weight that held him down.

Granddaddy stands over him, his arms folded across his chest, his feet planted wide apart. "Son, let's me and you go on back up to my place. This don't concern your mama. I believe you and me and my razor strop has got some long overdue talkin' to do."

"Yes, Sir."

Granddaddy leaves the barn without looking back at him. Bobby Ray scrambles to catch up, follows his grandfather's long strides up the path that winds up and over the hill. It doesn't matter now about the whipping. Granddaddy cares about him, that's what matters. And Granddaddy will fence him in.

Hilda rolls out pie crust, cuts two rounds, fits one into the waiting pie pan. She's done this so many hundreds of times that she can do it blind, and today her mind is certainly not on the task. Her heart has not yet settled from the start Will gave her when he walked into the house in the middle of the afternoon, went straight over and took his razor strap down from its hook behind the washstand and walked right back out the door. She followed him, her mind crackling with questions.

He nearly bumped into her when he stopped short and turned to tell her, "Just some business I need to tend to. I'll be back directly." He shooed her back into the house.

Watching from the door, she sees Bobby Ray standing slump-shouldered out by the door of the shed, kicking at the straw on the ground. She goes into the front room where Betty Crocker, turned up loud enough to be heard in the kitchen, has lost the attention of this house. She turns off the radio and goes back to her piemaking. She strains to hear something from outside, then tries her best not to.

She wonders what in the world has led up to this. It's probably the first whipping the boy has ever got. Gerty would never take a strap to Bobby Ray and would have a fit if Daniel threatened to. But then, poor Daniel, he would never think of it.

She pours the cut-up apples into the bottom crust, sprinkles on her special concoction of spices and sugar, covers it all with chunks of fresh-churned butter. She lays the top crust over the whole thing, tucks the edges under, and wipes the sweat of the hot kitchen off her face with the sleeve of her print dress. With a floury hand, she brushes back a straggle of her straight thick hair, tucks it into its rightful place in the bun at the back of her neck.

Will is headed back toward the house, Bobby Ray coming along behind, buckling his overalls. Hilda guesses that he'd rather stay in the shed a while, but it looks like Will intends for him to come on in with him, ashamed or not.

Why, he's almost as tall as Will! She's noticed it before, but it looks unnatural today with the little-boy face she sees on him now. She hurries to get the pie trimmed, hoping she'll have her back turned, putting it in the oven, when they come in, but she's too late.

At the door, Bobby Ray hangs back, ducking his head. Will pulls the boy's arm and shoves him on in ahead of him.

"Well," Hilda says, wishing somebody else would say something first. "Well. Are y'all hungry?" She wipes her sweaty hands on the front of her apron, not certain whether to look at Will or at Bobby Ray. "No, I reckon not," she says, "since you just had dinner a little while ago."

Will hangs the strap on its nail, washes his hands in the washpan. "When is it the preacher's brother is bringin' his tent to town, the one you've been talkin' about? When's that start?"

"Why, Sunday evenin', Will, but . . . " Surely Will hasn't forgot about Bobby Ray already. Whatever is he thinking about?

"Well, I reckon Bobby Ray here has a hankerin' to go with you."

Bobby Ray's head jerks up, his red eyes wide and his back far straighter than Hilda's ever seen on a grandson of hers.

"Yep," Will goes on, "Bobby Ray's havin' trouble keepin' himself on the straight and narrow here lately, and I reckon he's seein' the error of his ways and wants a whole lot to go with you. Ever' night. What'd you say it was? Two, three weeks?"

Hilda studies Will's face, expects to see his usual crinkly eyes, his wink at playing a joke on one of the grandkids. But his look at Bobby Ray is not playful—it's a stern one, as if he's daring the boy to cross him, to say one word.

"Why I'd be tickled to have him if he wants to . . . " Hilda says, saying the opposite of what she is sure is true. "Bobby Ray, Honey, are you sure . . . "

"Oh, he's sure. Ain't you Bobby Ray?"

Bobby Ray shifts his weight from one foot to the other, chews his bottom lip.

Will repeats, so much louder this time that Bobby Ray and Hilda both jump, *"Ain't you, Bobby Ray?"*

"Uh, yes Sir," he answers, with a gulp Hilda can see and hear clear across the room.

"Well, I'm happy to hear that." Will motions the boy toward the front door. "And not bein' much of a churchgoer myself, I'll be lookin' forward ever' mornin' to hearin' all about the sermon, as fascinatin' as they're goin' to be." He stops to kiss Hilda on the forehead. She pulls away from him with a frown. He could use a few sermons himself, the old reprobate, but she's almost given up on him.

She supposes a couple of weeks of tent revival meetings can't hurt the boy although she suspects he'd just as soon get another whipping instead.

She scrapes flour and bits of dough from the bread board. Maybe Gerty will go, too, if Bobby Ray goes. Hilda's always wished she could get Gerty to go more often, even though she's almost given up praying for a healing for her. The Lord must have his reasons.

"Now let's get back to work, Son." Will pushes Bobby Ray ahead of him out the door. "Looks like you'll have twicet as much work to do for a few days. But you'll do just fine, considerin' you'll be sittin' down of a evenin', singin' and prayin'."

With his fingers Will combs his skimpy hair over to the side and shoves his hat down to keep it there. "Well, maybe you won't be *sittin'* for a while. Don't you imagine Brother Earl will let Bobby Ray stand at the back for a night or two, Mammaw?" He winks at Hilda.

She turns her head quickly away pretending she didn't notice and puts the pie into the hot oven. She can't help a smile at her husband, the rascal, not that she'd have let him see it for anything. Only after Will and Bobby Ray are out of sight does she remember that she still doesn't know what this is all about. She supposes he'll tell her later at supper. She wanders back into the front room, turns on the radio to see if Ma Perkins is having a better day at *her* lumberyard.

The same afternoon

"Come on in, Mrs. Dunning! It's open!" Emma calls out from back in the kitchen when she hears the rattly knock on the front door screen. It must be Mrs. Dunning. She's the only customer expected all day. And even though Emma hangs out her sign right above the front steps every morning, *Emma Hartley's Dressmaking, Come Right In*, still, Mrs. Dunning is always proper about knocking.

When Emma first opened the seamstress shop in the front room of her home, there were plenty of customers. Materials were nice, and the challenge of each new creation was a pleasure for her. She was kept busy, with no time to while an afternoon away putting up a batch of jam back in the kitchen, like today.

Nowadays there's not much money to be had, and most of her business has turned to mending, letting out, taking in, making over. It still keeps her occupied and independent, and that counts for a whole lot, these days.

The likes of Lola Dunning can still afford new dresses, though not nearly as often or from as fine a material these days. But still nicer and more expensive than Emma could afford for herself, even if she had any place fancy to wear them.

She hears a shuffling on the porch, another knock. She tucks a loose straggle of hair into the net at the back of her head, hangs her apron on the coatrack.

"Good afternoon, Mrs. . . . . oh, Daniel, it's you! Why, you don't have to knock. You come on in!"

Her face goes hot as the thought slips through her mind, *I wish I'd put on a nicer dress.* As if Daniel would notice, and why should he?

Emma holds the screendoor open for Daniel, but he steps aside and Wayne comes up the steps behind him, slow and cautious.

"Lord, what's happened?" Emma rushes out to meet her son out on the porch, reaches to hug him to her, but he pulls back before she even touches him.

A big bandage covers his left eye, and the rest of his face doesn't look so good, either. And one arm hangs in a loose sling. *Oh, Lord, the saw! Thank the Lord both his hands are still there!* "What happened? Hon, what happened to your eye?"

"I'm sorry, Emma." Daniel backs away, stands holding onto his old hat, not looking at her face. "I'm afraid this wasn't exactly an accident." He sounds like maybe he's been making up a speech for her. "I'm . . . I'm ashamed to tell you that—"

"Bobby Ray did it!" Wayne butts in. "I'm sorry, Uncle Daniel. I'm so mad at that son of a . . . I'm sorry."

Daniel reaches for Wayne's shoulder, then backs off. "You've got every right to be mad. I'm sure your Mama is not feeling so kindly to my family right now, either."

Emma catches his glance just for an instant, but he snatches it away. He looks instead out toward the model-T. She can tell that is where he'd rather be right now.

"I'm surely ashamed of it, myself," he mumbles.

Emma helps Wayne into the front room, not sure where to touch her poor battered son. He points to his bandaged head, fingers it gingerly. "Doc Jessup sewed it up and he said we ought to put more ice on it. And he says my arm's not broke, just bruised up, but it sure hurts, clear up to here. That crazy idiot! Mama, what's the matter with him? He acts like a damn fool little kid."

Emma tries to shush him and looks back for Daniel, feeling his embarrassment for him, but he hasn't followed her into the house. He's already making his way back down the sidewalk.

"Daniel!" She dashes after him down the steps and out onto the walk to stop him, but when he turns around, she doesn't know what to say. She needs to say something. "Daniel, I'm . . . I'm so sorry!"

The look on his face says her words are not making any sense to him. "I mean," she goes on, "well, I . . . we're not mad at you . . . how could we be . . . I . . . oh, Daniel, you don't deserve this." Her hand from some wish of its own, reaches out and touches his face. Shocked by the intimacy of the caress, she jerks her hand back.

She suddenly feels naked in the harsh summer sunlight, turns and bolts back up the walk.

The sidewalk feels like it has stretched to a mile before she goes up the steps and reaches the screendoor, hurries in and pulls it shut behind her, struggling to catch her breath.

"Mama?" Wayne stands in the kitchen door, holding the ice pick and a dishtowel-wrapped bundle. "Mama, can I use this last little piece of ice? Charlie comes today, doesn't he?"

"Why, sure, Hon, yes." She tries to calm herself. Her sweet son is trying so hard to be a grown man. He's still not as tall as she is. Now he's so hurt and bruised. Tears fill her eyes. She wants to take him in her arms and hold him, and comfort him, and kiss him. *God forgive me but Gerty doesn't deserve Daniel!*

"It's all right, Mama. Doc Jessup says it's not as bad as it looks, and it'll look worse tomorrow. Granddaddy says I can stay home from the mill as long as I need to."

Emma manages a meager smile for her son. "Lord, Wayne, you do look a fright." She reaches out, hesitates, and settles for a tender pat on what she hopes is a solid place on his good shoulder. "Let's get you some clean clothes and you go lay down. I'll bring you some bread and nice peach jam I just made."

"That sounds good, Mama. Thanks." He hands her the ice pick and looks like he's trying to grin, for her, this sweet boy left to her as her only inheritance from the Great War and from J.D. Anymore, she sees in her mind not the real J.D., but the soldier picture on the chest of drawers, that even now shrinks into a tiny spot in the back of her mind. *Lordy, what a strange thought!*

Wayne starts his slow climb up the stairs, hanging onto the stair rail with his free hand, cradling the ice wrapped in the dishtowel in the other. "Oh, if it'll make you feel better," he says, "I reckon Grand-daddy went and whupped the hel—uh, the tar out of Bobby Ray."

Emma reaches up and pats the hand on the stair rail. "I wish we knew what's to happen to Bobby Ray, Son. I've been worried about him for a long time. You know your Aunt Gerty's not . . . she's not right."

"I know it, Mama. She's mean, and she's spiteful to Liam and Hildy. It don't seem like she's mean to Bobby Ray or to Little Will. So how come Bobby Ray's the one turnin' out so hateful? She lets him get away with anything."

"Don't you reckon maybe that's why, Son?"

The sound of Daniel's Ford pulling away draws her attention. She watches out the corner windows.

Her face is suddenly hot. When tears come close to the surface again, she turns her head away. *What on earth is the matter with me?* "Now, Wayne, you go on upstairs and lay down, all right?" She's pulled back to the window, but she can feel Wayne's gaze on her. She has to look at him.

He hasn't moved. His face looks curious, puzzled. "What is it, Hon? Are you hurtin' too much? Did Dr. Jessup give you some aspirins? I can get you some. Here, let me get you some."

"No, no, he did. It's startin' to feel easier. Mama, you know, you been a real good mama to me. And I reckon you done a pretty good job of bein' my daddy too."

There's no chance of hiding the tears this time, and no need to. These tears are just between her and her son.

She looks him straight in the eye and says with a smile that's a little too sparkly, "Now you get yourself on up to your room, young man, and don't you go makin' your old mama cry right here in the middle of the day. I've got work to do."

Wayne grins, his eyes shining too, and starts his way on up the stairs once more. She goes into the kitchen, leans with both hands on the sink top, gazes up the street toward the sawmill. After the speck of the model-T turns into the lumberyard, she closes her eyes and lets her mind speak out the words that her heart must have known for a long long time: *Oh, Daniel, you should have been mine, not hers!*

There are footsteps on the front walk again and she knows the foolishness playing inside her head must settle into its own place for now, out of sight. She splashes cold water on her face, pats it dry with the dishtowel, and practices stretching her lips into a wide smile.

Mrs. Lola Dunning is at the door knocking, late as she usually is for her dress fitting.

1937 . . . . . German helium-filled dirigible
Hindenberg arrives in New Jersey to
waiting crowds . . . . . Mayo Clinic reports
progress in search for serum against
infantile paralysis, also called polio
. . . . . Germany annexes Austria

Almost a month later
Summer 1937
Mahala, Kentucky

. . . leaning, leaning on the everlasting arms . . .

Bobby Ray slouches down in his wooden folding chair in the back row of the tent. Everybody else stands up, singing, clapping. He makes a face at a little girl scraping her wooden folding chair back and forth in the dust next to his. The girl's mother, a straggly-haired woman who is probably no more than twenty-five but looks twice that age, frowns down at Bobby Ray as if he were surely the source of the noise and the puffs of dust blanketing her shoes. As soon as the mother turns back to her songbook, the girl sticks her tongue out at Bobby Ray.

The piano pounds to a stop, and everybody shuffles around for whatever comes next. When they all get quiet, Bobby Ray wonders what's going on. He figures he might as well stand up and look. He tries to do it without anybody noticing—which is hard, big as he is.

The girl steps over on Bobby Ray's foot, stands on it, smirking up at him. He yanks his foot from under hers and she yells out, grabs hold of the chair and nearly falls over, chair and all. He knows she's not hurt—just raising a fuss—but everybody's looking back at them. The mother's accusing face turns to Bobby Ray again, but her rebuke suddenly disappears when she finds him now frowning down at *her*. She grabs the hand of the howling girl, goes down the row and leaves out the side of the tent, taking the congregation's attention with her.

Up at the front, a young girl about Bobby Ray's age with a scrubbed-shiny face and wearing a white robe comes up to sing. The congregation sits down, rustling their songbooks and fanning themselves with the cardboard fans made up new and given out by Teague's Funeral Parlor special for the revival.

. . . I come to the garden alone . . .

He thinks he's seen the girl before someplace, her blonde hair brushed and shining around her shoulders. Even with the robe he can see that her figure is filled out really nice, especially the way she stands with her chest pushed out like that.

. . . and the joy we share, as we tarry there . . .

She sings pretty, too. When the song is done, Brother Earl comes up beside the girl and puts his arm around her shoulder. "Praise the Lord, thank you Sister Connie Sue for that testimony! Hallelujah! And they all said . . . " he prompts, and the congregation says with him, "Praise the Lord! Praise be to Jesus!"

Connie Sue? That's Connie Sue Spivey? The little toadface turned into that pretty girl?

He grins and crosses his arms over his chest. Well, at least there's one good thing here to look at. Then he ducks his head as he catches Mammaw up in the second row smiling back at him. Granddaddy gave her the job of making sure he doesn't sneak out, he's sure of that.

Connie Sue takes her seat on the platform, and Brother Earl steps up to start the next song, another slow one that lets the regulars know the altar call is coming up. Bobby Ray's heard it plenty of times before, and the only thing good about this part of the service is that it's almost over.

At least the part he has to stay for. Granddaddy never said he had to stay until the last wrung-out and puffy-faced one gets up from praying through. The same ones, carrying on night after night, praying like they're black as the devil and can never get good no matter how long they pray.

He did stay a time or two, just out of curiosity, figuring it was better than going home.

And last night he stayed, wondering what all they had done to be such sinners, wondering if anybody ever got that way from somebody doing something to them that they couldn't help.

Curious to see if anything ever happened to take their sin away from them.

Just curious, that was all.

A Few Days Later

"Daddy," Hildy whispers, pulling Daniel from his woolgathering. Hildy stands at his shoulder, holding her plate, tilted, wobbly. "Me and Little Will, we don't like this old okry. Have we got to eat it?"

Daniel takes the plate from her and starts to put it up on the table, but Hildy snatches it back. She holds it down in front of her, behind him, out of sight of Gerty, who is over by the stove scooping up fried potatoes grease and all out of the skillet into a bowl.

Hilda sits on the other side of Daniel. She reaches around and steadies Hildy's plate.

"What's the matter, Honey? Did your Mama give you too much okry? Gerty, this is a lot of okry for one little girl."

Gerty sets the big bowl of fried potatoes down on the table with a thump and goes back to the stove. "What are you whinin' about now, girl? It's always somethin'."

Hildy huddles closer to Daniel. "I don't like it, Daddy."

"Well, I don't think you'll be needing to eat all that okra," he says. "Gerty, couldn't you boil the potatoes sometime, instead of all this grease?" He remembers Ma's potatoes, boiled with onions, steaming, filling the house with the aroma of butter and dill.

Gerty's look is cold. "That's the way Bobby Ray wants 'em."

"I hate okry, too," Little Will says from across the table. "It feels just like snot."

Over on the other side of Will, Liam snorts out a laugh then tries to cover it with his hand. Hildy giggles, hides her face in Daniel's shirtsleeve. Daniel tries to cover his grin, too.

But Will lets his laugh roar out. "By God, it does, don't it?" With that, Hildy and Liam allow themselves to giggle out loud. Little Will copies his grandfather's laugh, looks proud of himself.

"You get over here and eat that," Gerty yells, but Hildy backs around behind Daniel's shoulder, her laugh dried up.

"Now, Gerty," Hilda says, "I reckon anybody's got a right not to like at least one thing. I don't remember you or Emma was too crazy about it when y'all was little either."

Gerty puffs up, her mouth set into a pinched-up line.

Will asks, "Where is Emma this evenin', anyhow?"

Emma. Daniel's face feels hot; his fingers wander to his cheek.

"Well," Hilda says, with a quick look at Gerty, "Wayne's still not feelin' too good since . . . since he was hurt at the mill."

"Wayne was hurt?" Gerty brings over the huge platter of chicken. "I keep tellin' you them boys is too young to be foolin' around them saws, Daddy, I don't want Bobby Ray gettin' hurt, I told you."

"Them boys're just fine, Gerty," Will says, "They've got to learn the trade sometime, and Bobby Ray's near as big as I am. And it weren't on the saw that—"

"Your daddy's lookin' after the boys, Gerty," Hilda butts in, with a hard look and a shake of her head at Will.

"I'll eat it for you, Hildy," Little Will offers. "I don't hate it so very much."

"No," says Hilda, "you give me that okry and y'all have yourselves a pulleybone, and I'll make a wish on it with you when you're done. Here, let me find you one." She dumps the okra onto her own plate, then picks over the pile of chicken, pulls a piece from the bottom and gives it to Hildy, digs back in again for another one.

"Now Mama," Gerty fusses, "You know Bobby Ray likes pulley-bones. You save 'em for him."

Will piles four pieces of chicken onto his own plate. "Gerty, your mama killed three chickens, plenty for these kids to all have a pulley-bone apiece if they want one. Bobby Ray can have somethin' else."

He holds his fork up with a piece of chicken stabbed onto the end, winks at Liam. "Pass your plate on over here, Son, and let Grand-daddy fill it up."

Liam carries his plate around the far side of the table and takes the piece of chicken, fork and all, from Will.

Will dishes up fried potatoes onto Liam's plate before piling a big helping on his own. "Where is Bobby Ray anyhow? Never knew that boy to be late for supper."

"I don't know where he is half the time," Gerty complains. "He's gettin' so growed up, he does whatever he pleases. Bobby Ray's taller than Daniel already and him not but fifteen." The particular pleasure she gets from this last shows in the smirk she turns on Daniel.

Daniel looks away when he realizes he's been staring at Gerty. He can't imagine how she can be Emma's sister.

You don't deserve this. Whatever could Emma have meant? No, he doesn't deserve any of this, the farm, Will and Hilda treating him like family. But he didn't think Emma begrudged him that. Maybe she does. But her eyes—and her touch—said something more than that.

"Dan'l?" Will is talking to him. "Son, didn't you tell Bobby Ray to come on after he swept up? I reckon we ought to at least give him the evenin' off on Saturday, don't you?" Will chuckles.

Daniel turns his head to avoid Gerty's puzzled look.

"Besides," Will goes on, with a grin that looks like he's planning to stir up a hornet's nest. "Besides, he needs to clean up for meetin'."

"For meetin'?" Gerty frowns. "What—"

"Why, Bobby Ray's been goin' to the tent meetin' ever' night this week. Didn't he tell you?" Will grins over at Daniel, who cringes down, tries to hide his face. "I thought maybe you'd be wantin' to go too, Gerty, seein' as how your boy's gettin' right regular about it."

"Will," Daniel says with a guilty glance at Gerty, who's looking from one to the other in disbelief. "I think maybe Bobby Ray never told her—uh, anybody—he was going."

Gerty puffs up like an old hen again. "Mama, why didn't *you—*"

"Bobby Ray said you didn't want to, so I never bothered with sayin' anythin' to you. Lord knows I've give up tryin' to make you go a long time ago."

Just as the family is almost ready for Mammaw's berry pie, Bobby Ray stomps in through the back door, his face cloudy and sullen. Without a word to the family he goes straight to the waterbucket and drinks down two dipperfuls, then pours three more into the washpan and washes his hands, leaving the water dirty and the towel hanging above it streaked. Nobody's talking and everybody's watching him, but he picks out Hildy. "So what are you lookin' at, Runt?"

Mama struggles to her feet, bumping the table, rattling dishes. She hurries over to him. "Bobby Ray, Sweetie, why didn't you tell Mama you was goin' to meetin'? I always wanted you to go with me, and you never. You sit down here and have you some supper and Mama will go with you. Hildy, get in there and iron Bobby Ray a shirt." She reaches out to smooth his hair, but he jerks back.

Who told her? "Dammit, Mama, I don't want you to go, and quit pullin' at my hair!" He starts for the front room, but Granddaddy reaches out and catches his shirt sleeve.

"Bobby Ray, that's your Mama you're talkin' to."

"Granddaddy, please." He twists around so his back is to the others and talks through his teeth, "I don't want her goin'. Granddaddy. You know how she is." He turns to Hildy, finishing the last of her biscuit on the other side of Granddaddy. "Shut up, Runt!"

Hildy scoots closer to Uncle Daniel. "I didn't say nothin'."

"I'll bet you told her, you little—"

Granddaddy yanks the sleeve hard. Bobby Ray feels the stony glare on him. Still holding tight to Bobby Ray's shirt, Granddaddy says, "Now Gerty, I 'spect y'all could let Bobby Ray alone to sit with his own friends at meetin', now couldn't you?"

"I won't go if she's goin'!" Bobby Ray says.

Granddaddy pulls on the sleeve again. "Now Bobby Ray, you do have friends of your own at meetin', now don't you"—he yanks the sleeve hard— "that you want to sit with?"

Bobby Ray's face burns, knowing Hildy is standing there hearing all of this, and he turns his fury toward her, wishing he could reach her, just for a minute. Just a minute, that's all, and he'd pull those plaits right out of her head!

"Oh, Bobby Ray?" Mama takes on the wheedly voice that he hates, the one that makes him feel like she's pawing at him even from across the room. "Remember Brother Earl's little niece Connie Sue you was sweet on in the first grade? Well, she's back visitin'. I saw her at the store, and she's all growed up and turned out right pretty." Then her giggle turns to a pout. "But I reckon you already noticed her at the tent meetin'. Have you been sittin' with her?"

Little Will giggles, but Hildy solemnly hovers near Uncle Daniel's elbow. Liam shovels the last of his fried potatoes into his mouth.

Only Mama's fat grinning face looks right at Bobby Ray. His throat tightens; acid boils up from his stomach. And Granddaddy's grip on his sleeve feels like a trap clamped onto his body.

"Mama, shut up!" He wrenches his arm away from Granddaddy's grasp, ripping his shirt, and disappears into the dark front room. Let Granddaddy whip him. He doesn't care. He's not going to go back. He's *not* going!

Granddaddy follows him, stands in the doorway.

Bobby Ray closes his eyes and tries to hold back the sobs that are choking him. Granddaddy," he whispers, "please don't make me go with her."

The next week

. . . *What a fellowship, what a joy divine, leaning on the everlasting arms . . . hallelujah . . . praise be to Jesus!*

Bobby Ray slaps at the gnats that pester his ears, and he sucks on the last half of a cigarette. From where he sits on the low rise near the edge of the woods, leaning back on a big rock, he can see clearly into the tent set up in Ansel Grace's pasture, its side flaps rolled up to let in any stray breath of air.

The dusty metal-gray canvas takes on the form of an animal, standing on pole legs, lit up for all the world to see. Its insides sway and writhe to the music and most of the townspeople have been swallowed up. The ones up front are rejoicing for it; the ones in the back gobbled up when they got too close, because there wasn't any other entertainment going on in town.

Or because their granddaddies made them.

The muggy summer night air is filled with shrill voices, some of them on key and a whole lot of them not.

It's easy to see Mama in the second row of foldup chairs. How can he miss her? Little Will sits next to her, his nose in a songbook, and Liam and Hildy huddle down in the seats on the other side of Little Will. Bobby Ray imagines he can make out Mama's voice from here, singing out too loud, as usual.

"Hey, Bobby Ray."

He sucks in his breath so fast he nearly swallows his cigarette whole. "Dammit, Charles, you scared the shit out of me!" Bobby Ray flattens himself against the rock, breathing hard, sweating. "What are you doin' up here?"

Charles laughs. "Same thing as you—hidin' out. Only you ain't doin' such a good job of it 'cause I could see your cigarette from way down there. Got another'n?"

"Nah. I found this'n. Here."

Charles squats down facing Bobby Ray, takes a long drag of the last of the cigarette. "Your mama down there too?"

"Ain't ever'body's?"

"I didn't see you around here last night. Your granddaddy get you for it?"

"Nah. He said I didn't have to go no more."

"Yeah?"

"Yeah." Bobby Ray pulls his chest up higher, sticks out his chin. "Yeah, I told him I ain't aimin' to go no more, and there wasn't nothin' he could do about it."

"Oh, yeah, I bet."

"You callin' me a liar?" Bobby Ray grabs the front of Charles's shirt, knocking the cigarette from his hand onto the dry weeds. Charles scrambles up and stomps on the cigarette butt. "What's the matter with you, you fool? Can't you take nothin'?"

Bobby Ray sits back against the rock, his face stormy.

"Well," Charles brushes the grass and dirt off his overall pants. "I'm goin' on back down, before my mama comes after me." He starts off down the hill, then comes back up a few steps. "So how come you're out here if you ain't got to? You figurin' on *gettin' saved?*"

Bobby Ray scrambles up and starts after him, but Charles is far ahead of him down the hill, laughing. Bobby Ray picks up a rock and chucks it after Charles, then turns and stomps back up to his hiding-out place.

Damn Charles. Damn that old fool of a preacher, prancing in his big-city drummer suit, hollering about hell and sin.

Damn all of them. And especially damn Mama.

So what *is* he doing here? After Bobby Ray begged and pleaded, Granddaddy said he didn't have to come this last week of the revival. And there's nothing here he wants.

He presses his back up against the rock, wishes he had another cigarette. He wishes for anything except who he is and what he is.

He wishes he wasn't fifteen years old and bigger'n most grown men he knows. He wishes he was dead.

He doesn't belong here, but dammit, there's no place else that he belongs either.

He picks up the nearest thing his hand can find, a rock about the size of a walnut, and hurls it in the direction of the tent—the tent with its shouting and wailing, filling up the whole pasture, the whole town, the whole sky . . . *you crazy fool, you like to have killed me* . . . and he feels a strap, coming down again and again on his butt . . . and then the strange peace that lasts for only a second.

He grabs up another rock, throws it, hard, toward the tent. Then another one, and another—any direction, he doesn't care—until there are no more within reach. He crawls around in the dark, grabbing anything his fingers can pry loose, flinging it a.way from him.

But the black is still there inside him, swallowing him up, and he can't fling it away. It clings to his hands, rises up from within his chest, from within his very soul.

Exhausted, he flops down on the ground on his belly and sobs into the dirt and weeds. Why is he here? Simply because he has no other place to go.

. . . *where could I go, oh where could I go, seeking a refuge for my soul?*

He raises his head, his eyes suddenly dry, and looks around, as though somebody called his name.

The tent has quieted down now, and one lone voice comes soft like cornsilk fingers up the hill.

. . . *needing a friend, to help me in the end, where could I go but to the Lord* . . .

Later he doesn't remember going down to the tent, remembers only Mama swaying with her eyes shut, Hildy staring at him with her mouth hanging open, the preacher's pudgy face talking at him but no words coming to his ears. The altar bench hard under his elbows, the straw loose and yielding under his knees.

None of it matters, but that he is someplace.

And whatever there is for him, he will accept it, for he sorely needs something, and the voices murmuring at his ears promise much: *Accept Jesus as your savior, and He'll take away your burden. Lay it on the altar, Son, and He'll take it all away* . . . *tell Him all about it* . . . *to rid my soul of one dark blot, just as I am, I come, I come* . . .

A month later

" . . . for if the min-is-tra-tion of con-dem-nation be glory, much more doth the min-is-tra-tion of rig-rig-hit . . . " Bobby Ray wishes he'd paid more attention to his spelling books. "What is rig-rig . . . r-i-g-h-t-e-o-u-s?" he mumbles.

"Hi, Bobby Ray." The sweet, whispery voice wraps all around his body and the verses dissolve in front of his eyes. He closes his Bible—the one Brother Earl gave him, with his name in gold on the front. He leans back against the bench, out behind the church.

He thought he'd find some quiet to read First Corinthians, like Brother Earl told him to. There's no sense in trying now, not with her around. He wishes she'd go away. But he also knows he's been looking for her all afternoon.

"Hey, Connie Sue."

"Just *Sue*, Bobby Ray. Connie Sue is such a baby name, and I'm seventeen now. Well, I will be in two more months."

She sits down on the bench next to him, leans over to inspect the book on his lap. "What are you doin'?"

"Just readin' the scripture verses Brother Earl . . . I mean, your uncle . . . well, Brother Earl gave me." He runs his sweaty hand through his hair, bumps her with his elbow. "I'm sorry . . . I mean, I didn't know you was . . . I didn't mean to . . . " He hates when his voice goes all croaky like that.

His Bible slides off his lap and clunks onto the bench between them. He starts to pick it up, then changes his mind and leaves it. The Holy Bible between them feels . . . safe.

"Why, Bobby Ray, do I make you nervous?" She smoothes her soft cotton skirt, tucks her hands under her thighs, swings her feet back and forth under the bench. She stretches her lips into the kind of closed-mouth smile that shows off her dimples.

"Well, no . . . I mean, I reckon so. I mean, no."

"When you get to be a preacher," she says, "I think you ought to be *Robert*. Bobby Ray is so babyish. Uncle Earl says you're goin' to be a fine preacher some day. I heard him tellin' Daddy. He says he can tell, he can see it in a boy's . . . in a *man's* eyes that the Lord is callin' him. He says you'll have them people eatin' out of your hand, he can tell."

Bobby Ray can feel the red creeping up his neck and into his hair. He doesn't want to be a preacher! He never said he wanted to be any preacher!

"I'm gonna sing by myself again on Sunday," she says. "You know what I'm gonna sing?"

Is she expecting him to know the answer?

"Uncle Earl says I sing so sweet, it brings people runnin' to the altar, or to the offerin' plate, one. They don't know which one to do first." She giggles. "Bobby Ray—uh, Robert? Do you think I sing sweet?"

Bobby Ray thinks surely Brother Earl would never say anything like that.

"Do you think I do? Do you think I sing sweet?"

"Uh, yeah, I reckon so. Well, I mean, you have . . . " He tries to bring his voice down deeper. "You have a mighty fine singin' voice, Connie Sue." He's not at all sure why, but he wishes she would go away right now without another word.

She traces a fingernail along the seam at the knee of his overalls. His body reacts instantly to her nearness, and he grabs up his Bible from the bench between them and puts it on his lap.

"Robert?" Again, she looks like she's waiting for an answer. But to what? What does she want with him?

She scoots closer to him, reaches out and pushes his cowlick off his forehead. The faint scent of honeysuckle floats up in front of his face. Her lips open slightly, her tongue caresses the edge of her teeth. His whole body screams to reach up and grab the soft fingers, wants her to touch him with her lips, but something inside screams even louder, *Quit it, dammit!*

"Bobby Ray . . . Robert, have you ever . . . you know . . . been with a girl?"

"Let me alone!" He jumps up, feeling smothered and choked. He tries to hold the Bible in front of him, but his hands are sweaty and he drops it into the dust.

"Well, I was just askin'. I didn't think you'd be such a baby about it." Connie Sue's glance drops to the front of his pants, and her eyes flash with amusement.

She stands up, deliberately wipes her hands slowly down the front of her skirt, smoothing the wrinkles.

"What's the matter, you still tied to Mama's apron strings? I've seen her hangin' all over you."

"Get away from me!" he yells at her, his fists held tight at his sides. The old fury, the fury he's held down for a whole month comes screaming up from his gut, gags him, grabs his hair, shakes him.

"Do you hear me? Get away from me!"

Connie Sue's smile disappears. "Well, Bobby Ray. I reckon you really are just a baby after all."

He watches her walk away, not wanting to, but not able to will his eyes to look away from the sway of her hips. When she reaches the corner of the church, she turns back, raises her chin a little higher and flashes him a satisfied, dimply smile.

You like to have killed me . . . you like to have killed me! He grabs up the Bible from the ground, holds it out in front of him with both hands. "I thought you was goin' to help me!"

He slams the holy book onto the bench, then slumps down beside it. *I thought you was goin' to take it all away!*

Toward the end of summer 1937

It wasn't Bobby Ray's idea to have Brother Earl over to Sunday dinner after church. Brother Earl insisted on a visit to the family today and with Mama now attending his church almost every Sunday he didn't bother talking to Bobby Ray about it.

Brother Earl sits at the head of the long table, while Mama adds bowls of food from the cookstove. Mama's going on about how the house is not always this messy, blaming it on the kids, when most of the time it looks a whole lot worse, and it's nobody's doing but hers.

Brother Earl talks nice church talk, just as if Mama was one of the regular saints. "And where is your husband this fine afternoon, Sister Carmody? I thought surely he would be here with us today." Brother Earl pulls at his starched white collar, held sweaty and stiff to his pudgy neck by a polka-dotted bowtie.

There is not even a slight breeze from the screendoor to relieve the heat in the kitchen.

Bobby Ray sits down next to the pastor, wishes somebody would sit in the chair across from him. But nobody would be able to keep Mama away from it even if Daddy was here, and he's nowhere in sight. Not that anybody has expected him to be. Bobby Ray rakes his hand through his greased hair, then wonders what to do with the slippery stuff on his hand.

Mama brings over the platter heaped with slices of ham, making a big show of putting it in front of Brother Earl. She sits down across from Bobby Ray, pats down her hair, putting on that weasely smile she gets. Brother Earl goes on being nice to her, being her preacher.

Bobby Ray shivers at the sight of her face, the look he sees in his nightmares. But now her look is aimed at Brother Earl, and right in front of Bobby Ray's eyes, these two parts of his life smash together, like God and the Devil, bumping up against each other. He wishes

Brother Earl would just say something to put the Devil in his place once and for all.

But no, they go on with their everyday talk. "You kids get on over to the table," Mama says. "I'll swear they haven't got any manners at all, Brother Earl," she says with a giggle.

Liam comes over and sits in the first chair he comes to, leaving an empty one between him and Mama. Little Will takes it. Hildy hesitates, then stands across from Liam. Starting with the smallest, the younger children always stand up to eat when company comes for dinner, but Hildy doesn't seem to notice that there are enough chairs and the one next to Bobby Ray is empty.

Bobby Ray looks for something to say, words to fill the awkward silence. "He's over in the cornfield, I 'spect." Bobby Ray can't bring himself to say *Daddy.* "He's not here much." Can't Brother Earl figure it out? A coward like Daddy wouldn't stay here any more'n he has to.

"Ain't you proud of my Bobby Ray, Brother Earl?"

Bobby Ray looks down the table at the younger children, daring them to laugh. Instead, Mama is the one who giggles. "I reckon y'all call him Brother Carmody now. He's a mighty big handsome boy. Why I 'spect ever'body thinks he's my man."

Shut up, Mama! Just shut up your filthy mouth!

Brother Earl tugs at his collar again, his eyes aimed down at his plate. "Yes indeed we are proud of him, Sister Carmody. Well, now, *proud* is not exactly the word, for the scripture does say that we're not to have pride, but I am mighty pleased to see how the Lord is working in this young brother's life. I know the Lord is mighty pleased, too."

"Brother Earl," he says, "I been thinkin' on somethin'. Could I just be Bobby Ray at church?" He avoids looking at Mama's eyes. "Or Robert—Robert Ray? I mean, Bobby Ray sounds like a little kid. And Brother Carmody sounds . . . so . . . " *So stuck with Mama, that's what.* He sneaks another quick look at the kids, but Liam is concentrating on his empty plate, and neither of the twins is looking Bobby Ray's direction. They're listening, though. He can tell.

"Why, I think that sounds like a fine idea." Brother Earl smiles one of his preacher smiles at Bobby Ray, and Bobby Ray turns his head quickly away. Another hateful look at the younger kids: *you laugh and I'll wring your necks like chickens, I swear.*

"Help yourself to the ham, Brother Earl," Mama says. "It's been bakin' since early this mornin'." She takes a big slab and puts it on her own plate.

"Yes, I imagine it has." Brother Earl's look goes to the cookstove. He yanks again at his collar. "But first we're forgettin' to ask the Lord's blessin' on this fine dinner. Will your husband be comin' on in to join us soon?"

"Well, I reckon Bobby Ray and me are the ones you come here to eat with. Brother Carmody and Sister Carmody." She giggles at that. "Brother Carmody, Sweetie, you ask the blessin'."

Me? "Me?" Bobby Ray swallows hard, and his voice comes out with a croak. He hopes Brother Earl will rescue him, but Brother Earl smiles another preacher smile.

"I—I don't know what to say," Bobby Ray says.

Another preacher smile, waiting. "Now, Son, if you just let the Holy Ghost lead you, he'll fill your mouth with the right words."

Little Will is peeking sideways at Hildy, a grin pulling at his mouth, and Hildy has her head bowed with her eyes squeezed tight, biting back a laugh. *I'll kill 'em, I swear I'll kill 'em.*

Bobby Ray ducks his head obediently. He sucks in a deep breath and spits out, "We thank the Lord for this food we are about to eat, and for . . . and for . . . " *What are them fancy preacher words?* " . . . and for this food we are about to . . . to, uh, partake of. Amen."

"Amen," says Brother Earl, and he reaches for the plate of ham. "That was fine, Bobby Ray. That was just fine."

"You know Bobby Ray is my favorite one," says Mama, helping herself to fried potatoes. "He's not but fifteen, and already bigger'n his daddy and . . . and he's goin' to be a fine preacher, too, ain't he?"

"Why I do b'lieve you might be right." Brother Earl takes the bowl of potatoes offered to him. "I do b'lieve you might be right, Sister Carmody," he says. He winks at Bobby Ray.

Bobby Ray stares at his empty plate. His throat tightens up, his stomach churns up acid. How come everybody else is so all-fired ready for him to be a preacher? He never said he wanted to be a preacher!

" . . . aren't you, Son."

"What?"

"I say I reckon you're glad to see your Mama back to church, and all because of you? You're already bringin' souls to the Lord, bringin' your mama back in. You'll soon be bringin' your daddy in, too."

Bobby Ray feels like he's going to puke—he doesn't want to lie to the preacher, but having Mama pawing over him at church, too, is not something he's thankful for. And Daddy? He can't imagine it.

"Why, Brother Earl," Mama says, "I was always a good Christian, but Daniel, well, he never let me go to church." She smiles at Brother Earl. "He whupped me when I wanted to go."

Brother Earl doesn't answer her, but looks a question at Bobby Ray. Bobby Ray gulps. He glances at the screendoor, willing it closer.

"And when we was in Texas," Mama keeps going, "and my baby girl laid dyin'," I begged him to call my church so they could pray for her and the Lord would raise her up, but Daniel, he never, and . . . " Her face twists up, and she starts to make choking noises. "And then he wouldn't let me go to the funeral, and his heathen preacher came." She sobs into a fistful of apron pressed to her face.

Can't Brother Earl stop her? What's the matter with him?

Then just as if nothing had happened, she turns to Brother Earl and smiles that syrupy smile again, reaches over and paws at his hand. Brother Earl's mouth gapes, and the younger children sit like statues, not looking at anybody, not even each other.

The heat of the room squeezes Bobby Ray's chest so tight he can't breathe. He struggles up from the table, knocking back his chair, stumbles over it, lands tangled in its legs on the floor.

Brother Earl looks startled. "Son, are you all right?" He looks like he's not sure who to talk to, Mama or Bobby Ray.

Bobby Ray fights back the anger that is choking him. He stares at Mama's legs under the table, her rolled-up stockings pinching tight into the fat hanging over the tops, her hand groping between her fat thighs.

Right now, right this very minute, he hates her more than he can remember ever hating her before, and he would gladly kill her. And he knows that none of his repenting, or singing, or testifying has done one damn thing to lighten up the blackness that seethes inside him, or to wipe away her wickedness from his body.

He gets up and brushes off his pants. One thing he knows for sure. No matter what he does, crazy Mama always gets more power from his life than he does.

"Brother Earl, have some more of that good ham," she says, in that voice that makes Bobby Ray think of sticky sorghum molasses. She keeps smiling that sickening smile at the preacher and pulling at his shirt sleeve.

Instantly, it becomes clear to Bobby Ray what it is he wants to do—what he has to do, the only step up in power that he can take that Mama can't follow.

His fury settles back into its dark corner like a vigilant black cat, its eyes glistening in the dark. Bobby Ray picks up his chair, sets it upright at the table, stands and leans on the back of it.

"Brother Earl," he starts out, the strength of his voice surprising him. Yes, he likes the sound of it. He flicks his cowlick back from his face and stands up straighter. "Brother Earl, I been aimin' to tell you, the Lord spoke to me in a dream last night, and I think I have been called to preach."

For just an instant Brother Earl's eyes narrow a fraction, his mouth curves up the slightest, not a preacher smile this time.

Bobby Ray returns the look straight on, completely closing out any notice of Mama and her molasses grin, her filthy hands.

. . . there is power, power, wonderworking power in the precious blood of the Lamb . . .

Early fall, 1937
Mahala, Kentucky

Big Will leans his straight-back chair against the side of the sawmill office. "Dan'l, why'n't you go on home. They ain't much else to do here. Wayne can help me clean up and get on home in time for Amos 'n' Andy. You must have acres of p'taters left to dig."

Daniel smiles at Will's kidding, but behind the old man's eyes he sees the worry. The lumber business gets slimmer and slimmer each month. At least the gardens don't know the meaning of hard times.

Will seems like he's grateful for what Daniel brings over from his fields every day, enough for all three households, with plenty left over to put away for winter, and even some to trade in town for flour, sugar, coffee. Will's small plot and smokehouse keep the men in tobacco.

"You talkin' to me, Granddaddy?" Wayne is absorbed with some scraps of 1x4 that he has fastened together into the shape of a crude airplane.

"Your mama wantin' you home any time soon, Son? I was just tellin' Dan'l I could hear his p'taters callin' him."

Daniel picks up the broom and starts on the day's trifling of saw dust. "Liam's been begging to come help after school. Maybe we could let him?"

"Not much for him to do around here, but he don't get in the way. Y'all seen anything of Bobby Ray here lately? I reckon Spivey is makin' a real preacher out of him. Don't that beat all you ever seen, Wayne?"

Wayne scowls at him. "Well, as far as I'm concerned, I don't care if he grows himself wings, I'm not aimin' to turn my backside to him."

Will takes off his hat and scratches through his thinning gray hair. "I thought sendin' him down to that tent meetin' last summer would keep him out of trouble for a week or two, but I sure never figured on this." He closes his record book and gets up, stretches. "Well, you gotta admit, it sure did tame him down a right smart. Hell, it's got Hilda seein' some hope for me. And for that I've got no thanks to give to Bobby Ray. S'cuse me, *Robert* Ray."

Daniel sweeps, his mind an ocean and a lifetime away. *Liam, so much more like Uncle Sean, the priest. Or even Little Will, his sweet smile and kind spirit. But Bobby Ray, full of spite and fury? Who would have thought . . .*

Will breaks into Daniel's thoughts. "So why'n't you go on home and tend to your p'taters, Son. If I rustle up some business, I'll give you a holler."

"All right," Daniel says, "I think I will, then."

Will yawns, pulls out his pocket watch. "If you and Gerty want to bring some of them new p'taters, I reckon Hilda'd be glad to fry 'em up for us all." He hangs tools on their pegs over the worktable. "She put a big pot of beans on to soak this mornin' early, and she had me get her a couple of quarts of blackberries out of the cellar, so I'll bet she's got a pie or two in the oven."

Daniel scoops up the sawdust and dumps it into the trash barrel. "Little Will and Hildy'll be headed straight to your place from school to see about that pie," he says. "They'd as soon be around Hilda as anyplace in the world. Especially Hildy, when Gerty will let her." What would his family ever do without Will and Hilda?

"Wayne, tell your mama, y'all come on over for supper, too," Will says. "We ain't all had supper together in a long time. Is your mama doin' all right?"

Daniel picks up a scrap of 2x4 and studies it, then drops it into the barrel to take home for kindling. It has been a long time since he's seen Emma, and it makes him nervous to think about it. He doesn't have to look. He's sure Wayne is watching him again. Does it show on his face, he wonders, the uneasy feeling he gets about Emma?

"She's all right, I reckon," Wayne says. "Granddaddy, can I have twenty cents to go down to the show tonight after supper? I can work extra tomorrow if you want me to . . . if there's somethin' to do."

"Oh, so you're wantin' to see that *Greeta* Garbo woman again, are you? And you want me to pay for it?" Will's twinkling eyes give away his false sternness. Daniel sees it first and grins, but Wayne falls right into it.

"Aw, Granddaddy I'm not goin' to see *her.* Clark Gable's in it too, and I really like his actin'. And . . . and besides, I'm almost eighteen now, and . . . and what do you mean, *again?*"

Daniel turns his back, pokes the broom here and there in the dust. He sneaks to watch Will get the best of the boy without saying another word. He wishes he had Will's easy way with the young ones.

Will digs into his pocket, pulls out some coins. "Here, Son, you earned it. And here's another nickel in case any little yellow-headed girls is there you want to buy some candy or a cold drink for."

Wayne's neck and ears blush red. "Now who went and told you about Naomi, Granddaddy?"

Will's laugh bellows out into the mill yard. Daniel stands the broom in the corner, hiding his grin.

"Son," Will says, "when you goin' to learn you can't hide a thing from your granddaddy? Now, you go on home." He adds, in a mock-fear whisper, with a wink at Daniel. "Just don't go lettin' on to that preacher boy that you're goin' to that show, you hear?"

Three weeks later

"Bobby Ray!"

He knew it. He knew Granddaddy would be out here after him. Bobby Ray gets himself up from the floor of the hayloft and climbs slowly down the ladder.

Granddaddy grabs hold of Bobby Ray's overall strap and yanks him down from the second step. "Bobby Ray, I've told you time and time again, I'll not have you talkin' to your Mama like that. She didn't mean nothin' by what she said. She's proud of you, is all."

"Granddaddy she don't—"

"Now you hush, I'm not done talkin'." He loosens his grip on the overall strap and waits.

Bobby Ray straightens himself up and picks off the hay sticking to his clothes. "Yes Sir, but she don't—"

"Bobby Ray, your Mama fusses over you too much, I know it, but it don't give you no excuse to sass her like that, right in front of the family and the younguns."

I don't care what he does, I'm gonna tell him what she's done. I've got to. "But Granddaddy she never done them the way she done me! She's got no right—"

"Hush, Boy! You've been gettin' way too big for your britches ever since that preacher took you under his wing. But you just think about this: I was your granddaddy, and she was your mama, a long time before you got to be the preacher's fair-haired boy, and don't you forget about that. She's got the right to do whatever she thinks she ought to. She's your mama, do you hear me?"

"But Granddaddy . . . " Bobby Ray tries again, but he knows it's no use. Granddaddy's got his eyes shut tight about Mama. He'll never believe Bobby Ray. Never.

"But *nothin'*, Bobby Ray I ain't hearin' nothin' more about it."

"You *never* have heard nothin' about it! You don't know what she's done!"

Granddaddy grabs Bobby Ray's shoulders and shakes him hard. "Now you hush! Any more out of you and I'm gettin' my razor strop, you hear me? Now you come on back in the house and finish up your supper."

Granddaddy aims Bobby Ray's shoulder toward the barn door, but Bobby Ray balks, chokes out the words. "Can I just stay out here for a little while? I'll come on in a minute. Please, Granddaddy?"

"Well, then, you straighten yourself up and get on back in that house. I'll be watchin', and I don't aim to hear one bit more sassin' from you, you hear me?"

Granddaddy leaves for the house, and Bobby Ray sits down on a haybale. There's no use trying to find the words to tell Granddaddy, no use. And he's the only one. The thought of talking to Mammaw about it, well, he can't even think of words he could say to her. And she'd only believe him if Granddaddy told her to anyway. And he won't even believe Mama's crazy when everybody else knows it.

But Granddaddy's his only . . . fence. In Bobby Ray's dreams, he runs across a field, looking for a fence. He sees one over to the south and runs to it, and it disappears. Then he sees one to the north, and before he can reach it, it vanishes. And finally he looks up ahead, and there stands Granddaddy next to a fence.

Granddaddy keeps him fenced in. Bobby Ray's only thread of hope is through Granddaddy, but he only pulls the thread tight when Bobby Ray outsteps his bounds. But now he needs more than that, and Granddaddy's no hope at all.

Early spring 1938

"So how many acres of p'taters you puttin' in this year, Dan'l? Two, three hundred?" Will grins, pulls up the 2x4 that Daniel heaves up to him, stacks it on the truck bed.

Daniel grins right back and says to Wayne, "I was wondering when your granddaddy'd be starting in on me. He's running late this spring. The ground's been thawed out for two, three hours."

Big Will stretches tall and fans his face with his hat. "It don't get a rise out of you nearly like it used to."

Daniel picks up the last 2x4 and hoists it to his shoulder. "If you'd heard all the stories my grandfather told about the potatoes rotting, you'd worry too, I'll wager. And with times so bad now . . . well . . . "

"I 'spect so, Son." Will stands up on the flatbed, waiting. "But p'taters ain't ever gone bad here, not that I ever heard of. And I don't figure p'taters know enough about bad money times to get scared and go rotten!"

He laughs, then turns serious. "But no matter what the reason you done it, you was right, Son, and we was all grateful for what you raised last year. I'm sure hopin' times are gettin' better from here on up, and the mill can start bringin' in money like the old days." He takes off his hat, wipes the sweat on his sleeve.

Daniel looks away, embarrassed at Will's praise. "I . . . I mostly just like to be out in the sun," he says.

Will jumps down from the truckbed. "Let's get this stuff on over to old man Pyle, 'cause tomorrow I'm aimin' to take you out and show you that stand of timber I'm hopin' to get him to sell me. It's about ten, twelve miles out, so let's get an early start."

Daniel looks at Will, then Wayne, then Will again. *Me?* he starts to say, but no, he'd be talking to Wayne. Family business.

Wayne has one of his stick airplanes that he's swooping up and down through the air. "Granddaddy? You hear Howard Hughes flew clear around the world in less than four days?"

"Well, I doubt very seriously if *that* one's gonna make it out to the road yonder, even if you give it four years."

Wayne circles the sawhorse with his plane, and just as it comes in for a landing on the workbench, the wing piece falls off.

"So, you reckon you can take care of things by yourself here in the mornin'?"

"Sure, Granddaddy. First man'll give me fifty cents, I'll sell the place off and go to the show to see that *Greeta* Garbo woman. Then with what's left, me and Naomi will run off and get married."

Will gives the boy a sideways look, picks up a hammer and turns it over in his hand. Then holds it up, aiming it at Wayne's head.

"That's not funny, Granddaddy," Wayne says, but he grins just a little anyway.

"I'd watch out for that youngun," Will says to Daniel. "He's learnin' a real sassy mouth from someplace!" Will hangs the hammer up and heads into the office.

He pokes his head back out the door and says with a wink, "You don't reckon he's been hangin' around with that new preacher in town, do you, that Robert Ray fella?"

Early the next morning

"So the next mornin', dumb ol' Arnie comes out, just like ever' day the last three days, and they still ain't any baby pigs in the pen."

Daniel can't keep his attention on Will's words for staring at the road ahead. He wishes he could get Will to let him drive.

Will's glance darts back and forth between the windshield and Daniel's face. "So he's standin' there scratchin' his head, figurin' he's got to take the sow back up the road to visit Sam Higgins's hog ag'in, just like the last three days, and how maybe this just ain't workin' out like Sam claimed it would."

The old truck is in bad shape, but there's nothing much that can be done until tires and parts are available again. A door hinge broke off last fall, and the whole door had to be left off until times are better. It doesn't seem to worry Will that his whole side of the truck is wide open. He rides like he's on the back of a favorite old mule.

Will slows the truck down and looks around. "Keep your eye out for a rattleshack ol' barn with a Garrett Snuff sign on it. Leastwise that's how it was last time I was out here, four, five year ago. That's where the gravel road goes off."

The road is paved, but there has been no sign of life for more than five miles, the road lined with dense woods, dotted with paintbare roadsigns, most of them outliving the businesses they advertise.

"So anyways," Will goes on, "dumb ol' Arnie's just lookin' around wonderin' where the sow's gone to, when his old woman comes out on the porch and says, 'If you're lookin' for the sow, she's been settin' in the wheelbarrow since sunup, waitin' for you.'"

Daniel tries to keep his mind off Will's driving, instead shifting his interest to the dense woods along the highway. When he realizes Will's rambling has stopped, he tries to pull his attention back inside the truck.

Something feels undone, and he tries to pull Will's words back to his mind. "Now what was it, this friend of yours, he was wanting to raise pigs, and he took his sow up to a neighbor's to breed her?"

"Ya see, dumb ol' Arnie still didn't get how things worked with hogs. But the sow sure was enjoyin' findin' out, and . . . " He pushes his hat back off his forehead, scratches his head, grins. "Hell, Dan'l, you sure make it hard for a feller to enjoy tellin' a good yarn."

Will drives along, quiet. A few more miles on down the road he says, "I got somethin' kinda serious I want to talk to you about . . . about the Pyle place. I been wantin' this stand of timber of his'n for years. It was from his wife's family and he'd never sell it then, but now that she's gone and hard times are gettin' to him and he's hurtin' for money—well, ever'body is, but he's hurtin' enough to get shed of whatever he can, and he just don't have the heart for it anymore."

Will peers down the road, squints. "You ain't seen that barn? Just between you and me, my eyes ain't what they used to be."

Daniel thinks he'll keep his comments to himself for now.

"Now Pyle needs cash money and I know it. We ain't got much neither, but I've got a little put away. I never did believe in banks. I'm thinkin' maybe we could offer him just enough to get the back taxes up, and a little share of the business for it. Now, I know that ain't much of nothin' right now, but Roosevelt says things'll be different soon, and leastwise I reckon he can see better than Hoover ever did, him claimin' they wasn't no depression back there, and raisin' taxes on us." Will drives on, bouncing with every bump in the road. "I'm thinkin' Pyle'd be glad to just get shed of anything, to not have any taxes to pay, little as they are. It'd keep us in timber for years to come, and he's just enough of a gamblin' man to see that it could bring in some money later on. This depression can't last much longer, and he ain't makin' a dime on it like it is. It's standin' out there rain or shine, with no mind who it belongs to, timber just fallin' and goin' to waste."

Saplings crowd the road like children watching for a parade. The occasional cedar with its deep evergreen stands out in contrast to the bright emerald of the surrounding spring foliage. *Christmas trees,* Liam insists, no matter what time of year.

"Has anybody ever cut any of this timber?" Daniel asks. "It looks . . . old."

"Naw, it's not been cut since as long as I can remember. Folks come out here and hunt deer, is all. They's fine hickory and oak trees back in there that'd keep us in business from now on."

"It sounds like you've got your mind made up, then."

"Son, I figure it ain't just *my* mind to make up. You ought to have some say on whether or not you want to be any kind of partner with Charlie Pyle, since the mill's goin' to be yours one of these days."

Daniel turns to look quick and sharp at Will, then drops his gaze back down the floor. "But I thought . . . what about Wayne?"

"I used to figure on Wayne follerin' me in it, but I never talked to him about it. It's set up like that now, but I been thinkin' on it for a long time. He's done good in school and I'm hopin' he'll want to go on, maybe read law or somethin'. Or maybe learn doctorin'. Wayne's a good-hearted boy, and smart."

The left front wheel hits a rut that bounces them both to the roof. Daniel rubs the smarting spot on the top of his head, but Will doesn't seem to notice, staring down the road, his hat askew.

"They's bound to be more money one of these days, and I hope the mill can send all the younguns on for more schoolin', Chigger, too. So I aim to call Harry Gunn and change my will." His voice drops low and soft. "Dan'l, my only son died three days old in aught-three, and after Gerty, the doctor said they weren't to be no more. 'Til you come along . . . I never got to know Emma's J.D. . . . . I didn't have a real son. I'm proud of all my grandkids, and Wayne's a good boy but he'll find his own way just like the rest of the younguns, whether or not you and me like the ways they do it."

Daniel stares out the window, wishes he could say the words that fill his mind, but his throat chokes up, dry.

"You think on it a while. For now, just say 'nay' if you ain't in agreement to the Pyle deal, and we'll turn around and go home."

A rotted barn is visible on the right, the Garrett Snuff sign on the roof recognizable only by somebody who's looking hard for it or is remembering it from better days. Daniel points to it and Will nods, slows to turn the truck onto the gravel road. His arms drape over the steering wheel, and he appears absorbed in watching the road.

Daniel leans back, tries the best he can to relax a little, watches the trees passing by him, catches sight of an occasional dogwood in bloom.

After two or three miles of gravel, Will turns to Daniel. "You never talked about when you was a kid, or about your Mama. Or your Daddy."

Daniel shifts himself around on the hard seat, but he can't find a comfortable place for his long legs. "I remember him laughing and Ma, too, but when he got too carried away with it, she was the one who kept things sensible." The familiar lump of grief comes back up; he tries to swallow it down. "They both died the next year after they sent me to live with my uncle here. My baby sisters, too."

"What of?"

"I don't know. My uncle just said they died. He said I belonged to him, then, and he never let me forget how grateful I should be. There wasn't a lot to eat back home, and everybody was bad off. I guess I was one less mouth to feed. Ma wrote me every week, and they were goin' to come in a few years, but then . . . then they died. I guess I was too young to wonder why."

Will squints out at the road ahead. "Just seems kind of odd that they all died like that and he never said what of."

When Daniel doesn't answer, Will goes on. "I never saw my mama laugh. Her family was all mean. My daddy used to say they sized rattle-snakes for a livin'. She was mean and cold and hard, nothin' like Hilda. I don't know how I come to get me such a good woman as Hilda. My mama, I swear, she grew that old peach tree for one thing—for all the switches she broke off of it. I can't stand the smell of peaches to this day. My daddy he hightailed it out away from her when I was eleven. I never once blamed him, neither. I just wished he'd took me with him. If they's a hell, I don't doubt that's where that hateful old woman is."

The two men ride along the worn gravel road in silence for what seems like twenty miles to Daniel, but is probably no more than five or six. Then Will says, "You reckon they is one?"

"Is one?"

"A hell."

"Well, I can't picture my Ma anyplace but heaven. And I don't know if there's a heaven, that it means there's a hell, too."

"I reckon rascals like us don't want to think of they really bein' one. I all the time figured all that hellfire stuff was mostly how the preachers kept people in line. But you know, you can't help but wonderin' sometime, when you get closer to your own fourscore and ten." Will drives on, leaning on his arms on top of the steering wheel, his gaze glued to the road. "So, do you reckon they is one?"

Daniel realizes this very minute that whatever faith he's ever had has stayed with him only because nobody has ever asked him a question as simple as Big Will's. He surely has never asked such a question— *Is there really a hell?*—out loud, himself. How could he have, when to do so—to even *think* about doing it—would have brought wrath down on his head. Probably the wrath of God, but certainly the wrath of the priest and the nuns.

Here in the light of day, asked what it is that he believes, he knows that he not only believes almost nothing, but he has no idea when he stopped. But how can he turn loose of the belief in hell, if the hope of Ma in heaven goes with it?

"I honestly don't know, Will," he says finally and they both go on with questions no more answered than before.

Will brings the truck to a quick stop. Daniel's knees bump the dashboard. "Will, how about letting me drive?"

"Did you see a marker on that tree back yonder?" Will backs the truck up a few feet. "Oh, naw, it's just a broke-off piece of that dead tree." He shifts back into low gear and the truck leaps forward.

The road gravel thins, leaving only the deep ruts drying from the spring mud. As they bump along on the furrowed roadway, Daniel hangs onto the door and braces with his legs. He tries to watch the thick woods on both sides of the road, searching for a marker that he has no idea what it looks like.

Through Will's wide-open side of the truck, Daniel can see the deep gully where the spring runoff has washed away a quarter of the road, leaving very little for the tires. Will doesn't look like he's noticing. He's just staring directly in front of him, bouncing on every bump in the road, scarce inches from the whole outdoors. Daniel hangs onto the beat-up old door on his own side.

"One thing sure," Will says, "we'll have to do somethin' about this road."

"Look out!" A huge buck leaps in front of the truck, hits the hood with a loud BAM!

Will wrenches the wheel sharply, and the deer's body crashes into the windshield directly in front of the steering wheel.

The woods and sky are thrown askew, and the two men's bodies are thrown wildly in one direction, then the other.

Daniel comes to with a sharp pain at the back of his head, and his mind and body jolt to full consciousness at the same time. He hunches in the dim small space, almost blind with the pain in his head.

The truck lies on its side, and the space that used to be Will's wide open door is now a dirt floor under Daniel's feet. He tries to stand up, but bumps his head hard on the door above him. Shards of glass crunch under his step. He lifts his foot; stickiness sucks at his shoe.

"Will? Will!" he calls. The windshield is filled with the body of the deer, its rump protruding through the broken glass, held at bay by the steering wheel.

"Will!" he calls again, and hears a faint groan from near his feet, muffled, outside. Will is out! Will was thrown out!

On the dirt below Daniel sees two workboots set at odd angles. He gags. His stomach catches the coppery reek of blood before his mind registers it. Then it comes to him. He stands in a pool of Big Will's blood, and there is precious little else of Big Will to see.

Daniel pounds his fists against the door above him, He comes to his senses, twists the door handle. He heaves the door upwards and light floods in, stabs pain into his eyes. He pulls himself up through the opening, bracing his foot on the deer's body, on the window frame, on the gearshift hump. He pulls one knee up and over the running board, then the other, and he falls to the ground, scraping his backside on the exposed drive shaft. He lies panting, tries to get up, falls back in a wave of nausea.

He drags himself up to his knees, to his feet, and stumbles past the front wheels, past the stare of the deer's lifeless eyes almost level with his own, its body lying back in a grotesque sitting position against the cab of the truck. Around on the other side of the deer, the upper half of Will lies face down, growing out from under the top of the overturned truck.

Daniel throws his body against the cab of the truck, imagines his force growing mighty, a powerful heave and turning the truck upright, Will standing up, brushing himself off and walking away laughing at the monstrous joke. He rams the truck with his shoulders, his arms, his back, until his strength is drained and his will is exhausted. He drops down beside the gray head, the face a quarter submerged in the shallow muddy water that runs red down the gully. He looks around for something to put under it, but there's nothing. He rips his own shirt off, wads it and props it under the scraped side of the head.

Will groans, opens his eyes, tries to raise his head.

"Will . . . I'll go find help, I'll . . . "

As Daniel tries to get to his feet, Big Will's voice pulls at him. "Don't leave me, Son . . . don't leave me here . . . "

Daniel looks frantically around him with no idea of what miracle he expects—hopes—to see. There's nothing . . . no branch or broken trunk to use as a lever, no big rocks . . . no angels, no saints, no gods. There is nothing on earth that he can do, and heaven has turned its back on them all.

Pain holds his head in a vise and panic throttles his throat. He tries to clear his thoughts, needs desperately to come up with something he can do. He can't just sit there. There must be something. Through the pain in his head, thoughts bump into each other, trying to make some sense of what he sees around him. . . . *a priest . . . I need to get a priest . . . no . . . Hail Mary, full . . . no no . . .*

Will's muddy hand reaches out, grasping. Daniel grabs it, holds it tight . . . something . . . there must be something he can do.

"Dan'l . . . " Will's voice is weak, his eyes closed. "Son, reckon we might be . . . wrong about it . . . hell?"

Tears rush up into Daniel's eyes, and there's no reason to try to stop them now. "I don't know, Will . . . I don't know."

"I hope the Lord and Hilda . . . can forgive me . . . forgive me for not believin' . . . "

Daniel holds tight to the hand that grips his, as if he can hold onto a small part of Will's soul. Will groans and stirs, his eyes struggle to open. Daniel bends down so the old man can see his face, see that he's there.

He feels himself shrinking smaller, younger, helpless. *Don't leave me, Will, please . . .*

Will grins half a grin that twists into a pale contortion of the gentle wrinkled brown face of Big Will Tucker. Then the face relaxes into the peaceful look of sleep.

One last time the eyes open, but this time they seem to focus not on Daniel's face, but far beyond him.

Daniel turns his ear closer, so he can hear Will's faint whisper, " . . . the light . . . there yonder . . . look . . . "

Daniel looks up into the blazing midmorning sky, and the hand that grasps his falls heavy, lifeless into the mud.

"No! Don't go, Will! Don't leave me!" He lays his aching head on Will's back and moans, "No, no, no!"

But in the deep woods surrounding him—the hickory and the oak with just a scattering of Christmas trees, there is not a soul to hear his voice but a doe, standing with her fawn in her own grief by the side of the road.

He takes the shirt from under Will's head, wrings out the water and spreads the wet cool cloth over the gray thin hair. Daniel's right hand of its own accord reaches to his forehead, then his chest, but his mind cries *no no no.*

He sits back on his heels, not seeing or caring that his back is bare and his pants and shoes are filthy with mud, stiffening with drying blood. He rocks his body slowly, then faster and faster, as though the motion can keep his head from hurting, his mind from thinking, the truth from settling in. Here in the Kentucky woods, close to the woodland that he took for granted in the Ireland of his childhood and that he yearned for in Uncle Seamus's Chicago, here with Will's life drained away, Daniel has spoken his doubt out loud, and there is no faith left. He has the barest instinct to shrink down ever so slightly as though he still believed enough in something to expect to be struck down for his questions, for his refusal of the answers.

But he looks bitterly at the still body of the best friend he ever had, and even that fear is released. *If there was a God, wouldn't He have known to take me, and not Big Will Tucker?*

Daniel gets to his feet, straightens himself for the long walk back to the family.

The next day, at the cemetery

Daniel stands under a tree twenty yards away from the gravesite. He can't bring himself to join the family and most of the townspeople gathered there. The whiskey has done nothing to dull the reality, the headache, nothing to blur the deeper pain. The pastor's words drone on and on, but Daniel feels no part of this final goodbye to Big Will. The plain wooden casket smothered with wilting wildflowers is a far different goodbye from the one he endured alone by a pitiful trickle of a muddy stream.

The walk home from Will's body was endless, but he wished it to be so, because what waited at the end of it was unthinkable. As long as he plodded one foot in front of the other, he could give in to the numbness of his soul.

He stopped first at the sheriff's office to tell them where to find the truck and Will's body.

Then there was nothing left between him and the family but his stammered words and their dread of hearing them because the news might be as bad as they feared.

Hilda was hit the worst, he knew. She stood silently in her place by the stove, holding her dignity for the sake of the others, for the children, he could tell.

As the others drained out their grief with tears and anguish, Hilda came quietly out to the porch step where Daniel sought solace and rest for his blistered, torn feet.

A timid hand on his shoulder, and Hilda's desolate eyes peered down into his. "Daniel, I thank my Lord you was there with him." For the first time he sees tears glistening in her eyes. "Please, Daniel, did he say anything, there at the end? Was there time?"

At first no words came to the gray murk of his thoughts. But he nodded. Yes, there was a little time, yes, he did say something.

"Please try to recollect, Daniel."

He sensed that her plea was for something more than just the last endearing word or two on her man's dying breath. He searched the haze that enshrouded his thoughts and tried to pull out something, anything, of substance to give her. He couldn't let Hilda down this time, as he had done so many times before.

He stared down at his filthy shoes, the soles worn through, the dirt and stains on his pants, ashamed to sit here in Hilda's presence with Will's blood caking the creases of his clothes. He hoped that in the shadows of the porch she didn't see. "Ma'am, what he said was . . . well, he said your name, that you were a good woman, and then—and then he said that he . . . that he wanted the Lord to forgive him."

Hilda's eyes widened, and she raised both her hands, her tears overflowing down over her careworn face. "Oh, praise be to Jesus! Praise the Lord, praise His name!"

She dropped to her knees on the porch behind Daniel, encircled his neck with her arms, hugging him hard.

He winced at the pain in his bruised and sunburned shoulders, in the side of his head pressed against her bosom, but he didn't have the heart or the strength to pull away from her.

"Oh, Daniel, I am so grateful you was there, and to know my Will died saved. Now I know I'll see him when I go to meet the Lord!"

The pastor says his amen and solemn in their leavetaking, the towns-people pause in front of Hilda for a final pat, a sympathetic hug, until only the family is left.

The twins stand wide-eyed down at the end of the casket, Little Will holding his sister's hand, watching, with the bewildered look that

Daniel remembers from years ago, when a three-year-old Bobby Ray stared at his sister's coffin with no understanding of its meaning.

The Bobby Ray that he watches now, standing beside the pastor in the suit the church gave him, is a stranger to Daniel, no son he has ever known, as lost to him as the little girl left in the ground in Texas an eternity ago.

Without words, Liam joins Daniel in the shade of the big oak. Daniel pulls him close, awkward at first, but it is comforting—his real son, the one son who effortlessly reaches the parts of Daniel's heart that he cannot bring himself to give away to others.

Near the casket Emma leans on Wayne's arm. Wayne looks older, more somber in his dark blue suit, the suit Emma tailored for his high school graduation next month. She speaks something to Wayne and points over to where Daniel stands, then walks slowly towards Daniel, stopping a few feet away.

"Daniel, I—"

"Emma," he says, but he can't seek out her eyes.

Behind her, Bobby Ray approaches Wayne, but Wayne turns his back. Left in the awkwardness of the rebuke, Bobby Ray turns toward Daniel over by the tree. After a quick look back at the pastor, he starts over toward Emma and Daniel.

Daniel looks behind himself, hoping someone else has attracted Bobby Ray's attention, but there is no one.

Bobby Ray walks in front of Emma, stops right in Daniel's face, stands with his feet wide apart. Daniel can think of no words to say to this stranger.

But Bobby Ray has no such difficulty. "You let my granddaddy die and you didn't even try to save him! You are a wicked sinner, and the Lord will surely punish you!"

The hateful words stab at Daniel. Liam's body stiffens against Daniel's his bruised ribs. He tightens his hold on the boy's shoulders, but can offer nothing to Bobby Ray but a silent *no . . . no . . . no.*

He knows Bobby Ray's ears are closed to anything he could say back to him.

Bobby Ray turns to leave, his judgment delivered, but he meets Emma head on. Her mouth opens as if to say something, but nothing comes out. Instead, she slaps the boy's jaw hard. She looks as shocked at her own action as Bobby Ray does.

Wayne comes running over and pulls his mother to him, joining the circle of eyes glaring at Bobby Ray. Outnumbered, Bobby Ray backs off, rubbing his cheek. He flings a last vicious look at Daniel, and he stomps back over to the casket, where Brother Earl is hovering over Hilda and Gerty.

"Daniel, I'm—I'm so sorry!" Emma turns to hide her tears in the sleeve of Wayne's suit jacket. Wayne holds his mother awkwardly.

Then all their attention shifts to Gerty, who has been sitting dry-eyed and quiet on one of the folding chairs in front of Big Will's casket. "Come on over here by Mama, Bobby Ray!" her voice rings out above the muted voices around her.

Gerty. Daniel knows he should feel something for Gerty, but until now it has simply not occurred to him to wonder how she will cope with her father's death. She stands out like a garish yellow butterfly in a field of brown moths. There was no time for Emma to make her sister a new dress for mourning, and Gerty had a fit when Hilda offered to dye this one good church dress that still fits her.

"Brother Earl?" Gerty's voice jars the dismal afternoon. "Brother Earl, look here at my preacher man! Why, in that fine suit you gave him, he looks just like he's about to preach a funeral, don't he?"

Five days later

Wayne traces his fingers over the tools hanging on the board behind the workbench. Granddaddy's tools. He set such store by his tools. A sob comes up unbidden from deep in Wayne's chest before he can catch it and hold it back.

Emma looks up from her straightback chair that she has carried out of the mill office and into the sparse shade alongside the building. Hugging an open ledger book to her chest, she comes over, reaches out to touch Wayne's sleeve.

"Mama, it's just not right." Wayne turns a rasp over and over in his hands. "They're Granddaddy's tools, and this is *his* place. I can't ever think about 'em like they're mine. Hearin' it read out off a piece of paper is not the same as Granddaddy givin' me something himself. And even if he wanted me to have all this someday, it's just not right for it to be now, not this way, not yet."

"I know it," Emma says with a thin smile. "I keep thinkin' he'll be on over here any minute, and what am I doin' messin' with his account books. He always hung onto them and did them himself. Your granddaddy was good at figures. He was always proud of that, even if he didn't go to school but four years. He'd have been so proud of you, to see you graduate. It's what he wanted for all you kids."

She puts the ledger down on the worktable in front of him. Will Tucker's sprawling handwriting floats in columns across the pages, detailing the dwindling lumber transactions of the past few months. The last entry, *Charlie Pyle, 36 2x12s, white oak*, waits for a final dickered price. Wayne can't bear to look at it right now, not today.

Emma pats his hand. "Don't worry, I'm used to keepin' books, and I can do yours for you. I know it looks like a lot, but Granddaddy must've trusted you'd do a good job. I 'spect he counted on me . . . and Uncle Daniel . . . to help you."

Wayne hangs up the rasp, adjusting it to exactly the faint pencil outline Granddaddy drew last summer when Bobby Ray kept putting the tools up in the wrong places. "I'm worried about Uncle Daniel, Mama. He's not been here at all since the funeral. I think he's drinkin' more. More than he used to." He gets the odd feeling he always gets when he brings up Uncle Daniel around Mama. He can see her pulling inside herself at hearing the name. "I'm sorry," he says, but he's not quite sure why.

"What for, Hon?"

"Well, Mama, sometime I'm not sure if you—if you *like* Uncle Daniel or not. You act kind of like you're mad at him all the time. It wasn't his fault anything Bobby Ray did."

"Oh . . . well, no, Son. I just feel . . . " She turns her face quickly away from him. "I just feel sorry for him, is all." She opens the book and draws her finger down the last column. "Do you reckon on this Charlie Pyle order—"

"Mama, I don't know if I should ask him to help me, or if he doesn't want to work around here anymore. It'd be like he was workin' for me, and me bein' his boss and I don't blame him. He thinks I'm just a kid!"

He tries to turn away and hide the tears that blur his eyes. "This whole blame town probably thinks I'm just a snotnosed kid. And Uncle Daniel does too."

He leans against the shed and lets go of the tears that won't stay back any longer. Emma pats his sleeve, murmuring mother's words. Finally drained, he turns around. "Can we just go home now?"

Emma nods. "Tomorrow will be soon enough to worry about all this, Son. Let's go home."

1938 . . . . . Minimum wage raised
from 25 cents to 40 cents an hour

Two Months Later

"Why, Robert, what are you doin' in here, hidin' from the ol' devil?" Brother Earl makes his way down the aisle from the back of the empty church, grinning his pastor grin, to where Bobby Ray slouches on the bench in the second row. He straightens himself up as Brother Earl slides onto the bench next to him, his brown serge suit heavy with sweat and Old Spice.

Brother Earl puts his big hand on Bobby Ray's shoulder. Bobby Ray wants to pull away but he knows he can't. The preacher's just trying to be nice to him.

Bobby Ray wishes he was as good as Brother Earl sees him, but he knows better.

"No, sir, I was just tryin' to picture me up behind that pulpit. I—I'm wonderin' if this preachin' idea's not something I was too quick to talk about."

"Now you can tell me the truth, Son. Is that ol' devil tryin' to fill your heart with doubt? That's exactly what he'll try to do, because he hates to see a fine young brother like you reachin' out to serve the Lord. Why, he hates that worse than anything else in this world. But the Lord will be victorious if you just trust Him, for He knows your heart, inside and out."

That's what scares Bobby Ray the most. He has no doubt in his mind that he doesn't belong up there behind that pulpit. How will he ever convince Brother Earl, who seems like he has an answer from the Bible for everything?

"I don't know how I'll ever learn all them scripture verses. I never did real good with gettin' things by heart in school."

"But, Son, the Lord will help you, and the Holy Ghost will put the words right in your mouth. We'll start you out easy just testifyin' and such, and I'll write you out some words to practice on."

"But how come you're so sure I can do it?"

"Because Son, I can hear the Lord callin' you, and I have a vision of you drawin' sinners in to Him."

Brother leans in toward Bobby Ray. "Why, there are hundreds of young wom—young people out there who will listen to a fine young man like you, and will come into the flock."

Brother Earl always talks about visions and dreams like they were righteous and pure, but Bobby Ray Carmody's dreams are anything but righteous, and his daytime thoughts are not all that holy either.

Words. All the smooth words pour out of Brother Earl's mouth like sorghum molasses. How does he do that? "How did you learn all them fine things to say?"

"My brother Harold and me, we grew up under a preacher daddy who fed us the Word for breakfast, dinner, and supper. By the time we was your age, we was preachin' regular in his tent meetings. Harold turned out to be the one who traveled with Daddy and then he took over the tent after Daddy died. I married Mabel and settled into a church. But since she passed on, I like to travel with the tent crowd in the summers, and Harold's goin' to want you to travel with us, too.

"This revival comin' up next month, we'll just have you just do somethin' easy, you'll see. Why, when Connie Sue first started singin' when she was little, Harold had to hold her hand 'cause she was scared to death, but in no time we couldn't get her to hush up. By the time her mama died, she was so taken with it all, she took to travelin' ever'where her daddy went."

Picturing Connie Sue up there at the front of the church with him doesn't help one bit. Connie Sue knows him inside. She must, or why would she look at him like she does?

He turns and looks at Brother Earl. "I just don't know if I can do it. I'm just not—"

"Now there goes that old devil again. Get thee behind this boy, Satan! This boy is called of the Lord and you keep your filthy hands off of him!"

Filthy hands . . . filthy hands touching all the way down into his soul. How could Mama have touched him with her filthy hands, if he wasn't filthy too? He can't even remember when she first touched him like that. Was he bad already when he was born? She never told any of the younger ones to come and *help* her. Bobby Ray fights the tears back, but they're coming up too fast. He turns his head away from the preacher.

"Now what is this? You don't have to hide your tears from the Lord. The Lord can see down into your heart, Son."

Bobby Ray sits, biting on his bottom lip, not wanting to hear any more how the Lord can see inside him. His throat tightens up until he can hardly breathe, much less talk.

The quiet of the church bears down on him, just as surely as if the judgment of God was resting heavily on him, watching him.

Brother Earl has stopped talking. He doesn't know, but Bobby Ray does. There's no chance for him, none at all, no matter how much

Brother Earl talks, prays for him. There can't be, because there's too much nastiness that lurks inside him, peering at him, laughing at him from inside, heaped up in there, from all those years of filthy hands, and nobody can—

"Son, is it that mama of yours?"

Bobby Ray jerks his head up and sucks in his breath, his heart ripped opened wide and naked for everybody to see. *Brother Earl knows what Mama did!* Bobby Ray wants to run out of the church and slam the door behind him.

Brother Earl puts his hand on Bobby Ray's shoulder, holding him in place, and he smiles at him—not his preacher smile this time, but a quieter, softer one. "I kind of thought so, Bobby Ray. Your mama's a sick woman, and you've carried a heavy burden. I can see that in your heart, and the Lord can see it too, Son."

Bobby Ray buries his head in his arms on the back of the bench in front of him. Brother Earl tugs at his arm, turns around and kneels on the floor facing the bench, pulling Bobby Ray along with him.

The sin and the dirtiness Bobby Ray feels inside, it must be his fault, and everybody can tell, surely they can. Connie Sue, she can tell. She can tell he's full of sin and blackness, or else why would she seek him out? And why does he want her to?

And Mama. She knew he was bad, or else why did she make him touch her; why did his body act just the way she wanted when she touched him?

And the blackest part of all, why does he *want* his body to act that way now, on his own? Why does he *need* it to, when it had made him feel so nasty with Mama?

"I'll pray with you, Son." Brother Earl puts one hand gently on Bobby Ray's back. "Lord, look into our brother Bobby Ray's heart here today and help him in what he needs." Fear pushes up from Bobby Ray's insides, the terror that paints itself black over his heart, chokes him until he can hardly breathe. He'll burn in hell, he knows he will. He's sure of it.

"Ask Him, Bobby Ray. Just ask Him. Just say His name, Son. Call on Jesus."

Bobby Ray chokes, his voice held tight in his throat. "Jesus," he whispers.

"Say His name, Son. Go ahead, call on Him."

He can't. His throat won't open up. He's choking. He is being pulled apart, like the Devil and God are fighting for his very soul.

Finally the words scream out of his mouth—or are they just inside his head?—to God, to Brother Earl, to anybody: *Help me!*

He hears Brother Earl's voice somewhere that feels suddenly far away. "Lord, I hold our brother Bobby Ray up to you. In Your mercy, lift his burden from him."

The warm tears are finally released, the deep tears held in since he was a little boy, up from a place in his soul that no little boy could know was there. His body gives up its tears, its burden, and he rests his weary exhausted face on the seat, his cheek against the hard wood, slippery wet under him.

Brother Earl stays with him, his arm around the boy's shoulders as the last of the flood drains out of him in great shudders.

Finally Bobby Ray is drained dry. He sits on the floor, without words, embarrassed, hiccupping out the last remnants of his crying. His head hurts, his throat feels raspy, and he feels like he could fall down and sleep for a week.

Brother Earl pulls a clean handkerchief out of his pocket and gives it to him. Then he leans on the bench, pushes himself up from the floor. He sits back on the bench, rubbing his knees, breathing hard from the effort.

Bobby Ray follows, sits on the edge of the bench, leans again on the one in front of him. He listens to the silence, the calm that rests in the empty space filled so recently with rage and strife.

"Now, is that better, Son?"

He can't look at Brother Earl, is not sure just what he wants to say . . . or what Brother Earl knows. But for once somebody is listening, without blaming him. "Why . . . why is she . . . what made her the way she is?"

"Well, Son, I don't know. She might have a demon. Or it might be a sin of her mother and father, that she was born with."

"Oh, no, that's not so! It can't be. Mammaw is—well, you know Mammaw. And Granddaddy, he was—"

"Your granddaddy wasn't saved, was he?"

"Mammaw said he was, but I never knew of it. But that don't matter. He was a good man, I know it. The best one—I mean besides you. He just . . . well, he just couldn't see nothin' wrong with Mama."

"And what about your daddy? Can't he do anything with her?"

"Huh." Bobby Ray feels the disgust covering his face like a dark stain, and he turns it away from the preacher. "He can't do nothin' with her. He don't even care what she does. All he cares about is his bottle. He's got 'em hid everywhere, but Mama don't care if he drinks or not."

Brother Earl gets up to leave. "Well, I must get back to my message for Sunday, but you stay here for a while if you want to. And, Son, we must remember to pray for your mama and daddy both, that the Lord will change their hearts."

He looks up into Brother Earl's face. Change Mama and Daddy's hearts? Change *them?* "That's some job for Him to do." He puts his head down on his arms, the old darkness creeping back into the empty space in his heart, the void left from the crying. There's nothin' anybody can do . . . not even God, he's sure.

"Bobby Ray, we'll find an answer for you. You do the best you can and trust in the Lord. We'll find an answer. We'll save you, Son."

Bobby Ray lets out a deep sigh and settles back against the hard back of the bench, closes his eyes and nods. He'll try his best. But there's nothing anybody can do. Nothing, he is sure of that.

Early summer 1938
Lovelaceville, Kentucky

"Brother Robert?" Bobby Ray looks behind him to find the timid voice calling to him. A slight, stringy-haired girl about his age stands against the covered side of the tent, out of sight of the crowd that mills around waiting for the service to start.

He's seen the girl before, every night of the two-week revival. Her plain print dress with its high neckline, long sleeves, and long skirt do nothing to keep her body from looking like a skinny boy's.

"Brother Robert, I . . . I'm Hazel Mae Knight." She twists a dingy handkerchief around one finger. "Brother Robert, I—I've . . . you've . . . well, I been waitin' to talk to you, and now look, the Lord brought you right here where I am." Her nervous smile shows her gratitude for the miracle that has occurred before her eyes, but it quickly disappears behind her shyness.

What does she want with him? Bobby Ray can't even guess.

"I'm . . . well, I'm . . . I'm Hazel . . . but I've already told you that, and . . . and I . . . you probably haven't even noticed me, but I . . . I . . . been here every night, and your testimony, it blessed my heart, and . . . and . . ." Then out tumble the words that she has most likely practiced for several days and nights: "I had a vision and the Lord come to me and said that you was the one I was to marry."

Bobby Ray stares at the girl with no answer and the moment for any answer passes. Her moment of pumped-up confidence deflates like a punctured balloon.

"And I . . . " she starts, but when Bobby Ray doesn't respond the way she has surely prayed for, she loses herself in tears. She turns and runs, stumbling, around the corner of the tent.

He's still staring after her when Brother Earl comes up behind him, chuckling. "Another young lady with a vision of bearin' your children, Robert?"

Bobby Ray stands, still numb. "What's the matter with her? She don't even know me."

"No, Son," Brother Earl says, herding him away from the crowd that gathers at the side of the tent. "No, but she *reco'nizes* you." He stops and turns to speak right into Bobby Ray's face, his voice low and even. "Understand, she sees you as a way out of her limited life and out of this town."

"But she said she had a *vision*."

"Now tell me, Son, if you was her, wouldn't it be easy to stir up a vision or two if it might get you away from here?" His arm sweeps around to cover the small farming town, most of its hardworking citizens now taking their seats on folding chairs in the tent. A pudgy matron holds her purse primly in front of her, smiles and waves a girlish wave at Brother Earl. He nods and smiles back. "Why, good evenin', Sister Watkins," he calls over.

Back to Bobby Ray: "You have to be on your guard, always bein' kind, but protectin' yourself. Some young ladies might even get up more nerve than that, and offer you . . . well, offer you somethin' they figure you can't turn down, hopin' to lay claims on you later."

"But then why don't I just stay away from 'em?" Remembering Connie Sue's soft touch, her imploring mouth, his body stirs and he wants to run. "How come you even want me here?"

"Because, Robert, them women with their visions are the ones we need, to keep the Lord's work goin'. You'll understand it by and by. You just keep yourself in control . . . why good evenin', Sister Grace! . . . and remember, Son, you must be careful not to stumble. But even if you do, Robert, even if you do, the Lord will help you and forgive you, because you're His anointed and the temptations will be many. Remember that, you hear? Now come on in. Harold wants us to get this meetin' goin.'"

"But . . . but what should I say to her . . . them?"

"Well, you can always say kindly so as not to hurt their feelin's, 'Well, Sister, I will be waitin' on the Lord to give me the same vision, and then we will talk about it some more.'"

"Did it happen to you a whole lot, I mean when you were, you know, startin' out?"

Brother Earl guides Bobby Ray around behind the tent, toward the back of the platform where they will make their entrance.

A tightly corseted middle-aged woman rushes up, teetering on high-heeled shoes that punch holes in the bare earth. "Oh, Brother Earl, could I speak to you for a minute, uh, privately?" Her frown at Bobby Ray clearly invites him to leave.

The preacher tightens his grip on Bobby Ray's shoulder. "Why, good evenin', Widow Croft. Brother Robert and me have been tarryin' before the Lord for the glorious service the spirit is preparin' for us. Praise the Lord! We look forward to your testimony . . . in fact, might I call on you to lead the testimony service?"

She stands back. Her mouth shows slight disappointment, but her eyes have the look of having received a tiny secret message. "Why, uh, yes, of course, Brother Earl! Of course!"

The two men, the younger and the older, duck under the tent flap and take their places on the platform.

Brother Earl leans over and winks at Bobby Ray. "Oh, it still does happen to me, Son. It still does."

He walks up to the makeshift pulpit to start the evening's song service.

Bobby Ray looks over the congregation, sees the skinny young woman back in the sixth row, Hazel something, her face buried in her songbook. *Why, that pitiful little—she thinks she can use me to get what she wants.*

A darkness stirs up from deep inside him, as surely as the devil working on his soul. Why, he could take this girl who lays herself at his feet, and keep her or throw her away, whatever he wanted to.

Sister Hazel, I'm sorry if I was not properly, uh, polite to you before, but your news surprised me. Let's us go and find someplace where we can talk about it some more.

His body responds instantly in a way that is sure to embarrass him here in front of the congregation.

He sits down and grabs up his Bible to cover himself, thumbing through it as if he has been struck with unexpected inspiration.

. . . there is power, power, wonderworking power . . .

Six weeks later
Nortonville, Kentucky

The dream comes again, the fences, only now Bobby Ray runs toward a fence, and it turns into a row of young girls, with all the same sister-hazel face, holding hands.

Their smiles beckon to him; their bodies grow bigger, fatter, until only huge hands are in front of his face, growing darker and darker, reaching for him, grabbing at him . . . then a voice rises from the back of his head and mighty words bellow from his mouth . . . *get away from me, Mama!* . . . the hands explode and vanish, and the bodies behind them shrivel to skinny naked girls once again, who lie down on the ground and smile at him, beckon to him, beg him . . .

He flings the quilt aside, sweat soaking his hair. For a moment he can't remember where he is.

The bright moonlight from an unfamiliar window duplicates its image on the bare wood floor. Raucous snoring rumbles across the room, bringing Bobby Ray back to the upstairs bedroom of the boardinghouse where the two Spivey brothers and their helpers and families have been put up by the townspeople for the run of the revival. Tomorrow after the tent is folded and packed away on the truck, they'll be going on to Eddyville.

Bobby Ray gets up and pulls on his overall pants. Maybe it's cooler outside than here in this muggy room where his sweat refuses to dry in the sticky air.

He steps barefoot down the stairs, along the wall to avoid the creaks in the well-worn middles of the steps. He creeps out the front door, finally allowing himself a deep breath after he's safely on the front porch. He follows the dark old porch around the corner where it wraps around to the moonlit side of the house.

He wishes he had a cigarette.

"Why, Robert!" Connie Sue's whisper comes like a haunting voice that refuses to leave him. "Come on over here and sit in the swing with me." To hush her up more than to take part in her company he makes his way across the moonlit porch to where the wide swing hangs in the shadow of the vines that climb up past the sagging roof to form a loosely woven curtain at the end of the porch. A heavy aroma hangs in the air like a smothering blanket.

She makes no move to scoot over to the far side. "I just love the smell out here. It's night-bloomin' jasmine. I could smell it all the way in that tee-niney hot room they put me in back by the kitchen. Come on, sit down here."

As his eyes get used to the dimness of the corner, he notices she's in a nightgown, long to her ankles. Her shoulders are bare except for a bow tied on each side.

"Come on, Robert, nobody's lookin'. All the old fogeys are asleep." He eases himself onto the swing, tries to keep the chains from scraping against the rusty hooks.

"I'm so proud of you, Robert. You don't sound like you're still scared to talk in front of all them people at all."

"Oh, I am, some." He wishes he had put his shirt on. "Ain't— aren't you scared, standin' up there singin' by yourself?"

"I've been doin' it since I was *four.* Most I'm scared of is some-time I'll forget what song I'm singin' before I'm through." Her soft laugh is like the silky skin of her bare shoulders.

Her sweet perfume and the sluggish jasmine air pull at him. He sits still, not daring to let the swing move in the quiet.

Connie Sue runs a teasing fingernail along the bare muscle of his arm. He twists his body away from her but the chain grinds on the hook above him, whining out into the quiet.

"What's the matter, Robert? Don't you like me to touch you?" *Don't that feel good, Bobby Ray? Here, Sweetie, let Mama*—he jumps up from the swing, and Connie Sue is left to stop its wild swaying, the chains *screek-screeking* like a cat in heat. He leans on the corner post, the nauseating blossoms brushing his face.

When the night settles back into quiet, he looks to see if Connie Sue has gone, but no, she stands right behind him, her long night-gown hanging straight and thin in front of her, revealing the lines of her small pointy breasts. "You didn't look like you minded Mattie Lee Barnes hangin' all over you last week in Bowling Green."

"Well, she was the pastor's daughter, and Brother Earl said I ought to be . . . to be nice to her."

"And that homely little Jackson girl in Morton's Gap. I noticed you were bein' mighty nice to her, too." Connie Sue's fingertips flutter on his bare chest, and he shivers.

She reaches up to his face, then slips her hands around his neck, pulls him close to her lips. "I think you ought to be nice to me, too."

He grabs her shoulders and presses his mouth against hers with a fierceness that was surely not what she expected, but seems to delight her, anyway.

"Why, Robert!" She pulls away from him smiling, teasing, as he tries to reach her lips again. "Why, I think you do like me a little, don't you?" She brushes his lips again with hers, pulls away, then kisses him again. She guides one of his hands toward her breast, but he pushes her hand aside and yanks at her nightgown until one strap pins her elbow to her side, the other chokes up against her neck.

"Robert!" She slaps playfully at his hand. "You're choking me!" She straightens the nightgown, then looks up at him past her long lashes as she pulls at one of the ribbon ties. "You just be nice, now."

The bow unravels, letting one side of the nightgown fall open. One perfect white breast pops out into the shadowy moonlight. "Be nice," she whispers. "Robert, you're hurting my arm! Be nice!"

But he holds her arm tighter, and with the other hand he pulls his pants open, pushes them down over his hips. He twists her arm, forcing her down with him onto the paintbare planks of the porch floor, grabs a handful of her nightgown, yanks it upwards.

"Robert! Now stop it, Robert . . . wait . . . don't . . . you're hurting me!" She struggles to pull away, but he jerks her onto her back, kicks one foot free from his pants, and squashes her down with his body, smothering her protests.

He pins her feebly thrashing arms against the wood planks and forces one knee, then the other, between her thighs. Then in the five seconds that it takes to shove himself inside her with one hard, vicious stab, and collapse with an animal grunt onto the floor, he is done.

She shoves his deadweight arm off her and rolls away from him. Pulling at her nightgown to cover herself, she huddles on the floor near the railing. "Robert," she says, not bothering to whisper. "You didn't have to be so mean about it. You act like you despise me."

He pulls himself up onto the swing, the chain's noisy squawking complaints unnoticed. He tugs his pants on, hops on one foot as he untangles the free pant leg.

"But you do like me, don't you, Robert?"

He buttons his pants, starts back toward his room, now ready to get back to sleep.

She scrambles up from the floor. The bunched-up soiled gown falls in crumpled folds down the front of her. She holds the flapping side of her nightgown to her chest and stumbles along behind him. "Robert, please? You do, don't you? Just a little?"

He stops at the door, yawns, looks back at her . . . the silhouette of her thin body under the flimsy rumpled gown backlighted by the moon. A hint of air ruffles the jasmine, and a wave of the nauseating perfume makes him want to puke. Look at her . . . that molasses look on her face. She has the same look he saw on the Knight girl, and Mattie Lee Barnes, and all the others. They beg him to take them, and then they keep on begging. They're all the same, pulling him down anywhere just to hold onto him later. Of the devil, every last one of them.

Connie Sue looks quickly away and bites her lip, her honeyed expression turned to ashes.

He yawns, turns for the door, not even bothering to see if she is following him inside. "Yeah, Connie Sue. Sure. I like you."

The next week
Eddyville, Kentucky

"Robert, soon as we get back in tomorrow, I want you to see to it that your mama has what she needs." As he talks, Brother Earl continues to write on a big tablet with a yellow pencil. "I feel bad takin' you away right when the crops are comin' in, and your daddy is surely needin' you to help."

Bobby Ray stacks songbooks into a cardboard box. "My daddy, he don't care. That garden stuff is all his, and he don't want anybody else messin' with it."

"Now, Robert, your daddy is providin' for the family and you ought not be judgin' him so harsh. And with your granddaddy gone now, you remember, the Lord says to honor thy father and mother, now doesn't He?"

Bobby Ray wishes his daddy was dead, that's what he wishes. Him and Mama too.

"What was that, Robert?"

"Oh, nothin', Sir. Nothin'." Sometimes he almost sure that what he's thinking is hanging right out in the air where Brother Earl can hear it. He can't help it if God knows everything he's thinking, but it worries him a lot that maybe Brother Earl does too.

"Robert, your mama and daddy are doin' the best they know how to take care of you children."

Bobby Ray doesn't want to hear about Mama and Daddy. Why can't Brother Earl just let this alone? He knows how they are.

"Raisin' children is not easy. Look at my brother, raisin' Connie Sue by himself. If she was mine, I'd get her married off to a good

Christian boy who'd keep her in line." Bobby Ray can feel the preacher's stare on the back of his neck. Connie Sue wouldn't tell them about sneaking in with him every chance she gets, would she? He wishes he had more songbooks, but the box is nearly filled.

He should say something. Brother Earl seems like he's waiting for it. "Yes, sir, she does seem like she's sort of . . . well, kind of *worldly* sometime." He realizes that probably wasn't the right thing to say.

But it doesn't seem to Bobby Ray like Brother Earl is listening. The pencil keeps scratching on that tablet.

"How old are you now, Robert?"

"Sixteen."

Brother Earl puts his pencil down and turns to find something on the shelf behind him. Then he takes up the pencil again and continues his list.

"Yes Sir, I'd get that girl married off if she was mine, before she gets herself in trouble." Bobby Ray can hear the pencil even while Brother Earl talks.

"Robert?"

"Yes, Sir?"

Since Bobby Ray has run out of books, he stands with his hands in his pockets, looking at the floor.

"I want you to keep away from her, you hear me?"

The pencil stops.

"You hear me?"

Bobby Ray swallows the knot in his throat that is threatening to choke him.

"Yes, Sir."

. . . . . . 1938 . . . . . Nobel Prize for
literature goes to The Good Earth by Pearl
Buck . . . . . Pulitzer Prize to Thornton
Wilder for Our Town . . . . . Orson Welles
broadcasts War of the Worlds . . . . .
First feature-length
cartoon movie, Walt Disney's
Snow White and the Seven Dwarfs

Three months later
Mahala, Kentucky

"It's no use, Chigger, I can't figure it out. I'm just too dumb," Little Will says. The twins have their school lessons spread on the big kitchen table in the warmth of the cookstove. Little Will pulls his pocket knife out and sharpens the point of his yellow school pencil, then goes on to carve a precise double line up and around the pencil.

"It's easy, Little Will," Hildy says. "You just draw you a picture of some pies and cut 'em up, see? One-third is the same thing as two-sixths, and that way you can add 'em to the other sixths on the other pie there."

He adds cross bands and a head to the twin grooves and the two lines turn into a coral snake, coiled around the pencil, spiraling up to the chewed-flat eraser. Satisfied with his effort, he puts the pencil down and pockets the knife, goes on as though he'd never thought of it. "I hate arithmetic even worse than history 'cause even if it's not much use, history's got stories about people someplace." He stares at the circles Hildy has drawn, shaking his head. "Then why don't they just cut 'em all into one-sixths, then? Why don't they make 'em all the same size to start with?"

" 'Cause then you'd just have easy arithmetic problems like we had last year in the fourth grade." Hildy giggles, and he smiles at her crinkly eyes, the face that he can always depend on to laugh at his silly worries. Then her face darkens as her look goes past him to where Mama washes the last of the dishes from the pan on the stove.

"And besides," she whispers to him, her face aimed at Mama's broad backside. "Besides, some people always want bigger pieces of pie than other people."

She looks right at him again, then goes back to her arithmetic book. "And some people don't get any, so you don't have to add them in at all."

Little Will puzzles over his book. "I just can't figure it out. Don't you just add up the sixes and the threes on the bottom, and add up the ones and the twos on top?"

"No, look, let me show you." Hildy puts her pencil down, comes around to the other side of the table. She takes his pencil, and he shoves his school tablet over in front of her.

"Just draw the pie circles, like this, see?" She starts to draw, then stops to admire the snake. "You sure do whittle good, Little Will."

Mama looms over Hildy too late for Little Will to warn her. A hard whack lands on Hildy's shoulder, and Mama shrieks, "You get your own lessons and let him alone!"

Little Will tries to get between them. "Mama, she's helping me!"

Mama elbows around him and goes on, "You quit scribblin' all over his tablet!"

Hildy backs around to the other side of the table, rubbing her shoulder, her eyes glaring at Mama. Mama just keeps going, following her around the table.

"Mama," Little Will tries again, "she was just helpin' me!"

Mama ignores his pleas, keeping up her barrage at Hildy. "Little Will don't need you to help him. He got all G's on his report card."

"No, Mama," Hildy argues, "that was mine—"

"Don't you sass me, girl." Mama grabs one of Hildy's long braids, yanks it hard. Still holding tight to the braid, slaps her across her face once, twice, three times, the third time doubling her hand into a fist.

"Mama! Quit it!" Little Will is up on his feet, pulling at Mama's dress, tears pouring over his face. "Mama, quit it, quit it!"

With Mama's attention pulled back to Little Will for a second, Hildy manages to get her braid away from Mama's grip and run from the big kitchen into the dark cold of the next room.

Mama goes back to her dishes. As soon as her back is turned, Little Will goes after Hildy. "Chigger?" he calls softly into the dark room where the children's beds line the wall.

"She's over here," Liam's hushed voice comes from the far corner. Little Will finds his way over to the bed he shares with Liam. By the scant moonlight from the window he can barely see Hildy and Liam sitting propped against the wall at the back of the bed, huddling with quilts around them. He takes off his shoes and climbs over with them. Hildy opens up her quilt to take him in, but he stops and sits cross-legged in the middle of the bed.

Reaching for her face he can barely see, he touches her damp cheek. "Does it hurt much?"

She pulls back. "Nah, I don't care about it. I just . . . " The tears start again, and she hides her face in Liam's shoulder. "I'm sorry I got you in trouble, Little Will."

"It's not your fault I'm dumb. I hate school, and I'm quittin' just as soon as I'm old enough."

"You can't quit," she says. "Granddaddy said we're all to go to high school, and I want to, and if you quit, she'll make me quit too."

"Well, there's not much use talkin' about it," Liam says, "I'd quit too if Daddy'd let me, but he won't. You know how Daddy is. He does whatever he knows Granddaddy wanted."

"I reckon they neither one could stop Bobby Ray from quittin' when he wanted to."

"Nobody liked him. And he never passed anything."

"He's comin'!" The sound of Brother Earl's car sends Hildy scrambling to gather up her quilt and run to her bed. Liam dives for his pillow, grabs the end of his quilt and pulls it over him. The minute the kitchen door slams, Mama's voice starts in, whining to Bobby Ray what Hildy did this time.

"Mama!" Bobby Ray's voice booms. "Don't talk to me! I'm tired." Mama whines again, and Bobby Ray says "All right, I'll whup her, now let me alone, do you hear me? I'm goin' to bed."

"But don't you want no supper, Sweetie? I kept it for you."

"I told you to let me be. I ate at Brother Earl's." His heavy boots clomp across the kitchen and hesitate at the half-lit rectangle of the door. "Hildy!" Bobby Ray barks into the room where the children huddle in the dark.

No sound from Hildy; the only sound is Liam's faked snore. Little Will says, with a noisy yawn, "She's prob'ly down to the toilet."

"Well, when she gets back here, she's gettin' a whuppin'," Bobby Ray growls. He takes off his boots, and with a groan, he falls back onto his bed, and soon his snores grumble through the room.

Little Will hears Hildy's soft steps in the dark. The bed moves when she sits down on the side near him. He can hear her hiccupping back her crying, and he reaches out to touch her arm. "Hush up, now, you'll wake him up," he whispers.

"Nah," Liam says from over near the wall. "Once he's asleep he's like he's dead. Even when he's havin' one of them bad dreams, it don't wake him up. He just squalls about God and the devil and stuff."

"Yeah," Hildy says, "he surely does take the devil to sleep with him, don't he?"

Early 1939
Mahala, Kentucky

Little Will carefully notches and rolls the skin loose from a three-inch-long willow stick. He leans against the open door of the smokehouse, where outgrown clothes and broken pieces of furniture that were once piled against the back wall now spill out onto the whole floor. "Chigger, you ought not be into that stuff. And it's cold out here."

Hildy digs into a barrel in the corner. "Look here at this tee-niney shirtwaist." She holds up a faded calico garment riddled with holes, one that was obviously made for a slender young woman. "Lord, who do reckon ever wore this?"

Little Will carves a thin shaving all the way down the naked wood to the end. He slips the skin back on—a perfect willow whistle, almost as good as the ones Granddaddy used to make.

He looks up at the rafters at the smokehouse hooks, long unused and rusty. "I remember that time Granddaddy tried to help Daddy kill a hog. Granddaddy would try to show him how to stick the hog just right. Even when I was a little kid, I knew Daddy'd never do it. Liam, neither."

"Look at this sweater—it would about fit me." Hildy holds the sweater up in front of her and turns from side to side, then drops it into the pile on the floor. "Yeah," she says, "him and Daddy would go off to the spring and say they were goin' for water, but they never came back." Her muffled giggle comes from halfway down in the barrel.

"Not 'til Granddaddy had it all done and hung up out here." Little Will grins, then his face turns wistful. He squeezes the whistle tight in his hand and says with a choke in his voice, "I sure miss Granddaddy."

Hildy's studying a baby bonnet she's dug from the barrel. She perches it on the top of her head, tries to tie the faded pink ribbons in a bow under her chin, but they're not long enough. She comes over to where Little Will stands by the door.

He can't help grinning at the funny sight of his twin with the silly bonnet an empty floppy lump far above her ears, her braids hanging out underneath. The top of her head comes only to his chin. "Now take that thing off. You're not a baby."

"Sometime I almost forget that we're twins, Little Will," she says. "You've always been bigger'n me." Little Will is well on his way to being as big as Bobby Ray, and Hildy's reminding him of it makes him squirm. How come he's not like Liam and Chigger instead, or like Daddy?

"Do you reckon we ought not call you Little Will anymore? Now that Granddaddy is gone, you're the only Will there is."

He turns away to hide his eyes filling with tears.

"Little Will, are you cryin'? It's okay, you can cry over Granddaddy, it's all right." Her eyes are wet, too. Her sweet face opens the spring that Little Will has tried to hold shut for much too long, and he goes ahead and lets the sobs come up. Hildy holds him tight around his plump waist, and her tears wet the front of his shirt.

Finally, he pulls back from her and wipes his face on his shirt sleeve. "I don't go with nobody, seems like," he says. "You and Liam go with Daddy. And Bobby Ray and Mama, they go together. And me and Granddaddy, we went together, both bein' Wills."

He tries to swallow the tightness in his throat. Granddaddy would want him to act like a man. Dammit, he's a man, not a silly girl.

"But what do you mean, Little Will? You and me will always go together best of all. We'll always go together special, more'n anybody else does."

He has to take care of Chigger now. That's what Granddaddy would want him to do. He squares up his shoulders. "Chigger, you ought not be out here in this stuff, I told you. Mama might catch you, and that'd just give her another excuse to whup you. It's cold out here. Come on, let's go back in the house."

"She doesn't need any excuse. And she just throws all this stuff out here and never thinks about it any more. Daddy told her she ought to give it away and the mice will just eat it out here, but she says she's goin' to use all this stuff, and then she forgets about it." She sits down on a stool with one wobbly leg, folds her hands in her lap. "Sometimes she forgets all about me when I'm out here. Sometimes."

Little Will's eyes fill again, and he bites on his lip to keep the tears back. She looks so little with that silly old bonnet.

Hildy lets out a put-on laugh. "Besides," she says, "what does it matter to me what she does. She's crazy. Ever'body says it. But I don't care. And I don't care what they say about her at school neither."

"Well, I do . . . I hate the way she is. Yesterday evenin' when she was hollerin' and slappin' you over that gravy that spilled on the table, I even told her I did it, but it didn't make any difference."

"She won't do nothin' to you. She never does."

"Well, I'd let her, if she'd do it to me instead of to you. It makes me feel like a blame fool with nothin' I can do." He wipes at his face, but his shirt sleeves are soaked, and his eyes and nose still run.

"I'm sorry, Little Will. I just meant you didn't have to worry, she wouldn't hurt you."

He turns away from her, his fists tight against his overall legs, wishing he could beat on something, somebody. She can't understand at all. Mama never whupped Bobby Ray neither, but Little Will doesn't want to be in with him. He wants to be in with Liam and Chigger and Daddy. Why is he the only one who doesn't get hurt?

Later that afternoon

"Daddy, wake up!" Daniel pulls himself from his stupor, realizes Liam's face is in front of him, his hands shaking him. Pain crushes the side of Daniel's head, its weight pressing hard on his left eye.

The whiskey does almost nothing for his headaches anymore. They grow worse, lasting longer and longer each time. Odd, how often lately he can tell when one is coming, as though he wills it to come. When the pain comes, he can't think, and thinking is something he can no longer bear.

He drags his stiffening body up from his hiding place in the corner of the barn, the escape he's made for himself out of bales of hay, where he sleeps cowered into his heavy wool jacket.

The cold from the open barn door hits his face. First Liam's form is in front of him, then Little Will's, tugging at his leg.

"Daddy, Mama's whuppin' Chigger! She's goin' crazy, Daddy! Make her stop!" The urgency of Little Will's voice coming through the fog rasps on Daniel's senses. "She didn't do nothin', Daddy! Mama just went crazy! Chigger found an old baby hat in the smokehouse, and she was just playin' around with it."

"She went in the house with it," Liam says, "She wasn't doin' anything wrong, but Mama went crazy."

Daniel starts toward the house, propelled by the boys. His stiff legs balk at the kitchen porch steps, but Liam pulls at his arm, and Little Will shoves him from behind. Daniel stumbles up the steps and across the wood planks toward the open door. Hildy breaks out the door and down the steps, crawls up under the porch. Gerty thunders after her, her screeching piercing Daniel's head like a needle.

Liam and Little Will flatten themselves against the wall behind the screendoor that hangs from one hinge, a flimsy hiding place from Gerty's wrath.

"Gerty!" Daniel's hoarse voice batters at his own head like a club. He grabs at Gerty, but his fingers sink into the mush of her flesh and his hand pulls back in revulsion. No matter, he hasn't the strength to hold back her huge body.

Gerty totters at the edge of the porch, waves a scrap of yellowed cloth with faded pink flowers. "You got no right, you devil girl, you ain't Odessa! The devil took my Odessa away and give me you in her place . . . you got no right . . . you get away from here!"

Daniel backs up against the screendoor, mashing the boys against the wall.

Hildy's dark form is visible through the cracks in the porch floor. She huddles directly under Gerty, then makes her way down to the end of the porch. She creeps out and dashes for the open barn door, just as Bobby Ray pulls the preacher's Ford up into the dirt beside the house.

Gerty stares at the bonnet, her eyes dark and possessed.

Daniel motions for the boys to follow Hildy. They squeeze out from behind the door and run to the porch rail. They climb over, drop to the ground, and run past Bobby Ray as he saunters up to the back porch. He spits on the ground. "Go on back in the house, Mama!"

Gerty obeys, carries the bonnet into the house, muttering "Devil girl . . . she ain't Odessa."

Daniel wishes to be invisible. He hopes Bobby Ray will go on into the kitchen and leave him alone. His head hurts so that he can't think, doesn't want to be forced to try.

Bobby Ray takes the porch steps in two long strides.

"What are you doin' here?" he spits out at Daniel. "You drunken sot, you don't deserve to be here with decent people. Get out!"

Eyes hooded with pain, Daniel can only shrug.

Inside the open door Gerty drones on, "He went and got that heathern priest and they took away my baby girl, then they brought me that Stella's boy."

"Shut up, Mama!" Bobby Ray barks at her, but his eyes are still on Daniel.

There is a thought, a word, something Daniel means to say, but the pain has pushed it aside. It rushes to the surface, but before he can know what it is, or why it's important to tell this stranger standing over him who once was his son, the words tumble out: "She's crazy, can't you see it? She's mad!"

Bobby Ray shoves Daniel against the wall. Daniel slides down to a squat, but he doesn't try to get up. He welcomes the support of the wall behind him.

"She's mad," he mumbles, hanging onto the thought that has come so immediately clear to his focus, something that his sodden mind feels comfort in solving, as though the mystery of it had been haunting him all these years.

Bobby Ray's face, full of dark fury, fills Daniel's vision and the words hiss at him like vipers. "You just findin' that out? You just tellin' that to me?" Bobby Ray smashes his foot into Daniel's thigh.

The pain, no longer separate pains, throbs through his whole body. Another kick that registers a muffled thud against his jacket sleeve topples him to the floor. Now Bobby Ray's body towers over Daniel, his boots not a foot from Daniel's face.

"You're tellin' this to me? I'm the one you left to her a long time ago, this crazy woman, left her to dirty me while you kept your own self clean!"

Daniel can feel the familiar rage building in the oppression that looms above him, in the very air around him. *Danny, I won't have it. You belong to me and you'll do what I want!*

The full force of Bobby Ray's wrath slams into Daniel's ribs. He gasps, *huhn huhn huhn,* trying desperately to restore breath to his aching lungs.

Bobby Ray stands like a specter over him, his words spewing out in a stream of white-hot hatred into the icy winter air. "I've been the only man in this house for a long time. Why don't you go on to hell where your kind belongs!" Bobby Ray shoves his way through the door and elbows Gerty out of his way. "Mama, get in there and fix me somethin' to eat."

Left alone on the splintered planks of the porch floor, Daniel's body does not move, but his mind sways slowly, in the place where he has teetered for a long, long time.

He craves to find sanity in a place where madness is all around him, to walk into the kitchen and take his rightful place at the family supper table.

But another part of him—a much larger part now—yearns for rest, for a place free of pain and the need to think. For Ma. But there is no forgiving god that will allow him in. Surely not the god who takes Will Tucker and chooses to live in the likes of Bobby Ray.

The sky hangs heavy with the white-gray of snowclouds, their dampness creeping into his clothes. He hunches his shoulders and pulls his neck as far as possible into the heavy collar of the jacket, ignoring the knifepains in his chest that punctuate each breath.

But this feeble cocoon is not enough. He is still exposed, in this temporary nest that he will surely be forced to leave. There is nowhere that he belongs; he is finished but still undone. He craves something else, a final something else, for he wants for nothing but peace.

Maybe hell is where he belongs. If there is nothing better than this here, then whatever waits in any other place can be no worse.

If only they would allow him a peek into heaven, just one, to see Ma and Daddy and the wee ones before he goes.

"Please, Liam, go get Daddy up," Hildy pleads, shivering, huddling close to Little Will, her face and her lips darkening and puffing up on one side.

Feeling nothing of the cold, Liam starts toward the house, then he hesitates when Daddy drags himself up from the porch floor. Liam motions for the younger kids to stay back and walks out to meet him. Daddy drops an arm around the boy's thin shoulders, neither man nor boy capable of supporting the other.

With every step the two of them take, Daddy wheezes, grunts as though the mere putting down of a foot is unbearable. At the barn door Liam stands back until Daddy is inside, pulls the heavy door as far as it will go and ducks inside to take his position by the crack to guard against he knows not what.

Daddy stops at Hildy's side for a few seconds. Then he aims her gently toward Little Will, but she hangs onto his hand. He pulls himself free and walks past her, climbs stiffly up the loft ladder, and is gone for a long moment. Little Will and Hildy huddle, shivering, but Liam stands tall and silent, never taking his eyes off the top of the ladder.

Daddy's legs appear at the top of the ladder and he climbs slowly down, dangling a rifle—Bobby Ray's old .22 Liam barely remembers. Daddy rummages into his sleeping hole and pulls out a bottle, then a small wooden box.

Liam stands firm at his place by the barn door, watches each step as Daddy passes by the children and comes to stand by the door with Liam, not turning to meet their searching eyes. His head moves slightly in Hildy's direction.

"Take care of her, Son," he says to Liam, his voice nothing more than a whisper.

"But—"

"This is . . . here, you keep this."

Liam doesn't look at the box shoved into his hands. He stares at Daddy's face, as though he'll disappear if Liam doesn't hold him in his focus. "Can't I go with you?" Daddy shakes his head, no. Something dark and cold rises up inside Liam—he knows there is some deep worrying to be done here, and nobody to do it but him. Something invisible drops from Daddy like a blanket, falling around Liam's shoulders, but there's nothing warm about it. His body, his mind, fight off the smothering weight.

Daddy tries to push the heavy door open but the effort contorts his face, and he leans against the wood. He responds to Liam's soft tug on his arm by backing away, and Liam pushes the door open a few inches, scraping its bottom edge on the bare dirt.

The wind whistles into the opening. Daddy squeezes sideways through to the outside. Liam follows, and Hildy comes next, hugging close to Liam, shivering as the cold air hits her bare arms.

Little Will stands in the open crack and watches for a moment before he pushes the door open a few more inches, allowing him to squeeze through. He tries to shove the door closed behind him but shrugs, gives up.

Daddy struggles to set the bottle down, grimaces, and hands it to Liam to hold. He leans the rifle against the barn, takes off his jacket and hangs it around Hildy's shoulders, but he doesn't look her in the eye. "I . . . I've not done right by you."

Liam holds the quarter-full bottle tight against his chest, as if he could attach himself to Daddy, keep him close. But Daddy takes the bottle from him, retrieves the rifle, turns to leave.

Liam's voice surprises him, demanding, strong. "Wherever you're goin', I can go too, can't I?" Daddy stops, turns slightly, then walks on toward the trees.

"Tell me where you're goin'," Liam yells after him.

Daddy's mumbled answer sounds like, "To hell, I'm thinking."

Hildy tugs at Liam's sleeve, but Liam stares after Daddy, holding himself back from running after him. His body is rooted in its place, but he can feel his spirit straining, emptying, stretching to fill the lengthening distance between himself and his father.

"Where's Daddy goin'?" Little Will asks.

"I don't know." True, Liam doesn't know, but he still feels like he's lying. "I don't know. Huntin', I reckon."

"But I never saw him go huntin' before now. An' it's startin' to snow!" Hildy tugs on his sleeve again, her skinny arm reaching from under the heavy jacket. "Liam, what is a ol' dessa? Mama said I'm not a ol' dessa and I don't even know what one is."

A rush of shame fills Liam's face, shame that he wants to shove these children away from him and run after Daddy, to leave behind their pulling at him, their trusting, expecting eyes, their demanding questions. But the weight on his shoulders turns to rock, pins his feet to the ground.

Wet bunches of snowflakes stick to his face, snowflakes that he and the twins in other winters have celebrated, welcomed into their mouths as gifts from nature, pure and unsullied by the life that went on around them.

But today he swats them from his eyes, just as he refuses the tears that will distort his vision. He wills his focus to rise like a ghost above the children and keep his sight clear on the spot thirty yards away where Daddy's form hesitates only for an instant at the edge of the woods, and then disappears into it. Only after the spot blends completely with the trees around it does Liam let go of it and glance down at the box in his hands. He senses a movement beside him. Hildy shrinks into the barn door opening, bumping into Little Will.

Liam hurries to put the box behind his back, not ready to answer their questions about it.

But he realizes their notice is not on him. Down at the end of the porch, Bobby Ray stands smoking a cigarette, gazing out beyond the railing toward the woods.

Daniel tramps farther and farther into the woods, his monotonous plodding aimed not so much for a particular place as for a particular time. He has never held a vision of a far-off future, not since five years old, when he grew tall enough to see over the low garden wall. All he could see was another wall and another. America promised more, but with Uncle Seamus, life tightened and constricted, the choices fewer and fewer, until now there is only the one. Now he must leave, not because he has another place to go, but because he simply cannot stay any longer in this one.

In the bigger spaces between the trees the light snow has begun to stick, sugaring the ground. He comes to a clear circle in the trees, a place made by leprechauns, Ma would have said.

His numb fingers hold the rifle barrel and the icy whiskey bottle. His left hand grasp fails him, and the bottle clunks to the ground in front of him. He bends to pick it up, and the stabbing into his ribs forces his breath in sharply, intensifies the pain tenfold. He stumbles to catch his balance, stops himself against a tree at the edge of the circle. Each heavy breath ends in a sharp stabbing to his chest. He leaves the bottle in the middle of the circle where it lies, and he trudges on.

Snowflakes fall all around him, but he doesn't yet feel the chill through his shirtsleeves because it has not reached the depth of the cold inside him. A half-mile then another pass under his feet, one footprint after another, all the same, counting, counting, counting each step, each jab of the sword against his ribs.

With the setting of the sun the air temperature drops too cold for snow and patches of deep graying-blue appliqué the thinning clouds. A particular cedar tree catches his eye. White lace decorates its deep branches darkened to green-black in the twilight. *No, Son, it won't fit in the house, Son . . . way too big . . . way too big . . .*

Daniel accepts now, no longer ashamed, that he must turn his back on his children and trust them to the life that gave them to him. He wishes there really was a God, if only for them.

He drops to his knees and crawls, dragging the rifle under the low-hanging branches of the cedar tree. He lies down, each movement piercing his side. With his lying down, the sensation of falling departs him. The thick mat of composting cedar feels secure against the flat of his back. He lies still, breathing shallow breaths, stopping each one just at the edge of the pain. He contemplates the pressure of the ground on the back of his head, the pain settling in like an icy pool, slowly filling to just behind his eyes.

His body and his mind work together in some strange detached way that feels familiar, as though it were his natural state, the way he's always been.

When he opens his eyes, he is surprised that the sky has darkened to a white-black stillness all around him. He feels strangely at peace. His body slowly disappears in his awareness as the icy numbness moves up his legs. *The gun . . . remember the gun.*

With great physical and mental effort he pulls the end of the gun barrel to his chin with a hand that is only slightly warmer than the steel. He stretches his other arm along the side of it, his fingers already stiffening with cold.

What to do . . . something . . . there's something he must do before the gun will . . . what . . . in a minute when his mind clears, he'll know. He has arrived at the chosen time, and only one final thing needs to be done . . . just close his eyes for a minute . . . just for a minute . . . just for another minute . . .

࿓

A white fog surrounds him, strangely old and warm and timelessly familiar but at the same time new. A place and time he has not visited before, yet he is at home . . . again. He has a sense of sitting up, with no memory of painfully pulling his body up to that position.

But there's something he must do . . . something he must finish. He merely thinks to move his hand to the gun, and he immediately feels the hardness, the roundness of something made of cool, smooth metal. He pulls it close to his face.

A hand mirror, the one he gave Gerty for Christmas the year they married. He studies its shining silver back, then turns it over. In it he sees his own face, but not his own . . . older, yet younger . . . smiling.

"Find yourself a pitcher of your Daddy?"

Daniel grins, then slowly turns his consciousness around toward the voice, the laughter that falls all around him like raindrops.

"Horsey, Granddaddy! Horsey!" Big Will gallops away, his laugh roaring through the misty forest, the little girl in the white bonnet with pink roses giggling and bouncing on his broad shoulders.

Daybreak the next morning

In the dim light of the coal oil lamp, Bobby Ray stuffs three of last night's supper biscuits into his pocket. Gerty stands in the kitchen door. Her crumpled print dress sags open where two buttons have come off from sleeping in it.

"Get back to bed, Mama. It ain't even light out yet."

"Are you wantin' breakfast, Sweetie? Mama'll build a fire, and get you some—"

"I said get back to bed and let me alone, you hear me?" He doesn't bother to look in her direction. Gerty obeys, her mules slap-slapping back into the darkness.

He wishes he had let her build a fire. Coffee would have helped his headache, but nothing is worth having Mama in here. She'd never shut up, and he can't stand the sound of her voice. He watches out the kitchen window, chews on a biscuit.

As soon as he can imagine a silhouette of the apple tree out across the garden, he pulls his coat around him and buttons it tight, goes out onto the porch and pulls the door shut behind him.

At the porch railing he waits until his eyes get used to the dawn's graying around him, then he starts out across the dirt expanse toward the big oaks, past the Ford that sits ghostlike in its dust, reflecting none of the pinking sky on the night's eastern side.

He stops to look around him, then slips into the woods right at the spot where he last saw Daniel, at the beginning of the narrow trail that meanders for miles over in the direction of the old Manning Mill Road.

Among the trees the day has not yet begun. Maybe he should've waited until it was lighter. He shields his face with his arms against the intruding underbrush, shoves back branches and stomps down striplings covered with ice crystals.

He pushes on down the familiar path where he hide-and-seeked as a child. The cold brittle twigs snap at a touch, crunch under his feet. The temperature must be near zero.

He tosses his head back, flips his hair out of his face. "I should have run the coward off a long time ago," he spits out to nobody but an early squirrel startled from its early breakfast.

Another truth lies heavy on his mind, and his stomach responds with a surge of nausea. The leaden biscuits threaten to come back up, and he swallows hard to keep back the acid. His body begs for the sleep that escaped it during the night, tortured when his mind let down its guard and dozed, then bolted awake by the laughing demon as the gunshots from his dream echoed through the cavernous room.

On the path the light snow glows with an eerie whiteness. He can't bring his eyes to look straight ahead, to meet head-on whatever might be out there in the dimness. He stays to the footpath that widens out into a place he recognizes, the cleared circle where he used to play, a private place the other kids never bothered with.

He peers up through the trees, now dark against wisps of blue and orange in the sky. He was here once before at sunrise, once when he slipped away from Mama. The place that then drew him to its magic now chills him to his bones.

He pushes his hands deeper into his pockets and wishes he'd had that coffee. The brightest January stars are visible through winterbare trees. As he looks for a familiar constellation, his foot bumps something hard. He kicks it aside, sees a glint of glass and picks up the icy whiskey bottle, sloshing its ounce or two of liquid. A shiver creeps up his back and into his hair. As if the bottle had turned suddenly too hot for his hand, it drops it with a muted thud onto the snow-covered mulch. He pulls his shoulders up to force his collar higher on his neck and ears.

He looks to one side and to the other, moving only his eyes. An ice-brittle twig snaps, and he whirls to face the dark trees that lurk behind him. "Dammit, why didn't I wait 'til it was light?" He makes himself remember the half-inch of snow on the bottle—it must have been there a long time. He lets go of the breath he's been holding in and gives the bottle a nudge with his toe, almost expecting it to push back, to resist.

"Oh, hell." He bends and picks it up, wipes the snow and dirt off it with his coatsleeve, and wiggles the cork until it comes free. He takes a sip, remembering when he used to sneak the canning jar of homemade whiskey from down at the spring.

"I'm just drinkin' it to get warm. I'm freezin', is all," he explains to Brother Earl . . . or somebody.

The sky golds up gradually, and there is some light between the trees. He's glad to see it.

He tosses the bottle, then thinks better of it. He'll find a hole in a tree to hide it. He makes his way over to where he heard the bottle thump, squats to retrieve it at the foot of a tree.

There on the ground, rotting leaves are newly scuffed into bunches, lumpy under the thin layer of snow. A distinct outline of a bootprint shows, dug in deep as if somebody stomped down hard near a hickory sapling and stayed there for a while.

He slides the nearly empty bottle into his coat pocket, sticks his bare hand inside his coat. When there is a little more light, he can see more scuffing further on between the trees, in the leaves that are not touched by snow, from feet dragged more than stepped.

He pushes the low branches aside and takes up his quest into the woods again, driven to find what he came for, what he craves to see, but at the same time what he dreads. Sometimes he follows a clear track in the leaf mulch, its outlines filled with light snow. Sometimes a broken bush or tree limb. Sometimes he follows instinct alone.

Why can't he just let it be? That son of a bitch can just go to hell where he belongs, and Bobby Ray would be glad of it. But the mantra from the dream refuses to be quiet . . . *go to hell, go to hell, go to hell.*

Nightmare gunshots stalk close behind him even as he shakes his wide-awake mind to drive them away. He's gone a mile or more, he's sure, past the spot where he used to turn off to his swimming hole, the one he found the summer he was twelve, the one he saved just for himself and never told the other kids about.

Exhausted more of mind than of body, he looks around for

a place to drop, but everything is wet from the beginning of thaw as the sunlight filters in. Even in the morning light, it doesn't leave him, that feeling that somebody—something—is watching him from the dark. He tries to look every direction at once, steps back one way, then the other.

He creeps backwards to protect his backside up against cedar branches. He stumbles on something hard and falls back into the tree, its icy needles whipping against his head as he struggles to catch himself. His feet tangle again with something. The branches throw him forward, crashing him hands first to the ground. "Dammit!" he sputters and tries to get up, but his twisted wrist gives way and he crumbles to the ground.

He rolls over to sitting, picks cold wet pine needles off his hands. Beyond his hands he sees the bottoms of two booted feet, sticking out from under the tree. His own body jerks backward, its separate parts jostle one another to recoil from the sight, from the very image he has trudged through the cold to find. His nightmare explodes into the morning sunshine and the demons scream in his head to run, to get away from here.

All the energy that surges through his body spills into his stomach. It relieves itself of its meager burden, vomits bile and acid and the last of the soured biscuits onto the thawing ground. He heaves until his body is drained of food and the last of its hysteria.

He drops to the ground, spent, not caring that he lies in a puddle of mushy melting snow. The gunshots inside his head echo off into the woods, one after another after another, until at last the quiet of the woods lies heavy around him.

Bobby Ray has no idea how long he lay there wrestling with the truth: *he did this.* He caused the death of a man, even a man as loathsome as this one. It is done, and he is responsible for it. He did not fire the gun, but he killed this man, as surely as if he had.

And then the next truth: *he is glad.*

He takes in a deep breath, pulls himself to his full height and turns to face the boots. His mind races ahead, eager to see what he has hoped for, what his own voice through clenched jaws has prophesied. He bends to touch the cold stiff denim. He tugs at one of the boots, then drags the body a few inches out from under the tree. Something hangs and he can't budge it any further, so he drops the foot and pulls the lower limb out of the way. He stares, not at the sight his mind is prepared for, but at a gray, frozen mask, smooth, slack, at peace.

With one foot against a stiff shoulder, he dislodges the gun from the arm, rigid in its curve around the rifle. *My .22! What right did he have to take my gun and keep it? And for somethin' he knew I didn't do.*

He drags the body out into the clearing, leaving a wide swath in the light snow. He walks gingerly around it, peering from every angle, nudges the head with his foot, but it doesn't move.

There has to be something, somewhere. Muffled far back in his consciousness, he can hear the gunshots still. But there's nothing. Not a thing. His mind rebels. This stranger with the unmarked face is not his father after all! How could it be?

Then it comes to him. "He froze to death! The goddam coward didn't even have the guts to shoot himself. He just laid here and froze to death!" *He's got no right! This gun—my gun—it ought to have been what killed him!*

Bobby Ray grabs the gun up from the ground by the barrel, and swings it hard, smashes into the side of the head on the ground. "You deserved to suffer, you drunken heathen, you coward, you got no right not to suffer!"

Again and again he swings the rifle, ridding himself of the image of that face, that face that has no right to peace. "You never cared about me! You let her ruin me, and you never cared. Damn you! You were s'posed to save me from her!"

Finally drained of his fury, Bobby Ray drops to the ground. He buries his face in the leaves and dirt and sobs until exhaustion overtakes him. As his body cools, its rage spent, he hits his fist feebly against the ground. *Where are you, God? You were s'posed to save me from their sin!*

He gets to his feet, shivering, depleted, his head thick, his stomach a cold lump below the heaviness in his chest. He sucks the frigid air into his lungs and his whole body trembles in response to its bite.

He dares to pulls himself up and survey the small clearing, as the sun breaks through the mist-shrouded tops of the trees. A cloud lifts from him, and a new awakening arises in his mind, a verse of the many he has labored over . . . *neither will I be with you any more, except ye destroy the accursed from among you.*

He turns and looks again at the body, the damage that he has in his holy rage visited upon it. His new truth grows in the far deep pit of his being, in the hidden depth of his soul, rising up to his shoulders, pulling him up from the ground, taller, straighter. Didn't he himself prophesy this to happen? *You should be dead . . . go to hell . . . go to hell where the likes of you belongs.* He has overcome this evil. He has rid himself of this despicable sinner who didn't deserve to live among decent people. Surely this is the working of God's own wrath, smiting one who is not worthy. Bobby Ray has done nothing but speak this destruction into existence, that's all. Why, that's what the children of Israel did! They got rid of God's enemies for Him, didn't they? It was Bobby Ray alone—no, *Robert Ray,* God's anointed—who sent this sinner to his death, who destroyed the accursed by merely speaking its destruction into being.

The day is full upon the woods, and its light brings the immediate reality of the moment to Bobby Ray's focus: he has to do something with the body. He can't take a chance that anybody else will find it. They won't understand, and they'll persecute him, like they do to all of God's chosen.

But they can't take the satisfaction away from him, as long as he doesn't tell anybody. The ground is frozen, and there's nothing to dig with anyway. The swimming hole! He remembers the swimming hole. He picks up the feet, drags them across the clearing.

He can't leave the gun. He retrieves it from where he must have flung it in his rage—he doesn't remember—and lays it on top of the corpse. He unbuckles the belt and rebuckles it through the trigger guard.

The barrel points too late at the carnage that used to be the face. "There!" he says, "You brought it out here. You pack it. And don't go shootin' yourself, you hear?" A wicked laugh bubbles up from his chest.

Bobby Ray drags the body back through the woods to the place where a path snakes off to the east, where the winter-slowed trickle of the stream pulls him as the cool gurgle did in the summers of his youth. Making his way through the brush is no easy task. He stops more than once to clear some wayward brush away, scraping and cutting his cold-numbed hands.

The wide place in the stream is just the same as he always found it after the spring thaw. Rocks of all sizes are piled on the far side of the hole where, alone for days at a time when the other kids were in school, he patiently scooped the soft winter silt from the bottom until he had a wide pool, deep enough to cool himself waist deep.

He pulls the body parallel with the edge, where thick ribbons of ice still border the stream. He retrieves the gun. *You never gave it back to*

me, you son of a bitch! You had no right! With one shove, the body drops
into the three feet of clear icy water, stirs the mud at the bottom.

Bobby Ray pulls at the biggest rock until it rolls to the same spot
on the edge. With a huge splash, the rock sinks. He waits until the
slow-moving water clears.

Satisfied that the rock has landed firmly on top of the body, he
rolls one rock after another into the water, rocks that with much sweaty
struggle he heaved, rolled, hoisted and dragged from the stream in
the summers past, many times removing the same rock several times
before he finally made it do his bidding.

In those summers the stubborn rocks became playmates to dare
and defy, escaping his grasp and wetting his already soaked body
with their splashes, laughing at him from their reclaimed spots in the
stream. But he always had the last laugh over them, and they finally
stayed put where he commanded them.

Today he jumps back to avoid the splashes, but to no use. He's
soon drenched to the skin. He shivers; his teeth chatter. But he must
finish; he must stone this body, entomb it forever. He works until
every rock in sight, every rock he can pry loose, is on top of the body,
pushing it into the mud below.

He remembers the bottle in his deep coat pocket, pulls it out and
drinks the last few drops, then throws the bottle and smashes it on the
rock on the other side of the stream, a fitting epitaph for a drunken,
sinning coward.

Satisfied, Bobby Ray picks up the rifle and turns his back forever
on the playground of his solitary childhood. He tramps back through
the woods toward Mama's hot coffee and a roaring fire to ponder on
this power that swells in his chest, pulls his chin higher. The power—
yes, the very power that at the same time exhilarates and terrifies him.
After all, he is Robert Ray and he has with his very words sent this,
God's enemy, to hell.

Six weeks later

"Mornin', Wayne." Howard Fuller sticks his head in the doorway of
the sawmill office, where Wayne sits with the account book and waits.
There is very little business to be done, but Wayne has come to keep
his daily vigil.

"Mornin', Mr. Fuller." Wayne closes the book, weary already of
the routine that is starting to happen again.

He meets Mr. Fuller at the office door, and they both step out into the crisp winter sunlight. "Sure don't seem right without Will Tucker around this town," Mr. Fuller says.

"No Sir, it don't seem right."

Mr. Fuller takes off his hat, holds it in front of him. They used to show up to talk about Granddaddy just as if by talking about him, the truth that Will Tucker was gone would somehow still be open to change. One or the other of the men came by each day and one by one they all reached the amen to their pilgrimage: "Well, I don't need nothin' today. I just wanted to stop by." More often than not, they would add, "And you tell your Mama hello for me and the missus. And if they's ever anythin' . . . "

Their constant mention Granddaddy made it harder to get used to his being gone. But Wayne had to admit it, that after they stopped coming, the lumberyard was empty. Very, awfully, empty. One thing sure, Wayne wasn't the only one who felt the loss of his Granddaddy, and he was being called on to help everybody else through it.

But now this new thing, and they've started it up again. He can't talk to Mama about it. She acts so strange when he brings up Uncle Daniel. Today Mr. Fuller puts his hat on, glances around the lumberyard, his leavetaking held off, as if he's forgetting something but doesn't know what. They all do it.

Wayne leans on the worktable, giving all his attention to a rusty nail he's picked up, waiting for what he knows is coming next. He doesn't have to wait long.

"Say, um . . . " Mr. Fuller goes on, looking around. "Has they been any word from Daniel?"

"No, Sir, not that I know of."

"Oh." They all say it—"Oh"—as if they want to say the right thing, but none can figure out just yet what the right thing is. "Oh."

Then, "Well." Mr. Fuller shuffles his shoes in the sawdust on the ground, not glancing around anymore, like he's embarrassed that he had asked. "I reckon this here depression's made a lot of men up and leave town."

"Yes Sir, that's what I hear."

"Some of us, we was thinkin' maybe we ought to go lookin' for him, but none of us had any idea where to start. Then somebody heard it around town that Bobby Ray's claimin' he run him off."

Wayne puffs out a big breath. He was waiting for this part, and it always comes, dammit. "Yeah, well, Bobby Ray's got more mouth than he's got sense, always has. He doesn't scare me any, but I can't speak for Uncle Daniel."

And I'm tired of tryin' to, he feels like yelling out. Today he feels a little more reckless than usual. "If you ask me, Bobby Ray knows more'n he says. Guilty dog barks the loudest, I always heard. And I bet if he does, it's more'n just runnin' him off."

Mr. Fuller's eyes widen, and he leans closer. Then he takes a couple of steps back.

Wayne catches himself. He's said too much. "I'm sorry. I didn't have any call to say that."

Mr. Fuller looks nervous, uncomfortable. "Well, now, I need to be gettin' myself on back. You let us know, now, when . . . if you hear somethin'." At the front gate he turns and without giving it any notice, he takes off his hat again. That's what they all do, along about now.

"Daniel, he was a decent man. I didn't know him much. He kind of kept to himself, even when he was standin' right next to a fella."

His eulogy finished, Mr. Fuller puts the hat back on one more time and disappears around the corner. Wayne's nod is to the empty lumberyard.

Maybe it's easier for them to think Uncle Daniel might be dead than to swallow the idea that the likes of Bobby Ray has run him off. But Wayne can't put down the nagging thought that it could be both. He rubs the scar on his forehead and without even thinking about it, his glance goes to the tools hanging in their marked places. He knows Bobby Ray and his meanness only too well.

Back in the tiny office, Wayne sits at the little desk, picks up the account book, opens it to a page, any page, it doesn't matter which. Just looking at Granddaddy's scrawled writing comforts him some. There are no transactions to record for today, no figures to add.

"Howdy there, Wayne." Amos Teague pokes his head around the doorway of the office, his hat in his hand.

"Mornin' Mr. Teague." Wayne says, closes the book, gets up.

"It sure ain't the same around here without Will Tucker, is it?"

"No, Sir, Mr. Teague, it's not."

Spring 1939
Mahala, Kentucky

Liam leans against the smokehouse on the side farthest from the house. In the early stillness he starts this Saturday in no different way from the way he starts every new day, trying to find the best way to get to the end of it. The cornfield, strewn with last year's broken, sodden gray stalks, lays waiting. The ground ought to be thawed out just right for the corn planting by now. How can a new spring come around again without Daddy here to plant his corn and potatoes?

The waiting has become a part of Liam's being that he wakes up to and goes to sleep with, and sometimes it doesn't even leave him then. The image of Daddy stepping into the woods with the rifle repeats like an unconscious throbbing in the back of his head. But he can't turn loose of it, doesn't want it to go away. The image has taken over all the other pictures of Daddy, and if that goes away there'll be nothing left.

What bothers him the most is the curious forgetful part of his mind that says to him, *Daddy ought to be getting Granddaddy's old mule down here and—*

"You got any idea where Chigger's at?" Little Will pokes his head around the corner of the smokehouse. "I just wanted to warn her, Mama's lookin' for her."

"She's up in the apple tree yonder." Liam starts on over toward the tree where the bright spring leaves are barely far enough along to hide the brown winter branches. Little Will comes along behind. At almost eleven, he's two inches taller and quite a bit heavier than Liam's slender fourteen.

"Chigger, what are you lookin' at?"

Hildy grabs the limb that hangs over her head. "You 'bout scared me half to death!"

Little Will pulls at the lower branch, but he's too heavy to lift himself up so he gives up. "What are you lookin' at, anyhow?"

"Nothin'." She starts her careful climb down through the higher branches. "Nothin', I reckon."

Liam frowns up at her as she eases herself down limb by limb. When she gets down to the one just above Little Will's head, Liam says, "Here, want me to help you down?"

Little Will jumps up, bumps his head on the branch. "Yeah, you want us to help you down?" he says, rubbing his forehead.

She jumps down between them, lands like a cat on the softening spring earth. She stands up, pulls her skirt straight and brushes off the dirt and twigs.

"You ought to wear pants if you're goin' to climb up trees," Liam says. "You're too old to be showin' everybody your step-ins."

"Mama won't let me have any overall pants. And I can't wear yours and Little Will's, 'cause they're too big."

Little Will laughs. "Well, anyhow I only got one pair, and I'm not wearin' your dress while you climb up trees in 'em."

"And get your shoes on," Liam says. "Why're you climbin' up there with your shoes off? It's not summer yet."

"I can climb better without 'em." She sits on the ground, brushes the bark from her bare right foot before she sticks it into her shoe. "I wish I was a boy."

"Well, you're not," Liam says, "and you're not a monkey neither, so you ought to stay down out of that tree. But at least if you was a boy or a monkey one, you wouldn't be showin' everybody your step-ins like a little kid."

Liam leans back on the tree trunk, looks out toward the empty road, but just for a second. He glances back and meets Little Will's eyes. They both quickly find things on the ground to stare at.

Little Will squats on the ground next to Hildy. "He's not comin' home, Chigger. There's no sense in you always watchin' for him to come back."

She works at her shoestrings. "Who?"

Liam turns away, not wanting to hear anymore, but her voice is too bright and too loud, and he can't help looking back at her, puzzled.

"You know who I'm talkin' about." Little Will's voice is hardly more than a whisper. "Daddy."

Liam ducks around to the other side of the tree, picks up a rock, hurls it at the smokehouse, misses. Why don't they quit this game they keep playing?

"Oh, I wasn't watchin' for anybody," Hildy goes on, sounding almost cheerful. She pulls on her other shoe, yanks on the strings too hard, and one breaks off. She tosses it aside, leaving the shoe gaping.

"Chigger, he ain't comin' back."

Liam stares at her, but she's watching Little Will twist the piece of broken shoestring around his pudgy finger.

"You better quit that," she says, "or your finger'll turn purple." She pulls her chin a little higher. "I know he's not."

"You do? How do you?" Little Will asks.

"Well, how do *you?* You're the one said it, Little Will!"

Liam stands by the tree, the corners of his mouth twitching. He wants to say something to them, but he just doesn't know what

He picks up another rock and tries again for the smokehouse, harder this time.

"So why don't you let me alone, then? I can watch if I want to," Hildy bursts out, covering her face with her dresstail.

"Aw, Liam," Little Will begs, "I don't know what to do with her when she starts cryin' like this."

Liam comes over and drops to the ground beside her. "Now Chig, Little Will didn't mean nothin' by it."

"Me? I didn't say nothin'!"

"Hush, Little Will," Liam says. He puts his arm around Hildy's shoulder, and she leans into him. His own face puckers. He bites his bottom lip. No words come up to say to her that are of any use.

She wipes her face on the tail of her dress. "I'm sorry Liam. I made Daddy leave. I know he left because of me."

"Now hush. You didn't make him."

"Then why did he?"

"I don't know, Chigger."

"You do too! You know it was me. And he's never goin' to come back, 'cause I'll never be good enough for him to come back, never. I'll even go to hell and he'll never come back. I know it."

Liam says, "I don't know why he left, Chigger, but I don't reckon he blamed any of us. I don't reckon he would." He picks up a stray acorn that has bounced off the smokehouse roof, tosses it over to Little Will, who pulls out his pocket knife and starts to carve tiny, almost invisible lines with the tip. When he finishes a little grinning face, he hands the acorn to Hildy.

"Sometime," Little Will says, "sometime it seems like he never was here. Even when he was sittin' at the table."

"Yeah," Liam says, his lower lip trembling. "Yeah, but now he's *gone*, and *gone* is a whole lot different from just not bein' here."

. . . . . 1939 . . . . . First transatlantic passenger flight, Dixie Clipper, 23 hours, 52 minutes

Summer 1939
Mahala, Kentucky

"Wayne, how can you think about selling the sawmill? As if anybody had money to buy it, anyway." Emma sets the yellow bowl of butter beans in the middle of the table and goes back to the stove for the cornbread. "And don't you go sayin' anything about that in front of your Mammaw, you hear me?"

She goes to the back screendoor and leans out. "Mama? Come on in. Supper's ready."

"Well, I just don't see how I can handle it by myself, and I can't hire anybody to help me, and I've got no truck. And by myself, I can't promise anybody more'n a few piddlin' things."

Mama comes in with a bucket filled with ripe tomatoes. "They's still plenty of cucumbers out there. I'll come back over tomorrow and get started on them bread-and-butter pickles." She rinses two ripe beefsteak tomatoes, pulls out the bread board, slices them into thick meaty slabs and arranges them on a plate.

"But Dan . . . your Uncle Daniel can . . . " Emma starts, but here it goes again. Wayne's looking at her that way, and she doesn't want to hear what he's going to say. Why did she bring it up anyway?

Wayne ladles a big helping of beans onto his plate, puts the ladle back in the bowl, leans his elbows on the table. "It's been six, seven months. How long you reckon we ought to wait before we figure he's most likely dead?"

Emma feels the blood rush to her face, and she immediately needs to look in the icebox for something. Butter. She must get the butter. She stares into the icebox at the butter, not seeing it. "I can't believe that, Wayne, and I don't want to hear you talk like that."

"Now where else could he be but dead? He didn't just go travelin' off to Florida or somethin'. Nobody's heard anything."

"Well, I just can't . . . I just won't believe he's . . . he's not comin' back." She comes back to the table empty-handed.

"Wayne, would you get us some butter from the icebox?" Mama says, softly, almost a whisper.

Feeling her mother's puzzled look, Emma's face feels hot.

"Sure, Mammaw," he says. "I think we've got to start believin' he's dead." He comes back to the table with the butter and the pitcher of buttermilk, sits back down to his supper and keeps right on. "I can't wait on him to do something with the mill. I miss him, too, but you know he wasn't a whole lot of help anyway after Granddaddy died."

"Be careful, Wayne, I just took the beans off the stove." Wayne's fork clangs to his plate and he grabs his milk glass with both hands.

Emma shakes her head, grins at Mama. "I swear I have to tell him that every night. He's always starvin' and can't wait."

Wayne drains the glass of buttermilk and pours himself another one. "Well, maybe next time you could tell me a little quicker."

"All right, then, I'm tellin' you tonight for tomorrow night. You heard me, Mama, I've already told him for tomorrow night."

Mama laughs, brings the plate of tomatoes to the table and forks up a fat slice for Wayne's plate.

"Thanks, Mammaw."

Emma takes her place at the table and dishes up a big plate of beans for Mama and one for herself. She hates to open the subject up again, but they need to decide something or Wayne will keep this up until she can't bear it anymore. "Wayne, what if I was to help you until things are better? I'm strong, and I can carry planks."

"I won't hear of you doin' men's work, and besides that, you've got your own business to tend to. And right now your sewin' is takin' care of you and me both." He breaks off a piece of cornbread and reaches for the butter. "Mammaw, don't you reckon Granddaddy would—"

"Wayne," Emma interrupts, "I told you I don't want you givin' up what Granddaddy left for you. When times are better, we can hire somebody. And when Daniel comes back, he can help."

Wayne puts down his fork, leans back and crosses his arms over his chest. "I can't figure it out. Can't you see Uncle Daniel's not goin' to be that much help to anybody, even if he's not . . . even if he does come back? I don't know why you're always takin' up for him, like he was your husband."

But he should have been! Emma jumps up, rattling the dishes on the table, goes again to the icebox. She feels suddenly naked in front of her son and her mother. She can feel both their stares on the back of her neck, but she can't turn around. "I . . . let's not talk about it anymore."

"Well, Wayne," Mama says. "Maybe you ought to just shut the mill and leave it 'til times are better. Couldn't you just do that?" Emma's grateful to Mama for the aiming the conversation away from Daniel.

"Don't you reckon one of Granddaddy's friends, like maybe Amos Teague," Mama says, "don't you s'pose one of them might give you some work to hold you over 'til things get better?"

"But Mammaw, they can't give me a job if they don't have any jobs to give. But, yeah, that's what I was thinkin', about closin' it up. And maybe I could join the Navy."

Emma runs water into the dishpan, sets it on the stove. "Now Wayne, we been through that a dozen times. I gave them your daddy already, and I'm not givin' them you too." She comes back to the table for the bean bowl.

"But Wayne, Honey," Mama says, "they're talkin' over the radio that we might get into the war. Lord, my mama would turn over in her grave if she knew the way her homeland was headin'."

"Aw, I don't reckon Roosevelt'll take us into a war that's not any of our business. But even if we did, I don't reckon they'd send me anywhere, considerin'—well, considerin' I'm the only man around here in this family now, as far as I can see. Wait—don't take that bowl yet, Mama. I want some more."

She waits for Wayne to scrape the bowl clean. "That's what your daddy told his mama, in the Great War, but the next thing we knew they sent him across the waters and we never saw him again."

Mama says, "Your granddaddy'd understand if you wanted to shut up the mill, don't you reckon, Emma, until money's better?"

Yes, and then it would still be there for Daniel, when he comes back! Emma turns her attention back to the table, avoids their eyes, tries to sound calmer than she feels. "Well, if that's what y'all both think, I reckon it's all right by me." She picks up her own half-empty plate and takes it to the stove, stoops to scrape its contents into the dog's bucket. "But I don't want to hear about the Navy again, do you hear me? I don't mind takin' care of both of us until you can get a job."

"Well, now that I'm a man, *I* mind. And Granddaddy would have understood that, too, wouldn't he, Mammaw?"

"I expect so, Wayne," Mama says, standing up. "Let's get this food cleared away and out of the heat."

Wayne brings his empty plate over to Emma. She piles dishes into the dishpan on the stove. "All right, I'll see about a job first," he says. "But me and Naomi can't even think about gettin' married if I've got no way to support her. And if I can't find anybody who'll give me a job, well . . . "

"Why, Honey!" Mama comes around the table behind Wayne, hugs him. "Are you and that sweet little Naomi wantin' to get married? Lordy, Emma, I can't think of Wayne old enough to get married. But then Will was not but seventeen when we run off either."

"Well, I can't live off of Mama's sewin', with me a grown man, sittin' on my hind end . . . I mean, sittin' out at the mill. I'm pretty sure Granddaddy'd understand that."

"Well, all right, Hon," Emma says, trying to sound a little brighter. "Let's us do that then—close up the mill—and I'll finish out your books, and we'll see who we can talk to about some work in this town." She wipes the oilcloth on the table with the dishrag. "And maybe by next summer we can plan a nice little weddin'. Wouldn't that be nice, Mama? Naomi's such a sweet little thing."

"Uh, y'all care if I go over to—"

"Only if you bring her back here for your Mammaw's good berry pie. Go on! Shoo!"

Mama comes over and picks up the dishtowel. Emma hands her a wet plate. "I swear, Mama, I don't know why he keeps talkin' about the Navy. He knows we're not going to hear of it." Mama smiles and wipes the plate dry. "What are you grinnin' about, Mama?"

"I was just thinkin', that boy may not look a bit like his grand-daddy, but he surely reminds me of him sometime."

Almost a month later
Nashville, Tennessee

"Come on in, Robert, and sit down." Brother Earl points Bobby Ray toward an empty chair. Bobby Ray sprawls back into it with one leg thrown over the arm.

"The others will be on in here soon," Brother Earl says.

The others? Bobby Ray sits up straight, puts his feet on the floor. "Is there somethin' the matter? I've got to get back to my message for tonight."

"You'll have plenty of time for that, Son. We've got some family business to talk about."

Brother Harold Spivey appears at the door.

Brother Earl takes a quick look down the hallway, but before he closes the door, he asks in a low confidential voice, "Will she be joinin' us now?"

"Not yet, Earl, not yet." Brother Harold nods toward Bobby Ray without looking at him, takes a chair on the other side of the room.

"Now, Robert, like I said, we've got several family matters we need to discuss with you."

"But I'm—"

Brother Harold leans forward in his chair and wags his finger at Bobby Ray. "You'll listen to us, young man, and do as you are told!"

"Now, now, Harold, let's keep our heads about us here. I'm sure our Brother Robert is perfectly willin' to do whatever the Lord has led us to tell him. Isn't that right, Robert?"

"Well, sure. All I meant was . . . " Bobby Ray shrugs.

Brother Harold slumps back into his chair while Brother Earl paces to and fro between him and Bobby Ray.

"Now, Robert, here is what the Lord is speakin' to us to do. First, Brother Harold is startin' a radio broadcast from here in Nashville, and I'm goin' to be movin' down here and joinin' him, and takin' over the tent revival circuit as soon as they can get a new pastor for my church over home."

Bobby Ray starts to get up from his chair, but Brother Earl gently pushes him back. "Now don't you worry, Robert. The second thing is, I want you to move here with us and be my helper, just like you have been, but permanent. Now what do you think of that?"

Bobby Ray scoots to the edge of the chair seat. Stay with Brother Earl permanent? And never have to see Mama again?

"But we are feelin' amiss," Brother Earl goes on, "We have taken up most of your time this summer, and we are feelin' that restitution must be made to your poor Mama for this, with her bein' left alone after your father's—well, until your father comes home."

"He's not comin' home," Bobby Ray answers too quickly.

"Now I don't see how you can be sure, Robert, unless—has there been some word? Has anybody heard anything?"

Bobby Ray feels Brother Earl's stare and slouches into the chair. "I don't know. He might be dead. Yeah, I reckon he might be dead. He just—well, I don't know."

"In any case," Brother Earl says, resuming his pacing, "your mama ought to be taken care of, and we plan on givin' her a pension and some groceries each month, in exchange for takin' you with us."

Bobby Ray sits up straighter again. His eyes dart from one of the Spivey Brothers to the other. "What— "

Brother Harold is up from his chair, pointing a finger at Bobby Ray. "You just sit right there and listen, Boy!"

"Now, Harold, just calm yourself." He nudges his brother back to his chair. "Brother Robert is just anxious to know what we have in mind for him, aren't you, Son?"

"Yes sir," he says. He wonders why neither one of the preachers is looking him in the eye.

"Then let's all keep calm and we'll get to the point." Brother Earl takes his own chair and sits back, steeples his fingers in front of him.

"Robert, we think it would be best that you come and live with us, but we plan to take care of your Mama, because the Word does admonish us to do that, now doesn't it?"

If they're taking him away from Mama for good, how come Bobby Ray's feeling like a June bug with its leg tied with twine?

"Of course we will have *you* deliver the pension and the canned goods to her each month. That would be the most fitting way to do it, so that for all appearances' sake, the son will be takin' care of his poor deserted mother . . . or widowed, if that be the case."

"Well, yes Sir, but—"

"Get on with the rest, Earl." Brother Harold shifts restlessly in his chair, looks at his big pocket watch.

"Yes." Brother Earl comes over and sits on the edge of the table next to Bobby Ray "Yes, Robert, to the other matters."

Brother Harold sits back, arms folded in front of him.

"Robert, you like Connie Sue, now don't you?"

Brother Harold is up from his chair again. "I don't see as that has much to do with it!" Brother Earl waves him back.

Bobby Ray squirms. Has she been tattling to them? Well, it's her doing, not his. They know how she is!

"Robert, it seems that Connie Sue has gotten herself into a little trouble, and—well, we have prayed over the matter considerably, and what we'll do is, we will marry y'all two here this afternoon, and make things proper in the eyes of the Lord. Of course, we won't have to let on to anybody that this is just happenin' *today.*"

Bobby Ray is up on his feet, glaring at Brother Harold, who glares right back at him. "But she— you can't—"

"Yes, Robert, we can," says Brother Earl, with a preacher smile that covers his insistent words. "We have agreed that this would be best, and then we can groom the two of you for the revival circuit and the radio broadcast. Robert and Connie Sue Carmody, Sweethearts of the Lord. Yes, I b'lieve people will take to that. Yes, I do believe they will take to that just fine."

As Bobby Ray slumps into his chair, words tumble through his head, but none make enough sense to spit out. Finally he leans back and stares into the faces of the Spivey Brothers. He blows out a deep breath that he feels like he's been holding for hours. It'll get him away from Mama for good. The rest he just won't think about right now.

Brother Earl offers Bobby Ray his hand, shakes it and pulls him up from the chair in one motion. "Now, Harold, shall we get the little bride on in here and get this over and done with?" Brother Harold gets up and starts for the door.

"Uh, Brother Earl," Bobby Ray says, and Brother Harold stops, looks around, his obvious impatience digging a deep groove between his eyebrows.

"About that *Brother Carmody*. I been thinkin' on this a long time. Is there any way I can change it to Ray, instead? Just Robert Ray?"

"Harold, can that be done, do you reckon?" Brother Earl asks.

Brother Harold huffs out an irritated snort and goes on out the door, and down the hallway.

"Why, I'm sure that it could, "Brother Earl says, with his preacher grin. "We could talk to the lawyer about it. Robert and Connie Sue Ray, the Lord's Sweethearts. Yes, I b'lieve I like the sound of that."

Ten days later
Mahala, Kentucky

Hilda stands up, rubs her stiff back. All around her, withering tomato plants lay tangled, dotted red in the August heat. "Gerty," she yells over to where she sits in the porch swing in the shade. "Have you never pulled up a weed one out here? They's quarts and quarts of t'maters out here rottin' away under this mess of weeds. Bring us the waterbucket!" Gerty goes inside, comes back with the waterbucket and the dipper. She waddles down the porch steps and sets them down out at the edge of the garden, then goes back up to the porch swing.

Will, our two girls turned out like day and night, didn't they? Hilda thinks. More and more often these days, she feels her Will's presence close and comforting, like when he used to lie beside her in the dark.

"Mama," Emma says, stopping to wipe sweat from her face with her apron. "You and me both know if poor little Liam didn't pull up the weeds, they wouldn't even get thought of." Emma picks up her bushel basket, half full of red ripe tomatoes. "None of this would've even got planted if it hadn't been for him."

Hilda holds the two corners of her apron and fans her face with it. "You know how the heat bothers Gerty." *Our family is changing, Will . . . you gone, and Daniel . . .* She feels uneasy at the thought of Daniel. With Will she has reached a peace and was at least given the chance to put him away properly, assured she would be with him in the sweet by and by. When Big Will died, everybody acted the same as everybody else, pretty much, and they could all cry together. But with Daniel, they're all different. The family waited, watching his absence until they forgot how to wait. But one thing they've each silently learned is how much they can wonder out loud to the others.

You can talk to Hildy about it, Will, and she accepts it. No, Will, you know what it is? It's playacting at accepting it, that's what it is. And Little Will, you know him—he always looks like he's sufferin' inside himself. No matter what you talk to him about, he keeps right on whittlin'. Liam? Liam always looks like he's holdin' a lid on himself like a pot of steam. Now, Bobby Ray . . . Bobby Ray don't seem like he's belonged to us for a long time. And Gerty. I'm glad you're not here to see, Will . . . you always turned your head to it, but something's wrong with Gerty. It ain't right for a woman to forget about her man so soon. And Wayne, he misses you and Daniel, too. But he's growin' up fast . . . and little Naomi helps, bless her heart.

Emma squints up into the sun. "Lordy, Mama, it must be at least a hundred out here. What we don't get canned today, I 'spect will all be rotten by tomorrow. Wayne! Y'all come on and take the rest of these tomatoes in the house!"

Wayne and Liam leave the bushel baskets of potatoes they've dug up on the hill, and lope across last year's cornfield now covered with potato vines drying in the hot sun.

Wayne teases Liam, and Liam chases along after him, with a grin that Hilda has not seen on his face for a long time. *Look at 'em, Will. They look a sight more like brothers than Liam and Bobby Ray ever did. Poor little Liam, tryin' to be a man. He's takin' Daniel's leavin' awful hard.*

Wayne runs up to Emma, huffing to get his breath. "Mama, now you tell me. Don't you think that hill over there has sunk down a whole foot since we dug out all the potatoes Liam planted?" He socks Liam on the arm and races to get out of his reach.

Emma laughs, shaking her head. "Mama, what're we goin' to do with these two?"

"But ain't it sweet to see 'em grinnin'." Hilda watches the two of them, bites her lips tight together. *Wayne, your favorite, I know it, Will, not that you'd ever say, but I knew it . . . and Liam, so much like Daniel.* "Let 'em play. They've too soon been made the men of the family," she says to no one in particular.

As though her thoughts have reached over and tapped the two of them on the shoulders across the open air of the garden, Wayne and Liam abruptly stop their chasing and their faces drop the little-boy grins. Sobered, they both start toward the baskets of tomatoes waiting to be carried inside, washed, cooked, and canned. Wayne stops, lets out a long whistle, points out toward the road. A new-model Buick slows and turns up into the dirt beside the house.

Hilda and Emma stop where they are, not even remembering to set their baskets down.

"Must be somebody lookin' for the Dunning place. Somebody had better aim them back at the other side of town."

"They must be—" Hilda is cut short by the sight of Bobby Ray getting out of the car on one side, Brother Earl on the other.

Up on the porch Gerty struggles to get up from the swing, her face lit up. "Bobby Ray, Sweetie, is that you?" she calls out. "Why, you're dressed up so fine, and you've growed taller, too!" Bobby Ray looks like he's going to jump back into the car, but Brother Earl nudges him forward.

"Sister Carmody! And how are you this fine afternoon?" Brother Earl's preacher smile is at its best.

Emma and Hilda set their baskets down and walk cautiously up toward the porch. Liam and Wayne hang back.

"Sister Tucker! And this—isn't this your other lovely daughter, Miz . . . ah, Widow, uh . . . "

"Emma Hartley." Emma stands with her fists shoved into her apron pockets, her eyes narrowed and looking downright mean.

"Why, we didn't expect to see y'all today, Brother Earl," Hilda says, brushing the straggles of gray hair out of her face. "And Bobby Ray, you do look nice. And what . . . what a big fine car."

"It's my brother Harold's," Brother Earl says. "You remember my brother Harold." The preacher makes his way over to the shade of the porch, Bobby Ray following close behind. "We have family business to talk over with Sister Carmody, and you ladies are welcome to join us." Brother Earl takes the old wicker chair down by the swing, and Bobby Ray sits on the porch railing close by.

"Robert, give your grandma a hand there." Bobby Ray jumps up and reaches an awkward hand out toward Hilda, who waves it away and takes a spot on the top step.

Emma stands by the porch, her fists still jammed into her apron pockets.

Liam and Wayne wait out past the Buick barely in polite listening distance of the porch, making no move to come closer to the house. Wayne points at the car and elbows Liam, who slaps his hand over his own mouth. Hilda's stern look stills them both.

Gerty says, "Bobby Ray, Sweetie, you look so handsome! Look at my preacher man there, Mama, my preacher man." Bobby Ray scoots closer up behind Brother Earl. His slicked-down hair, clean white shirt and brown worsted pants and shiny shoes stand out in contrast to the work clothes of the family.

"Don't he look pretty, Mama?" Gerty sits in the swing with her hands folded proudly in her lap.

"He surely does, Gerty." Hilda swallows hard, runs her finger along a faded gather in her print dress. *But Will, I liked him better in his overall pants, with that cowlick hanging in his eyes.*

Emma hasn't moved from her spot. "I reckon there's money for such fine things in *some* pockets these days," she says.

"Emma!" Hilda is surprised. What on earth is wrong with Emma, to say such a thing!

Look at her, Will—not so much as a blink of shame!

Brother Earl smiles directly at Emma. "The Lord's people take care of his chosen ones, Widow Hartley."

Hilda watches the preacher, seeing him from a ways off, as surely as if she'd risen up to the rooftop, as if she could see him through Emma's narrowed eyes. *Will, I never noticed how slimy Brother Earl has gotten to sound, since he went off with his brother.*

"Yes," Emma comes back, "I am quite sure people can always find money from someplace to pay for their sins, even durin' hard times."

Lord, Will, she sounds just like you! "Emma, I don't think . . . " Hilda's words hang useless in the hot sticky air. Neither the preacher nor Emma shows her any notice.

Brother Earl's face drops its preacher grin, and his answer is soft, obviously aimed at Emma alone. "*Especially* durin' hard times, Sister Hartley."

The big preacher smile comes back, and he turns to Gerty. "Now Sister Carmody, we have waited before the Lord for the answers to some burdens we have had, and we have come to tell you what He has given us to do."

His preacher grin is too wide, next to Bobby Ray's somber eyes that never meet anyone else's. "Sister Carmody, we feel real bad that we—the Lord has taken your son into His ministry just now at a time when you must sorely miss havin' his help here on your farm. Now, we don't question the Lord's timin' on such things, but it's a shame that you have also been left alone by your husband's passin'."

Emma gasps. She turns and walks quickly over toward where Wayne and Liam wait. Hilda starts to get up to follow, but realizes she has no idea what to say to Emma.

Brother Earl goes on, talking to Gerty. "The Scripture says that His church is to take care of its orphans and its widows, and we intend to take good care of you."

Gerty's face looks like a light has just come on in her reasoning. "Am I a *widow*? Why, I never—" Gerty looks around at the others, smiles. "Mama, Brother Earl says I'm a widow, too, just like y'all are."

"Well, by *widows* of course I mean all women who have been left alone, uh, for any reason," Brother Earl recovers. "Our Brother Robert is sorely needed in our ministry, but we aim to see that you are taken care of. He will be stayin' with us, but he is to come once a month, bring you store goods and money, and see to it that you are not in need of anything else. I see that your family and the other children are helpin' you with your garden." Hilda looks down at her apron, stained with dirt and tomato juice. Brother Earl goes on, "You have two other good-sized children . . . twins, I b'lieve?"

Gerty's blank face stares at the preacher, then turns to smile at Bobby Ray just as if nobody was talking to her.

"They started to school today," Hilda offers when it looks like Gerty is not about to answer. "Liam there, he starts to high school next week. My husband Will, he always wanted his grandchildren to go to high school, and well, Liam, he's small for his age, but he's fourteen, and he's done good in school." She catches a smirk on Bobby Ray's face before he turns his head away.

"Is it time for school already?" Brother Earl stands up, brushes off his pants, looking back at the chair he has just left. "My, how the summer flies by. I'm sure they will be doin' their share of chores after school. Well, then, it's all set. Robert, if you will give your mama the money we—you brought, and there is a pasteboard box of canned goods in the car, along with some sugar and coffee."

Bobby Ray gets up and starts toward the steps, looking relieved to have something to go and do.

"Robert?"

"Oh, uh, yeah." He pulls some bills out of his pocket and leans over toward Gerty from where he stands. She stares at the bills, reaches for them. He turns loose too soon and one of the bills flutters down to where Hilda sits, but she just looks at it, making no effort to pick it up. Something seems . . . wrong about it, but she can't place what.

Bobby Ray jumps from the porch railing past her and rushes out to the car. "Oh, and Robert?" Brother Earl calls after him. Bobby Ray stops in his tracks, looking like he's been caught at something. Again.

"Robert, I do b'lieve that you have neglected to tell your family your happy news."

"I didn't . . . "

"Robert has some mighty fine news for you, Sister Carmody, and for his grandmother here, too." Brother Earl nods toward Hilda.

Bobby Ray scuffs his shiny shoes in the dust. "Well, I . . . Connie Sue and me, we got married . . . "

"Robert and my brother Harold's little daughter Connie Sue, they run off and got married last Easter without tellin' any of us! And now there's a grandchild on the way. Widow Tucker, it must be your first great-grandchild, then?"

Bobby Ray, married? So that's what has brought all this on!

From the confused look of Gerty's face, Hilda knows she'll need to explain all this to her. But for now, she can't help smiling. *So Bobby Ray's about to be a daddy . . . and married last Easter he says. Why, Will, that's what we told my mama, remember that? I know she didn't a bit more believe it than anything, but she never once let on, bless her heart.*

Hilda eases herself up from the step and starts toward Bobby Ray, but he looks like he's eager to get to the car.

"Well, ladies, we must be on our way," Brother Earl announces. "Uh, Widow Tucker, would you be so kind as to send one of your other grandsons over to get a box out of the back of the car?"

The boys stand over on the other side of the car, Emma between them, and neither of them moves as Bobby Ray hurries past them to get into the passenger side.

Emma looks straight at the preacher. Finally Brother Earl opens up the back door, takes the box out and struggles with it over to the porch steps, where he sets it down. He gets back into the car and starts it up. With a wave and a broad preacher smile, he eases the big black car backwards out into the road.

Early the next week
Mahala, Kentucky

"Now, Wayne, there's no sense in goin' on about this." Emma can barely bring herself to try to calm Wayne down when she's just about as mad as he is.

"Well, it makes me so mad, Mama, I can't stop thinkin' about it. Naomi and me are workin' and savin' up to get married, and he's ridin' all over in big ol' Buick fancyin' himself a big preacher." Wayne sits at the table over a plate of biscuits and egg gravy that he still hasn't touched. "I can't help it, Mama. Him and his whatever-her-name-is are traipsin' all over in fine clothes, and Naomi and me probably won't be able to take a honeymoon trip at all, even with me workin' two jobs."

"Wayne, listen to me. What Bobby Ray does hasn't anything to do with us. As far as I care, he's not been part of this family for a long time, and good riddance. Now go ahead and eat your breakfast before it gets cold."

Wayne picks up a biscuit, jabs it at the air in front of him. "And besides that, Mama—"

"Wayne, that's enough. We're not havin' Bobby Ray for breakfast another day." She sets her plate on the table, goes back to the stove for the coffeepot.

"Besides, I've got something else I want to talk about." She pours two mugs of coffee and sets one in front of Wayne.

"Now, I've been thinking, why do you and Naomi have to wait until April? You were lucky enough that you got one part-time job, let alone two. I 'spect you need to count your blessings for Granddaddy's good name and his good friends in this town."

"I know it, Mama." He puts four heaping spoonfuls of sugar into his cup. "Well, me, I'd just as soon run off tomorrow, but she's already plannin' on April, and you know how fussy girls are about wantin' to have everything just right. She's savin' up all her waitressin' money for a fancy dress. But me, I'd just as soon run off, and save the money."

"Don't you dare! I never forgave myself for doin' that to Mama and neither did she." She stares out the side window over at the sink as she sips her coffee. "Now don't y'all go doin' it to me. I don't even want to hear you jokin' about it, you hear me?"

She sounded sterner than she meant to. Bobby Ray has always managed to could keep the whole family riled up over one thing or the other. She brings the coffee pot over to the table, sits down across from Wayne.

"What I was thinkin' about was, why don't I talk to Naomi and see if I can't help her more? I mean, would she mind, do you reckon, since she doesn't have a mama of her own? I thought it might be nice to get married on your birthday. It's on a Sunday this year."

"But Mama, we won't have enough money to get married in just a month." He starts to get up. "Have we got some more butter?"

"Here, I'll get it." She's already halfway to the icebox. "So what do you need money for that can't wait? They say two can live as cheap as one, so surely three can live as cheap as two, right here. I'll give y'all my big room and I'll take yours. And I was thinkin' . . . if you're wantin' a nice ring, I'm sure Naomi would be proud to wear the one your daddy gave me."

Emma glances down at her hands, now bare. Last year on what would have been her and J.D.'s twentieth anniversary she quietly slipped off her ring and put it away with his photograph, and no one noticed its absence. At least nobody mentioned it.

Wayne sits quiet, sopping up egg gravy with a biscuit. "But Mama, would it be proper, so soon after Granddaddy, and, you know, Uncle Daniel . . . "

Emma looks quickly away. *I won't say anything . . . I won't.* "Hon, I reckon Mammaw would be as glad as I would to have something for the family to be happy about for a change. A weddin', and maybe a baby next year."

She watches his face for a reaction to that, but he's cleaning the last of the gravy off his plate. "I know I'd like that," she says, "and I think Mammaw would too."

A hint of a smile starts playing around the corner of his mouth. "Thanks, Mama." He shoves the last bite of biscuit into his mouth and gulps down the last of his coffee. "You mind if I—"

"Don't talk with your mouth full, Wayne. You go right ahead, Son. Unless I'm mistaken, Naomi'll be as tickled to hurry things up as we would."

· . . . . 1939 . . . . . Germany invades Poland
. . . . . Britain and France declare war on
Germany . . . . . FDR fireside chat: "America
will remain neutral: I have seen war, and
I hate war" . . . . .

Early October 1939
Mahala, Kentucky

"It sure is pretty, isn't it? Lordy, I never imagined havin' such a pretty weddin' dress."

"Mmm-hmm," Aunt Emma says, biting off her basting thread.

Hildy looks up from the catalog and her tablet, where she has marked a long list of numbers. Standing on the stool while Aunt Emma fusses with the waist of the dress, Naomi looks as pretty as the ladies in the Sears 'n' Roebuck catalog. But Hildy isn't going to say so.

"I didn't know Aunt Silvie had Grandma Rose's dress," Naomi goes on, "and then I about died when I couldn't button it up. I was worried I was goin' to have to get me one of them lace-up things like Mammy put on Scarlett." Naomi giggles. "Can you find me one in that catalog, Hildy?"

Puzzled, Hildy is not sure what to say. "But I don't reckon there'd be time, would there?"

"Hold still now, Naomi," Aunt Emma says. "I can't believe your grandma could've been even tinier than you. Nobody will notice the gussets, soon as we take a strip of lace off the bottom to piece together and cover them with. It's a good thing your grandma was taller than you, too. She must have been a regular beanpole to be littler than you."

"Well, it's the first time I was ever glad I don't have big bosoms!" Naomi giggles at Hildy again. "Oh, Miz Hart—uh, Emma—Lord, I won't ever get used to callin' you that. You sure you want me to?" Naomi bends to run her hands down the fine lace of the skirt.

Aunt Emma smiles up at her. "Hon, you can call me whatever feels right to you. Even Mama, if you want to."

"I sure appreciate you doin' this. I'd've died if I couldn't have worn it, but I never did learn much about sewin', and I surely didn't know there was any way to make a dress *bigger*."

"I could teach you to sew, if you want me to. Now stand up straight, so the hem won't be crooked when I'm done. Hildy's learnin' to be a fine seamstress, aren't you, Hon."

Aunt Emma cuts a piece all around the lower edge of the dress. "You can't find lace like this anymore. Somebody must've brought it with them when they came over from Germany or someplace like that. Turn around this way. I'm almost done. Mama always used to tell me about the fine lace her grandma had that was made in Germany."

She holds the strip of lace, running her finger over the pattern. "Hildy, I'll bet your grandma in Ireland made pretty lace, too." Aunt Emma hands the strip to Hildy. "I hear they make real pretty lace in Ireland."

Hildy studies the lace strip, the swirls and flowers embedded in its pattern, puzzles at the look on Aunt Emma's face. Aunt Emma busies herself with the long row of buttons on the back of Naomi's dress.

"There, now, you go pull it off and I'll hem it and finish up these gussets, and we'll be all done. And be real careful, 'cause they're just basted in. Hildy, why don't you come watch? We might not get many chances to work with fine lace like this."

Hildy shrugs, drapes the strip over the arm of the chair, watches Naomi absorbed with her own reflection in the mirror. She goes back to her catalog, wandering from one page to the next. Naomi can watch this time. After all, it's *her* "fine lace."

Aunt Emma stands up and stretches, bends first one way and then the other, rubs the small of her back. "Umm, I must be gettin' a touch of the arthritis. Hildy, whatever are you doin' in that Sears 'n' Roebuck catalog? It looks to me like you're makin' out a mighty big order. Are you expectin' to get rich any time soon?"

Hildy erases a number from her long column of figures on her tablet page, ripping the page with a rumpled up triangle where the metal tears through. "I'm just playin' like what I'd do if I could spend twenty-five cents on a page, what I'd pick out. On some pages I don't pick out anything, so I can save up."

Naomi twists and turns in front of the mirror. "Why, that sounds like fun, Hildy. I'd save up all my twenty-five centses together and buy me one of them new coats that look like they're made out of lamb's wool. Would you pick me out one? And with a hat to match?" Naomi swishes the full lace-covered skirt around her. "I'll wear it to Atlanta, to see Gone with the Wind."

Aunt Emma says, "Now Naomi, you go in and pull off that dress before Wayne gets here. We can't have him seein' you in it before Sunday." She sits on the couch next to Hildy and pulls the catalog over, points to the open page. "Now would you look at that. Five-ninety-eight for a crepe dress almost like the one I'm makin' for Mrs. Dunning. I need to start chargin' her more. So which dress did you pick out of these?"

Hildy turns the page back. "I couldn't make up my mind. I liked this silky taffeta one or this rayon one with the puffy sleeves. But it only comes in petal rose or romance aqua, and the silky taffeta one comes in black like I wanted. But it's $3.98."

"But Hon, the rose or the aqua either one would go really pretty with your dark hair. Why on earth would you want it in black?"

She pulls her fingers through Hildy's wavy hair. When she catches on a tangle, Hildy flinches. "We need to do something with your hair.

Would you like me to put it up on rags for the wedding?"

Naomi comes in carrying her grandma's dress over one arm, smoothing down her own straight blond hair with her free hand. "Can we get my hair to curl up like Scarlett's? I never was quite sure what ringlets are. It says her hair hung in ringlets. Do you know what that is, Miz . . . uh, Emma?"

"Oh, I was aimin' to tell you, Naomi, with you lovin' that book so much. Mrs. Dunning is goin' to Atlanta in December to spend Christmas with her sister. Isn't that when the movie is comin' out, about then? Seems like that's what I heard over the radio, that it was comin' out in December."

She pats Hildy on the arm. "Maybe that crepe dress will get worn to something real fancy."

"Oooooh," Naomi swoons. "I'm so jealous. I told Wayne I'd give anything to take a honeymoon trip to Atlanta and see it. But I can't imagine them pickin' that English girl. It won't make sense, Scarlett soundin' like an *English* girl. Now does that make any sense to you? It sure doesn't to me. Now, Bette Davis, she sounds just like Scarlett ought to. She sounds just like I imagine Scarlett, just like her."

Hildy crosses her eyes and the catalog page blurs into two. She knows what Scarlett would say to Naomi: *My, you do run on!*

Aunt Emma takes the dress from Naomi, hides it away in the chifferobe next to Mrs. Dunning's unfinished crepe.

"I was just telling Hildy," she says, "if you two want some fancy curls for the wedding, we could roll it up on rags. Come on in the kitchen and I'll show you."

Hildy looks after them as they disappear into the kitchen, then she goes back to picking out her wardrobe from the catalog, along with aprons for Mammaw at two for seventy-nine cents, and maybe this fancy hat for Aunt Emma, with a *wimple*, whatever that is. It must be that thing than hangs down around the shoulders.

Naomi can save up her own twenty-five centses for an $8.98 half-wool and half-rayon play-like Persian Lamb coat.

Three months later, in the middle of the night
Nashville, Tennessee

Bobby Ray rummages through the pantry for matches. He still feels like an intruder in Brother Harold's house. The only time he can sneak a cigarette around this place without being preached at is in the middle

of the night. In the middle of *this* night, he sorely needs a cigarette.
His hair is soaked with sweat. He rubs his hands together to keep
them from shaking. The dream was a really bad one. The girls—one
after the other he took them. First they smiled at him, then they yelled
no no no until he smashed their faces, and then they smiled again, and
all the faces blurred together and turn into one fat Mama face with
the molasses grin, her eyes glittering black, and—*where are the damn
matches when you need 'em?*

He yanks at the curtain of the pantry shelf, almost knocking over
a jar of peach preserves.

He didn't imagine what it would be like living in Brother Harold's
house, hearing on and on, every day, every suppertime, slick silver
words about the wages of sin, how a man of God has no business
partaking of the devil's pleasures.

Connie Sue stands in the kitchen door, yawning, scratching her
swollen belly through her pink chenille robe that barely meets in the
middle. "You had another one of them bad dreams?"

"What do you know about my bad dreams?" He tries to hide the
cigarette. "Get on back to bed."

"Well, Robert, with all your takin' on in the night, I figure you
were either havin' bad dreams or you got a demon. Or both. You got
another cigarette?"

"You know where they're hid."

She sits down at the table, pulls at the front of her bathrobe. "It's
cold in here."

Bobby Ray digs into the pantry again, finds the match box
behind the lard bucket, goes ahead and lights the cigarette in front of
her. "Go on to bed and let me alone." He turns his back to her and
looks at the reflection that returns his stare from the black.

The chair scrapes on the linoleum. When he hears Connie Sue
get up, he lets out a relieved sigh along with the blue smoke that he
blows at the reflection. But she's not leaving. He feels her faint touch,
one finger, one touch on his back, and he shivers all over, not just
from the chill of the room.

When they were first married, before her face puffed up and she
took on the shape of a rainbarrel, she came to him in the dark. It was
a relief to have her any time he wanted to without sneaking around.
But afterwards when she tried to slip over closer to him, trying to hang
onto him, to own him, just like Brother Earl said, he shoved her away
and got up.

Now she makes it known she doesn't want him to touch her. *The baby,* she says . . . *the baby . . . the baby.*

And that's fine with him. He hasn't wanted to touch her now for a long time anyhow. She's ugly and fat, and he wants nothing to do with her, feels trapped by her and her father. There's no lack of skinny little girls wanting him, and next summer at revival time, there'll be more than he can use.

So now he just rolls over on his back and leaves his wife out of it, rocking the bed with its squeaking springs until he's done and the only sound is Connie Sue sniffling into her pillow. Then he gets up to pace through the house until he's exhausted enough to sleep.

But still, once in a while she rolls over close to him in her sleep, warm and smelling of jasmine toilet water, his body betrays him, remembering her thin warm body from last summer. In his half-sleep he punches his pillow with his fist. First it's Connie Sue, then it's Mama. Once in a bad dream it turned into Daddy, screaming inside Bobby Ray's head . . . *killed me . . . killed me!*

That night he roamed the house and smoked until daylight.

"Robert," she says, startling him. He forgot she was there.

She starts, "Why couldn't we at least just try to be decent to each other? Maybe it would be easier to act all lovey-dovey in front of everybody if we didn't act like we despised each other at home. I kind of thought bein' married, well . . . "

This girl that he first thought was so pretty, now he can't stand the sight of her. He wants to squeeze his eyes shut tight, cover his ears—anything to keep her whining voice from invading his head. "It's fine with me the way it is," he says.

"Well, what's our baby gonna think, with its mama and daddy actin' like this?"

Our baby. He refuses to hold the idea. Well, this beats staying at home with Mama. But not by a whole lot, with Brother Harold at him all the time. Connie Sue's floppy mules shuffle away from him, and he turns around. She stops at the door, pushes the straggly hair from her puffy face.

Look at her standing there pawing at her belly, trying to claim some special notice for doing what any sow can do.

He turns to the reflection in the window again, mashes out the last of his cigarette on the windowsill. "What do I care what that youngun thinks? I'm probably not its daddy anyhow."

"You bastard, Brother Robert," she says, "you know you're its daddy. I'm just hopin' it doesn't turn out nearly as mean as you, or I'll be the one with the demon to worry about."

> ..... *1940* ..... *U.S. life expectancy*
> *established at 64 years* ..... *Because*
> *of war in Europe, the Olympics, the*
> *Davis Cup and Wimbledon suspended*
> ..... *U.S. gives 50 outdated*
> *destroyers to England* .....

After midnight, midsummer 1940

"I thought she was goin' to stay at it all night." Bobby Ray drops onto a folding chair on the empty platform. The tent flap behind him hangs still in the listless midnight air. "She was up here every night this week."

"Now Robert," Brother Earl grins from up at the pulpit where he counts out money from the baskets. "Good old Sister Florrie waits for us every summer to get rid of the sins she's saved up all winter. If it takes her the whole two weeks to do it, it's not any skin off our teeth, now is it?" Brother Earl comes over and sits down, stuffs the last of the bills into a canvas bag. "You reckon by next summer she'll be used to takin' care of her sins over the radio, one at a time, and not savin' 'em up and wearin' out her knees in the sawdust ever' summer?"

Outside the crickets chirp their sinless chorus, no longer needing to compete with the groans of human souls beseeching their god for forgiveness. Brother Earl grunts and stands up. "The radio program is up to us now, Robert. I'm dependin' on you and Connie Sue to help me carry it on. We might not do it exactly the way Harold had in mind, but he didn't leave me much to work with. Of course, he didn't expect to go so quick like that, neither."

It wasn't quick enough for Bobby Ray. He goes over to the open side of the tent where he can see the full moon, now high in the sky. The old fool Harold nearly drove him nuts.

"Is Connie Sue holdin' up all right? So soon after the baby, I was real worried about her. She was always her daddy's little girl."

"Yeah." *Yeah, Daddy's little bitch in heat.*

"Well, I think y'all will do fine on the radio program. Ever'body here's takin' to you and that sweet little girl. I'll bet you little Molly will be singin' as sweet as her mama before long. I remember when Connie Sue was just four, Harold would hold her up so everybody could see her, and she'd sing out, 'This little light of mine, I'm gonna let it shine.' "

Brother Earl goes on and on without even looking around to see if anybody's paying attention. He's starting to sound just like old Harold did. He pulls some bills from the bag. "Now, I want you to go on out to see your mama tomorrow before we move on, and take her this here money, and see to it she has whatever she needs. Is she holdin' up all right too?"

Bobby Ray takes the money and shoves it into his pants pocket. "She always seems about the same to me."

The next day
Mahala, Kentucky

Emma makes her way carefully up Gerty's back porch steps, carrying a dozen ripe peaches in her apron gathered up into a pouch. When she sees Bobby Ray's Ford parked in the dust out by the side of the house, she changes her mind about going in. Emma is in no mood to see Bobby Ray today.

Just as she turns to go, she hears his voice from the kitchen: "Mama, is that the only rag you've got? Get Emma to make you some decent clothes. What does she do with the money I bring you?"

Emma's in even less of a mood to *hear* Bobby Ray. She swears he sounds snottier every day. She's not about to let him go unanswered, so she squawks open the screendoor and marches in.

"And what on earth do you think I do with it?" Emma clears a spot on the big table and one by one sets out the peaches, next to the box of store-bought groceries Bobby Ray has dropped right on top of a dirty plate.

Gerty fusses with her faded yellow dress, pulled tight across her bosom. The middle button is gone and her dingy underslip shows through. "But Mama put it on just for you, Sweetie. It's the one you always liked the best."

"I never cared what you had on, Mama, and that's nothin' but a dirty old rag. Emma, I bring her good money. Why don't you make her up something decent to wear?"

It's all Emma can do to keep from slapping his smirky face right off his head. "With your precious money we pay for electric and coal and whatever she needs from the store. And you're the one traipsin' around in the big cities. You might bring her some piece goods if you're all that worried about her dresses. We're in a depression, not that the likes of you would know it."

"Emma, you always did try to tell everybody what to do."

"Well, if anybody ever told *you* what to do, I never saw it do much good. And my name is still *Aunt* Emma to you."

"Emma, Bobby Ray brought his mama a radio!" Gerty chirps. "My Bobby Ray is a preacher on the radio."

Bobby Ray puffs himself up taller. "Connie Sue and me are on the radio every Sunday night. I'm more interested in that than if Mama gets new dresses or not. You ought to listen to it, Emma."

Emma stares him down. "And who might this be, this Connie Sue? I don't recall seein' anybody by that name around here lately."

She goes back to lining up the peaches on the table. "I reckon we'll have to miss out on the Self-Righteous Piss Ant Hour at our house. We already listen to Jack Benny and Fred Allen on Sunday."

Bobby Ray walks over and helps himself to one of the peaches. "Well, y'all had better leave that worldly business alone and start thinkin' about your eternal salvation."

Emma glares at him. "I reckon we'll manage just fine without your sermons, here or on the radio." She picks out two of the peaches for herself and starts for the door. "And I suggest you start practicin' what you preach, and start takin' better care of your Mama."

She stops at the door, turns to talk to Gerty but her glare never leaves Bobby Ray's face. "Gerty, you might have your big preacher man here bring along his wife and his little girl for you to see, and you might tell him his Mammaw ought to get to see her great-grandbaby before it's too late."

Gerty beams from one to the other of them. "My Bobby Ray is a preacher man, Emma. Y'all ought to listen to him on the radio."

Bobby Ray's small victory is written in his sneer. He takes his time ambling back over to the stove, bites into the best part of his peach, looks at it with disgust and drops it into the slop bucket. "What place is it of mine to take care of her? She had a no-account husband who ran out on her."

How dare him! Before she can stop herself, Emma hurls a peach at him, barely missing his head. It splats on the wall behind the stove.

"Daniel was a better Christian than you'll ever be, Bobby Ray!"

She steps out onto the back porch, smacking the screendoor shut behind her. She stomps down the porch steps, breaths heaving in her chest. *What right does he have to even mention Daniel's name?*

She makes her way up the dusty hill toward home, stifles the tears that gather in her eyes. She absently bites into her last peach, and the warm summer juice runs unnoticed down her bare arm. She tosses the seed into the bushes, wipes her mouth and her hands on her apron. The satisfied feeling of putting Bobby Ray in his place drains away. Behind that arrogant preacher face, she can't help seeing the towheaded three-year-old that Gerty and Daniel brought with them from Texas, peeking around Gerty's dresstail at his cousin Wayne for the first time.

Oh, Daniel, whatever happened to us all? I wish we could go back to then. She's ashamed of letting Bobby Ray goad her like that. She'll go back and clean up that peach mess. But not until he's gone.

"Mama!" Wayne's running down the road toward her. "Hurry! The baby's comin'!"

A month later
Mahala, Kentucky

Emma stops in the middle of the road, pulls Hildy over to a shady spot under a tree. "Here, Hildy, sit down a minute. I really do want you to come with me to help with some sewin' like I told your mama, 'cause Naomi's still not up to it. But there's somethin' else, too."

Hildy tilts her head to the side, with that suspicious frown she gets when she's puzzled.

Emma pulls out a letter from her apron pocket. "It's from Liam. He's all right, you can tell Little Will. And you'll need to help me with something—well, here, you just read it." Emma swats the dirt off a big rock and sits down. Hildy sits on the ground, pulls the lined tablet sheet out of its envelope.

> Dear Aunt Emma,
>   Im sorry to run off but I reckon
> you heard that Bobby Ray whupped me.
> I always kep my mouth shut when he
> was home but I couldnt stand hearin

him go on about how he run Daddy off
I was so mad I wanted to kill him and
I wisht I did. Mama went crazy even
more than she always is. She said I
was to blame for her baby girl dyin and
Aunt Emma I never did know what that
desser is she keeps hollerin about. do
you know? Mostly I couldnt stand being
there no more with Daddy gone.

I didnt aim to tell anybody where I
went I thought I would be better off not
knowing about everbody but its a whole
lot worse. Tell Chigger to write me.
This farm where I work they let me
sleep in the barn and they feed me good.
Mr Goodaker is a horse doctor and he
fixed my arm where it was growen
back wrong. They even give me a shirt
that belong to their son that died, but he
must not of wore it much for it looked
brand new. I reckon it was too little for
it fits me fine. Mrs. Goodaker makes me
think of Mammaw. She thinks I aint
got folks Im sorry to have lied but I
had to. She give me the paper and pencil
for this letter I told her it was for a
girl back home now that part was not
exactly a lie was it.

If you could get Chigger to find you
my wood box Daddy give me. She knows

*where its at. Its got a gold watch in it
dont you worry its not stolen or nothin.
Daddy showed it to me when I was 10
and he said it would take care of me
when he was gone. I reckon he knew he
was goin for he said that many a time.
Well hes gone and I need it now if you
could sell it for me and dont tell Mama
or Abby Ray but send me the money. And
tell Chigger I aim to send for her some
day when I can if she can hold out till
then.*

Hildy finishes reading over the letter quickly but holds it still in her lap for a long while. Emma studies her, the thin face and long brown braids. *Lordy, she looks so much like Daniel!*

Hildy folds the letter carefully and hands it back. "Well," she says, after a deep breath. Nothing else, just "Well."

"Wouldn't you like to keep it? I reckon it was really for you."

"I've not got a good hidin' place in the house, only out in the smokehouse where the mice would chew it up."

They start out walking toward town; the dust of the road puffs up with each step. "Well, then," Emma says. "I'll keep it and you can read it over any time you want to. And if you want to write him one back you can do it at the house. I'll give you a three-cent stamp and mail it for you."

They walk on quietly for a long while, neither of them finding any need to talk.

Emma takes a sideways peek at Hildy from time to time. Sometimes her face looks pleased and relieved. Other times her forehead bunches up into that look she gets when she's thinking on serious things. Like one of Daniel's headache looks.

Across on the other side of the dried-up stream bed that follows the curves of the roadside, the year's blackberry briars are parched brown and bare. When Emma was a girl, she hopped from rock to rock along this same creek, exploring the rounded-out hollows in the sandstone, her sturdy legs as brown as Hildy's and her mind as busy.

Where are the children to jump this stream, to chase along the roadside, to pick the berries In the springs to come? She and Daniel could have had a dozen like this one.

"Aunt Emma?" Hildy's eyes narrow with suspicion, but a little mischief shows through. "Do you reckon that nice woman made that shirt up just for Liam?"

Emma laughs. "I can picture your Mammaw sneakin' and doin' that, not expectin' her reward until she got to heaven. I'd say that Miz Goodaker must be a fine Christian, too, just like your Mammaw."

Hildy plods on in the dust, her tough bare feet treading on rocks and dirt alike with no notice. Then she reaches out her slim hand, tucks it shyly into Emma's large-boned coarse one.

Emma smiles down at the deep blue eyes, so like Daniel's that she quickly looks away. "Yes, a fine Christian," she says. "He's lucky to have a fine Christian woman to take good care of him."

Hildy's face puckers into her thinking look again. "And do you reckon some fine Christian woman is takin' care of Daddy, too, wherever he went off to?"

Almost a month later
Mahala, Kentucky

Dear Aunt Emma and Chigger and little Will, How are you fine I hope. Aunt Emma I got the 10$ and I think its a fine idea that you keep the rest for me and send it when I need it this will last me a good long time.

I didn't know it would be more than 10$ for the watch anyways, that it would get such a good price.

You asked me about the picture in the box of the baby. Daddy showed me it a long time ago and said to not tell anybody but I reckon he meant Mama. He *had it took of me I dont know why but he just said that people ought to have a picture of there baby. Chigger wanted a picture of me but I dont know where to get one so let her have that one its the only one there is.*

I drempt about Daddy last night and I thought he stood there and grinned at me like he used to when I was little.

Sometime I think on what it would be like if I was to find him he would be as surprised as me. I cant help it, I think he is dead because if he wasnt dead he would of come back or wrote us by now dont you reckon?

Emma puts the letter down. No, no, Liam mustn't talk like that. Daniel's not dead, he's not. He will come when he can. He *will.*

She takes the wooden box from the desk drawer, opens it and tenderly lifts out the watch. Liam needn't know. She'll pay him for it piece by piece. She holds it, closes her eyes for a second. She remembers the photograph, pulls out the tiny rectangle of paper, the baby in the dotted dress, in an oval.

Yes, poor dear Daniel, he would have done this, of course he would. In his grief for the little girl, he would have made sure there was a picture of Liam. He would have done this.

"Aunt Emma?" Hildy calls from the open front door.

"Come on in, Hon!" Emma quickly drops the watch and shoves it back into the drawer, then goes to meet Hildy in the front room.

"I told Mama you had work for me, but I . . . " Her eyes brighten when she sees the letter Emma waves in front of her.

"And I have something for you in here Liam wants you to have, to keep."

Hildy pulls the folded page from the envelope and sits cross-legged on the braided rug to read it.

Emma savors the photograph a moment more, before she has to give it up, to give it to Hildy.

Yes, Daniel would have done this, yes, dear Daniel . . .

A month later
Mahala, Kentucky

Hildy closes the Bible, traces her finger along its worn edges. Mammaw pushes the covered chamber pot back up under the bedstead and sits down on the edge of her featherbed. She smoothes the sunbonnet quilt with the thin paper skin of her fingers. "I thank you for comin' over to sit with me, Hildy. I dearly love to hear you read out of the Bible. Your granddaddy was always proud of how good you read."

"I don't know all them big words. Did them people really talk like that way back then, like *verily I say unto you?* How come they talked so fancy like that?"

Mammaw lies back on her pillow, tucks her feet under the quilt, chuckles. "Why child, that was a ways before my time."

Hildy helps pull the quilt up under her grandmother's thin arms. "I didn't mean you was as old as one of them old Bible people, Mammaw." She didn't mean to hurt—but wait, Mammaw's eyes are sparkly. Her feelings aren't hurt—she was just teasing!

Hildy takes her place back in the big rocker pulled up to where it almost touches the bed, near the big bolster pillow.

"Mammaw, do you remember when you was eleven, like me?"

"Why I surely do, like it was yesterday. Why, I was not any more than that when I first laid eyes on your granddaddy, and he wasn't but fourteen, and I knew then he was the only boy I wanted some day. He was so big and tall, but he was real bashful."

Mammaw reaches over and runs her frail hand down Hildy's tanned arm, tucks her fingers around the girl's slender hand. "You saw your granddaddy laugh a lot in your time, but it took him a long time after we was married before he would do that. When I first saw him, he was quiet like you. Or more like your daddy. You wouldn't a thought that, now would you?"

At the mention of Daddy, Hildy tries to pull her hand away, but Mammaw holds onto it. "Hildy, has they ever been any word at all about your daddy? No, I 'spect not. Your daddy was a troubled man, Hildy, but he was a good man. I hope you can keep a soft place in your heart to forgive him for goin'. He couldn't help it. He wasn't strong enough to help himself. He was a good man, your daddy. Just not strong . . . "

Hildy rubs her loose hand over the pebbly surface of the old Bible. Her mouth twitches at the sides. "I know he left because of—"

"What, Honey?" Mammaw rolls onto her side, reaches over and holds Hildy's hand with both of hers.

Hildy only shakes her head. She knows it was because of her, because she's so wicked. She knows she'll never be good enough for Daddy to come back, no matter how much she prays, never. She's too too wicked. The two of them sit quietly in the softening light of the late afternoon, listening to the *squeak squeak* of the rocking chair.

"Well." Mammaw says. She gives the hand a squeeze and lets it go, settles back on her pillow "I'll wager you're already lookin' at the boys for a sweetheart, ain't you, just like me when I was your age."

Hildy shakes her head again.

"Now, don't go tellin' me the young fellas at school ain't already noticin' that pretty face of yours."

"Me?" *Is Mammaw getting so old she's blind?*

Mammaw raises up on her elbows, looks all around the room. "Why, is they some other pretty girl in here?"

"But I'm—I'm homely."

"Child, whatever are you talkin' about?"

"Mama always says. And Daddy, he never looked at me at all."

"Hildy, you're not to pay any attention to what your mama said. She's not . . . she don't always know what she says. She never meant to be hateful to you." Mammaw drops back onto her pillow, looks even more tired. When she turns back, her eyes are sparkly again, but not the same teasing way as before.

"Now, you go get me my lookin' glass over yonder on my dressin' table. Go get it and bring it here to me."

Hildy gets the mirror, then on second thought brings the hairbrush, too. "You wantin' me to brush your hair?"

Mammaw reaches out and pulls Hildy's arm, motions for her to come up and sit on the bed next to her, leans back on the pillow, pants some for the effort.

"Now I want you to look in there and tell me what you see."

Hildy holds the mirror up in front of her face, but her puzzled look is still aimed at Mammaw.

"Look in there, child. What do you see?"

"Just . . . just me, is all."

"You see anybody in there that makes you think of me, or your Granddaddy?"

"No, Ma'am." She doesn't look like anybody except maybe a little bit like Liam.

"No, that's not a Tucker face. I 'spect you look just like your *other* grandma, and I'll wager that outside of her, your daddy thought you was about the prettiest girl he ever seen."

Hildy peers into the mirror for a long while, but there's nobody looking back except her own homely face, her eyes too dark. The devil's eyes, Mama said. Mammaw must be wrong.

"Hildy, I don't ever want you to forget you're my most special granddaughter."

"But Mammaw, I'm the only one you've got."

"Well, even if you wasn't, you'd be the special one. You're the one named for me, just like Little Will was named for your Granddaddy. That'll always be your special thing. You hold your head up high. You hear me?"

Hildy sits looking at her hands. Mammaw reaches up and nudges the girl's chin and their looks meet for only a second.

"You hear me, Hildy?"

"Yes Ma'am."

"And the Lord loves you, too, you remember that."

Oh, no, how can that be?

"Hildy? You hear me?"

"Yes, Ma'am."

But Bobby Ray says Hildy's wicked, and he's a preacher. Mammaw, she just doesn't know!

. . . . . *1940* . . . . . *FDR defeats Wendell
Wilkie for unprecedented
third term as president
*. . . . . *Pulitzers for Hemingway's For
Whom the Bell Tolls, Sandburg's Lincoln
and Steinbeck's Grapes of Wrath* . . . . .
Congress passes Selective Service Act . . . .
40-hour work week goes into effect

. . . . .

A month later, winter 1940
Mahala, Kentucky

Dear Liam, How are you fine I hope. Is it cold in Nebraska? It has been real cold here.

I am awful sorry I have gone and lost your picture. I had it in my spelling book and I have looked and looked and its not anywhere. Little Will helped me look for it, but I cant tell anybody else, even Aunt Emma. Im ashamed to. She wanted to keep it for me and I should have let her but I wanted to look at it.

I miss you but I am glad youre not here. I hope I can come see you someday but I cant go to stay even if you send me money like you said without Little Will. He is sweet to me and tries to help but he cant do anything with Mama neither. I wish he would quit thinking he can. You know little Will, he is not real smart.

I hate to say that but he is sweet and I love him and cant ever leave him. He needs me the most but he doesnt know it.

Bobby Ray just gets meaner and meaner. Connie Sue she never comes with him. I reckon she is too good to come. Being married or being a preacher neither one didnt change him much, only made him meaner.

Every time he comes Mama starts in telling him what I did and most of the time I never heard of it. You know how she never remembers anything right. Im just glad when he gets the whipping over with. I never holler out no matter what he does and I know it makes him mad.

Im sorry we couldnt find you in time for Mammaws funeral. I miss her, but Aunt Emma said Mammaw was just lonesome for Granddaddy, and wanted to go on and be with him. She left me her radio I reckon cause I used to listen to PepperYoungs family with her. I dont have any place to listen to it now because they turned off the electric out at Mammaws place and I cant bring it home. Aunt Emma said Mammaw wanted me to have her little looking glass too but I dont know why. Naomi she was jealous cause she likes looking glasses.

Her and Waynes baby Billy Wayne is sitting up by himself now. He looks just like Naomi. We dont any of us know who Bobby Rays little girl looks like, he never brings her.

Little Will said him and me are the only Will and Hilda left now. I dont reckon he meant to make me cry.

Love, Hildy

.....January 1941.....
FDR addresses Congress on four freedoms:
freedom of speech, freedom of worship,
freedom from want, and freedom from fear

A cold January day in 1941
Mahala, Kentucky

Gerty watches the road, down the slope from her front porch and out past the old oak tree by the mailbox. She's waited all afternoon, but for what she is not really sure. A black Ford passes the house, slows down for just a moment, then makes its way slowly up the hill toward town.

"Bobby Ray, Sweetie?" Gerty struggles to get up from the swing. The chains screech against rusty hooks. She steadies herself on the side of the swing and pushes her ponderous body off onto wobbly legs, then pulls herself up the chain hand over hand until she stands upright. She wipes the rust flakes from her hands on her dirty apron, satisfied with her effort.

The car is gone. A gust of cold north wind howls around the end of the porch, agitating the shriveled brown oak leaves on the bare ground in front of the house. "Bobby Ray, you come on in now," she yells out into the silent yard, the now-empty road. "Mama needs you to help her. Bobby Ray you hear me? Mama wants you to help her." Gerty waddles across the groaning porch planks to the railing that creaks in the winter chill, wet from melting frost in the pale sunshine. She peers out to the barn. Its door sags open and scrapes in the wind. "Bobby Ray?" *Where has that boy gone to?*

She gives up her mission, not sure now what it was. She shuffles back into the house. She's just about to shove the front door closed when a corner of paper catches her eye in the thin sunlight, something stuck under the edge of the tattered linoleum. She hangs onto the door knob and bends, grunting, to pick it up.

Her breath catches in her throat. Odessa! The melancholy face of the baby ghost stares up at her, its face caught forever still on the tiny rectangle of paper. It's Odessa! Her baby Odessa!

She clutches the photograph to the front of her faded print dress, pushes the door shut and leans on it, panting, as though to capture the tiny being and not let it escape. Memories hopscotch through her, a tiny girl in a white bonnet, toddling in the dry patch of Texas yard, a wind coming up just like this one, but hot, hot . . .

"Bobby Ray, you get your sister and bring her on in here now this wind is gettin' too hot . . . too cold . . . Bobby Ray, you hear Mama?"

Gerty hugs the picture to her bosom, wanders into the kitchen. "Are you hungry, Odessa, Sweetie? Mama's makin' you and Bobby Ray snowcream."

There's a noise at the door. Gerty looks around the big kitchen, worried, afraid. Emma's voice calls in, "Gerty?"

No! Emma can't have Odessa! Gerty scurries into the front room, digs through the pile on top of her chest of drawers, not sure now what she's looking for. She spies her worn old Bible, grabs it up and stuffs the photograph between its pages, hides it under the dirty garments heaped in the corner.

Satisfied, she wipes her hands on the front of her dress and goes to the kitchen. Emma can't have Odessa. She won't get her this time.

"Gerty, has Bobby Ray been in with your money yet? We need to pay your electric and get you a load of coal before you run out."

Gerty brightens up, the photograph forgotten. "My Bobby Ray's comin' in today?"

"Well, he ought to have been here already, *last* week. Maybe you had better give me his address where I can write him."

"What do you want with him?" Gerty peers at her sister, her eyes narrowed, suspicious.

"Gerty, I want to write him and find out when—well, Lordy no, I don't *want* to write him, but he's got to take better care of you."

"Bobby Ray, he loves his mama. Bobby Ray brought his mama a radio." She can't understand Emma's cold look. Emma's so hateful.

"Well, he better start takin' better care of you. That's all I'm goin' to say about it."

"You don't like my Bobby Ray, Emma. No, you don't."

Emma's looking at her cold again. What's the matter with her? *Daddy, Emma's being hateful to Bobby Ray again. Whup her, Daddy!*

Emma starts for the door, turns back. "Well, Gerty, now that you said it outright, I reckon I don't. Your Bobby Ray has grown up into a mean man, and no, I don't like him. He doesn't give a body much to like. But whether I like him or not, he's got to start takin' better care of you."

But Bobby Ray does take care of his mama. He brought his mama a radio, didn't he?

Spring 1941
Mahala, Kentucky

Little Will looks up from his spelling book. "Chigger, you ought not be sneakin' out. Mama's goin' to ask me—what am I s'posed to tell her then?"

"Little Will, let me alone. It's not any of Mama's business. I'm almost thirteen years old, not a little kid." Hildy stops at the back door. "I'm sorry, Little Will, I didn't mean to be hateful to you. I'm sorry." She comes back to the kitchen table and pats his hair, runs her hand over his arm, but he twists away from her and gets up from his chair. She treats him like he was a puppy or something.

"You're always lookin' out for me," she says, "but I wish you'd quit it. I'm the one Mama's goin' to whup. She won't blame you."

Little Will jumps up from his chair and whirls around to face her, hot tears brimming in his eyes. "Dammit, nobody cares what I say! You never listen to me! It don't *matter* if she blames me. I wish she would, and get off of you. But you make it worse by just tryin' to get in trouble. You act like you *want* her to tell Bobby Ray all that bad stuff about you."

Hildy eases into the chair next to his and looks at her hands for a long time.

Little Will watches her, waits. He finally gives in and takes his place back at the table beside her.

"I reckon . . . " she starts, but at the sound of Mama's lumbering footsteps in the front room, Little Will shoves his spelling book over in front of her. They both play at studying until the sound wanders away. She pushes the book back to him. "I just don't care one way or 'nother what she tells him. No matter what I do, she tells him things I never did. I figured I 'bout as well go on to the show and have some fun anyway, 'cause I'm gettin' whupped no matter what."

Little Will doesn't answer. He sniffles, wipes his face on his denim shirt sleeve.

"Do you need me to help you any more with your lessons?"

"No. I can do it by myself."

"I'll stay if you want me to."

He sits with his arms folded in front of him and won't look at her. She doesn't care what she does. Why should he care?

"Well, I'm goin', then. Charles said if I get to the moviehouse for the first show, he'll buy me a cold drink. If Mama asks you, you just tell her I went to the toilet or I went to bed and she won't even think about me."

She gets up, stands by his chair a few more moments, then goes on. When she's almost at the door, he can't keep quiet about this any longer. "Chigger, that Charles Sisk's not a fit boy for you to be around. Why can't you go with somebody like Aaron?"

"Oh, Aaron! He makes me think of a mouse, peekin' around in people's face then runnin' off when they look at him. He hasn't got any gumption at all."

Little Will bites his lip, trying his best not to comment on that. Maybe she thinks *he's* like a mouse, too, with no gumption. Well, maybe he is, but somebody's got to stand between his twin and the trouble she's always asking for. "Well, Aaron does good in school, and he likes you. That ought to account for somethin'."

"He likes me? How do you know that, Little Will?"

"Don't you reckon I know that's why he hangs around me? Why can't you go with him instead of somebody like that fool Charles Sisk?

He's hateful to you—you don't even know if he'll be there, no matter what he says, and you'll have to walk home in the dark."

"I'm not scared of the dark." She goes over and stands in front of the old shaving mirror over the washstand, combs her fingers through her long hair that ripples to her waist the way it does after being braided up all day.

"I know he kind of forgets, but he's not real hateful. He said he was sorry that time he slapped me and he says he won't ever do it again. It's just that he got mad 'cause I—"

"Chigger, I think you're *wantin'* people to be hateful to you."

"I'm not either. You think I've not got good sense?"

It's no use. She's going, anyhow, and he can't stop her. She won't listen to him anymore.

"You've got good sense. I know it." He puts his spelling book back into his book satchel. "But I don't know why you want to throw it away on Charles Sisk when there's boys like Aaron that would be good to you."

Later the Same Month

Little Will walks along behind Hildy, holds tight against his chest the two books he's brought from school. Lord, sometimes he wishes girls would all just shut up.

But Hildy doesn't shut up. "That prissy Gaynell Putnum thinks she's so pretty. I hate her." Hildy huffs along the dusty road, twists around to reach the book that is ready to fall from the stack under her arm. "She just makes me mad, she's so stuck up. And she—"

"Chigger, I don't care about Gaynell or if she's stuck up or not. And I don't know why you care, neith—" Little Will stops short, stands in the middle of the road, looks up past Hildy toward the house.

The wayward book finally gets away from her and drops into the dust. She stops to pick it up, drops another one. "Well, you wouldn't like it if she lied about you."

Little Will grabs her arm with his free hand, points up to the house. Bobby Ray's car is parked in the shade, close to the kitchen door steps. "Now Chigger, don't you go in there and say nothin' and get him goin'. You hear me? Just don't say—"

"Hildy! Get in this house right now!" Bobby Ray is leaning on the front door frame.

His words hit Little Will's stomach like a fist. He hates this. He can't stand any more of it!

She picks up her books, pulls herself up tall, sticks her chin out that stubborn way she does. "I reckon it's too late to worry about that."

"Hildy! You hear me? Get in this house!"

Little Will hangs back, but Hildy heaves a big sigh, starts up the path to the front of the house. Bobby Ray meets her out at the edge of the porch, grabs her hair and pulls it hard, sending her books scattering down the porch steps. "Mama's tellin' me you been whorin' around in town at that showhouse again."

"I didn't do nothin'! Ow . . . let me loose!" Bobby Ray holds onto her hair, and with his other hand, slaps her hard across her face.

As soon as the screendoor slaps shut behind them, Little Will scrambles up to the front porch steps and picks up his sister's books. Chigger sets such store by her schoolbooks. He piles them on the chair by the door, bites back his own voice as he hears Bobby Ray inside.

"You get down there on your knees and repent to God, you hear me?" Little Will's body lurches in response to the thump he hears from inside the front room. He knows Hildy's on the floor and not of her own doing.

"You hear me? You repent to God, you little harlot."

"But I—I—don't—I didn't—"

"If you don't know how, you better listen here! You'd better beg God to forgive you. You're a no-account sinner, and you're goin' straight to hell."

"But I didn't do nothin. I didn't, I swear!"

Little Will huddles outside the screendoor, hears the first *Crack!* of Bobby Ray's belt, the sound he knows too well. "Chigger, quit it!" he whispers, "Quit fightin' him. Just do what he says."

"Scream out, you heathen! Scream out and repent to God. If you can't do it, I'll make you!"

Crack! "Say it! Say it, 'I'm a sinner, God!' Say it!"

With each blow, Little Will's body jerks, and the tears flood down his face. "Just do what he says, Chigger, do what he says!"

Crack! "I—I'm a . . . sinner . . . I'm a sinner."

Crack! "Say it! Say 'I'm a black ugly sinner'!"

"I—I'm a . . . black . . . ugly . . . sinner . . . "

After the clumping of Bobby Ray's boots fade into back of the house, there's no sound except for the soft whimpering from the front room and the *thump thump thump* in Little Will's chest as he tries to control his own urge to cry out.

He peeks through the screen into the dimness of the room, then slips as quietly as he can into the house. He sits down on the floor next to Hildy, reaches to pull her over to him, but she resists.

"I told you, don't say nothin'. Why don't you listen to me?" Little Will wipes his face fiercely with his sleeve. He pulls at her again, and she lets him cradle her head in his lap.

He runs his hand over and over her tangled hair, tenderly touches the bruise forming on her cheek.

Her voice is tiny, almost a whisper. "Oh, Little Will, I hope I don't go to hell."

"You're all right, Chigger." He can't keep his glance away from the door. At every sound from the back of the house, his body tenses, pulls at him to jump up, to run. "I just wish you'd listen to me and quit fightin' back at him."

"I'm no good, I know it, but I don't mean to—"

"Now you hush. You're as good as anybody." He doesn't care if Bobby Ray comes in here or not. He'll kill him, that's what he'll do! "You just don't know to keep your mouth shut, is all. I keep tellin' you, but you won't—"

The car door slams just outside the window, and every muscle in Little Will's body shudders. Then the engine starts up, and Bobby Ray is gone in a roar down the road. Little Will slumps in relief.

"But you don't understand, Little Will." Hildy gingerly pushes up from the floor onto her knees, then stands up. "I know I'm a sinner, I know it. I mean to be better, but I just don't know how to be good enough." She wipes her face on the skirt of her dress, then tries to smooth it down the front, grimaces as she straightens up.

Little Will hangs onto the iron bedframe and pulls himself up off the floor. He looks quickly away from her swollen eye. "But Chigger, it ain't right. It's just not right."

"I'm tryin' to be better." She wipes her face with the back of her hand. "I try to be better, so he won't have to whup me so much."

. . . . . 1941 . . . . . Lend-Lease Bill to lend
democratic countries goods and munitions
. . . . . Ford Motor Co. signs contract to end
strike by CIO at River Rouge plant . . . . .
OPA established to recommend price controls

. . . . . Immediate freeze on steel prices . . . .
U.S. Savings Bonds and stamps go on sale . . . . .
. . . . . After 56-game major league record,
Joe DiMaggio's hitting streak ended
by Cleveland Indians . . . . .

Summer 1941
Mahala, Kentucky

Naomi sits in the porch swing nursing her new baby, keeping herself modest with a diaper covering her breast and the baby's face.

"We've been wonderin' when you were comin' by to see the baby, Hildy. Come here and sit by me and I'll let you hold her soon as she's done nursin'."

"I been . . . real busy." Hildy doesn't move to take a place on the swing, but sits down instead on the top porch step. "I meant to come by to see it, but I had a lot of lessons . . . uh, chores. Is Aunt Emma here? I was wonderin' if there's any . . . you know, any letters."

"Oh." Naomi's face shows her disappointment. "I couldn't wait 'til you could come to see the baby, 'cause we got somethin' special to tell you about. I wasn't sure you'd like it, but Emma—"

"Why, there you are, Hildy!" Aunt Emma steps out on the porch, carrying one-year-old Billy Wayne. "We've been wonderin' how you were doin' and what you were up to."

Hildy jumps up to meet her. Aunt Emma takes the spot on the swing next to Naomi. Billy Wayne wiggles down from her lap and staggers a few steps toward Hildy.

Naomi shifts the baby to her shoulder and buttons her housecoat with her free hand. "I was just goin' to tell Hildy what we talked about namin' the baby, but she's wantin' to know about her letter first."

Aunt Emma takes the baby from Naomi. "Rosie, you come on to Grandma, you sweet thing, you. Billy Wayne, you come back here now. You'll fall. I swear, he'll walk right off the porch into the rainbarrel."

"Now, Emma, you're spoilin' her," Naomi protests, but Hildy can see by her grin that Naomi's not really too worried about spoiling that baby girl.

Aunt Emma's grinning too. "Why, now, I thought that's what us grandmas were for." Then over the baby's head, she says to Hildy,

"Hon, there's a letter in there on the table for you."

Hildy slips into the front room and picks up the envelope with Liam's writing on it. Colorado. She sits in the rocker and peels up the flap on the envelope, pulls out the one tablet sheet, folded up small.

Dear Chigger and Little Will,

It's real pretty here, I wish you could see it. Theres mountins with snow on them right where I can see them. My pal Henry and me are thinken about catchen a train to California where I hear theres always something to pick even in the winter time. Can you imagine picken oranges and lemons off of trees? Henry says the trees have got blossems and oranges both the year long. Me and him and 3 other boys and 2 girls named Earline and Jonelle stick together and watch out for each other. Henrys brother joined the army and hes wanten to join too. I hope he dont go. Id miss him but I wouldnt blame him. Hes hopen we'll get into the war and he'll get to go and fight the Germans but me it sure does sound good to not have to worry about something to eat and warm clothes. It will be a while yet before I can join cause nobody believes me that I'm almost 16 let alone 18. Henry he

*can get away with it cause he looks 20
but hes 16 too.*

*Dont write me here. I wont be here
long for theres not much work. Would
you ask Aunt Emma if there's any
money left from the watch? Ill send
a new address as soon as I settle
someplace.*

"Hildy, did you get lost in there?" Aunt Emma's voice comes from the porch. Hildy supposes she should go look at the baby. She folds her letter, puts it in her dress pocket, and goes back out to the front porch.

Aunt Emma twists around to show the sleeping face nestled on her shoulder. Hildy reaches out to touch the tiny fingers, not knowing what else to do. She wonders if babies open their eyes right away, or if they stay closed for ten days, like kittens. She can't remember if Billy Wayne did or not.

When she can't think of anything else to say, she says, "I reckon you wanted another boy."

"Why no—" Aunt Emma and Naomi both answer at once, but it's Naomi who goes on, "We all of us were hopin' for a little girl, and we picked out the name Rose for my grandmother. We didn't even have a boy's name picked out."

Hildy wonders why they would want a girl.

"And we thought it would be nice," Naomi goes on, "well, since your grandma died, it would be nice to—" Naomi flusters, turns to Aunt Emma.

"We thought it would be nice to name her for my mama, just like her other grandma, so we . . . well, Naomi and Wayne named her Hilda Rose, for both of them. So you see, you two have got something special together, both bein' named for my . . . for your Mammaw. We thought she'd . . . we thought you'd . . . "

Under Hildy's stare, their words wind down to a whisper, as if they just ran out of things to say. Naomi jumps in with some words to fill the awkwardness. "Oh, but we'll keep callin' her Rose so as not to mix y'all up and all."

As Hildy stares, her chest squeezes, her words yell out in her mind, but are held tight in her throat. *No!* Mammaw said it was *her* special name! She backs toward the porch steps. "No!" She spits out the word, bolts from the steps, stumbles, catches herself and runs down the front walk.

"Hildy?" Aunt Emma calls after her from the porch, but Hildy keeps on going.

It's not right! They can't give that baby her name! Mammaw said it was hers, special!

More than three months later

"I don't want to hear about it, Wayne." Emma snaps the radio off, without waiting to find out what attachments come with the $15.95 Electrolux vacuum cleaner. She goes back to hemming Mrs. Dunning's gray wool skirt, invisibly attaching the gray tape to the inside of the soft fabric, but it isn't calming her nerves like her needle-work usually does.

"Well, Mama," Wayne says, "there's no sense hopin' we won't get into the war, the way things are goin'. It looks to me like—"

"Wayne, with two babies, surely they're not about to call you up," Emma says. "And I don't want you worryin' Naomi either. Between Rosie teethin' and you and Gabriel Heatter goin' on about Hitler, her nerves are fallin' apart. And mine aren't in such good shape either."

"Well, we all had to register, babies or not, even old man Fuller, he had to, and he's forty-five. And on the newsreels last week they said Hitler is goin' to—"

"Wayne, I told you I don't want to hear it!"

"I'm sorry Mama, but it's goin' to happen, and there's nothin' we can do about it. I'm figurin' at least if I'm goin' to get called, I'm goin' to join the Navy. I at least might as well do the one I'd rather do of the two, if I have to go."

"Ouch! Now look what you made me do!" Emma sucks the end of her finger where the needle missed the thimble. She turns on the radio again, hopes for anything except war news. But the radio sides with Wayne and vomits out world events she does not want to hear.

Why do they think she wants to hear every little detail, twice? At least Gabriel Heatter sounds like he's winding down for the day. She wishes she could say the same for Wayne. Isn't it time for Fibber McGee and Molly?

"The world has got a whole lot bigger lately, seems like," she says. "Used to be, if it wasn't somethin' you could see from right out on the front porch, you couldn't be sure it was out there, or if it was just made up, like Wistful Vista."

She dumps the wool skirt onto her chair and jabs the needle into the cloth. "I liked it a whole lot better back then." When Peggy Lee comes on, singing "Little fool . . . little fool . . . " Emma snaps the radio off again. "Fools . . . that's what the world is full of! Fools!"

"But Mama—"

"Wayne, I wish you had a button on you like that radio!" She reaches over and twists his nose . . . but not very hard. He looks just like J.D. did, that last time she saw him.

She settles back into the rocker and closes her eyes. When she opens them, Wayne stands with both hands in his pockets, staring at the red coals in the fireplace.

"Why don't you take Naomi to the show and get her out of this house for a while," Emma says, "I'll look after these babies. We'll likely have to give Rosie some more paregoric to ever get her to sleep tonight. Naomi was sittin' here asleep in the rockin' chair herself this mornin' when I got up."

"It's gettin' kinda late. The show's goin' to start in ten minutes."

"Well, you'd better hurry up then. Lord knows we don't want you to miss out on the newsreels, so you can have plenty to say about Hitler for breakfast in the morning."

. . . . . December 1941 . . . . .
Japanese attack Pearl Harbor in the
Hawaiian Islands . . . . FDR: "A day that will
live in infamy" . . . . .
U.S. declares war on Japan . . . . . Germany
and Italy declare war on U.S. . . . . . Wake
Island falls after 15-day standoff . . . . .
Rubber rationing starts today; tires top list
. . . . 1942 . . . . . Manila falls; MacArthur
troops trapped on Bataan peninsula . . . . .
MacArthur ordered to leave . . . . .

Spring. 1942

Emma can't—refuses to—believe what her boy has done. He's talked of nothing else but joining up ever since December, but she hoped she had him talked out of it for the last time.

"I told both of y'all we had to plan on this," he says, "but you never believed me."

"It's not fair!" Naomi wails. Four months pregnant again, she's in tears for at least the third time today.

But the morning's routine disasters were simply practices for this one that Wayne has brought home this time.

Emma can usually be counted on to calm Naomi, but now she is far too upset herself to even *listen* to Naomi. "I can't believe you'd do this to us, Wayne. They're not draftin' men with kids."

"No, Mama, but they will, and I wasn't goin' to wait for the army to call me. I told you that a hundred times."

Emma keeps moving the iron back and forth, back and forth, thinking any minute now her hand will jump up by itself and throw the iron across the room, and she won't be able to stop it.

"Well, even if they do," she says, "everybody on that draft board knew your granddaddy. They know you're the only son I've got and the only man we have in this house."

Wayne comes over and gently takes the iron from her, sets it over on the stove. "Mama, everybody else is goin', and they need all they— well, I want to go, too. I need to."

"Wayne, I swear, what is the matter with you men, gettin' so all-fired excited about war? You sound just like your daddy!"

Naomi sobs, "I thought I'd have you the whole rest of our life, and now . . . oh, Wayne, it's not fair!"

Emma has the urge to slap her daughter-in-law. Today Wayne is no longer Naomi's husband, but Emma's son alone, and she wants to take him and run away with him and hide him somewhere, even from Naomi.

Wayne tries to comfort Naomi, but she turns an angry shoulder to him. He shrugs, turns back to Emma. "So I went over to Paducah and joined up, like I told you. I knew if I told you first, y'all would throw a fit. I mean, worse than the one you're throwin' now."

Well, at least on one thing Emma agrees with Naomi. It's not fair. She gave them J.D. already! It's not fair! And that damn radio. The same radio that used to keep Wayne happy with Captain Midnight and his baseball games, interrupting once in a while with weather bulletins and hog prices, now it sits there entertaining itself by spitting out war news. Then without even a hiccup, it switches back to Fibber McGee and Molly.

And today, especially, the radio's blank mask of a face offers no sympathy that Emma's boy Wayne is going off to war. She wishes she could slap Naomi for her crying and complaining, when that's exactly what Emma feels like doing herself.

About three months later

Dear Liam,

How are you fine I hope. Sometime I dearly wish I could come and be with you. It sounds exciting riding on them trains but I cant leave Little Will. Hes trying so hard to be a man around here, but Mama just doesnt pay any mind to him. He is getting as big as Bobby Ray but she treats him like he was still a baby. Naomi is having another one this summer baby I mean. That is not anything new any more is it ha ha. Wayne is leaving for the navy and Naomi and Aunt Emma are always fussing so I just stay away from there out of their way.

It was real nice of that Woody Guthry to play his guitar and sing his songs for yall on the train. I wish I could of heard him. Did he sound anything like Roy Acuff? Little Will and me we have Mammaws old radio hid and we listen to grand ol opry on saturday night till it goes off. Bobby Ray never comes in on Saturday or Sunday because he is a big preacher on the radio now. But we dont listen to him. We listen to Roy Acuff.

Love, your sister Hildy Mae
P.S. today Little Will and me are 15 years old. You have been gone a long time.

.....*1942* .....*Japanese march American*
and Philippino prisoners to death on
Bataan peninsula . . . . . *Jimmy Doolittle*
bombs Tokyo in daring raids . . . . .
U.S. wins battle in the Coral Sea . . . . .
Philippine island of Correigidor falls to
Japanese . . . . . *Midway Island defended*
with great loss to Japan . . . . .
Marines land on Guadalcanal . . . . .
Gasoline and coffee rationing begins . . . . .
First jet plane tested

More than six months later
Nashville, Tennessee

"Turn that radio off!" Bobby Ray yells. "I'll not have that worldly music in my house. It's of the devil, you hear me? Turn it off!"

Connie Sue makes a face at Molly, who sits next to her on the vanity bench, her blonde hair wrapped with cloth strips intended to produce Shirley Temple curls in the morning. Connie Sue reaches over and turns the volume down slightly, then goes back to smoothing cold cream onto her flawless plump cheeks.

Molly digs her fingers into the big cold cream jar, smears cream on her own cheek. "I pretty too, huh Mommy."

"Yes you are, Sugar." Connie Sue looks up at Bobby Ray in the mirror, standing behind her in the doorway.

"I told you to turn that radio off." He says it in that teeth-gritting smooth way he has about him when he's trying to control himself. Connie Sue continues her nightly face ritual, giving her husband only a glance in the mirror. Bobby Ray goes on, "And get Miz Nevins in here to put that baby to bed."

Molly ducks closer underneath her mother's upraised elbow. "I not a baby, Mommy. I free years old." Pouting, she holds up five fingers.

"Almost, Sugar." Connie Sue glares at Bobby Ray in the mirror over the little girl's head. She takes her time wiping the cold cream off Molly's hands with a tissue. "Now you be Mommy's big girl and go tell Miz Nevins to give you a cookie and tuck you in, and Mommy will come in and read you a story. Go on, now." With her nightgown flapping around her bare feet, Molly scoots through the door, pulling it closed behind her.

Bobby Ray stomps over to the radio and snaps it off. "I told you to get this thing out of here, if you can't listen to anything but this no-account shit."

"Robert, I figure as long I'm Sweetheart Sister Connie Sue on the radio on Sunday, I can do whatever I want to the rest of the week. Just like everybody else around here."

She brushes her platinum hair in long strokes, keeping her eye on Bobby Ray in the mirror. "You might as well save your sermon 'til tomorrow," she says. I heard it a hundred times already. Good Lord, to hear you preach, you'd think the only sinners in the world were women. Why don't you lay it onto the men sometime?"

"It's the women that's chasin' after soldiers, just like whores, and I'm just preachin' what the Lord lays on me to preach."

"Well, I don't see as how women can chase after soldiers if the soldiers don't run." She speaks in the slow measured way she knows makes him furious. "And I doubt if any of them are runnin'."

"The girls get what they're wantin', and it's the wantin' it that I'm preachin' about."

She opens a jar, sniffs its contents, puts it aside and chooses another jar. "Well, I'm sure they're not the only ones that are wantin' *or* gettin'."

Bobby Ray stops at the door. "Are you still peroxidin' your hair after I told you to quit it? You look like a whore yourself."

Connie Sue turns deliberately to face him, her eyes mocking and wide. "I do? Now how would I have any idea what a whore looks like?"

"Connie Sue," he says, his words hissing through his teeth, not nearly as reined-in as before, "one of these times . . . "

"One of these times . . . what?" She makes a point of looking at his fists, clenching and unclenching, then stares him in the face. "Let on to Miz Nevins that you're not that sweet Robert Ray, God's gift to the world? I don't think you will."

He slams his fist into the door jamb, then stomps into the bedroom. She flinches as the door slams behind him, then goes back to smearing pink sticky paste on her face. To the bedroom door in the mirror, she says, "And you would surely be the one to know what a whore looks like, now wouldn't you, *Brother Robert*."

Two months later
Nashville, Tennessee

Bobby Ray drops into a chair just inside the door of Brother Earl's tiny office. He mops his forehead with a used handkerchief. "Were you listenin'? That one ought to bring us in a bushel basket or two full."

Sweat streaks his shirt front and underarms. He looks around for something to do with the handkerchief, lobs it into the wastebasket by the desk. He pulls his sticky shirt away from his chest, sniffs and makes a face. "I could sure use me some new shirts."

Brother Earl quickly gathers up the sizeable stacks of bills in several denominations spread on the top of the big oak desk that fills a quarter of the room, pulled out from the wall to make space for his ample waist. He stuffs the money into his cash box and locks it, scoops the opened envelopes into the top drawer of his desk.

Bobby Ray throws his leg over the arm of the chair and laughs, but Brother Earl's hasty concealment of the money rankles him. The old fool acts like Bobby Ray's going to jump him and take all of it.

"Any good letters from my girlfriends?"

"Robert, I don't consider that funny." Brother Earl leans back in his chair, his arms folded across his chest. "I work hard to take care of the requests of our listeners with a delicate hand, and I don't reckon you should pay it any mind."

Bobby Ray chuckles. The old fool. Listeners? They're listenin' to Robert Ray, that's who! "Well, you told me once that I should always encourage them, 'cause we needed their, uh, *support*."

Brother Earl swivels his chair around and faces the window behind his desk. "Robert, I told you a whole lot of things once, but I can't say you always took 'em the way I meant 'em. I will keep on considerin' it my job to encourage our givers, and you'd best not bother yourself with any of it. I don't reckon I need to remind you of what happened in Murfreesboro last summer."

"Yeah, but she was just like all the rest of 'em," Bobby Ray says. "And all it took was a little bit of money to make her see it different. They're all alike. If they can't get me, they'll settle for money."

Brother Earl opens his mouth to say something, then apparently decides against it. Then he does it again. He looks like a catfish gulping for air, Bobby Ray thinks.

He stands up and stretches, yawns, leans on the doorframe. "So what's eatin' you, Earl? Looks to me like you had plenty of money there to make you happy today. How much you figure we got in today? Five, six hundred?"

Brother Earl as usual doesn't answer about the money. He turns his chair back around. "I was listenin' to your broadcast, Robert, and I have to say, you've got me worried some. My brother Harold used to be a stern fellow most of the time . . . I'm sure you remember . . . but he always said we needed to make sure there was plenty of honey in the word, too, not just the vinegar. We have to give them some promise of reward, too, preach the love of Christ, not just hit 'em with hellfire and that's all. Sometimes you sound like it's your personal right to judge. Remember, the scripture says *judgment is mine, sayeth the Lord*."

Bobby Ray scratches his head and yawns again. "Yeah, well, I don't ever remember old Harold usin' any of that honey on me."

"Robert, I'll not have you speakin' ill of Harold. He was a serious man, but he had a heart of gold and he had a good thing in mind for this radio broadcast. I want to see that it goes the way he saw it."

Bobby Ray reaches for the doorknob. "Well, like you always said, Earl, just open up your mouth and the Holy Ghost will fill it. I just preach what the Lord lays on me to preach, just like you always said."

Brother Earl looks at him without a word, but Bobby Ray stares him down. Brother Earl drops his gaze to his desktop and he heaves a heavy sigh. He retrieves an envelope from the drawer and comes around to lean on the front edge of the desk. "Here's your household money for this month. Connie Sue was by a while ago and I gave her some to take with her. She said her and Molly needed new coats."

Bobby Ray folds the envelope and stuffs it in his shirt pocket. "She's always whinin' about needin' something or other. She's got more clothes than any three women, and she's spoilin' that kid rotten."

"Well, I promised the Lord I'd take care of them for my brother, and I aim to. And speakin' of that, how long's it been since you were out to see to your Mama? I was thinkin' maybe I should mail her money to your aunt, thinkin' you've been too, uh, *busy* lately to get up there?"

Bobby Ray huffs out an irritated snort, reaches for the second envelope Brother Earl holds out to him, and turns his back to leave. "I'll go up there tomorrow."

"You know, Robert," Brother Earl changes the subject, returning to his chair. "I was readin' about somethin' the other day, made me think of your mama."

Bobby Ray grits his teeth. Let Brother Earl take care of Mama himself if he's so all-fired worried about her.

"It was somethin' new they're doin' for people like your mama, people who . . . well, for people that's— that's got problems. Somethin' they do with electric shock. Now I don't rightly see how that could help anybody, myself, but they say—well, they started it in Italy or France or somewhere over there, and now they're doin' it over in places like Midwestern State, where they've got so many to look after. It makes 'em happy and calms 'em right down, they say. Oh, now, I'm not sayin' your mama's like them people. Don't get me wrong. I didn't mean . . . "

"So how much do you reckon something like *that* would cost?" Bobby Ray says with a pointed look at the cashbox.

"Why I . . . I don't know, Robert. But if there's something we can do to help her, the Lord will provide enough money to pay for it, I'm positive." Brother Earl gets up again, looks out the window behind his desk, pulls at his chin.

"Well, now I didn't mean—I just thought it was interestin'. You tell your mama I'm prayin' for her, and you tell her I asked about her, all right?"

. . . . . *1943* . . . . . *Battle of Bismark Sea in the Pacific, 22 Japanese ships sunk, 40 planes shot down* . . . . . *Shoe rationing announced—only 3 pair a year per person* . . . . . *Rationing begins on canned goods, meat, fat, cheese* . . . .

Later the same month
Midwestern State Hospital

Bobby Ray points to a small group of patients who sit on benches under the trees, accompanied by a bored-looking attendant. "Now Dr. Milvey, what are you tellin' me, that this electric shock you give them people out here, you're tellin' me it makes 'em act better by makin' 'em more . . . simpleminded?" Bobby Ray and the doctor continue walking up the long sidewalk through the spacious lawn of the brick hospital, the biggest building Bobby Ray has ever seen in his life.

The doctor chuckles. "I wouldn't have said it exactly in those terms, but yes, that does describe it. By disabling, as it were, the parts of the brain that allow the schizophrenic behavior."

"The what?" Bobby Ray can't take his eyes off the woman who sits to the side in a wheelchair. He follows her gaze to find what she's looking at, and there's nothing but the high fence twenty yards beyond the trees.

But she sits there, smiling, apparently enjoying some sight that nobody else around her can see.

"Schizophrenic—combative, depressed," the doctor explains.

Bobby Ray is still not sure what the doctor is talking about, but he is ashamed to ask. But *combative*—well, that sounds like somebody who's hard to get along with, and that fits Mama.

"By destroying the part of the brain that allows this behavior, we enable them to become more docile, yes, simpler-thinking, happy. None of these people you see out here could have been allowed outside even a month ago, but now look at them."

The doctor points in the direction of the group under the trees. "Take Pearl, over there. When she first came to us, she was hostile. We had to restrain her to her bed. After only one series of shock treatments, Pearl now enjoys being outside in the sunshine. Her daughter is pleased with her progress, claims she's a completely different person. We might even be able to let Pearl go home after another treatment or two. Her daughter shouldn't have any further problem with her."

"It sounds like some kind of miracle."

The doctor smiles. "Yes, I guess we here in our business have a different means of exorcising demons than you have in your business, but I do suspect at times the results are similar."

"So you reckon my mama— my *mother*, this treatment might help her?" Bobby Ray stops walking, but he can't bring himself to look directly at the doctor.

"We will have to examine her personally, of course, but from what you've been telling me, she sounds like an excellent candidate for electroshock treatment, with her delusions, anger, depression . . . "

"And nobody else would have to know about it? You know how it is. Some people might . . . and my daddy . . . my father, he's, uh, he's dead, so I'm the one left to make up my mind about it. And . . . and I've got plenty of money to pay for it."

"I understand. Yes, unfortunately some people, especially in rural areas, hold some old-fashioned beliefs about mental illness. We can take care of your mother, and I assure you everyone in the family will be happy with her improvement."

Later the same month
Mahala, Kentucky

"Naomi, are you foolin' me?" Emma sets the grocery bag down on the kitchen table, brushes her hair back from her face. "Billy Wayne, you get away from that! Hon, he's got to stay away from my sewin' machine. He likes to ride on the treadle and he keeps my thread all knotted up. You mean to tell me Bobby Ray came here to my house?"

Naomi, carrying seven-month-old Sissy on her hip, goes and gets Billy Wayne from the front room and pulls him by one arm through the kitchen, nudges him out the back door.

"Now you play out back with Mutt and be quiet," Naomi says. "Don't you go and wake Rosie up." She goes on, "He said—I swear he did—he said he was takin' his Mama back down to Nashville with him. She was sittin' out there in his car wearin' some pink dress I never saw before and she was grinnin'. Once she looked like she was goin' to get out, but he hollered out there and told her to stay in the car. Oh, and he said for you to look after her garden."

Naomi puts the baby into the paintbare wooden highchair, the one made for Wayne when he was born.

"I hate to say it, Emma," she says, "but I never did much like that Bobby Ray."

"Well, Hon, you can say it all you want to say it. You know I've never lost any love on him. Lord, I can't believe it. He says he's takin' her home with him?"

"Uh huh, that's what he said. And that they'd be back in a week or two." Naomi gives Sissy two soda crackers, one for each hand. "Was there any mail?"

Emma pulls the mail out of the top of the grocery bag. "Now you know I wouldn't forget that, Hon. Here's two letters for you and one for me. Looks like he mailed them all three the same day." She sets the rest of the groceries out on the counter, puts the milk in the icebox. "And there's your allotment check. Let's go over this afternoon and see if Green's got in any outing to make you up some more diapers. Now that the weather's warm, we can let Rosie run around outside without any on. Then she gets to where she likes bein' dry, and she won't wet herself. If we can at least get her broke, finally, that'll help."

Naomi has already ripped the first letter open. She looks relieved, like she always does when she gets a letter from Wayne, just as if she'd not had two letters yesterday, too. "Oh, this makes me so mad," she says and she looks like she's going to cry again. "They keep cuttin' big holes in his letters—I keep tellin' him to quit tryin' to tell me where he is. I don't even want to know, then I won't keep lookin' them places in the newspaper or listenin' for them over the radio."

Emma skims through her own letter, relieved to hear nothing new from Wayne. "I swear, he never really tells me anything. I reckon he only writes me because he thinks otherwise I'd want to read yours." Her mind finally registers what Naomi has said. "Now, you don't want that. Then you'd worry about every bit of news you heard from the whole Pacific Ocean, instead of just the part he's in."

"Oh, Emma, sometime I feel like I never had a husband!"

Emma reaches over and pulls Naomi into a hug. "I know it, Hon. Seems like he's been gone way more'n a year."

It's no time to remind Naomi that Emma has been in the same place before, that she spent many a month sitting with baby Wayne on her lap with no word about his daddy until the letter came from his commanding officer.

"But just look around," she adds, laughing to cheer herself up as much as Naomi, "with all these babies, you can't very well forget you got a husband for long, can you? Now you go on upstairs and lay down a few minutes and read your letters over again. I'm goin' to start some supper. Look, I got us a half a pound of stewin' beef."

Naomi looks grateful as she disappears up the stairs. Emma's sure it's for the offer of a minute's peace more than the stewing beef, even if it is the first of the rationed meat they've had this week.

Emma pulls out from the pantry the one jar left of last summer's string beans. Good thing the new vines are already well up the poles. "They call 'em 'victory gardens' now," she says to Sissy. The baby stops banging the tray long enough to look up and laugh. "But it's the same old garden I used to plant before the war."

Emma takes a look out the back screendoor to make sure Billy Wayne and the puppy are occupied out by the garden fence.

"Now don't you go away," she says to Sissy, then unlocks the cellar door and dashes down to the cool bin.

When she comes back a minute later with six potatoes, Sissy smiles a relieved smile. "We're goin' to have a nice supper tonight. I feel like celebratin' for some reason, don't you, Sissy?"

She tickles the baby's neck, and gets a dimply giggle in return. Sissy's attention goes back to the soggy pieces of crackers scattered on the highchair tray.

So Bobby Ray took Gerty home with him. Well, miracles haven't quit happening, have they? She's gotten after him enough about taking care of his Mama. But she still doesn't believe it.

"Sissy, we'd better go over and tell Hildy and Little Will to come here for supper while she's gone. That'll be nice, won't it?" Sissy smacks the highchair tray with both hands, making crumbs fly.

The following day
Midwestern State Hospital, Tennessee

"My name's Lloyd, Reverend . . . Ray, is it? Now we don't usually let family come in with the patient, but since you're a preacher, I guess we can make an exception. They should have her ready for me by now."

Bobby Ray follows along behind Lloyd, looking around at the dingy gray hospital walls, the scuffed linoleum. He shivers. The place makes him feel like there's something evil peering from the corners, ready to leap out onto his skin.

Another intern comes toward them, leading a patient who looks plainly scared of approaching Lloyd.

"You been good today, Ernest? Need to come in and see me for some more shocks?" The patient looks frantically up and down the hallway, until he's led away by his keeper, who shoots a disapproving glare back at Lloyd.

Bobby Ray lags behind, watching. Lloyd waits for him to catch up. "I'm not very popular around this place, as you can see," he says. Bobby Ray looks at him, puzzled at his grin. Behind his hand, Lloyd says, "They know I'm the one that gives them what I call their 'electric spankings.'"

Something black and icy leaps up inside Bobby Ray. "Their . . . the what? They . . . what did you say?"

Lloyd's laugh stirs the darkness, and Bobby Ray shivers again. With a touch on the arm, Lloyd aims him on down the hallway talking low, close to his face. "Maybe I shouldn't have said that, with you being a preacher, but . . . well, between you and me, I've got my own theory. You see, most people in here, it seems like to me, are wallowing around in some kind of guilt—if anybody'd know the kind I mean, you would. And it's my own private opinion that they secretly want the electric shock because they know they deserve to get punished, and that's one reason why they feel so much better after. That's just my own opinion."

Lloyd chuckles and waves him on after him down the long hallway. "So I just give 'em what they're looking for. Kind of like you do, when you tell 'em in your sermons what they're in for, I'll bet."

Bobby Ray hesitates, stares after Lloyd. Upon some shadowy permission from this man's words, Bobby Ray feels something stirring from the place where the dreams hide in the daytime. His stomach churns up acid. Ever since he went and picked Mama up in Mahala, his stomach has been a wad of nerves.

The last two nights the dreams have been especially vivid. This morning he woke up soaking wet, not only from chilling sweat but from the shameful wetness that his body spewed out as the dreams brought themselves to their unholy climax. He was ashamed, and yet along with the shame there stirred in him a tremor that made his heart feel like it was being pounded, that he could die from it. And somehow he wouldn't care if he did.

Lloyd stops at a closed door, stands with his arms folded across his chest, as if guarding the entrance to a forbidden place. "Now I have to warn you, you may want to change your mind. Me, I'm used to it. But sometimes it gets . . . well, a little ugly to see. But don't worry, the patient doesn't feel any pain. It's just the body's reaction, and she . . . they don't remember it after they wake up. I mean, you can change your mind if you're not—"

"No!" Bobby Ray answers too quickly, tries to recover. "I mean, uh, yes, I'll be, uh, I'll be all right." For an instant he feels naked to Lloyd's eyes, as though this cocky young man can not only see right inside him, but also claims some kinship with and approval of what he sees in Bobby Ray.

Lloyd motions with his head for Bobby Ray to enter the small treatment room with him. Bobby Ray is startled at the huge mound of Mama's body, on its back, strapped to the table and covered with a green hospital sheet. Her mountainous breasts flop on top of her body, stretching the sheet indecently tight across her chest. Wires run from the machine to the head, attached to shaved circles on both sides. An assistant ducks past Lloyd with a nod and disappears out the door.

At first Mama lies still, but when Lloyd speaks to her she opens her eyes, struggles to get up. Bobby Ray turns his head away, forces down the gagging in his throat. He moves down to the end of the table where he can't see her eyes. Lloyd stands ready to proceed, his hand on the machine at his side. "We'll use a lower current at first," he says to Bobby Ray over the mound, "then we'll determine how much to increase it."

Without any further warning, Mama's body jerks with a spasm that strains the tethers holding her to the table.

Bobby Ray feels Lloyd's stare and pulls his look up to meet it.

Lloyd smiles. "See? It causes a convulsion, like—well, you ever see anybody have an epileptic fit? There was a kid I went to school with that had 'em."

The mountain of flesh writhes on the table, strains at the leashes. One arm breaks loose from its strap and thrashes out against the table with a cracking sound.

The flailing on the table stops abruptly, bringing Bobby Ray's attention up short. "It kills off all the bad brain cells," Lloyd says. "Getting rid of her demons, so to speak." Even without looking directly at Lloyd, Bobby Ray can hear the sneer in his voice.

"We'll let it rest a minute, then give her another one." Lloyd says, then he comes around to Bobby Ray's side of the table and adjusts the straps, snares the dangling arm again.

On his way back around the table, Lloyd stops to look right into Bobby Ray's face and, without a word, nods to him.

As surely as if an arrow leaped across between them, Bobby Ray feels a peculiar oneness with Lloyd. He wonders what kind of a mama Lloyd had.

Again, the current wracks the body on the table, as Bobby Ray stands with his arms folded in front of him, watching.

From far down inside a dark place a craving rises, a craving Bobby Ray knows he shouldn't have, and yet he doesn't want it to leave him.

He is ashamed of the way his body stirs. He's glad Mama's body is between him and Lloyd's eyes.

The feeling draws up with it a power, the same power that he feels behind the pulpit. The same power that he feels in the dreams of the skinny girls, the wicked whores of Babylon.

The revelation comes clear to him, and he does not disown it: This very day he is to have his complete power over Mama.

The whole creature inside him, everybody he has ever been, gathers to watch.

Here in his own presence and the presence of an almighty God is the punishment Mama deserves, and he himself is the one who has purchased it for her, has delivered her to it.

*. . . . . 1943 . . . . . FDR: "All essential
workers must stay on their jobs" . . . . .
Polio epidemic kills 1,511, cripples thousands
more . . . . . Large scale production of
penicillin can now be produced after mold
on cantaloupe found in Illinois proves to
yield ten times as much as previous sources
. . . . . U.S. Supreme Court. rules that
children cannot be forced to salute flag if it
against their families' religion . . . . .*

Several days later, summer 1943
Mahala, Kentucky

"Why, Gerty, nobody told me you were home. Why didn't you come by and tell me?" Emma comes up on the porch where Gerty sits in the swing, slowly pushing her feet against the floor, back and forth, back and forth. Emma drags an old wicker arm chair over closer to the swing and sits down, takes off her shoe and shakes out a pebble, puts the shoe back on. "So you went to Bobby Ray's house, did you?"

Gerty answers with a tentative smile, a questioning look.

"What was it like? I been dyin' to hear about it."

"What?" Gerty raises her arm with its cast and shoos away a fly that has landed on her nose.

"Gerty! What happened to your arm?" Emma jumps up and grabs the swing chain, stops it with a jolt, sits down next to her sister.

"Good Lord, Gerty, what on earth happened to your arm?"

Gerty looks at the plaster of paris cast as though she's never seen it before, smiles at Emma. "It got broke. Bobby Ray said."

"Bobby Ray said? Don't you remember it yourself?"

Gerty smiles down at the cast.

"Gerty, did somebody hurt you?"

"It got broke, I told you." She smiles. "Bobby Ray's got a big old house, Emma."

"Gerty, I want you to tell me what happened."

"No, I won't tell you." She giggles. "It's a secret. Bobby Ray said. My secret. My secret and Bobby Ray's secret."

What on earth is wrong with Gerty? She's actin' so peculiar. Emma goes back to the chair, takes a peek at Gerty's face. It looks the same as always, framed by her long dark hair, parted in the middle and loosely draped back into a bun at the nape. But something's different . . . strangely different.

"Well, what're his wife and baby like?" Emma tries to keep her voice calm and friendly, but she can't help staring at the cast.

Gerty frowns, as if she's trying to remember something, then smiles again, shakes her head. "He don't have a baby, Emma. His baby, Odessa, she's gone, don't you remember?"

Don't I remember? Emma feels sometimes like she can remember Gerty's life better than Gerty can. Emma's learned better than to let Gerty get started on one of her distorted rantings and ravings on this subject.

She gets up and goes to the screendoor, peers into the house, hopes for something different, something to explain the strange feeling gnawing at her. Everything looks the same, except for the cast on Gerty's arm and the gaudy pink rayon dress.

Gerty pumps the swing, back and forth, back and forth. "I don't like Bobby Ray's big house, no I don't." She smiles.

Back to her chair, still puzzling, Emma says for want of anything else to say, "That's a mighty pretty dress, Gerty. Did Bobby Ray's wife get you that? I wish she'd got you something more practical than rayon. I could have made you three for what she paid for it."

"It's for Sunday."

"Well, tomorrow's Sunday, so do you reckon you ought to pull it off and wash it so it'll be clean for tomorrow? We'll have to wash it out by hand. If you put rayon through the wringer, it'll draw up."

Emma's staring at Gerty's face, but Gerty doesn't seem any more self-conscious about it than Sissy would be.

Emma gives up. What does she care what Gerty wears to church? "I've got to get back. I just came by to look after your tomatoes, but I've got a new customer comin' by in a few minutes. I looked this morning, and you've got plenty of canned goods left. You ought to use up your string beans. The new ones should be comin' in by next week, and we'll need to get the jars washed." Emma gets up, brushes off the back of her skirt. "I've got some little crook-necked squashes already. I'd have brought you some if I'd known you were home."

Emma still feels like she should be able to see something, some-where, that makes sense. Nothing. "I'm goin' to have Dr. Jessup come by and look at that arm. It looks like somebody fixed it all right, but I want him to look at it. You don't remember what happened to it?"

Gerty smiles, holds up her cast as if she's as proud of it as she is of her new pink rayon dress. "I don't like Bobby Ray's big house, Emma." She smiles.

"Well. I'll stop back by directly and you can tell me about it some more. When Little Will and Hildy get home from school, you send one of them over to get you some of them squashes. There's goin' to be worlds of 'em."

With nothing more to say, but a lot more pondering to do, Emma starts back toward the road. Something is different. Besides the cast and that awful dress . . . something else is different, and she can't put her finger on it.

Why, of course. It's the smiling, that's what it is! She has not for years seen Gerty smile so much.

Well, whatever it is that Bobby Ray's done, if it makes Gerty this contented, it can't all have been bad, she'll have to admit that. But she still doesn't trust Bobby Ray any further than she can spit. No, she doesn't.

> *. . . . . 1943 . . . . . Race riots in Detroit . . . . .*
> *Jive, a danceable form of jazz is popular,*
> *jitterbug the most popular. Variation called*
> *Lindy Hop said to be the*
> *"true national folk dance of America"*
> *. . . . Allies invade Sicily . . . . . Rome bombed*
> *by allies . . . . . After Italy surrenders,*
> *Mussolini turns and declares war on*
> *Germany . . . . . Victory for U.S. on island*
> *of Rabaul . . . . . U.S. troops land on Tarawa,*
> *step closer to Japan homeland . . . . .*

Midwinter, 1943
Mahala, Kentucky

"It won't do any good, Chigger," Little Will says, stuffing his other shirt into a pillow slip. He hands her his pocket knife. "Here, you keep this. Where I'm goin', I won't be needin' it anymore."

Hildy takes the knife, drops it on her bed. "But you *can't* go."

He can't bear to look at her face, at the black-and-purple bruise that wraps around her closed eye. "I've got to, Chigger. I can't take no more." His own shoulder and arm move stiffly and painfully as he tries to gather his few belongings. "I always hoped I'd find some way to help you, and I swear I was goin' to kill him, I was. But you can see where it got me."

"He didn't mean to, Little Will. It was just because you got in his way and—"

"Chigger, for God's sake stop makin' excuses for him! I was tryin' to *help* you! If you don't care if he whups you, then I'm not goin' to stand there and let him whup me just so he can get to you."

He can't help checking the window, even knowing that Bobby Ray's car went up the road an hour ago. "I'll catch a ride out to Camp Campbell, and they'll tell me where to go. I'll write you when I get to wherever the army sends me."

Little Will stops at the door, his half-filled pillow slip slung over his shoulder. "I've been thinkin' on this for a long time. Chigger. I can't stand it anymore bein' nothin' around here. I might not be but fifteen years old, but I'm a grown man and I've got to do something to help you. Maybe I can find some way in the army. Maybe they'll let me send you some money, then you can leave too, I don't know."

"But you're not old enough, Little Will." She sounds to him like a little girl, but then when has she not been a little girl in his mind? Even when they were in the first grade, he was her big brother.

He wants to grab up his twin and take her with him, but it's not possible, where he's going. "I can lie, and they'll take me," he says. "Sandy Teague's three months younger'n me, and not even as big as me, and he did it."

She doesn't make any move to come closer. He waits, almost hopes, but the moment passes.

"Well." He makes his sorrowful way to the door. He knows that if she would ask him not to go one more time, he might not be able to do it. But she just stands there, not saying a word, just looking at the floor. He'd be grateful if she would say something, but he's even more thankful that she doesn't.

He can't bear to look at her battered face, although God knows he's seen it plenty of times before. He doesn't want to remember her that way, but as hard as he tries, already he can't picture her face any other way.

He walks out to the road, then for one second looks back, thinks she at least might have followed him out onto the porch. He sees a slight movement at the window, and to snap the chain that pulls at his heart, he breaks into a run toward town.

. . . . . 1943 . . . . . General Dwight D. Eisenhower named Supreme Commander for the Invasion of Europe . . . . . 1944 . . . . . Allied troops land at Angio, Italy, to outflank Germany at the Gustav line . . . .

Early January 1944
Mahala, Kentucky

Dear Liam,

How are you fine I hope.

I have been waiting for a letter for more than a month and I have not got one so I hope you get this one. Little Will has run off and joined the army. Wayne has been gone for nearly two years so I reckon Little Will will be gone for a long time too. If you still want me to come where you are I will come and stay till he gets back. If you could send me some money for the bus like you said or I could hitchhike if you will tell me where you are. Aunt Emma would never let me come or I could ask her for the money.

Mama wont care. She doesnt care about anything anymore. She sits in the swing and grins and talks about Bobby Rays big house. She doesnt bother with me anymore either, I dont reckon she even sees me. I wish I could say the same thing for Bobby Ray but he comes looking *for me. Sometime I think its the only reason he comes in.*

Love, Hildy

Satisfied with the letter, she signs it and folds the tablet page, puts it in the pocket of her sweater.

Then on second thought, she pulls it out and unfolds it, adds

P.S. I reckon he is trying to git me saved, but I dont feel much like I am.

Afternoon of the same day

"Lordy, Girl, what are you doin' out in this cold?" Emma scolds Hildy, who comes up the walk with no headscarf and just a sweater, and with snow clouds crowding in. "You come on in here by the fire. I've got two letters for you."

Hildy follows Emma into the house. "I've not had one from Liam in so long. I was coming to mail him this one."

"I was aimin' to bring them over as soon as Naomi gets back. She's over at Green's seein' if they've got any shoes in. I swear, Billy Wayne wears them out worse than his daddy did. Naomi's had to use her own shoe rations for him."

Emma gripes more for her own enjoyment than for Hildy's. The girl has obviously not been listening since she ripped open Liam's envelope postmarked Oklahoma. What an odd thing. She would have thought Hildy would read Little Will's first. Emma starts toward the kitchen, but Hildy's "oh!" draws her back.

"Hon, what's wrong?"

Hildy bites her lip, and she turns her face quickly away. Emma takes the letter from her.

Dear Chigger
Im sorry I havent wrote sooner but you will be suprised when you hear that I have joined the army and I have got married both. I joined up on my birthday

and me and Jonelle got married that same day. We was the only ones left of our gang that stayed together. I hated to leave her by her self and I thought this way I could still look after her and she can get money from the army too. When we was always moving I told people she was my sister but I cant tell the army that.

I almost did not pass because my teeth and my eyes are bad, but I reckon they need everybody. I dont know if they will send me overseas or not.

Right now I work on jeep motors can you picture that. Closest I get to farming now is peeling potatoes. ha ha It feels good not to worry anymore about food and a place to sleep.

Me and Jonelle we live in a little bitty house near Ft. Sill in a bunch of five of them and they each one have a sign on the door with the name of one of them quints. We live in the one named Cecile. Jonelle says thats a french name. I thought they was from up north someplace but she knows more about that than me. Shes real smart. Shes got herself a job already.

Write me, Ill be here till they ship me out if there going to but Jonelle will know where to write me.

Your brother Liam and his wife Jonelle.

PS Jonelle says to say hi. She says I shouldnt call you Chigger anymore because its silly. If you think its silly I wont.

"Why, Honey," Emma says, "You had me thinkin' it was bad news," She puts her arm around Hildy's shoulders. "Now, I don't like to hear about any of our boys bein' in the army, but maybe for poor Liam it will be all right. I've been worried about him wanderin' the country like that. And here he's gotten married, too, now isn't that a nice surprise."

Hildy shakes her head but doesn't answer. Her face has clouded up just like the sky outside.

"Now why don't you open up that letter from Little Will and let's see how he is. Lordy, now *that* was a surprise to me, him joinin' up, and him not but fifteen."

Hildy hands the second letter to Emma without a word. Emma carefully pries up the flap, pulls out the single sheet, but hands it back to Hildy. "Here, Hon, why don't you come on in the kitchen and read it out loud to me, all right? Let's see if his news is as good as Liam's." Hildy shrugs, but doesn't take the letter, so Emma reads it.

DEAR Chigger,

It is just as well I don't know what I'll be doing next or when because I wouldn't be sposed to tell you anything about it if I did.

I don't know how long we will be here or where we're goin. Nobody knows anything, but that don't keep everybody from talking about it all the time.

I'm sorry I had to leave, Chigger. Please write me.

Your brother Will
PS They don't call me Little Will here.

Emma looks into Hildy's sad face, its mournfulness too large to be hidden by any efforts to keep it in. Surely this girl has carried enough.

Emma silently gathers her into her arms. It's been so long since she has done that. The little-girl body, still too thin, has rearranged itself into a young woman.

But still, even at fifteen years old, Hildy should be worrying over nothing more than learning *The Deacon's Masterpiece* by heart for Addie Stanfill's English class.

Emma holds the girl's slender body close, remembering the time when her tiny arms responded by wrapping around her neck. Now Hildy holds to herself, and all Emma can feel are the faint hiccups from deep inside her. *Oh, Daniel, she's so much your little girl.*

Finally, Hildy heaves a deep sigh and pulls away. She takes the letter, stuffs it with Liam's letter into her sweater pocket and starts for the door.

"Don't forget about the letter you came in to mail. I reckon you'll need to change the address on it now. Here, let me get you another envelope." Emma goes to the desk in the corner, shuffles through the top drawer for an envelope and a three-cent stamp. "Oh, and while you're doin' that, let me go up and get you a headscarf—"

The front door thumps to a close, and Emma turns back to an empty room. A bright spot in the fireplace catches her eye. A sheet of tablet paper with Hildy's handwriting scorches brown and bursts into flame.

The front door pops open again and Naomi bustles in, drops her bundles on the front table. "Lordy," she says, "It's goin' to snow out there any minute now. Was Hildy just here? I thought it was her I saw, but she didn't answer me. Is Billy Wayne up? We promised him we'd make snowcream if we get enough."

. . . . . *1944* . . . . . *800 Flying*
Fortresses bomb Berlin with 2000
tons of bombs . . . . . *Allied forces enter*
Rome . . . . .

June 5, 1944
Aboard a ship docked off the coast of England

> Chigger I couldn't go on watchin you get
> hurt and me not belonging anyplace. I
> couldnt stay there and see it no more. If
> I could have got hurt instead of you I would
> of but it didn't stop you from gettin hurt and
> maybe made it worse.

"You got a picture of her?"

"Huh?" Little Will looks up from his paper, propped on a book on his chest, the V-mail paper he's been writing and erasing on all afternoon, trying to find the words to explain to Hildy what he has barely begun to understand himself. He's almost worn the V-mail sheet through. He hopes he doesn't have to copy it all over.

"Now don't go telling me this one's to your *sister*, too. It's got to be a girlfriend." Joe Rossi laughs, takes the last drag of his cigarette, drops it, stomps it out. He digs out his pack of Lucky Strikes, lights another one, and goes back to pacing the small space between the berths.

"Nah," Little Will says. "Same one."

"You think I'm gonna believe that? Nobody writes to his *sister* all day." Joe runs his hand over his stubble of dark hair, stops to lean on Little Will's berth. "Man, I hope we go on out tonight—I can't stand much more of this damn waiting. They're holding another mass up on deck. I think I'll go. At least they're supposed to when the rain lets up. That's what they said anyway. I wish they'd tell us for sure what's goin' on." He paces to the far end of the narrow aisle. "What do they think, we'd run tell the Germans or something?"

Little Will goes back to his writing.

"Dammit, man, how can you lay there like that?"

Little Will sticks his pencil behind his ear, lays his paper face down on his chest.

"Oh, listen, buddy, I'm sorry," Joe says. He pulls out his cigarette pack again, offers Little Will one. "I can't stand this waiting."

Little Will takes the cigarette and accepts the light offered along with it, lies back and takes in a long drag. "Yeah," he says, "I reckon everybody's about as restless as an old hound waitin' to go huntin'."

Joe disappears; his voice comes from the lower berth. "So, do you have any other sisters or brothers? You southerners always come from big families. They always do in the movies." His head pops back into Little Will's sight. "Oh, now don't get me wrong. I didn't mean anything by that. I mean, hell, nobody comes from bigger families than us Italians. I got three sisters and four brothers—I must've told you all about 'em already. I just never heard *you* say."

Does Little Will have any brothers? It seems like there was only the two of them, him and Chigger, all his life.

Joe is up on his feet pacing again. "Dammit! I wish they'd tell us something."

Little Will takes another drag on his cigarette and watches his friend through the smoke. He knows Joe's already quit listening. He's fretting out, the only way he knows how, his own fear of what tomorrow is going to bring.

Brothers? Well, one that he despises, that he wishes was dead. And the other one that he hardly knows, who ran out on him just like Daddy did, who might just as well be dead. No, Little Will has no brothers. Only one sister that he has hurt more than he ever could have helped.

> Its been stormy and cold ever since
> I got here, Chigger. I don't think I been
> warm once. They don't tell the wether over
> the radio like they did back home cause they
> dont want the Germans to know.

Little Will hopes they go out tonight, too. It's time. For him, there's nothing to dread about tomorrow. He crushes out the half-smoked cigarette on the wall behind him. He knows what he's come halfway around the world to do. "Joe?"

"Yeah?"

Little Will stares at the empty berth a foot and a half over his head. "If we do go out tonight, and I don't come back, will you go see my sister after you get out?"

"What are you talking about, man? I mean, quit talking like that. We're all coming back. We'll whip them Germans and be back home for Thanksgiving turkey."

"Well. But if I didn't, would you do that?"

"I don't want to hear—okay, okay, yeah I will. But cut out that kind of talk, you hear me? It's bad luck."

Little Will nods just once and goes back to his letter.

My buddy Joe is goin to come see you. Hes a good friend, the best one I ever had except you. Well I have got to go now. I dont have nothin else to say.

                              your brother Will

.... *June 6, 1944* ..... *D-Day of Operation Overloard* ..... *Allied forces land on beaches at Normandy in France* ..... *4,000 ships* ... *3,000 planes* ..... *millions of troops* .....
summer 1944 ..... *U.S. Superfortresses bomb Kyushu, Japan* ..... *Saipan taken after 25 days of fighting. 25,000 Japanese killed, 2,359 Americans killed, 11,000 wounded* ..... *Guam taken back after 20 days of fighting, 1,214 Americans killed, 6,000 wounded. 17,000 Japanese killed, 300 taken prisoner* .....

Five weeks later
Mahala, Kentucky

"Is it in yet, do you reckon?" Hildy gets up from the porch step when Aunt Emma appears at the screendoor. Back in the kitchen, Sissy howls, and five-year-old Billy Wayne bursts out the screendoor, careens around Aunt Emma's legs and crash lands on his belly on the porch swing seat. His chubby legs barely reach the floor for a running push, then he pulls himself up into the seat..

"Hon, Mr. Hite never gets the mail in 'til after noon anymore, but you can go on over and wait if you want to. Why don't you do that? Let me get you my stamp book and you can pick us up some sugar if he's got any in." Aunt Emma goes back in, calls behind her, "Billy Wayne, you come on back in here now!"

Hildy supposes she should come over and help Aunt Emma with the kids. Since Naomi got word that Wayne was wounded on his ship, she cries all the time. Hildy would rather help with the sewing like she usually does, but Aunt Emma's not getting a whole lot sewing done this week.

Billy Wayne has climbed up onto the porch swing and looks like he's proud of it. Hildy makes a face at him, but he just grins at her, then yawns and rubs his eyes with his fists.

She'd like to slap his face, sitting there grinning like there was nothing in the world to worry about, nothing at all. Here his daddy is on a ship with one of his legs cut off, and Billy Wayne runs around acting foolish like nothing's wrong.

Naomi comes out onto the porch with the ration stamp book, her eyes red and puffy. "Did Billy Wayne come out—oh, there you are, Precious." Naomi sits down with him in the swing. "Y'all haven't heard anything from Little Will yet, have you?" she asks.

"No." Hildy starts down the steps. She should say something about Wayne, but she doesn't want to start Naomi crying again.

"Well." Naomi pulls Billy Wayne over against her, runs her fingers through his hair. "At least if you haven't heard anything, then he's probably all right. I expect you would've heard by now if he was hurt or . . . anything."

Hildy picks at a thread she finds hanging from her dress sleeve. "They didn't lose any time lettin' you know about Wayne bein' hurt." She glances up to see Naomi shaking her head, pointing at Billy Wayne, now nestled in her lap. Hildy stares at her, puzzled. Do they reckon Billy Wayne won't notice one of his daddy's legs is cut off when he comes home?

As the boy's eyes droop toward sleep, Naomi keeps her voice calm and steady. "He keeps tellin' me they'll ship him home as soon as they land somewhere. Can you imagine, a ship havin' a whole hospital in it?" Naomi's voice sounds cheery and hopeful, but Hildy can see she's putting it on. Holding onto Billy Wayne with one hand, she hides her face in her other arm on the back of the swing. "Oh, Hildy! He's goin' to be a cripple the rest of his life!"

Hildy stands on the top step, with nothing to give this girl whose man is coming home, who writes her letters every day.

There is no comfort left inside Hildy for anyone else, no pity left in the dread that started as a cold pinpoint, and now has spread all through her heart during the seven weeks that Little Will has answered none of the letters she writes him day after day.

> *Little Will, why don't you answer my letters?*
> *I hope I didn't say something to make you mad at*
> *me. I hope you still like me, Little Will. Do you?*
> *I know you left on account of me, because I didn't*
> *treat you good enough.*

Without another word, Hildy makes her way down the steps and heads in the direction of the Hite's grocery and post office.

"Mr. Hite, have I got—"

"Any mail? You surely do. We got a whole lot in today. You want Miz Hartley's and Wayne's wife's, too?"

"Look, Sue Ann, there's Hildy." The voice comes from the small group of stragglers congregated over by the potbelly stove that sits gathering summer dust. Most these days are waiting for some word, hoping it comes by V-mail and not by telegram.

Mrs. Suggs bustles over to the counter, leaving Sue Ann in the corner with the baby. Sue Ann is looking a whole lot older than she did in the tenth grade last year, before she quit school and married Dwight Suggs just before he was sent overseas. Now she waits with her mother-in-law for word from the war, just like most of the rest of America waits for news since the big invasion last month.

Mr. Hite gives Hildy the handful of letters from the cubbyhole on the back wall. Two V-mails for Naomi from Wayne and one from him for Aunt Emma. And one for Hildy addressed in Little Will's handwriting!

Mrs. Suggs is at her elbow. "Oh, Hildy, have y'all heard something from your brother? I was just tellin' Sue Ann that surely we'll be hearin' from Dwight any day now. You know we've not heard from him since the invasion, just like you." Hildy can barely hear Mrs. Suggs rattling on. She pulls open the tiny envelope, pulls out the folded page. She brushes right by Mrs. Suggs and runs out into the sunlight, sits down on the first bench she comes to, skims over the words. Where is he? Where is he? Near the very end, there's something:

It's been cold ever since I got here. I don't
think I been warm once . . .

In the summertime? Where?

Mrs. Suggs has followed her out of the store and sits down on the bench beside her. "I'm so glad you heard from him, Dear. I'm sure your mama will be relieved to hear. How is she holdin' up? Oh, I hope your brother's not in France. I keep tellin' Sue Ann, I hope Dwight's not in France."

Hildy stops reading any sentences—her search bounces from word to word:

watchin you get hurt . . . my buddy . . . got to go.

She tries to find something to calm the pressure that builds in her chest, the dark feeling that something is very very wrong, but she can't find what it is.

"When did he write it, Dear?"

Up in the corner, in Little Will's small printing made smaller in the photographed V-mail, Hildy finds the date.

June 5.

More than a month ago. The day before the big invasion.

Almost a month later

Hildy uses the last clothespin to hang her one good princess slip on the clothesline that runs from the corner of the smokehouse, all the way down to the toilet. She pulls up the forked stick that props the middle of the sagging line and hoists it as high as it will reach up into the sticky August heat.

She wipes the running sweat from her forehead with her bare arm, lets her eyes rest on the summer green leaves of the apple tree against the deep blue of the sky. If only she could push with her bare feet and rise up into that blue, above Mama's big dingy underdrawers that hang limp and motionless in the heat, above the dishrags dripping from one clothespin apiece.

"Are you doin' all this washin' by yourself?" Aunt Emma's voice jolts Hildy from her daydreaming. Aunt Emma comes around to the side of the house where the two big wash tubs were set up in the shade this morning. Now the shade has long past and the depleted soapsuds, reduced to a dirty film on top of the wash water, reflect only the heat of the afternoon sun.

"I'm sorry Hon," Aunt Emma says. "I didn't mean to scare you. Doesn't Gerty—doesn't your mama help with any of this?"

Hildy lifts the washboard out of the tub and leans it against the smokehouse. "I'd just as soon do it without her. I let her be and she lets me alone. Did the mail come in before you left? I was goin' to walk into town as soon as I got done."

Aunt Emma grabs the other side of the wash water tub and they dump the water onto the bare ground. "I was over there at noon," she says. "It's gettin' later and later all the time, seems like." They move to the second washtub and dump it over. The murky rinse water floods out over the already soaked ground. Aunt Emma jumps back to spare her sandals, but Hildy lets the tepid water run over her bare feet.

Aunt Emma takes one of Hildy's wet hands and looks at it, then the other. "Honey, your fingers are bleedin' from that wash water. And Lordy, Hon, you've bit your fingernails down to the quick. Have you got any of that Jergens lotion I gave you?"

Hildy pulls her hands back, takes off her soaking wet apron and wipes her hands with it, then drapes it over the empty washtub to dry. Her wet dress feels cool for now. "Did the mail come in yet?"

"I just told you—"

Hildy takes in a sharp breath at the sight of Mr. Latham's car parked out at the road.

"Hon, what's wrong?"

Mr. Latham never stops here with mail anymore, not since Aunt Emma told him to keep it in town for them to pick up, so Mama wouldn't get it and lose anything important. Hildy didn't mind. It gave her a good excuse to stop by Aunt Emma's on the way home from school, or to make a trip into town on other days.

Hildy shivers. Maybe she should change the wet dress. Aunt Emma puts her arm around the girl's waist and starts out to meet Mr. Latham, but Hildy holds back. Something inside her pulls her to run the other way. Mr. Latham huffs his way up the rise from the road. "I'm glad to see you're here, Miz Hartley," he says, catching his breath.

Hildy stands rooted, stares at the yellow envelope in his hand.

After only a nervous glance at Hildy, Mr. Latham continues talking to Aunt Emma. "I brought this out here, you see, because I'm, you know, supposed to give it to Miz Carmody personal, but I'm glad

... I mean I'm sorry ... well, it's good that you're here, uh, with her. I saw her sittin' in the swing around yonder. Maybe you could, uh ... " He hands the telegram to Aunt Emma, then he runs the palms of both hands down the front of his shirt. "I ... I don't know what ... I didn't know what to do ... " He shrugs, turns to go, looks back at the two women. "I wish they wouldn't make me bring them things. That's three of 'em today."

Hildy stares after him as he trudges to his car, gets in without turning back to them and drives away.

"Oh, Hon ... " Aunt Emma pulls her close, smotheringly close, and Hildy can feel the choke in Aunt Emma's voice, feel the dampness of her face. "Oh, Hon ... "

Hildy pulls herself away from Aunt Emma's arms and snatches the yellow telegram to read for herself:

> WASHINGTON DC AUG 1 AM 1100
>
> MRS GERTRUDE CARMODY
>
> ROUTE 2
>
> MAHALA KENTUCKY
>
> THE SECRETARY OF WAR DESIRES ME TO EXPRESS
> HIS DEEP REGRET THAT YOUR SON PFC WILLIAM
> CARMODY WAS KILLED IN ACTION ON SIX JUNE
> IN FRANCE LETTER FOLLOWS
>
> THE ADJUTANT GENERAL

Late the next week
Mahala, Kentucky

Hildy sits up in the apple tree. Her gaze is aimed out toward the road, but she's not seeing it. It's been many months, maybe a year, since the last time she climbed the apple tree. At sixteen, her long slender legs don't fit into her favorite sitting place anymore. She hugs the branch like a walkingstick bug, all knees and elbows, but not nearly so well concealed from view.

She used to hide from Mama up here, but there's no need to now. Mama sits on the porch swing, talking to herself, staring at nothing at all. Liam always knew where to find Hildy, but he usually knew to leave her alone.

She meant to stay with Little Will always, but who would have thought he'd be the one to leave her first?

Dogdays hang heavy and still. Sweatbees buzz around her ears, her eyes, and she swats at them without thinking.

The Army said Little Will is buried in France. They said they'd send his body home after the war, if Mama told them to. But what will Mama care if he comes back or not? She hardly noticed he was gone.

It seems like he ought to be right here, grinning up into the tree at her, whittling an acorn into a little smiling face. *Here, you keep this,* he said about his whittling knife. *I won't be needin' it anymore.* How did he know?

Sorrow swells and catches in her chest, but she refuses to let it make her cry. What good does crying do? It never brought Daddy back, and it surely won't bring back her brothers. The only one who comes back without fail is Bobby Ray, and crying never helped that either, did it?

She carefully picks her way down, branch by branch, and jumps the last four feet to the ground. What happened to that knife? She probably lost it too, just like she has lost Liam's picture. Now she has nothing to remember either one of her brothers by. Nothing at all.

"Hildy?" Aunt Emma's voice comes around the side of the house. Hildy brushes off her skirt, stuffs her feet into her sandals, not even bothering to bend down and pull up the heel straps.

Aunt Emma hesitates at the corner of the house, sets a paper sack down on the ground, comes on over to where Hildy hasn't moved from beside the apple tree. "Hon, I was thinkin' about you, wonderin' how you were." Aunt Emma reaches awkwardly toward her, but Hildy makes no move to respond. She glances half-curiously at the paper sack, but it doesn't hold her interest long.

"If you want to come on over to the house," Aunt Emma says, "Hon, you're welcome to any time. I really wish you would. It might be good for you. Billy Wayne and Sissy are always askin' for you."

Hildy shrugs. "Oh, no, I reckon not." She shrugs again.

Aunt Emma pats Hildy's arm, settles her hand on Hildy's hand, but Hildy feels no need to respond. "I know it's always a madhouse there, with the kids. But sometimes it's good to get away for a while."

Why? Hildy stares at Aunt Emma, blinking, and can't think of anything to say, or any reason to answer at all.

After a few awkward moments, Aunt Emma says, "Well, I've got to get back."

She nods toward the paper sack. "I brought something by for you. But, Hon, I'll take them back if you want me to. Naomi thought I should just put them away, but I didn't reckon I had any right not to give them to you. They're rightfully yours." She puts her arm around Hildy's shoulders and pulls her gently along with her to where the sack is waiting. "Now, Hon, Mr. Hite gave me these. They all came back at once, and if you want me to keep them I will. Maybe I should." But she moves to let Hildy stoop by the sack and pull it open. "Hon, what it is, is that they all got there too late for him to get them, so they have to send them back, the post office says they have to, but if you want me to, I'll . . . "

Hildy pulls the first bundle from the bag and drops it hard on the ground as both her hands fly to her mouth. The band around the bundle breaks and two dozen letters scatter on the ground, all addressed in Hildy's handwriting *PFC William Carmody*, and each marked across the front with a big red stamp, **DECEASED**. She sucks in a sharp breath as if a ghost had appeared before her eyes, and her "oh!" is muffled behind her hands.

Aunt Emma drops to her knees and hurries to gather the scattered letters, stuff them back into the bag. "Oh, Hon, I'm sorry! I shouldn't have brought them, I *knew* it! I didn't know if you'd want them . . . I'm so sorry! Whatever was I thinking about?"

Hildy rocks back and forth on her knees, stares at the bag. Then she sighs a deep shudder of a sigh, stands up, smoothes down her skirt, squares up her shoulders.

"I'll take them and put them away for—"

"No, I . . . I want them." Hildy snatches the sack from her and holds it tight against her chest.

"Well, if you're sure. But I should have waited, I know I should have waited until you were over at the house, but Hon, we haven't seen you all week."

Hildy walks away toward the back porch, clutching the paper sack close to her chest.

.....*August, 1944* ..... *American*
*7*th *Army lands in South of France*
.....*Paris liberated!* .....

Mid-August 1944
Nashville, Tennessee

"Why, Uncle Earl, you don't need to knock. You come on in here!" Connie Sue hugs Uncle Earl and stands aside to let him pass. "Molly, Sugar, look who's here," she calls down the hallway. Four-year-old Molly peeks around the corner, then runs to Uncle Earl, her eyes shining from recent tears. He picks her up, and over the girl's shoulder he looks a question at Connie Sue. But Connie Sue turns away, ashamed to admit how glad she is to have her argument with Bobby Ray interrupted.

"I'm sorry to disturb your breakfast, Connie Sue, but I've got something I need to talk to Robert about." Connie Sue points toward the kitchen. Uncle Earl bends to put Molly down, but she hangs onto his neck. He switches her to the other side and carries her with him.

Connie Sue goes to the cupboard for a coffee cup for Uncle Earl. Bobby Ray sits at the kitchen table finishing his breakfast, as if nothing of any importance to him has happened.

"Hey, Earl, what are you doin' out so early? Connie Sue, get him some coffee. Earl, I was wantin' to talk to you. I need some extra money this month, 'cause I've got to have me a new car. Mine's—"

"I told him there's a war on," Connie Sue interrupts, "and I told him nobody's makin' new cars. They're makin' *tanks.*" She gives Bobby Ray a smug look. "I read that in the paper." He'll get her back later, she knows, but he won't dare do it with Uncle Earl here.

"You've got a fine car, Robert. What's wrong with it? We can get it fixed if there's something wrong with it, if they can get any parts."

Connie Sue busies herself with the coffee, pretends she doesn't see Bobby Ray's cold mean look.

He turns back to Uncle Earl. "Well, I should drive a better car, that's all. When are they goin' to quit this blamed war? I'm gettin' sick of hearin' about it."

As Connie Sue passes by with the coffee pot, Bobby Ray holds his cup out, but she walks right past him. He elbows her in the behind, making her stumble.

She turns and fawns, "Why, did you want more coffee, Robert?" She'd like to pour it down his neck, but she's sure he knows that. He puts the cup down on the table for her to fill. Maybe she should just spill it all over his hand instead. "Uncle Earl, did you have breakfast? I can fry you up some grits real quick."

"Now, Earl, you watch out. She probably wants somethin' from you. You know how they act—sweet as molasses 'til they get what they want. She's got this nice big house on account of me, and she don't appreciate me at all for it."

Oh, Lord, he's going to go back to the argument, right here in front of Uncle Earl!

Uncle Earl shakes his head in answer to Connie Sue's breakfast question. His eyes plead for her to keep quiet.

She nods a tiny nod back at him, sorry to have worried him like that. She should try to be nicer. If Bobby Ray would just drop it and be nice, she would try, too. But he keeps her so riled up she could just scream, if Molly wasn't here. And now Uncle Earl.

"Molly, Sugar, why don't you go find Puppy and give him this last little bit of grits and eggs." She scrapes the food into a bowl. Molly wiggles down from Uncle Earl's lap and, skirting Bobby Ray's chair, comes to get the bowl.

"Yeah," Bobby Ray goes right on, "I bring in all this money, and she acts like it was all her doin'."

"Robert," Uncle Earl says, "I'm sure you both—well, all of us— I'm sure we are all grateful for how the good Lord has blessed us."

"Yeah, well, they'll use whatever they've got to get what they want from men." Bobby Ray sips his coffee. "You're the one told me that, remember?"

Uncle Earl? Connie Sue can feel the color rise in her face. *Why, surely he'd never say something like that!*

"Now Robert . . . I never . . . if I ever . . . Robert, out of respect for your wife, please!"

Bobby Ray laughs, but his laugh sounds wicked, with no respect for anybody. "Well, I reckon we both know how she used her little tail end to get what she wanted from—"

"Robert!" Uncle Earl explodes. "You're bein' vulgar! That's too far! Now stop it!"

Connie Sue turns her head away, and blinks back the tears that blur her eyes. As she gathers dirty dishes, the clinking of bowls and cups is suddenly loud and irritating.

"Robert," Uncle Earl starts, pulling a letter out of his suit coat pocket. "The reason I came was this. I don't know when you were out at your Mama's last, but it sounds like it's been a long time, accordin' to your Aunt's letter here."

"That nosy busybody's writin' you letters?"

"She says she doesn't have an address for you, so she sent it in care of the radio program."

"Well, if she's whinin' about the money, I *mailed* it up there. If Mama's lost it, I can't help that. I got better things to do. Connie Sue, get me some more of this cow piss you call coffee."

Connie Sue glares at him and refuses to move until Uncle Earl's imploring eyes break her stubbornness. She brings the coffee pot over to the table and puts it down barely within Bobby Ray's reach.

Uncle Earl clears his throat and starts again. "No, the reason she wrote me was that there's been bad news from the war front. I hate to be the one to tell you this, but your brother was killed in the invasion of France. I'm sorry."

Bobby Ray barely looks up from his coffee cup. "That little runt Liam was old enough to join the army? I can't picture that."

"Well, no, it wasn't him, it was the younger one, William. One of the twins, is—wasn't he?"

Bobby Ray reaches for the last biscuit on the plate. "Don't seem to me like any of them kids could be old enough to join the army. Here, Earl, you want half of this last biscuit?"

"Robert, you need to . . . it seems to me . . . you ought to go out and see how your Mama is holdin' up. It must be a bad time for her. And your little sister."

Bobby Ray slathers butter on the biscuit, takes a big bite, washes it down with a gulp of coffee. "That little whore. She's—"

"Robert! You stop it!" Connie Sue throws the wet dishrag at him, but misses. It lands in a sloppy wet lump on the table.

"That's enough, Robert," Uncle Earl says. "I don't want to hear any more of it, you hear me?" He dabs at the spreading wet spot on the tablecloth.

Bobby Ray gets up from table, picks up the dishrag, throws it back at Connie Sue. It slaps against her blouse, leaving a wide wet spot before dropping to the floor. He heads up the stairs.

Uncle Earl sits with the letter in his hand, and Connie Sue tries to swallow back the dry web that clogs her throat.

Bobby Ray reappears, stuffing the tail of his clean shirt into his pants. "All right, I'm goin' up there, so y'all will get off of me about it." With a pointed look at Connie Sue, he says "Don't anybody appreciate me here anyway." He slams the front door behind him.

Connie Sue mops at the wet spot with a dishtowel. She wonders if it's doing anybody a favor to send Bobby Ray to his family, the evil mood he's in. But then when is he ever *not* in that mood anymore?

The door opens again, and Bobby Ray says, "Oh, and Earl, when I get back I want to talk about the money. I figure if I'm bringin' in all this money it's my right to have a say about where it's goin'. And Connie Sue, you keep your nose out it. Money is men's business."

Uncle Earl starts to get up from the table. "Robert, we have to consider what Harold—"

"This hasn't got anything to do with Harold any more. It's got to do with me." Bobby Ray slams the door again.

Uncle Earl sits with his elbows on the table, rubs his forehead. Connie Sue comes over and sits down next to him, but she has no idea what to say, except "I'm sorry Uncle Earl. I . . . I just can't help myself sometime."

He reaches over and takes her hand, squeezes it, then quickly pulls it away. They sit in silence for a long while, then they both start at once.

"Connie Sue, I'm—"

"Uncle Earl—" She stops and lets him go ahead.

"I've been torn up over somethin' for a long time, and it may well be this is as good a time as any to talk about it."

He reaches for his coffee cup, but it's empty, so he sets it back in the saucer. Connie Sue hurries to get up and refill it, but he waves his hand no and she sits back down.

"I don't know how to do it," he goes on, "but I want to get out of the radio program. But I can't leave you in it with him, you and Molly. He's right about one thing. It's got nothin' to do anymore with what Harold started, and I can't stop what Robert's made it into, or where he'll go with it after I'm gone. But I don't have to be part of it any more. I just don't know what to do for you."

Connie Sue wipes her eyes hard with her palms, but the tears come anyway. "You know how mean he is to Molly and me. I hate livin' in this 'Sweetheart' lie with him. I don't want me and Molly to have any more to do with it either. But I thought you . . . well, you know, you and Daddy . . . "

"Maybe it wasn't my . . . our . . . your daddy and me . . . maybe it wasn't our place to make you marry him. We didn't have any idea what demons were drivin' that boy. I just can't live anymore with what I helped make Robert into."

She folds a napkin again and again, her fingers intent on forming a perfect square of it, but her mind is not on it at all. "It wasn't all your fault. Much as I hate to admit it, I set out to get him and I did. Whatever way I had to."

"I know, I know. It's the way girls are taught." He reaches for her hand again, covers it with his. "I reckon I thought by puttin' you two together, it would save you both."

"Well." She gets up and gathers dirty dishes from the table. "I'm goin' to put on a new pot of coffee. It sounds like we've got some talkin' to do."

They wait in silence until she sets out the steaming cups of fresh coffee. Uncle Earl pours some into his saucer, blows on it, takes a sip. "I'm goin' to talk to the lawyer this mornin' and find out what I have to do and how much I have to give Robert. I don't care about me, but I have to make sure you and Molly are taken care of. And that it don't depend on Robert to provide it, like he does his mother."

He takes another sip from the saucer. "And I have to see to it that she's taken better care of, too. You understand that, don't you Connie Sue? I promised that to her, that the church would take care of her, back when we took Robert into the ministry. I thought Robert would follow along, but he doesn't seem inclined to. And with his daddy and his other brother gone off somewhere, and now the younger one." Uncle Earl stares down at his coffee cup. Connie Sue can't bear to look at his pained face.

"I always had the uneasy feelin'," he continues, "that Robert knew more about his daddy than he ever said, I don't know why. Anyways, with the younger brother dead in the war now . . . you do understand, don't you, Honey? I reckon Harold would, too. I can't ask the Mahala church to take over where we—where I—have failed."

Somehow it's hard to imagine Robert having family, Connie Sue thinks. His poor mama, and his poor little sister. What must his little sister be like? She should have made him take care of them. She should have gone with him. She nods. Yes, she understands, but now it feels sad, as if it's too late.

"I 'spect Robert will fight me on it, but I have to see that enough money is set aside for her, maybe put in war bonds or somethin'."

Connie Sue pours herself another cup of coffee. Uncle Earl has hardly touched his. "Are you sure, Honey, really sure that you want to leave it too, the radio program?"

She sets her cup down and leans on her elbows on the table. "Uncle Earl, I don't just want to leave the program. I want Molly and me to leave Robert."

He looks down at the table for a long time, shoulders sagging. He nods. "Yes, I s'pected that's what you meant."

"Could you talk to the lawyer about that today, too?"

His eyes close. He nods again.

"Uncle Earl? What Robert said about the money—I know it's not my business, but he's always talkin' like that. He never seems like he's satisfied. I hate to say it, but I reckon he means to get his hands on it all someday. And if he did, I doubt if he'd care all that much about takin' care of you or me and Molly, if it was up to him, let alone his mama. He's that hateful. I can see it."

Uncle Earl leans back in his chair, absently drinks his coffee, stares off across the room. "Connie Sue, I wish I could say you were all wrong about that. I truly wish I could."

"He talks like there's a lot of money." Connie Sue gets up, starts for the refrigerator with the empty cream pitcher. "Is there?"

He looks surprised that she would ask such a question. "A lot of money?"

"I know, money is men's business. But I just wondered. Is there a lot? From the program, I mean?"

"I've tried to be a good steward, to not be foolish with it. I wait on the Lord for just where to use it, and . . . well, my mind's not been on the Lord's work much here lately. But yes, there is a great deal of money, with more comin' in every day."

"Well, does Robert know exactly how much there is? I mean, what if after all the widows"—she sweeps one arm out to cover the whole city of Nashville—"and the women with no husbands and the fatherless children, and"—she pats him on the shoulder—"the older folks had bank accounts to take care of them, what if there wasn't any money left for Robert to buy fancy cars with?"

Uncle Earl studies his coffee cup for a long moment, then drinks the coffee down. It must be cold by now, but he doesn't seem to notice. When he finally looks back at her, his eyes look a little more alive, more like the Uncle Earl she remembers as a kid, back before Robert. "Why, I don't know, Honey. I'll just have to talk to the lawyer and see what he says."

Later the same day
Mahala, Kentucky

Bobby Ray pulls his Buick up into the shade next to the kitchen porch. He gets the box of canned goods and sugar from the back seat that

Earl put in his car last week. Damn, he forgot and left the money envelope.

Mama sits at the kitchen table with a paper sack and a bunch of scattered envelopes.

He drops the box on the table, fishes out a can of vienna sausage and one of pork and beans. "Here, Mama. Heat this up. I'm hungry."

Mama hurries to obey, and retrieves a pan from a hook on the wall, digs through a pile of utensils for the can opener, pours the beans into the pan. The stove is cold.

"Don't you have any fire in there? What do you do around here all day? What's the matter with you? You ready to go back and see that doctor?" Gerty shakes her head, backs away from him.

"Here, gimme that, and wash me a spoon."

She fishes a spoon from the cold dishwater and dries it on her apron. He takes the pan, looks the spoon over, wipes it on his sleeve.

"Yeah, I reckon you're about ready for another trip to the doctor, you crazy old woman." He laughs as she cowers away from him. He pulls a chair out and turns it around, straddles it, eats the cold beans out of the pan. He points his spoon in the direction of the pile of envelopes. "What's all this here?"

Gerty sits down across the table, sighs a heavy sigh and smiles. "Little Will sent letters to his Mama." Then a puzzled looks comes over her face. "I don't know where that boy went off to." She looks around her, as though he might be in the next room. Bobby Ray picks up an envelope, turns it over.

PFC William Carmody. "You crazy old woman, these are not from him, they're *to* him." He studies the rounded handwriting, the return address . . . *Miss Hildy Mae Carmody* . . . the **DECEASED** stamp. A chill prickles the hair on the back of his neck. "Where'd you get this?"

A smug little twitch keeps her mouth busy as her mind has apparently wandered onto a thought of great pleasure to her. "I named him Little Will for my daddy. Daniel, he didn't like it, no he didn't."

"Oh, shut up, Mama." Crazy old woman. He puts his pan down and opens the envelope, pulls out the tablet page.

Little Will, why dont you answer my letters? I hope you still love me, Little Will. Do you? You left on account of me, because I didnt treat you good enough, I know it. When you come back I want to make up to you that I didnt treat you right.

A burning starts behind his rib cage, and the beans turn to a rancid lump in his stomach. "That little whore. That no-account little whore." He rips open another envelope.

Sometime I wish we could get married and then we could stay together forever, you and me just like we always were, and I could take care of you.

Why, that little harlot, crawling after her own brother! "Hildy! Where is she, Mama?"

Gerty stares at him. "Little Will, he—"

"No, I'm askin' you where is Hildy."

Mama looks around, her eyes round with fear. Bobby Ray jumps up from his chair and shakes her hard by the shoulders. "Where is that little heathen of yours? Where. Is. Hildy."

"She went to the spring. To . . . uh . . . school. She went to, uh, school." Gerty smiles, nods.

The waterbucket is missing from the sideboard.

Down the hill at the spring the empty bucket sits on the ledge, but Hildy's nowhere in sight. Where has that little bitch run off to? From downstream he hears a splash.

He pushes aside the low-hanging branches. At a wide place where the stream has dug under the roots of a big oak tree perched on the far bank, Hildy wades in knee-deep water, her dresstail tucked up into her underpants, her thighs white and naked in the afternoon shade.

"Get out of there, you little whore, showing yourself half naked. You hear me? You get up here, right here!" He points to the ground next to his feet.

She loses her footing and struggles to catch herself. "I . . . I didn't do anything. I . . . I didn't . . . I've not done anything!"

"Get up here right now, you hear me?" She makes her way to the near edge, slips in the shallow water and catches herself with a hand on the muddy bottom, drenching the front of her dress.

Bobby Ray jumps back but not before his brown gabardine pants are speckled with muddy water, his brown leather shoes soaked.

As she reaches the edge, he grabs her hair and yanks her up onto the bank. He slaps her face hard, lets her fall to the muddy ground. "You are wicked in God's eyes, Harlot! His punishment is upon you!"

She struggles to her knees, tries to crawl back toward the water, but he grabs a handful of her dresstail and holds her back while he wrestles with getting his belt off. The first blow with the belt sends her sprawling in the mud, and most of the worn material of the skirt rips off in his hands.

"You filthy little whore, smelling after your own brother!" The belt cracks again. Hildy curls herself into a ball, but Bobby Ray grabs an ankle and twists her leg, forcing her to her back . . . *just like all the rest . . . just like all the rest . . .* the blackness rises up inside him . . . *except ye destroy the accursed from among you . . .* the fury swells inside him, filling his skin, straining at his clothes, the nightmare alive in front of his face . . . *skinny naked girls, crawling, craving, begging.*

Before he realizes he has done it, he has freed himself of the garments that restrain him, letting his hard fury free, a sword of judgment on the wicked.

She tries to scramble backwards, kicking at him with her free foot, but he is on her, holding her down to the muddy ground.

All alike, all after the same thing . . . *filthy whores of Babylon . . . filthy . . . filthy . . .* the vision looms in front of him, naked skinny girls . . . filthy hands grow bigger, bigger, blur into a bloated face . . . the face turns frozen and gray, a skeleton face . . . its evil mutilated grin taunts him . . . the skinny body resists, refusing, refusing the very thing that he knows she craves. He rips the flimsy material of her underpants. She'll not resist the punishment of God. She'll have no hold on him, for he is of the Lord and she of the devil, and Robert Ray will again see to it that judgment will take dominion over the wicked whores of Babylon.

His vengeance spent and rage diminished, he pulls himself from her, away from her wickedness. He is disgusted at the look of her, lying whimpering on the ground, pulling at her meager clothes now reduced to rags to cover her nakedness, her blood. He yanks her up by one arm and shoves her to the edge of the water. "Wash yourself of your filthy sins, you harlot!"

She splashes, struggles, choking, gets herself upright in the water. She huddles on the far side where the water is deepest, at the root of the big tree and she hangs onto the biggest loop of root, sinking shoulder-deep into the cool muddy water, hiding her face in the curve of her arm against the root.

Bobby Ray picks up his pants and shoes, takes them with him back to the spring. He fills the waterbucket and pours dipperfuls of water over his body, grunts at the shock of sudden cold. He shivers, rids himself of the remnants of her sinful body, then he pulls on his pants and stuffs his feet into his ruined shoes.

Not yet halfway up the endless hill back to the house he has to stop, exhausted. When something dark and evil rustles near his ears, he shivers, his jaw clenches. He won't listen. No! He refuses the whispering. "She's just like all the rest of them!"

He is Robert Ray, called of the Lord God to be an instrument of judgment, to destroy the accursed among His people . . . *there is power power in the blood . . .*

But from somewhere deep in the pit where the power cannot reach, a skeleton face grins, leers from out of the dark.

No! He rejects it, he will not listen to it, holds his hands tight against his ears, but he can't suppress the voices inside his own head. He screams out, "She was just like all the rest!"

He scrambles, panting, to the top of the hill. Without stopping to peer into the screendoor at the crazy old woman, he gets into his car and slams the door, starts the engine, roars out onto the road.

The next day
Mahala, Kentucky

"Now, Miz Hartley, just calm down." The sheriff comes around and sits on the front of his desk. "All I'm sayin' is that I don't tell people how to raise their children, and since she don't have a daddy and her mama's—well, you know—I reckon it's as much her brother's place as anybody's to keep her in line."

Emma is up from her seat again. "Russ, that's about the stupidest thing I ever heard of! You come and look at this girl, see her bruises for yourself. With her face like it is, she's not goin' to be able to start school next week. What he did was not called for. That self-righteous bully has got no right to get away with that! It's your place to keep the law in this town, and I want you to do something about it." She struggles to keep the tears back.

The sheriff takes out a cigarette and lights it, blows out a long stream of smoke. "Look, Miz Hartley. Emma. Between you and me, I've pretty much stayed out of your family's business ever since—well, your daddy was a hardset man, and as long as he saw to it that his people behaved, we pretty much stayed out of each other's way."

"Russ, my daddy's been gone for six years now, and this hasn't got a thing to do with him. I'm the one askin' you to do something about this."

The sheriff puts his arm around her shoulders. "Now Emma. Sheriffin's my job. You go on home and tend to your sewin' business, and I'll—"

She jerks her shoulders free. "Don't you try usin' your charms on me, Russ. I'll not be talked out of it, so you're wastin' your time and mine tryin' it."

He finishes off his cigarette and drops the butt on the bare wood floor, crushes it out. "Listen. All I can say, Emma, is I wasn't there and didn't see him beat her. She could be lyin' for all I know. There could be a boyfriend, or . . . " He shrugs.

Emma snatches up her purse from the chair. "Well, I'll wager you if it was your little girl we were talkin' about here, you'd have him strung up outside the courthouse by sunup, on no more than a hunch that he was the one who did it." She glares at him until he finally looks the other way.

When he looks back, his eyes have gone softer, his voice gentler. "Emma, listen. Why don't you take her to stay at your place, and be sure she behaves herself and keeps out of his way. That's what I'd do if I was you."

"Well, Russ, you don't have to tell me that. I was a fool for not doin' that a long time ago. But I'll tell you one thing, if he comes around my house, you won't have to bother with him, because I'll shoot him dead myself."

Early September 1944
Mahala, Kentucky

Emma stops at the foot of the Gerty's front porch steps, sets down her peck basket of blackeyed peas and listens. A man's voice, then Gerty's silly giggling. A knot tightens in Emma's stomach—Bobby Ray? It can't be him. There's no fancy car pulled up by the side of the house. But the voice is familiar. She picks up the basket and goes around back to the kitchen porch. "Gerty?" she calls through the screendoor, and the man in the red-and-blue checked shirt turns around, jumps to his feet and holds the screendoor open for her. "Well, good mornin', Miz Hartley. We were just talkin' about you. Here, let me take that."

Earl Spivey? What in the world? He looks like Earl Spivey, but in overall pants, with his hair disheveled? And Gerty already has a big pile of blackeyed peas in the middle of wide kitchen table. "But where did . . . why . . . " Emma waves her arms foolishly at the peas, at the screendoor. The knot in her stomach twists tighter and tighter.

How dare him come here! Earl has never done anything to her personally, of course, but Bobby Ray's not here, and she has to blame somebody. After all, aren't Brother Earl and his kind responsible for the devil Bobby Ray has turned into? How dare him come and sit here like nothing's happened?

Earl sets the basket on the table and takes his place back in front of his bowl of shelled peas, much smaller than Gerty's. "Sister Gerty was just showin' me how to fix these things. I picked all the rest of the peas out there, but I had no idea there'd be so many when we dumped them out here. It just seemed like they needed pickin', and now with the basket you brought . . . "

Emma's stomach knot unravels, all the ends breaking loose at the same time. "Well, I can't take care of everything! Lord knows I've got enough with my son comin' home crippled from the war, and three grandbabies to help with, and now Hildy to look out for!"

"Little Will went off to the war, Emma," Gerty says, nodding.

"Oh, no, Miz Hartley," Earl says, with an odd glance at Gerty. "Please, I wasn't meanin' to criticize, no I wasn't. I was just wantin' to help out, and I confess I don't have any idea of what to do."

"What are you *doin'* here?" It comes out harsher than she means for it to, from the anger pit in her stomach.

Gerty's mouth gulps open and closed like a catfish, looking from one to the other of them.

"Here, Miz Hartley, why don't you sit down and I'll get you a cup of coffee. I brought some for Sister Gerty. You know how hard it is to come by, and—"

"Well, not hard to come by for the likes of you and Bobby Ray, I don't reckon." He pulls out a chair for her, but she still can't budge from the doorway.

"I am sorry," he goes on. "I do b'lieve I may be gettin' in the way here more than I'm helpin', but that's what I wanted to do. I just wanted to help out around here."

Gerty smiles. "Brother Earl picked all them peas, Emma."

"Yes, Gerty, I see 'em," Emma says, but her glare never once leaves Earl's face.

"I'm sorry, Miz Hartley. I'm bein' foolish, when I need to explain to you. Please, would you sit down?"

She sits on the front edge of the cane-bottom chair, her arms tight against her chest. Earl pulls a chair up to the other side of the table, and looks a *May I?* at Emma. She turns her head quickly away, not willing even to give him the permission to sit down in her presence. He stands by the cookstove, his hands behind him. "I have come back here to Mahala to live. I'm rentin' a room from Miz Darnell— you know Miz Darnell, do you?—and I am hopin' to be asked to take some small part in my old church again, since I have, uh, retired from my work with Robert and with the radio program."

"You what?" Emma's reflexes are faster than her grudges.

Earl leans on the back of the empty chair, hurries on. "But I don't want you to worry. I . . . uh, the church is still goin' to see to it that your sister is taken care of."

Emma expects to see Earl's preacher grin spread across his face, but it doesn't. She huffs out a big sigh and tries to rearrange her face to something more pleasant. "Well, I reckon I would enjoy that cup of coffee, if it's already made."

Earl smiles . . . a real smile . . . and gets a cup from the clean ones stacked on the washstand. It looks like he's been helping out with the dishes, too. Lord knows Gerty doesn't do a very good job it herself.

Gerty pouts, "Emma, she don't like my Bobby Ray, Brother Earl, no, she don't."

Without turning to look at her, Emma says, "Gerty, do you reckon there's any apples ripe out on the tree yet? Why don't you go look and see?"

Gerty obediently gets up. As soon as she's out on the porch, Emma goes on, "So, is he comin' back here, too?"

Earl sets the cup in front of Emma. "I can't speak for him, but it's not likely. He's already signed on at another radio station, one out of Memphis."

He goes over to the screendoor, looks out, cradling his coffee cup. "I haven't spoke to him since we decided to go our different ways. Our three different ways, by the by. Connie Sue and the little girl are stayin' with family in Atlanta. There's nothing left for me on the radio. I never had the heart for it after Harold died, and besides, Robert's the one they want."

Emma tips her coffee cup, watches the coffee come precariously to the edge before she uprights it. "So we can count on not seein' that bastard nephew of mine around here anymore?" Without moving her head she looks at his back to see his reaction.

His shoulders move slightly, then visibly slump, but he doesn't turn around. "I thought sendin' him up here to take care of his mama would be good for him. I reckon I've made a lot of mistakes in what

I thought." He turns to her, his eyes heavy and old. "He acted pretty bad here, did he?"

She runs her finger around the rim of her coffee cup. "We can both do without me tellin' you all about it."

He shakes his head. "I was afraid of that. Miz Hartley. I don't know what else to say. I wish I could go back and change things, I surely do. But since I can't, I hope you'll tell me what the church can do here to make up for his not doing right by his mother."

She shrugs, points to the chair. "Why don't you sit down here and we can talk. And thank you for this good coffee, Earl."

Before he sits down, he retrieves the coffee pot from the stove, puts it on the table between them. "I would like that, Miz Hartley."

"Emma."

"Yes, I would like that, Emma."

A month later
Mahala, Kentucky

Hildy dumps her armload of books onto the porch swing, then holds the slice of light bread in her mouth while she slips her arms into her blue sweater. Across the street, gossipy old Mrs. Brown sweeps orange and yellow leaves off her walk, but the brisk October breeze dumps some more every time she turns her back.

Hildy claimed she wasn't hungry for breakfast, but the truth is she didn't want to hurt Aunt Emma's feelings. Nothing on the table smelled very good. But the light bread might help settle her stomach.

It's odd to be alone at Aunt Emma's house. The noise and fuss that usually go from daylight to dark make her want to scream, herself. Billy Wayne loves to yell out for no reason, just to make everybody come running to fuss over him. And the babies are always into something. Now Naomi is worried that Wayne's being crippled will keep her from having any more babies. Good Lord, what does she want with more babies?

Early this morning Aunt Emma took them all over to Mammaw and Granddaddy's old home place, to fix it up for when Wayne gets home. They probably would've asked her to watch the babies, but she pretended she was really tired and needed a nap. Funny thing, she did go to sleep for a little while, but it was too quiet in the house and she woke up.

She half-heartedly pokes through the stack of books that Mrs. Stanfill left for her yesterday. Mrs. Stanfill was her favorite teacher in ninth and tenth grades, and she promised that this year they'd get to read more books. Literature, she calls it. Such a pretty word when Mrs. Stanfill says it: *Lit-tra-chure.* Hildy picks up the first book on the pile: *Julius Caesar.* She slaps the book shut and tosses it aside. All that fancy talk. Like the Bible. Nobody talks like that now.

Mrs. Stanfill says she's positive Hildy can still catch up if she comes back to school soon, but it's already time for the first six weeks tests. Maybe next week she'll start . . . if she feels better.

Silas Marner. She peeks at the first page . . . spinning wheels . . . deep in the bosom of the hills . . . in that far-off time . . . It sounds old-fashioned, too, but not like Julius Caesar. More like a fairy tale.

Hildy shivers at the mysterious sound of it, although she has no idea what "unwonted" means. Mrs. Stanfill will know.

" . . . to the peasants of old times, the world outside their own direct experience was a region of *vag-ew-ness* and mystery: to their un-travelled thought a state of wandering." The words sound soft and milky when she reads them out loud. Her stomach even feels a little better.

She skims through the first few pages and picks out phrases that catch her eye . . . the eccentric habits which belong to a state of loneliness . . . an odd word, *eccentric.* She wonders if she has any of those funny kind of habits, whatever they are. She looks at her own chewed, ragged fingernails.

She flits over the nutting or birdsnesting . . . the snug, well wooded hollow . . . well-walled orchards and ornamental weathercocks . . . until her focus settles into the feeling of the story.

She moves the books to the far side of the swing and tucks her feet up under her, almost forgetting to nibble on her bread.

Poor Silas. Surely he is innocent . . . but nobody believes him. Poor Silas. Hildy's chest tightens and sadness presses up into her throat.

But I didn't do anything! her own voice screams out in her head. She smacks the book shut and looks around her. Mrs. Brown stops sweeping and looks up. Could she have heard it too? She picks the book up again and shuffles through, looking for her place. How do I know what you may have done in the secret chambers of your heart, to give Satan an advantage over you? Silas's friend asks. Hildy's own voice echoes *You are wicked in God's eyes* . . . inside her own head she is sure. But she peeks to see if Mrs. Brown is looking again.

She reads on, not surprised when the church's lottery proves Silas guilty, no matter that he isn't. And when Silas claims there is no God that hears witness against the innocent, Hildy nods, feels sad for Silas, poor Silas. Wonder what his *eccentric habits* were that he had in his *state of loneliness*? For truly Silas was lonely, Hildy is sure of that. Why didn't he just run away from those hateful people?

Yes, on the very next page, Silas departed from that town. Lucky Silas found a place to go. It sounds like his loneliness went along with him to Raveloe, though. At least it was a different place to be lonely.

If only she had a Raveloe to go to.

" 'S'cuse me, Miss?"

Hildy sucks in her breath so hard that she nearly chokes on it. "You 'bout scared me to death!"

The young man out on the walk, his army jacket slung over one shoulder, rushes up to the porch railing and peers through. "I'm sorry. I didn't mean to! I thought you saw me. They told me up at the DX station that I'd find Hildy Carmody up here at the yellow house." He stands back and looks at the house again, as though he can't decide if it's yellow or not. "Could you tell me where she might be?"

"I'm Hildy Carmody. But who are you?" He's surely not anybody from around here.

The young man looks puzzled. "You are? Uh, I'm Joe Rossi. You never heard of me, but I . . . really? You're Hildy? Well, hell, he never told me you were so pretty. I expected his twin sister would be . . . " His hands measure somebody much taller and wider than either of them.

Pretty? What's the matter with this boy? Is he blind? Her foot pushes absently against the porch floor, and the swing moves. Her stomach sways with it, and she stops the swing abruptly.

He takes the porch steps two at a time. "I'm sorry. I didn't mean to be a jerk." He drops his jacket onto the porch railing, wipes his hands on his pants and offers his hand. "I'm Joe Rossi . . . oh, hell, did I say that already?"

Yes, Will did say something about Joe, she thinks she remembers. "He told me you'd be comin'. I reckon I forgot."

"He did?" Joe looks puzzled again. "But he only made me promise to come see you if—oh, now don't get me wrong, I'm glad I came, not just because he asked me to or anything. I mean, I was thinking maybe I'd like to anyway." He stops, takes a deep breath, runs his hand through his dark hair. Hildy guesses it's curly when it isn't so short.

He looks like he's going to start over, but he shrugs and smiles. "I had a whole speech made up, but I forget it now. Damn. I wish he'd told me how pretty you were."

A little smile plays with Hildy's lips, too, and she can't look him in the eye. He's such a good-looking boy and not a bit bashful. "Well, Joe, he could've told me what you looked like, too." Tears come up warm in her eyes, and she tries to look away before he sees.

He scoops up the stack of books, drops them on the old wicker armchair, takes a seat beside her on the swing. "I'm sorry . . . did I say the wrong thing? I did, I must have said something stupid."

"No. I just was thinkin' about Little Will, and you bein' with him when he died."

Joe laughs, then catches himself. "I'm sorry. *Little* Will? You said *little*—I'm sorry. I didn't mean to laugh, really I didn't. He—he was a good guy, one of the best. I only knew him a few weeks, but we hit it off." This part sounds like he's found the words to his speech, but his eyes are still crinkly. His grin turns shy and he scratches the back of his head. "Hell, he didn't—I mean, heck, I sure wish he'd told me . . . "

She can't help grinning, too, even with her eyes still wet. His laugh is soft and sweet. She can tell it's not the making-fun kind of a laugh.

But then his face turns somber. He leans his elbows on his knees and runs his hands through his hair again. "Yeah, I was with him."

Hildy waits. It seems like he wants to say some more. He's staring off across the street, but she doubts he's seeing Mrs. Brown's porch, but something else in his mind. "We were all scared," he starts out, finally. "Oh, nobody admitted it . . . they all claimed it was just seasickness . . . the way they—well, we— we were all throwing up. But I won't lie to you. I was scared. I mean, the Germans were shooting at us, and we weren't even up to the beach yet! When we left the lander, it was a mess. Nobody told us what to do . . . we got separated from our CO, and we just stayed there in the water, not knowing what to do next. I mean, most of us had never seen combat before. Guys were getting hit all around me. Some of 'em I'll bet might've made it, but they fell there in the water and probably drowned, I don't know. One of our buddies got shot right away and went down. I grabbed for his gun in the water, and . . . and his hand came with . . . his hand was . . . " Joe closes his eyes and it looks like the war is right there behind his eyelids. Hildy's pretty sure he's gone past where he was aiming for his speech to go.

"It's all right, Joe. You don't have to tell me if you don't want to." To tell the truth, she wishes he wouldn't. She's afraid she's going to puke, herself.

Joe takes in a big deep breath and it comes out in little bumps. He takes in another one, looks off across the road again. "I'm sorry," he says, sitting up straighter. "I didn't mean to dump all that out on you. I'm sorry."

She can't think of anything to say to him. Her glance wanders to the window, the front door, the porch floor.

He goes on, "Will was a swell guy but kind of quiet. You'd never take him for the big hero type, but he sure had me fooled. The rest of us tried to find something to hide behind out there in the water, but he started on up toward the beach. I yelled at him to get down, to wait, but he just looked right past me and just kept going . . . honest to God, I don't think he was scared. I still don't understand . . . "

Joe looks like he's not only forgetting the speech again, but has forgotten Hildy is sitting there. He shakes his head, repeats, "But I still don't get it . . . "

Hildy swallows hard, tries to think of something to say to this nice boy sitting so close to her, this boy who spent time with Little Will after he left her, who was there when her brother died.

Joe, he may not understand, but she does. Little Will left because she let him down, because she wasn't a good sister to him. And that's nothing she can explain to Joe.

His attention and his voice come abruptly back to the porch. "Anyway," he says. His shoulders straighten. He reaches over and takes Hildy's hand, and somehow this seems like it's part of the speech, too. "I didn't find out for sure what happened to him 'til later in the hospital. I was hit, too, after we got up past the sea wall and up the cliff. My whole shoulder and my arm were all busted up. That's why I didn't come sooner. I was back in England for a month." He rubs his shoulder. "At first they thought they were going to have to cut . . . to *amputate*, but—I'm sorry. There I go again. Well, anyway, I remembered he made me promise . . . I mean, I promised him I'd come if anything—" His forehead wrinkles with that puzzled look again. "He told you I was *going* to come, just like that? Now that doesn't make any sense."

He drops her hand as though now that the speech is over he has no reason to hold it, and wipes his hand on his pants leg again. He jumps up from the swing. Hildy holds both feet solid on the floor to stop the swaying. Joe digs a cigarette out of the jacket pocket, lights it and leans on the porch post, looking off down the street where a dark Ford is parked. "Or, you know," he mumbles, "maybe it does."

"What?" Hildy says.

"I'm sorry. Are you all right? You look a little . . . white."

He sits on the railing, and she's relieved that he didn't make the swing move again. And his cigarette smells *awful.*

"I'm sorry," he says again. "I guess I just had to get it over with. It didn't go like I meant for it to." The hand with the cigarette in it shakes a little.

"Well, I reckon it made you feel better for tellin' me," she says, wishing she could say the same for herself, for hearing.

He puffs on the cigarette until it's about half gone, then drops it, grinds it out with his shoe. "Listen, I can leave if you want me to. But tell you the truth, I'd like to stay and talk a while. And if there's someplace we could go and I could buy you lunch? I mean, if you want to."

His voice is kind and soft, even if his words are shorter and his talk faster than she's used to. He must be from up north, someplace where they call dinner *lunch.*

She wonders what kind of voice Silas Marner had.

"That's all right," Joe says, picking up his jacket. "If you don't want to, I mean, I can go." But he still looks like he doesn't aim to leave any time soon, if he can help it.

Her stomach is starting to settle a little. "Where is it that you live, Joe?"

"Philadelphia. Born and raised there." He hesitates, like he's still not sure if he's being invited to stay or not. "I've got four brothers and three sisters. You'd like my sisters, I'll bet." He grins. "And as for my brothers, well, the devil with them. I saw you first."

She smiles. "I wish you would stay a while. I like listenin' to you talk." She'd like to hear about Philadelphia. She wonders if it could be anything like Raveloe.

Dusk the same day

Emma drops into the porch swing and pulls off her headscarf, letting her hair fall loose to her shoulders.

If the mosquitoes will leave her alone, she'll just sit for a minute and catch her breath before she goes in to gather up some supper to take back over to the old house. Naomi at least can get a little more done over there while the little ones take naps on Mama and Daddy's old featherbed.

It's sweet, watching Naomi make a home for Wayne and their babies in the kitchen where Mama cooked up so many good suppers with blackberry pies, fresh-churned butter. They'll have to get a cow, she thinks. She stretches her weary legs out in front of her.

How strange it will be with Wayne and Naomi and the kids out of the house. She'll have some peace and quiet for the first time since, how long? Since before the war started. She can have some nice long talks with Hildy without a dozen interruptions.

"Hildy, Honey, I'm out here!" she calls in the direction of the front door. Surely the girl's not asleep again. Maybe Doc Jessup can give her a tonic or something, so she can get back to school.

Emma notices the books and the radio—Mama's big old radio—in the wicker chair. Now whatever possessed Hildy to bring the radio out here? "Hildy?"

Loretta Brown comes scooting across the street toward Emma's porch. Emma gathers her hair up into one big handful on the top of her head, and rubs her stiff sore neck. The last thing she feels like is having Loretta come over for a one-sided hour of gossip.

"Emma!" Loretta starts, huffing up to porch. "I've been watchin' for you to come home!"

"Well, come on up and sit a minute, Loretta." A *minute* is all she can offer—if only Loretta would take her invitation that way.

"No, I have to get back to Malcolm's supper, but I had to tell you that little niece of yours, she left with a soldier boy I've never seen around here before. About an hour ago. I didn't know what to do and I didn't know where you were!"

"Now Loretta, I'm sure it must have been one of her friends from school." Not that any friends have been by to visit Hildy before. And most of the boys are overseas. Nadine McBride did mention her boy was coming home on furlough, but Loretta would know that already. She probably knew that before Nadine did.

"No, no, Emma, I'm sure it wasn't. Malcolm said the boy stopped in at the DX, right from the highway and asked where to find Miss Hildy Carmody. He sounded like he was from up north. Malcolm was sure he was *Eye*talian. And then he sat out here on the porch with her most all day, the boy did, well except for a little while at dinnertime when they walked down to . . . " She waves her arm over toward the town's main street. "well, I don't know where. Then about a hour ago I just happened to look out the window . . . just happened to, mind you, and I saw them leave in his car. It was a Ford, well, that's what Malcolm said, with out-of-state plates . . . I don't know where . . . I couldn't make out . . . I mean, I didn't notice. Before that, they went in the house and she came out with a big paper sack and he was carryin' that radio, but then they put it down and left. And Emma, I saw them, well, you'll never guess, he . . . " Her voice drops to a raspy whisper. "He kissed her on the cheek, right there on the porch in broad daylight, he did! Why, I never! Young people this day and age—why until we was married, Malcolm never touched—"

"Now Loretta, I'm sure there's a good reason." Although Emma can't imagine what it might be, and a cold wad is gathering at the back of her throat. She leaves the swing while her body is still willing, rubs her aching back, picks up the radio.

"I'll let you get on back to Malcolm's supper. I have to get some supper together myself. But I thank you for watchin' after things so close here while I was gone."

Emma ducks inside the screendoor, watches Loretta waddle back across the street. Then she sees the note propped on the hall table:

Dear Aunt Emma, I am going to Philadelphia. Joe Rossy and me we are going to get married. I will write you. Love, Hildy.

Good Lord! Married? Philadelphia? And with a stranger—why, he might be a lunatic! A broken voice rises up in her throat, a dry cackle that causes her to choke on her own words. What chance is it that Philadelphia will be any worse than what she's left behind here?

Emma shuts the front door and leans on it, suddenly feeling out of breath, exhausted, drained. She hugs the big radio to her. She'll put it away and keep it for Hildy. Her Mammaw wanted Hildy to have it, and Emma will see to it that she does.

Oh my Lord, what has she done? She meant to take care of Hildy for Daniel!

. . . 1944 . . . . . Battle of Leyte Gulf, largest naval battle yet, Japanese suffered heavy losses . . . . . FDR elected to 4th term, Harry S Truman vice president . . . . .

Relief reaches Allied
forces in Bastogne,
German columns destroyed . . . . .
Allies push on to Berlin after Battle
of the Bulge . . . . . Major Glen Miller's
plane reported missing in flight
from Paris to London . . . . .

Early 1945
Mahala, Kentucky

Tugging her coat closer around her against the chill, Emma trudges through the remnants of last night's snowfall, up the dirt path from the gravel road to the old home place.

She carries a lard bucket packed full of warm cookies. At least they were warm out of the oven when she left the house. Even this late, the temperature has not risen much above freezing, and the winter sunlight barely holds its own against the approaching storm that is sure to bring on another early night.

Good thing for the workboots of Daddy's that Emma found when they spruced up this old place for Wayne's family. They're a little too big, but with shoe rationing tighter and tighter, they'll do for cold-weather walking until the war's over and there are new ones to be bought, and better yet, tires for the car. What a luxury it seems like now, to drive the mile out to the old home place and back and think nothing of it.

She pauses a few steps from the porch. Electric light brightens the windowpanes against the peeling gray weatherboarding of the house, so much smaller than she sees with the younger eyes of her memory. For a moment she could swear she sees the flicker of the coal oil lamps that Mama used to keep vigilant on the mantel.

Wayne's voice booms from inside the house, "Billy Wayne, get down from there!" but Emma's ears hear Mama's soft reminder, *you look after your little sister, Emma . . . don't let her fall in the fire . . . Yes, Ma'am.*

It seems like that's what she's done all her life—look after other people. And what good does it do? No matter how much you look after them, life itself drives them away from you. And if that's not enough, war comes and takes away your boys, and if they come home at all, they come home crippled.

There were two more this morning from Mahala. The Hargis boy, his bomber shot down over Germany. And Freddie Hite's body was found, so he's no longer missing in action, his brother already gone at Midway Island. The youngest boy Clyde is still at home, pestering his folks to sign for him early, not wanting to wait for his turn with the draft. Emma was at the grocery store waiting for the mail when Mr. Hite took down the blue star from the window and put up the second gold one. At least now since the Sullivan law, they won't take Clyde, no matter how much he's begging to go.

Thank the good Lord the Hites are not like that ignorant woman on the radio from Chicago who said she was proud to give her son, and she wished she had another one to give.

Lord, if this war is driving the women—even the *mothers*—crazy, who else will be left?

The war takes every thought and twists it into a War Effort. The enemy—not the Germans and the Japs, but the war itself— has blurred the lives of every family she knows, including their own. Poor Little Will, like a doll sitting on a shelf, never to change or grow or say another shy word or smile another sweet smile.

The war casualties, do they include Daniel, too, from another time and place? Emma can hardly picture his face anymore. Yes, the blue star that hangs in the back corner of her heart for Daniel is fading to gold, and she hasn't the wherewithal to stop it.

The deep breath she takes in and blows out hangs as a frosty cloud in the winter air. As she starts up the steps, the door flies open and Naomi hurries out, pulling the heavy door closed behind her with a bang. "Oh. Emma!" Naomi quickly wipes her face with the back of her hand. "I didn't know you were comin'!" Emma can see Naomi's been crying, or trying very hard not to.

"Why Naomi, are you comin' out here in this cold without your coat on?"

Naomi leans back on the door. "I . . . I just need a little bit of air." She sits down on the top step and tucks her long, full skirt around her bare legs.

Emma sits next to Naomi, opening her coat to wrap part way around them both.

When Naomi leans into her, Emma can feel sobs gathering, ready to pour out. "Is it anything I can help with, Hon?"

Naomi explodes. "Oh, Emma, what is the matter with men, any-way? Wayne won't shut up about the Jap planes and his ship and . . .

and . . . and Billy Wayne, he's eatin' it up, all the time shootin' us with his broomstock gun Wayne made him, and makin' the girls cry. I'm so tired of it! Wayne heard over the radio his ship is at some island, E-wo somewhere, and you can tell he wishes he was there. You'd reckon this war was the only excitin' thing that ever happened to him!"

Emma hugs Naomi closer to her and lets her cry, rocks a little, tries to hold back her own sobs, waiting and ready to be called up at any time. "You know, Naomi, it probably is. About the biggest thing he ever had before was his baseball games on the radio. And Captain Midnight."

Naomi pulls back and digs a well-used hanky from her pocket, dabs her eyes. "Well, to listen to him, you'd think it was all the same thing. He's even sayin' now that if this baby's a boy we're goin' to name him Marcus something or other after his commandin' officer because he turned on the lights on the ship, or some silly thing."

"Hon, men don't have any way to get their feelin's out like we do. Seems like no matter what they're worried about, or scared of, or mad at, as long as they can keep remindin' the whole world that they're still men, then they can get along all right. I 'spect the only ones they need to remind is their own selves. With his bein' crippled now, he might need a lot of remindin' for a while. It's the way men are, Honey."

The door bursts open and Billy Wayne runs out, shooting his stick back over his shoulder. Wayne's voice roars out the door after him, "Naomi, can't you make these kids be quiet? I'm tryin' to listen to the radio!"

As Billy Wayne dodges around them to the lower steps, Emma grabs the stick and points it back toward the door with the boy hanging onto it. He charges back into the house for another attack and the door slams behind him.

"Lord, Lord," Naomi says, shaking her head, with just the hint of a smile. "And how many of them reminders do you reckon he needs, Emma?"

"Oh, here," Emma says, pulling a slim envelope from her coat pocket. "What I came to tell you was, we finally heard something from Hildy! Here's her address, so now I can send her the insurance checks. She got another one of them today. That's more than $200 she'll be surprised to get. It was just like Little Will to put her name on the insurance. He always tried his best to take care of her, bless his heart." It's a lot of money, Emma thinks, but even $55.10 a month the rest of her life would never make up to her what she's paid for it.

Naomi blows her nose and stuffs the soggy hanky back into her pocket. "Does it sound like she's . . . you know, happy?"

"Well, you know Hildy, she won't say much about herself. But she's goin' to have a baby too. Can you picture Hildy married, with a baby? She didn't say when, but I'll bet it must be about the same time as what is his name? Marcus?"

Emma gets up and smacks the twigs off the back of her coat, picks up the bucket. "Now let's get you back in the house before you freeze and let me give the kids the cookies I brought 'em before I head on back. You know how Wayne used to love his Mammaw's sugar cookies. I hope he won't notice they don't have as much in 'em as they used to. I used up all the sugar I'd saved up." At the door, she adds, "And you know, Naomi, maybe a little Marcus will help bring Wayne home from the war."

Naomi looks like she's considering the idea, but her eyes are not convinced. "Well." She finally gives in, with a weary sigh, pushes a long strand of hair behind her ear. "Some baseball games on the radio this summer won't hurt any either, will they? If anybody's left at home to play. But he's probably a little too big for Captain Midnight, don't you reckon?"

. . . . . *1945* . . . . . *Movies enjoyed greatest year*
in box office history last year . . . . .
U.S. Army taskforce lands on Luzon in
Philippines, 100 miles north of Manila . . . . .
After 36 days of bloody fighting,
island of Iwo Jima falls to Allies. 4,000
US marines killed, 15,000 wounded,
20,000 Japanese killed . . . . .
FDR, age 63, dies in Warm Springs Georgia
of cerebral hemorrhage.
Harry Truman sworn in
as 33rd president . . . . .
United Nations conference opens
in San Francisco with 50 nations represented
. . . . . *Victory in Europe* . . . . . *Hitler dead!*

PART THREE

May 12, 1945
Philadelphia, Pennsylvania

Hildy shifts one way and then the other, trying to get comfortable in the hospital bed, but it's no use. She's never spent so much time in bed in her life.

The baby stirs awake, opens his mouth against the front of the bed jacket that covers Hildy's tightly bound breasts. She stretches to reach the bottle from the night stand.

Two young mothers at the far end of the ward whisper, and one giggles. Let them laugh. Hildy doesn't care one bit.

A familiar form appears in the rectangle of light from the hallway. A young blonde woman in a maternity nurse's uniform peeks into the dimly lit room. Hildy's been hoping Peggy would stop by. Peggy's the only one who's been friendly to her the whole six days that she's been here.

"Hi, Kiddo. I had a hunch you'd be awake. I'm glad somebody got smart and let the mothers feed the babies at night. What few nurses there are left, they can't do everything." Peggy plops her very pregnant self into the chair in the corner near the bed. "How are you feeling tonight? Are you sleeping any better?"

At the other end of the room, the two young mothers are quiet, but when Peggy glares at them, they quickly turn to the business of feeding their babies. Hildy pretends not to notice them. "A little better, I reckon."

Peggy's voice drops to a whisper. "I hope it didn't embarrass you that I heard it all this evening. I almost marched in here and choked that lily-livered husband of yours."

Hildy hasn't thought to be embarrassed. She knows the other girls in the ward whisper about her, but why should she care what a bunch of strangers think? She's never seen any of them before. And she'll never see any of them again either. Who cares what they think?

Peggy says, "Lord, what I'd give for a cigarette. They ration everything else, but it's not fair to take our cigarettes. I'm going nuts." She grunts as she struggles to pull at a shoestring, uses her toes to force the shoe off. "I saw your mother-in-law down there yesterday, looking in the nursery window. She was telling everybody how that baby certainly didn't look like anybody in her family. I was never so glad to see old Battle Axe Filmore go after somebody. I thought she was going to drag that woman to the stairs and throw her down them. I hate to think what you've put up with living with her all this time."

Hildy sets the bottle on the night table and puts the baby to her shoulder. "I reckon she had somebody else all picked out for Joe to marry and she was mad when he brought me home. She used to ask me 'bout every day how far along I was, and count on her fingers."

"Gee, a real witch, huh? I betcha some people wouldn't spell it that way. So, wasn't it . . . I mean he's obviously full term, and . . . listen, I'm sorry. I didn't mean to be nosy."

When Hildy tries to shift the baby to the other shoulder, her pillow slides out from behind her and onto the floor. Peggy reaches over and nabs it with her toes, raises it barely high enough off the floor to grab it with her outstretched fingers, then struggles to get herself up from the chair. "Here, Kiddo, let me have him and you put this back the way you want it."

Hildy's grateful for a chance to rearrange her bedding. She feels awkward holding the baby, as if she doesn't have enough arms.

Peggy wanders to the window, one shoe on and one shoe off, humming softly to the baby. She pulls back the curtain and peers out the window. "They're still celebrating down there. A hundred years ago when I was still young, I'd have been out there dancing with them." To the baby she croons, "William Roosevelt Rossi, you don't know it yet, but you were born on a real important day. They're calling it V-E Day, and by the time you're old enough to know it, this war will be in your history book, thank God." To Hildy, she says, "Are you going to call him Billy?"

"Will," Hildy says. "Will, for my brother."

A huge shadow fills the doorway, and Head Nurse Filmore peers into the dimness. "Nurse!" she barks at Peggy, "whatever are you doing here? I'm quite sure you have other duties elsewhere!"

"No, ma'am, I've finished my shifts—two of them today—and I just stopped by to see my friend before I go on home. She's had a rough day today."

Nurse Filmore squints and leans into the doorway to look at Hildy, then rolls her eyes. "I can just imagine she has," she mutters and heads on down the hall.

Peggy chuckles, hands the baby back to Hildy. She sinks into the chair, pulls at her other shoestring. "So the old witch . . . the other one, I mean your mother-in-law . . . is she really going to make him get the marriage annulled? I can't believe he'd be so gutless and not stand up for you. What a mama's boy."

"But Joe, he can't help it, he's not—"

"Oh, Hildy, don't make excuses for him. He fought the Germans! He should be able to fight off his own mother. You're way better off without him. Blood's thicker than water, especially Italian blood."

Peggy manages to get one foot up across the other knee, and massages her stockinged toes. "So have you thought about what you're gonna do? Now that's a silly question, isn't it? That's probably all you *can* think of. But don't you worry. I think I've got an answer for you. Well, what it is, is an answer to prayer for *me*. My aunt keeps my little girl for me at night when I'm here, and I had no idea what I was going to do when this new baby came. Aunt Carrie wants to go live with her own daughter in Kansas, and she's stuck with me."

She puts the one foot back on the floor and struggles to lift the other one. "So it occurred to me, what if you came home with me next week? You could stay as long as you want, 'til you decide what you want to do. We could help each other. We haven't known each other very long, but I can tell we'd get along fine, can't you?"

The baby starts to fuss, and Hildy wonders what to do. What do babies want? How can she tell?

"Rub his back, Kiddo. He just needs to burp, that's all."

Hildy moves her fingers on the baby's back, and he rewards her with a belch. She lays him down across her lap and tries to smooth down his nightgown. "But won't your husband be comin' home soon, now that they've done fightin' over there?"

"They're saying the boys in Europe will just be sent right to the Pacific. But even if he isn't, since he's an officer, he'll probably stay until after the regular troops are sent home. I wish he could be here when this baby comes, but I'm not even going to hope."

She tries to stuff her feet into her shoes, but has no luck. She finally gives up and sags back into the chair. They both sit quiet for a few minutes. Peggy rolls her head from side to side, rubs her neck, and Hildy just stares unseeing at the open door.

Peggy yawns, stretches her legs out in front of her. "I'd rather he'd be stuck in Germany for the whole occupation than sent to the Pacific." She shivers. "At least he'd not be going to fight those awful Japs. I heard their women don't cry at all, that they're *happy* to have their boys die in the war."

A nurse about Peggy's age appears at the door. "Mrs. Rossi, I'll take your baby back to the nursery now." She tucks a stray lock of brown hair back under her cap and smiles. "Lucky you, going home. I've got . . . " She looks at her watch. " . . . three hours and twenty-two minutes more to go."

"Well, you better not enjoy it too much, Sarah. Old Battle Axe is in a foul mood tonight."

Sarah lays the baby in the middle of the receiving blanket and swaddles it tightly around him, tucks him expertly into the crook of her elbow and scoops up the empty bottle. She stops at the door and peeks out, then whispers back, "Oh, yeah? And when is she not?"

Hildy leans back on the pillows, pulls her knees up, tenting the sheet. "I've got money, so I could pay you. Joe gave me money. He snuck and did it behind his mama's back. And I've got my brother's war money every month." She pauses a moment, looking down at her hands. "I've been thinkin' a lot about him today. He always said he would find some way to send me money, but I didn't know the only way would be for him to . . . do this." She takes a deep breath, dabs her eyes with the corner of her starched sheet.

Peggy stretches her hand out and Hildy, puzzled, realizes Peggy wants her to take it. She leans over and accepts it. Peggy squeezes her hand and says, "It's so sweet that you named your baby for him. I'm sure he'd be proud."

Hildy lets go of Peggy's hand and leans back against her pillows.

"Anyway, Joe's mama said we should give it to her, the money, I mean. Joe said no, I ought to keep that for the baby."

"Well, I'm glad to hear he had *some* nerve about him. And he's right, you save that for your Will. Just being there with Rhonda would be more than enough for me, and we can even trade off. But to tell you the truth, your stamps would really help. We could do real well, putting them together. Maybe we can get a can of Spam *every* Sunday! Lord, when this war's over, if I never see another can of Spam 'til I'm a hundred, it'll be soon enough."

"His mama told him I ought to get the doctor to find somebody to adopt my baby out."

"Oh, Kiddo, you'll do just fine with him. Lots of girls are raising their kids by themselves. Gosh knows I feel like I am, too."

Hildy stretches her legs as far as she can, runs her hands over her now-flat belly. "Well, all I know is he's mine, and not hers to decide about."

"That's the spirit, Kiddo. Listen, I'd better be getting on home before I go to sleep in this chair. You think about what I said and let me know tomorrow."

She studies her flopping shoes. "Do you suppose if I could get my feet up on that bed railing one at a time, you could lean down and tie my shoes?" She smiles, looks at her watch. "Otherwise I don't know how I'm going to get to the bus in time, like this." Hildy reaches down and ties the shoe offered her, then the other one. She leans back onto her pillow and watches Peggy push herself up from the chair, then struggle to put on her coat.

"Uh, Joe and me? You wanted to know?" Hildy says, "We just got married last October."

Peggy's face goes blank for a couple of seconds, then she leans in close and whispers, "Listen, Hildy." She looks pointedly at the young mothers across the ward and says, "Don't you go thinking that's anybody else's business but yours, okay?"

She smiles and pats Hildy's shoulder. "You let me know in the morning, all right?"

Early the next week
Philadelphia, Pennsylvania

Hildy pushes up the sleeve of her smock and shakes a few drops of milk onto her wrist, the way Peggy showed her. The maternity smock she wore from the hospital this morning hangs limp and loose on her. Only ten days ago, she almost filled it up. She listens to the voices from the other room. "Aunt Carrie, Hildy and I will do just fine. You go right on ahead to Jeannie's, and don't think another thing about it."

Hildy waits at the kitchen door until they notice she's there, then brings the bottle over to the bassinet—Peggy's bassinet, with new blue lining and ruffles, all ready for the baby boy she's hoping for. Baby Will is waking up, just starting to fuss. Hildy changes his diaper, then settles onto the sofa to wait until it's time to feed him.

Peggy's aunt is all right. A little bossy, but nice. She's not like Joe's mama at all.

Aunt Carrie goes on, "Well, when I was your age, girls didn't live alone without a chaperone, even . . . " She nods in Hildy's direction. "Even widows."

"Aunt Carrie, things are different now. Lots of war brides and, uh, *widows* are putting up together and helping each other out."

Hildy's mind registers their word . . . *widows?* Peggy gives her a tiny headshake and hurries on, "So just don't you worry, Aunt Carrie, and you give Cousin Jeannie my love, all right?"

Aunt Carrie fusses with the doily on the coffee table, reaches for the little red cereal bowl, but Peggy beats her to it and helps herself to the last of the dry cereal. "And you're spoiling Rhonda Anne," Aunt Carrie insists, "letting her have that breakfast food. The Book says they shouldn't have that foolishness."

Will's fussing gets louder, more urgent, and Peggy wanders over to the bassinet. Hildy sits on the sofa with the bottle.

"Hildy," Peggy says, looking at her watch. "You go ahead and feed him. You don't have to wait."

Aunt Carrie comes bustling over. "Now, see what I'm talking about? The Book says to make him wait until the proper time, and let him cry. Crying is good for babies . . . it's their exercise. You girls—"

"Aunt Carrie!" Peggy interrupts. "You go ahead and feed him, Hildy. He's a big baby and he knows when he's hungry. Aunt Carrie, we'll do just fine."

"But the Book says—"

"Well, I think a baby knows more about when he's hungry than some damned old book that's been around since about 1800." Her voice rises to cover the baby's wails. "I read an article by a new baby doctor that said Holt was too strict, that you can listen to your baby. He knows what he needs."

"That's ridiculous! Any decent mother knows Dr. Holt is—" She is interrupted by a loud honk from the street.

"There's your taxi. Now, Aunt Carrie, thanks so much for all your help. I could never have made it without you."

Hildy picks up the baby, who sucks angrily on first one fist and then the other. His cry is so frantic that she has to force the bottle nipple into his mouth before he realizes it is there and attacks it.

Aunt Carrie heaves a disapproving sigh, conspicuous in the sudden quiet. She snaps the suitcase closed, gives Peggy a perfunctory hug and turns to Hildy. "I'm so sorry to hear about your husband, dear, and you so young and . . . " She pats the baby's head. "And everything."

Behind Aunt Carrie, Peggy touches her finger to her lips. Hildy says, "Oh, uh, yes ma'am, thank you, uh . . . you have yourself a good train trip now." The baby sucks greedily until he has to stop to take a snort of a breath.

Aunt Carrie's eyebrows register her protest of the early feeding. As she bustles to the door with her suitcase Peggy follows and holds the door open for her. The older woman starts down the steps, and Peggy closes the door gently until it clicks. "Kiddo, I'm sorry. I thought—"

The door pops open. "I don't suppose I should wake Rhonda Anne and tell her goodbye," Aunt Carrie says. But before Peggy can answer, her aunt turns and goes out the door again, mumbling, "No, I guess it's easier this way."

"I'll tell her you're going to come back and visit soon," Peggy calls after her aunt, "And you will . . . won't you . . . " Once more, she closes the door, but waits, as if she doesn't trust it to stay closed.

Hildy sets the empty bottle down and pulls the baby up to her shoulder. She's getting a little better at this. Seems like he already feels heavier than he did last week.

Still peeking back at the door, Peggy eases herself onto the sofa and props her feet on the coffee table. "I love her dearly, but we've been around and around about this for the last month, and she was really starting to get on my nerves. She's never approved of my finishing nursing school while Donald's gone, 'cause she's sure he'll just want me to quit as soon as he get home. 'A woman's place is in the home', you know. And she's always—well, you saw most of the rest."

"What was that book she's always talkin' about?"

"Oh, it's the damned old baby-raising book that's been around forever. Says you can't hold your baby or rock him, 'cause you'll *spoil* him."

"My Mammaw always used to rock us, but I don't remember her ever readin' any book about it. Least I don't reckon they talk about it in the Bible."

She puts the baby back into the bassinet, and he goes to sleep, exhausted from his frenzied lunch.

"Too bad." Peggy laughs. "'Thou shalt rock thy children'. But you know some oldtimers would probably take that to mean the same as stoning them."

"What did she . . . your aunt . . . what did she mean—"

"Oh. That. I'm sorry, Kiddo. She kept wanting to know more about your husband, and I just told her he died in France. I really didn't think she'd actually mention it. Sometimes it's easier just to lie a little than to get into the truth."

She reaches over and pats Hildy's knee. "You might think about that yourself, Hildy. You keep that wedding ring on as long as you want to. It's not anybody else's business."

"Mommy?" Peggy's almost-three-year-old daughter Rhonda comes down the hall from the bedroom, her blonde hair matted and her face flushed pink from sleep. She heads straight for the red cereal bowl on the coffee table. "Mommy! Somebody ate 'em all up!"

With both her hands braced on the coffee table, Peggy pushes herself up from the sofa, straightens her skirt and takes the bowl from her daughter.

"Do you s'pose it was Goldilocks? Come on, Rhonnie, Mommy'll get you some." Over her shoulder, she says to Hildy, laughing, "You'll do fine with Rhonda, as long as we've got plenty of Cheerioats. And as long as that damned old book stays out of it."

"Mommy doesn't like the *dammo* book," Rhonda says. Peggy's laugh rings out from the kitchen. Shyness overtakes Rhonda, and she scampers after her mother.

At the kitchen door, Peggy says, "I almost forgot. We found that box over there on the front step this morning with your name on it. Some things of yours they sent over?"

Hildy drags the cardboard box over to the sofa, pulls out the blue sweater and the print dress she wore the day she left Mahala with Joe, the night they stood in front of the justice of the peace. The dress his mother said looked too *country* and insisted on picking out some proper clothes for her.

Rhonda sits at the edge of the oval braided rug, content with her red bowl of dry cereal, but Peggy comes back to the sofa. "Is this . . . all they sent?"

"I told him all I wanted was what was mine." Hildy digs into the box and brings out her hand mirror, the one Mammaw left her, and oh! *Silas Marner*. She hasn't thought about *Silas Marner* for months. She really shouldn't have taken it. It belonged to Mrs. Stanfill, but Hildy wanted to finish it.

Mrs. Stanfill. The name sounds strange and unfamiliar now. That was all such a long time ago.

"Well, Kiddo," Peggy says, picking up the dress, "I don't think this is going to fit you anymore. You're filled out some from the baby, I've got plenty of dresses I'm not using—let's find you something." She folds the dress and puts it back into the box. "And if you don't mind, I could probably get a few wearings out of that smock you have on. See? We can help each other out all kinds of ways, can't we?"

. . . . . *June, 1945* . . . . . *Japan surrenders*
Okinawa after 2 months of deadly struggle.
100,000 Japanese killed, almost 13,000 Americans
killed, 40,000 wounded . . . First atomic bomb
test detonated in Alamogordo New Mexico . . . . .
August 6, 1945 President Truman: "Today, an
atomic bomb dropped on Hiroshima, a naval base
in Japan . . . U.S. will continue to bomb until
Japan's ability to wage war is destroyed". . . .
Nagasaki bombed, city leveled . . . . .
Japan surrenders! WAR IS OVER!

Four months later
Mahala, Kentucky

Dear Hildy,
Hon, I have worried so about you, not hearing
from you since last winter. I wish you would have
written us that your husband was lost at Okinawa.

I would have insisted that you come on home so we could take care of you until your baby came.

I am so sorry Honey. Joe was a good boy, I'm sure of it. Such a shame he didn't live to see his baby boy.

We all thank the Lord every day that the war is finally over. So many were lost, eleven in all from the county. Honey, I hope you will think about coming on back home as soon as you and the baby are able to travel. You didn't say what day he was born, but we would all love to see him, and you too. I'm glad you named him for Little Will. I know he will be a blessing to you in your grieving. And your granddaddy would have been proud too, for as you know your brother was named for him.

Wayne and Naomi have a new baby too. They named him Marcus and he was one month old yesterday. That makes four now. Your mama is the same as always.

I'll close for now, but Honey I wish you would think about coming home at least for a little while.

      Love, Aunt Emma

. . . . . *September 1945* . . . . . *First Nobel Prizes awarded since 1938, Peace Prize to the International Red Cross and to former Secretary of State Cordell Hull for his part in the establishment of the United Nations* . . . . .

October, 1945
Philadelphia, Pennsylvania

Hildy pulls yet another clean diaper from the mound on the floor, folds it and adds it to the top of the stack on the coffee table. Who would have thought three dozen brand new Birdseyes could make somebody so happy? Peggy was so excited when she brought them home— but then Peggy gets excited about everything, seems like. She was right, though. Another few months of shortages and they'd have to do what the dammo book says and potty train the babies at five months whether they liked it or not.

Peggy's three-month-old Judy, propped into the corner of the sofa on pillows, blows sleepy bubbles on her fists. Hildy can feel five-month-old Will's stare from his pillow nest at the other end of the sofa. Why does he watch her like that? She ought to say something to him, but what do people say to babies?

When the front door latch rattles, Hildy hurries to the door. Peggy struggles in with two big sacks of groceries. Hildy takes the biggest one on into the kitchen, but Peggy sets her bag down on the coffee table. "Hi, Sweetie, how's Mommy's angel?" Judy coos, sucks her fist, flashes a sleepy smile.

Peggy calls to Hildy, "It's almost fun to go to the store again. I was so sick of counting out stamps and points." She kicks off her shoes. "And where's our Willyumyum—there he is!" Will crows like one of Mammaw's old roosters.

"Look," Peggy says, digging into the bag. She pulls out a white paper-wrapped package. "I got us a pot roast! Can you believe it? And look what else!" She pulls out butter, the *Family Circle* magazine, two cans of carrots, a pint carton, then a second one. "Next to bananas, I've missed ice cream the most! And Willyumyum, you're going to have it, no matter what that dammo book says!" Will kicks his feet and waves his arms wildly, smacking himself in the face, startled, then he laughs at his own silliness.

"I swear, Hildy, I think he understands every word we say to him! That's what I said, Yumyum—that dammo book!" Will laughs outloud again and inhales the rooster noise. Hildy goes back to her stack of diapers. "Seems like I just scare him when I talk to him."

Peggy takes the ice cream cartons into the kitchen, yells back to Hildy, "There was something in the mailbox, but my hands were full. Want to get it?"

Hildy comes back with the letter just as Peggy is making herself comfortable on the sofa between the babies.

"Why don't you try singing to him?" She turns to Will and sings, "Hush little baby, don't say a word . . . Mama's gonna buy you a"—she pokes a finger into his chubby belly—"dammo book!" Will giggles, ducks his head, suddenly shy. "See?" Peggy says, "That dammo book is good for something—just to make our babies laugh!"

Hildy sits back on the floor by the coffee table, pulls at the flap on the letter. "I never could sing good."

"Oh, Hildy, babies don't care. They just love to hear our happy voices." Judy has dropped off to sleep, but Will struggles to sit up. Peggy takes his hands and pulls him up. His chubby legs go rigid in her lap. "You're such a good baby, Yumyum." She snuggles him into her lap and kisses the top of his head. Then she says to Hildy, "Didn't your mother sing to you when you were little?"

Hildy stares at the envelope, but her memory searches for singing. The only singing that comes to her mind is the music at the church. And of course the Grand Ol' Opry on Mammaw's old radio. She wishes she'd brought the old radio with her, but Joe said he'd get her a newer one. He never did.

She pulls out the folded sheet of yellow stationery with roses and Aunt Emma's familiar handwriting. Another sheet of paper, lined with writing she doesn't recognize, drops out onto the table. She looks over Aunt Emma's stationery, then unfolds the tablet page.

"Nothing from Donald," Peggy says. "I really didn't expect it. He's acting like such a stinker and I don't feel like arguing with him today. You know something, Kiddo? I counted up last night, and altogether Donald and I have only been together twenty-seven days. In almost four years of being married, we've been together not even a month. We knew each other two weeks when we got married, then off he went, and I was left here by myself, pregnant. You think Aunt Carrie was down my neck last summer? You should have seen her then!"

Will has melted into a sleeping lump on Peggy's lap. She gets up, rearranges his pillows and lays him down, moves to the easy chair. "And then there was the furlough before he shipped overseas last year, and he was off again. And of course I was pregnant. Again."

She picks up the tiny framed photograph from the end table. "Sometimes it seems like I'm just married to this picture." She blows dust from the photograph, wipes it with her sleeve, and puts it back. "You got another letter from back home so soon? Everything okay?"

"Everybody's all right. Aunt Emma says the trees are real pretty this year. She knew how much I always loved the yellow and orange leaves in the fall. She sent a letter from Liam—well, from his wife. He never did much like to write." She pushes herself to her feet, scoops up the stack of diapers, hugs them to her. "They're movin' to California as soon as he gets discharged, but his wife's not goin' to let him farm like he wants to. She's goin' to make him get a job in a store or something."

Peggy props her feet on the coffee table, rubs her forehead hard. "Shoot, I'd never get away with that with Donald—trying to tell him what to do! No, he'd be 'way too busy telling *me* what to do." She's up from the chair again. "It makes me so mad, the way some girls *want* that! Deanna, one of the student nurses, said she can't wait 'til her husband gets home, so he can tell her when to breathe in and when to breathe out. She even sent him the checkbook when she couldn't get it to balance, and him off in a foxhole! If I had my choice, I think I'd rather be like your sister-in-law. At least she's willing to try to get what she wants."

Hildy chews on her thumbnail, watches Peggy pace. She wonders if anything would ever make her as excited as Peggy gets over some new Birdseye diapers or damned old books or student nurses and what they're wanting.

Peggy fishes a cigarette and lighter from her purse and plops down into the chair again. After a few puffs, she puts it out in the ashtray on the end table, settles back into the chair, puts her feet up again. Her anger is gone as fast as it came, but her eyes are cloudy. "You know," she says, "I hate to admit this, but I'm kind of scared of how it'll be when Donald gets back here. I'm going to miss things like they are now, with just you and me and our babies." She reaches over and strokes Will's wisp of brown hair. "I hope you stay here close."

"Lana . . . well, you know, my friend Lou Ann . . . she changed her name to Lana . . . she's talkin' about me movin' to California with her. She says maybe when she's in movies, I can get a job sewin' her fancy dresses like Joan Crawford wears. You know, the sparkly ones she wore in Mildred Pierce."

"Oh, Hildy! I wish you'd stay away from the likes of her, with her Hollywood airs. As if selling tickets at the show makes her some movie star material. She's cheap, Hildy—and those awful boys she tries to fix you up with! This Charlie she's been bringing around—Kiddo, I know his type. He's only after one thing!"

Charlie's not so bad, Hildy wants to say, but maybe she'd better not. He drinks a little too much, but he's not so bad.

Peggy piles the rest of the groceries back into the bag, leaving the *Family Circle*. "Take a look at this. It's got a swell article about kids' toys. Says it's okay for boys to play with dolls. Oh, Donald would go for that . . . you bet he would! I thought I wanted a boy and a girl, but I'm glad now I got my two little girls. Maybe at least he won't want to raise them like little soldiers, like he was talking—*his* son was going to do this, *his* son was going to be like that. I hope he's over that before we have any boys."

"Mommy?" Rhonda's sleepy voice comes from the bedroom down the hall. Peggy goes to retrieve her. Hildy studies the envelope on the coffee table in front of her, pulls out Aunt Emma's yellow stationery sheet again.

> Wayne was going to college over in Bowling Green on the G.I. Bill, but Naomi has talked him into taking a job with her family's furniture business over in Asheville. Wayne says he'll do it if I quit my sewing business and go with them. I am going to be 50 years old next year and the arthritis in my fingers is getting worse so I reckon I wouldn't mind having some time to grow some roses.
>
> We are selling the sawmill and my house in town both to Sam Luther, a veteran Wayne knows from Bowling Green.
>
> Do you remember old Brother Earl Spivey? He wants to look after your mama, so I am going to keep the old home place and let him live in it. I don't know why he feels like it's his place to see to her. He says everybody has a place and mine is with my grandkids so I should go and not feel bad about it.

"Tell you what." Peggy comes back, with sleep-grumpy Rhonda trailing along behind her, wearing just her panties. Peggy sits on the edge of the coffee table, pulls Rhonda to her, tries to match little girl legs to the overall legs. "Let's save the i-c-e-c-r-e-a-m 'til later when the babies are up, and if you don't mind, I'll take Rhonda over to the park for an hour or so. We're not going to have many more pretty days like this. And I think she's feeling a little j-e-a-l-o-u-s."

"Mommy, I want a-e-o-o-s," Rhonda whines.

Will stirs, and Hildy heads for the kitchen for his bottle. Too late—he's already working up an angry fuss.

As she heats the milk, she listens. Peggy's words are for Rhonda, but she has taken on the sound she uses for fussy babies. Will settles into an impatient whimper.

Hildy pulls the rubber nipple onto the bottle, stops on her way back to the living room to watch. Rhonda tickles Will's bare foot, and Will rewards her with a giggle. "See, Mommy? That means he loves me," she says, nodding with three-year-old authority.

Peggy buttons Rhonda's overall straps, and Will starts to fuss again as Hildy comes in with his bottle.

"He doesn't love Aunt Hildy," Rhonda says.

With an embarrassed look at Hildy, Peggy picks up the crying baby and hands him to her over Rhonda's head. "Oh, Kiddo, you know how kids say things."

She leads Rhonda back to the chair and picks up the hairbrush. "Honey, of course he loves his own mommy. Babies always love their own mommies!"

After the house is quiet and Will's most urgent hunger is satisfied, Hildy allows herself to settle back onto the sofa, shifts the baby's weight from her lap to the plump cushions. He stares cross-eyed at the bright rickrack on the front of her dress as he sucks lazily at the bottle.

Why don't you try singing to him? Words call to her from the time when she was little, from a far off time that was for another little girl, a tiny girl that Hildy feels no kinship with. Back to the only singing she remembers, when she was not much bigger than her baby is now.

Standing standing standing in the needoprare . . . whatever were they saying? All around her, feet stood only on the same sawdust-covered ground that she stood on. She knew those feet well. When everybody stood up, tiny Hildy was lost in the forest of legs and feet, all claiming to be standing in whatever this *needoprare* might be.

Over on the other side of Liam, Mama sang loud, "it's me, it's me, it's me, oh Lord, standin' in the *needoprare*" . . . and Hildy looked puzzled at Mama's fat feet, pouring over the sides of her shoes. On this side Brother Renshaw sang even louder, "it's me, it's me" . . . and Hildy looked at *his* feet. It must be a funny game . . . whatever was it?

Then old Sister Hubert's voice behind Hildy claimed *she* was the one. "It's me! It's me!" Hildy forgot Mama and the preacher and climbed up onto her folding chair on her knees, gazing up at Sister Hubert, who stood so close to the chair that the belly of her dress hung over the back of it, wiping softly against Hildy's hands, back and forth as the old woman swayed with the music. Sister Hubert smiled and stopped clapping long enough to pat Hildy's cheeks, but her jaws kept up with the music and her bare gums mouthed the jumble of words, "it's me, it's me, it's me oh, Lord . . . standin' in the *needoprare.*"

Hildy touched the warm place where soft old fingers had touched, and she giggled.

A yank on her dresstail, and Liam insisted, "Get down!" just before the hard whack on the back of her legs. Mama's face leaned over in front of Liam. Her big hand whacked again at bare legs.

Biting her lips tight together, Hildy turned around and sat still in her chair, not looking to either side, pulling her shoulders up nearly to her ears. The soft caress on her cheek was gone. Now the sting of red welts on her legs was all she could feel. Above it all, the screeching and the loud music hurt her head. She pressed her hands to her ears to close out the silly, silly words. Who cared what a *needoprare* was anyway?

After the last of the milk is drained, baby Will gums the soft rubber nipple hanging from his mouth, and settles back against Hildy.

She closes her eyes and lets her body sway softly with his heartbeat that she can feel where his head presses against her breast.

Another far-off memory pushes itself gently into her mind: her own ear nestled against a hard chest, rough fabric against her face and a sweaty arm around her tiny shoulders.

Then a different time, the weight of a coat, heavy on her little shoulders, and a muffled voice echoing from far back inside her heart . . . *take care of her . . . take care of her.*

A soft tear slides unbidden down her cheek, and the soft voice whispers from farther and farther away. A memory-picture of her Mammaw lingers for an instant just inside her eyelids.

He loved you, Hildy.

Hildy's arm tightens around her own baby and she awkwardly

bends to kiss him on the top of his head. At the touch he struggles to twist himself to look up into her face . . . the expectant stare, but softer this time.

Why don't you try singing to him?

Barely more than a whisper . . . her voice cracking at first . . . she starts the only song that comes to her mind, "just as I am, without one . . ." The words slip into that shadowy place behind her memory. After a few *hmmmm-hmmmmms* they trail off to nothing.

Will stares at her, and the bottle nipple drops unnoticed from his mouth. With a giggle that surprises them both, Hildy blurts out, "without that dammo book!"

Will grins and buries his face shyly in the front of her dress. She squeezes him so tightly that he grunts and struggles to get free.

He loves you. You hear me, child?

A tear escapes and slips down the side of her face.

Yes, Ma'am.

Early 1946
Philadelphia, Pennsylvania

Hildy finishes drying the few dishes that she used for their simple supper—her own soup bowl, Rhonda's divided dish with clown faces around the edge, the baby bottles from all day.

She checks the coffee table. With nine-month-old Will pulling up to everything, they don't dare leave anything in reach of his grabby little hands.

She's not really interested in hearing music, but she twists the dial on the radio until she finds some that's not too noticeable. It's just that the house is so quiet. She could go on to bed, but sometimes Judy still wakes up around midnight, Peggy's usual time home from the hospital. With Peggy gone for the night, Hildy wants to get Judy from the bedroom before she wakes up the other two. What would she do with all three crying at once in the middle of the night?

So peculiar, how Donald wanted Peggy to meet him somewhere without bringing Rhonda and Judy. Peggy said she wasn't sure if she should be mad, or just glad to see him alone first. After all, there was a lot to talk about. She took her overnight bag, figuring they'd both be back here tomorrow.

Knowing Peggy won't be home tonight makes the house seem so much quieter. And the night so much longer.

Hildy dreads meeting Donald. It means she's going to have to find a new place. She pats the cushions on the sofa, smoothes the dents in the well-worn seats. Such a cozy house, Peggy's—her mama's, before she died. Her mama must have been a good woman.

A key turns in the front door lock and Hildy jumps, startled.

"Oh. Hi, Kiddo. I assumed you'd be asleep." Peggy gives her face a swipe with her coat sleeve, manages a little smile. "I must look a mess." She does look like she's been crying. She drops her overnight bag by the closet door and takes off her coat, retrieves her lighter and a cigarette from her purse before she puts it in the closet.

Hildy takes a place at the end of the sofa, holds her questions, waits for Peggy to collapse into the chair. "There's some coffee left if you want it," she says.

"Oh, no thanks." Peggy nods toward the bedroom. "Kids all right?" She doesn't look too worried about the answer. She takes off her open-toed pumps, pulls up her skirt and unhooks her garters, slips her stockings off.

"Okay," she says. "I might as well tell you all of it right now." She takes a deep breath and stretches back into the chair, wiggles her bare toes out in front of her. "You know how Donald has stopped arguing about my going to school and—well, everything, lately?" She lights the cigarette, takes a long drag from it and blows the smoke out across the room. "Well, turns out all this time he's telling me he doesn't know when he'll be sent home, he's got a girlfriend he met in Paris last fall. He's brought her back with him and he wants me to give him a divorce."

She gets up, anger rising in her voice. "So, this stranger that I've been having second and third thoughts about being married to sits across a table in a restaurant telling me he doesn't want to be married to me either. And you know what? It made me so mad that I threw a cup at him! He was lucky they hadn't poured the coffee yet." She laughs, but it sounds like she had to think about it before she remembered how.

Once again Hildy feels half of herself drawing back from Peggy's burst of emotion, and the other half drawn like a moth on a coal oil lamp chimney trying to reach the flame inside. She shivers, wraps her arms tightly across her chest.

Peggy says, "I was halfway home in the cab before I figured out what made me so mad. It was because *I* never would've had the nerve to ask *him* for a divorce. I'd have gone right on twisting myself out of shape to be what he wanted. And I darn sure wouldn't have cheated on him." She jabs the cigarette butt into the ash tray, goes to her purse for another one. "So it's *me* I'm mad at, not him! Doesn't make much sense, does it? I hardly know him, but I know me only too well, don't I?" She forces a laugh, but tears puddle in her already red eyes.

Peggy looks at the cigarette. "I hope you never start smoking. Hildy. We all thought it was cute back in my rebellious youth days. Of course, to hear Aunt Carrie tell it, I'm still in 'em." She puts the cigarette back into her purse. "I can just imagine what she'd have to say about it now. Most likely 'I told you so!' "

She comes back to the chair, once again calm, but she looks old and haggard.

"Anyway, Kiddo, we've got a lot more to talk about tomorrow morning. I hope you didn't come up with any other plans yet, like running off to Hollywood with"—she waves her hand and bats her eyelashes—"la-de-dah Lana. Shoot. Next thing, she'll be trying to talk you into changing your name to Hedy." Her laugh sounds like it's rattling around in the bottom of a bucket. Hildy's sure this doesn't mean the same as funny.

"Charlie says—"

"Hildy, I hope you see through that Charlie character before he talks you into anything. Is he still running around in that uniform? There's not much call for war heroes when it comes to getting jobs. His type is only out for one thing." She leans her elbows on the coffee table and rubs circles into her temples. "Shoot, they're *all* only out for one thing."

Hildy chews on her bottom lip, runs her finger along the flower pattern in the arm of the sofa. "But he says he wants us to get married . . . someday."

Peggy comes around and sits on the edge of the coffee table in front of Hildy, takes Hildy's hand in both of hers. "Hon, I can tell you, he's not the marrying kind. I've met too many of them. And I'll bet he's not wanting to wait 'til someday for . . . *you* know."

Hildy turns her head away, can't look Peggy in the eye. Charlie loves her. He says he does, and he promises he'll always stop before it's too late, that he won't go all the way. Peggy means well, but she doesn't know Charlie. She doesn't understand. "But he says I'm the best thing that's ever happened to him."

"Kiddo, you're young, you don't have much experience with men, even if you are divorced and have a kid." She drops Hildy's hand and stands up. "Oh, yeah, you bet you're the best thing that ever happened to him."

"But he . . . he says he needs me."

"Well, you don't need him. Your baby boy, he needs you."

Peggy disappears into the kitchen. Hildy can hear her rummaging in the silverware drawer.

She brings back two bottles of Nehigh grape soda, opened. "I'm sorry, Hildy. I don't mean to be telling you what to do. But you're like a little sister to me, and I don't want to see you get in trouble again."

Hildy feels like she's going to cry, and if she does cry, she doesn't want Peggy to see her. She takes a sip of the soda pop and swallows with a noisy gulp that she's sure Peggy can hear.

"Just curious," Peggy says. "How long did you know you and Joe know each other before you got married?"

As Hildy chews a fingernail a familiar nauseous rumbling starts in the bottom of her stomach. "The same day," she says.

"Oh." Peggy takes a long drink of her soda. "So, did your old boyfriend, did he ever know about the . . . know you were pregnant? And you were only, what, sixteen? How old was he?"

Hildy stares at the coffee table. Images squeeze themselves into her focus like a crowd of ghosts, shadowy things, all moving their lips, but none making itself into words.

One figure forces itself to the front, but it is only a fuzzy outline. Somebody familiar, but she can't quite make out . . . who. She hugs her arms to her chest, suddenly feeling chilly.

"Hildy?"

Hildy knows she should answer and she means to, but nothing comes to her mind in real words to say. She intends to answer, but there's . . . no . . . answer . . . there, and she can feel her body—but not her body, really—pulling back from Peggy's voice.

She tries to remember Peggy's question, but it's strangely not there to remember.

Peggy scoops up her shoes and stockings from the floor and starts for the bedroom. "I'm sorry Kiddo, it's none of my business. I'm just trying to say that you've been lucky so far, getting out with no scars and a beautiful baby boy. But you've got to be careful, that's all I'm saying."

She stops at the bedroom door. "Well, I can promise you one thing. I'm going to find me a guy who treats me right, and who loves my little girls, and who doesn't try to tell me when to inhale and exhale.

And if he's not out there somewhere, well, then, I'm not settling for any other kind. I'll just go it by myself, first."

Hildy tries to manage a smile, but doesn't feel much like smiling. She can feel Peggy watching her, waiting for her to look up, so she forces herself to raise her eyes. Peggy holds up her pop bottle and says, "Like Mildred Pierce said, Kiddo, cheers to the men we have loved—the stinkers, all of 'em!"

"I don't think it was Mildred, it was—"

"I know. I know. Whoever it was." She yawns and that makes Hildy yawn, too.

"You go on and get some sleep, Kiddo," Peggy says. "Big Sister is home, a hundred years older, and free. And maybe by in the morning she'll have sense enough to be more relieved than mad. Then we can make us some big plans."

. . . . . 1946 . . . . . ENIAC, first electronic digital computer dedicated. Weighed 30 tons, filled a 30x60 foot room . . . . .

Spring of the same year
Philadelphia, Pennsylvania

"You swing, Mommy!" Rhonda scrapes her shoes on the bare ground under the playground swing and jumps out as it lurches to a stop. Peggy obediently takes her place on the swing and Rhonda scampers around behind her to push.

Hildy keeps her own feet rooted firmly on the ground, but it's no use. She thought a swing would be a comfortable place to sit, but her stomach feels even the slight sway from the almost nonexistent breeze. She climbs her hands up the swing chain and stands up, pulls the wide strap of a swing seat away from her backside and tries to straighten her smock.

She finds herself an empty spot on the pallet under the tree where the babies nap, exhausted from their day in the fresh air.

"You're too big, Mommy," Rhonda announces, with her hands on her hips. Peggy gives up the swing and joins Hildy on the pallet.

"Kiddo," she says, "you look a little green around the gills. Let me find you a cracker or something." She digs into the picnic basket and comes up with a baby toast. "With both of mine, I was feeling pretty good by four months. Were you sick a lot with Yum?"

Hildy pulls at her memory but her first pregnancy is a shadowy blur . . . funny, she can't even remember when she first thought about it. The first image that comes to her is Joe, impatient, asking her questions. "I don't think I was," she says.

"How could you ever forget? I threw up three times a day with both of mine, in the beginning."

Ten-month-old Judy's eyes pop open. She sits up with the frantic look of a baby surprised at finding herself in the park and not in her own bed. Her face brightens with relief when Peggy reaches for her.

"Well, we thought you two were going to sleep all day long, Juju. As soon as Yum wakes up, we can have his birthday surprise."

Will is one year old. How can that be only a year ago? Sometimes it seems more like a hundred years ago. Hildy can hardly picture Joe now . . . barely hear his anger that she couldn't answer his questions. Far back in her memory she hears his voice deciding that well, at least his mama didn't have to know, did she.

Peggy pulls a diaper out of the bag and lays Judy down on the pallet. "Oh, Kiddo, that reminds me." Holding the wiggly baby with one hand, she stretches to reach her purse. "Look in there. I bought us something."

Hildy puzzles at the big purse shoved at her, then pulls it open. Stuck into the top are two paperback books, both the same, *The Common Sense Book of Baby and Child Care*. One copy looks brand new, the other has pages dog-eared already.

"I got us both one—they were only a quarter. That's that baby doctor I'm always telling you about, the one who writes all those good magazine articles."

Hildy takes out the dog-eared copy. *Spock.* What a funny name.

"Look there what he says about potty training. Just like I thought. He says—look, there, read where I turned it down."

Hildy reads the marked sentence, "The best method of all is to leave bowel training almost entirely up to your baby."

Rhonda comes running over. "Mommy, can I go in the water, can I please, please?"

"Oh, no, Hon, we don't want you to get polio. Hildy, we'd better get on home before the bugs get bad. We can have our cupcakes at home, all right?"

Hildy swats at a buzzing noise near her face. "Liam says there's not as many mosquitoes in California. And it gets cool at night, even in the summer. But there's no lightnin' bugs."

Peggy gathers toys and dishes, piles them into the picnic basket. Then she stops, stares off toward the duckpond, runs her tongue along her top teeth, like she does when she's working on an idea. Or an idea is working on Peggy, Hildy's not sure which. She thumbs through the doctor book, but she watches, waiting for the words to come jumbling out of Peggy's mouth.

"Ooooo, listen to this. Why don't you and I and the babies take a vacation trip? Why don't we go to, say, California?"

"California? But you said California was—"

"Oh, not the part where the War Hero and the Movie Star ran off to. Didn't you say your brother lives up near San Francisco someplace? We've got new tires, and there's plenty of gas, and it wouldn't cost much more than staying at home. We could see the ocean, and . . . and . . . "

Hildy's getting used to Peggy a little, but sometimes she feels like a 'coon staring into Granddaddy's carbide hunting lamp. In five minutes Peggy can plan a whole summer. In ten minutes, she could probably come up with a whole life, like a movie.

Peggy rushes on. "And what if we even liked it so much there that we just stayed? I could sell the house. God knows everybody's crawling all over everybody else trying to buy houses. And we could buy one of those cute little house trailers. Can you imagine, oranges for the babies, right in our backyard? And—and—I could finish nursing school there, and you could sew fancy dresses for rich San Francisco society ladies."

Hildy can't help a little grin. It didn't even take ten minutes. She heaves out a big breath, realizes she's been holding it in. At least Peggy gets excited about happier things now, with summer here, and being away from Donald and all.

"It's not such a stupid idea, do you think?" Peggy asks. "Well, maybe it is, I don't know."

"I reckon it would be nice to see Liam again. It's been so long since I've seen him, I don't even know what he looks like now."

With this little encouragement Peggy picks up speed again. "And we could stop at Aunt Carrie's on the way. Oh, but we're gonna have to come up with something for you. I don't think Aunt Carrie will believe *two* husbands who died in the war!"

A doubt nibbles the edges of the trust that Hildy has allowed herself. California? She never imagined going as far away as California. She hands Peggy the doctor book and nudges Will to wake him up.

Peggy laughs and gives the book back, points to a line on the first page. *Trust yourself. You know more than you think you do.*

"What do you think? Is it a sign?" Peggy laughs again, but Hildy isn't quite sure what the joke is. "Hey, Kiddo!" Peggy gives Hildy a friendly smack on the shoulder. "Who else are we gonna trust but us? All the Stinkers and the Movie Stars and the War Heroes?"

Hildy smiles. Peggy's laugh is catching, not like polio but the same way. Hildy tries this once to relax and just give in to Peggy's excitement, to let it wash over her instead of drawing back from it. *Trust yourself. You know more than you think you do.* Maybe this baby doctor with the funny name is right. And it always turns out that Peggy knows what to do. She was right about the dammo book, wasn't she?

*1946 . . . . . United Nations accepts gift of 8
million dollars from
John D. Rockefeller for permanent
headquarters in New York City . . . . . 1947 .
. . . . Enrollment of veterans in American
colleges under the G.I. Bill of Rights exceeds
one million . . . . . President Harry Truman
says housing shortage the "foremost problem
in the nation" . . . . . 1947 . . . . .
Jackie Robinson first Negro
admitted to major leagues 1948
. . . . Supreme Court rules religious
education in public schools unconstitutional;
violates first amendment freedom of religion
. . . . . Bernard Baruch says world is
in a "cold war"
. . . . . Harry Truman elected in close vote
over Dewey. New York Times jumps the gun
and declares Dewey winner in
morning-after headlines . . . . .*

1949 . . . . . Minimum wage upped to
75 cents and hour . . . . 1950 . . . . .
After North Korea crosses
38th parallel to invade South Korea,
Truman orders
American troops to join U.N. effort
to drive them back
1951 . . . . . First color TV broadcast.
Unfortunately, no color sets are owned
by public . . . .
MacArthur relieved of
command in Korea
. . . . . First atomic-powered generator
begins producing electricity . . . . .
1952 . . . . . Republican
Dwight D Eisenhower elected president
over Adlai Stevenson . . . . .
Supreme Court rules unconstitutional
government seizure of steel mills to
prevent strikers from shutting them
down . . . . . 1953 . . . . . Senator Joseph
McCarthy grabs headlines with charges
of communist infiltration of
U.S. government . . . . .
Protests around the world as
Julius and Ethel Rosenberg
first civilians executed for espionage
. . . . . Chuck Yeager breaks speed record
at 1600 mph in Bell X-1A
rocket-powered plane . . . . .
St. Louis Browns become
Baltimore Orioles
. . . . . Yankees win World Series
5th year in a row

PART FOUR

Hildy parks her old Ford and walks past the four other spaces to her trailer, where Stan's motorcycle is parked in the middle of the parking spot next to the patio. Why didn't he just walk over from his trailer?

She struggles with a bag of groceries and the hangers of the wool dresses—"woolen frocks," Mrs. Brandenberg calls them. Hildy was tempted to leave the dresses in the car and go back for them, but at the grocery store she could almost feel Mrs. Brandenberg's cold stare on the back of her neck at the idea of leaving her very expensive "frocks" unguarded.

After a long day of alterations at Weinstein's in The City—everybody calls San Francisco "The City", as if there was only the one—Hildy persuaded Mrs. B. to let her bring home the last four dresses to be hemmed, so she could avoid some of the late-Friday traffic. The one dress should have been let out in the hips, too, but snooty Mrs. van Wrightwood insisted it was just fine and she even refused to wear a girdle with it. Oh, well, she's the one with her fancy society pictures in the *Chronicle*. If she wants to look like a sack of potatoes, it's all right with Hildy.

Then there was the big accident on the Bay Bridge, and she's late anyway. She hopes Stan won't be too mad.

She hasn't told him yet that Peggy asked them all over for supper to make up for being on duty and missing Rita's seventh birthday party last weekend. Stan's never liked Peggy, but she always includes him when she asks, just like she's always done with the other men Hildy has gone with. But to tell the truth, they always have a lot more fun when Stan doesn't go.

Rita meets her mother at the wide-open front door, her reddened eyes wet with tears.

"Yeah, run tell Mommy, you little crybaby." Stan's baritone voice comes from the end of the trailer that triples as a dining room, living room, and Hildy's bedroom when everything else has settled down for the night.

Hildy tries to shift the grocery bag to the other arm, but she can't manage it with the heavy wooden dress hangers, so she gives the bag to Rita, pushes the girl's curly bangs out of her eyes. She'll have to find time to cut them this weekend. "What's the matter, Honey?" she asks Rita, avoiding looking up at Stan.

Eight-year-old Will takes the bag from his sister and puts it on the tiny counter by the sink, shoving aside three beer bottles. He has that stubborn look that Hildy knows so well, when he's trying fiercely to keep from crying.

"Mommy," Rita starts in, hovering close to Hildy, whispering. "He said I have to sit on his lap, and I don't want to."

Stan pulls himself up from the couch, saunters over to the sink counter, and digs into the grocery bag. "Mommy's little crybaby," he mutters.

Will inches closer to Hildy. "She is not! Mom, he said—"

"Now you shut up, you little twerp. You're a bigger crybaby than she is." Stan piles the box of macaroni and the can of tuna out into the sink, still filled with breakfast dishes. "Hildy, where's my cigarettes? Shit. I guess I'll have to go get 'em myself, like I always do." He stomps out the open door. After his motorcycle roars off, the trailer seem suddenly twice as big.

Hildy hangs the dresses in the closet space between the kitchen and the kids' sleeping space in the back. During their—hers and Peggy's—first two years in California the little trailer was crowded with toys and diapers, but it never seemed too full back then. They even had company over sometimes, cooking outside and using the trailer park picnic tables. Peggy could always find a co-worker or two from the hospital to join them, and Liam came down often from Sacramento, sometimes with his wife Jonelle but not often. Jonelle usually had something else she had to do at home.

Then after Peggy married Richard and moved to her big house in the Berkeley hills, the trailer felt empty, for a while. But no more. The walls are closing in again. Sometimes she dares wish for a Richard—or a Liam—of her own, but they always turn out to be Stans.

The motorcycle is back. Stan pokes his head back in the door. "Gimme a couple of bucks. I spent the last one I had on me some hamburgers. There wasn't anything here fit to eat."

"There was peanut butter and jelly. The kids—"

"Well, I'm not one of your *kids*."

She digs into her purse and hands him two ones.

"And if that's what you're making for dinner," he says, waving his arm toward the scattered groceries, "then don't look for me to come back here."

"That's for lunch tomorrow. Tonight I want to—"

"*You* want to? You never asked what *I* want." He slams the door, then it pops open one last time. "You always have to have everything your own way, don't you?"

She could have mouthed it along with him, if she had the energy. It's the last line of an imaginary movie she has seen a dozen times in her mind. She twists herself like a pretzel to be whatever it is they want, and in the end it always comes around to *You always have to have everything your own way, don't you?* It used to be a shock, like being slapped in the face, but lately it happens after she's too weary of it to care, and all she can feel is relief.

She knows their eyes are on her—Will's and Rita's—watching to see what she'll do next.

"Stan lost his job again," she starts out with an excuse that already sounds even more feeble than she knew it would. "I thought maybe if he stayed with you he'd feel more like we needed him."

Will puts his arm around Rita's shoulders. "Well, we don't! We can stay by ourself after school."

"Yeah. We can stay by ourself," Rita echoes. She leans against her brother, her dark curls barely reaching his shoulder.

"But he seemed like he was crazy about you kids." Before the words are out of her mouth, Hildy knows this was just something she wished in her heart.

"Mom," Will says, "he's mean to you, too. Why do you like people that are mean to you?"

She can hardly bear to look at her Will's face, so much like his namesake, so long ago. *Chigger, sometime I think you're wantin' people to be hateful to you.* She eases herself onto the couch. Her head is starting to throb. She never listened to Little Will either.

Rita strokes her mother's shoulder, tugs at a strand of her hair. "Mommy, do you want me to make you some tea? I can do it. Aunt Peggy lets me make it when I'm over there."

"Not right now, Honey. But I could use an aspirin." She manages a little smile to go along with a change of subject. "Oh, and we're going over there for supper."

Rita looks suspicious. "Just us three?"

Hildy nods. "Just us three."

Rita's face brightens and Will looks relieved, but Hildy can see that Will's not done with what he has to say. He stands with his arms crossed over his chest and his chin quivers a little. "Uncle Richard's not mean to Judy and Rhonda. Or Aunt Peggy either."

Hildy motions him over to the couch, and he grudgingly comes after Rita elbows him out of the way so she can fill a glass at the sink. He perches on the far edge of the couch. Hildy wants to reach and touch him, but she knows he doesn't want it. She feels somehow guilty that she is relieved. It still feels foolish and awkward to pat and hug her children the way Peggy does.

"Stan seemed like he needed somebody to take care of him," she says, then lamely adds, "and I guess I thought he'd help take care of us." As soon as the words are in the air, she hears Peggy's words again, *Well, Kiddo, you don't need him. Your kids— they need you, and they come first.* How many times has she heard this from Peggy? And why does she keep doing this same thing over and over, anyway? Will softens, scoots closer to her. "Mom, me and Rita, we'll take care of you."

Rita brings over the aspirin and a glass of water, sits on the floor at Hildy's feet, rubs her hand on her mother's smooth stockings. "Yeah, Mommy. We'll take care of each other."

Hildy swallows the aspirin, then drinks down the whole glass of water with her eyes closed. She knows that when she opens them, her children will be staring at her, looking to her.

It has happened again and again, and now once more: when she finally muddles to the end, when she realizes that the man who has just stomped out of her life is far from the man she has made him out to be in her mind, her children are the ones who are waiting there for her. Seems like they know all the time, and they wait patiently until she finds out for herself.

Her whole face fills like a sopping sponge, and her eyes spill over. Before she even realizes it's there, a sob comes up from deep inside her and pours out, then another, and another, and she cries until she feels all squeezed out.

She sags back on the couch, drained, embarrassed that the kids have seen her cry. Will has retreated to the far side of the couch again, glaring at the door, then back to his hands in his lap.

Rita twists the hem of Hildy's skirt. "Mommy, I'm sorry."

Hildy fumbles for a tissue on the little built-in shelf behind her, blows her nose. "What for?"

"You know," Rita nods toward the door. "For you and him. I mean, I know you . . . *love* him."

Will shoots his sister an angry look, and she wilts back a little, but she looks him straight in the eye.

Hildy reaches out for their hands, and Rita gives hers a little more willingly than Will does. "No, not any more, I don't think. I'll be all right. We all will, won't we?"

Rita stands up and pulls on Hildy's hand. "Come on!"

"What? Where?"

"Just come on!"

Rita opens the tiny refrigerator, takes out the last two beer bottles. "What should we do with his nasty old beer?"

He'll be mad, Hildy's instinct warns, but she shakes her shoulders free and manages a laugh. "It's not his beer. It's my beer. I bought it, didn't I?" She finds the bottle opener in the sink, opens a bottle and pours its contents down the drain, holding her nose.

A giddy feeling starts in Hildy's stomach and chuckles up into her throat. Rita giggles and takes the other bottle, struggles with the opener, and the bubbly stink from the second bottle disappears down the drain.

"Hey, save one for me!" Will stands at her elbow, grinning, but he swipes his wet face with his sleeve.

"Oh my gosh! It's getting late!" Hildy remembers. "Aunt Peggy's probably wondering if we're all right!" She grabs her purse as the kids scramble for their jackets and shoes.

At the door, she helps Rita zip up her blue windbreaker. Rita says with a triumphant look, "And Mommy, we *are* all right, aren't we!"

. . . . . *1954* . . . . . Salk polio
vaccination begins
Polls show 60% of U.S. males and 30% of
females smoke cigarettes . . . . . U.S.
explodes first test hydrogen bomb, 1,000
times more powerful than atomic bomb
that destroyed
Hiroshima . . . . . Army McCarthy
anti-communist hearings deemed a
witchhunt by the national press . . . . .
Brown vs. Board of Education Supreme
Court ruling outlaws supposed "separate
but equal" schools . . . . . State of Virginia
shuts down public schools rather than
obey anti-segregation ruling . . . . .
3 days of violence
after first enrollment of a Negro
at the University of Alabama
. . . . . *1955* . . . . .
Actress Grace Kelly marries
Prince Ranier III of Monaco . . . . .
1956 . . . . . Ike re-elected by a landslide
over Adlai Stevenson . . . . .

Almost four years later, June 1957
Richmond, California

"Let me get my toolbox out of the jeep," Liam says, "and I'll fix this leakin' faucet for you. It'll just take me a minute." He enjoys Hildy's kitchen. It feels more like home than his own.

"Let me get it!" Will drops the potato masher, scattering lumps of potato on the counter. He races out the door after Liam, almost bumping into him on his way back in.

Liam reaches under the sink and turns off the water. "You need to have you a good man around here."

Hildy laughs. "It looks like I've got me one."

"Mom," Rita tattles, "Will didn't do the potatoes."

"Rita? Do you want to finish 'em?" She hands Rita a stack of plates from the cabinet above Liam's shoulder. "Then you mind your own business, young lady."

Will lugs the heavy toolbox in and tries to heave it up onto the counter. At twelve, he's already almost as tall as Liam, but still has an eager little-boy face and the clumsy gait of a big puppy. "Can we go for a ride in the jeep?"

"After supper," Liam says. He takes the toolbox from him and sets it on the floor, squats to dig into it for a pipewrench and big safety pin of rubber washers of all sizes.

Hildy turns chicken pieces in the bubbling Crisco. "It's nice to have so much room to work in the kitchen. I'm spoiled already."

"I am too, with all these big Sunday suppers." He wrenches the faucet loose, cleans around the hole and drops in a washer.

"I'm glad you talked me into gettin' a house," she says, "but I've been kind of scared to ask the landlord to fix that." She shoos Will away from Liam's elbow and back to his potato mashing.

Liam tightens the faucet base, ducks under the sink to turn the water back on. "That's what landlords are for, Hildy." The water spits and sputters as he turns it off and on several times to test it. "So, like I said, how come a good-lookin' gal like you hasn't got a good man of your own yet?" Both kids look away and Hildy idly pushes the chicken pieces a half inch each direction, not changing anything that Liam can see. He grins, shakes his head. He always wondered why women do that, anyway. He even remembers seeing Mammaw do it.

"I've about given up findin' one that suits these kids," she says.

Will's potato mashing has slowed to a stop again. "We don't need any men around here," he grumbles. A guilty look comes over his face. "I don't mean you, Uncle Liam! You're not mean like them."

Rita collects silverware from the drawer. "Yeah, we don't need 'em, do we, Mom."

Hildy spreads a paper grocery sack on the counter next to the stove. "I don't think they all meant to be hateful." She forks smaller chicken pieces out onto the paper to drain.

Liam closes the toolbox, wipes his hands. "Well, there's not any excuse for a man bein' hateful to women and kids. No matter what kind of problem he's got, that's no way to fix it."

Will drops his potato masher again, grabs for the toolbox. Liam hangs onto it, sets it by the back door and points the boy back to his potato bowl. Hildy digs into the other paper sack and sets out the tomatoes, corn and cucumbers that Liam brought from his garden in Sacramento. "We sure do appreciate all this," she tells him, again.

"I hope you can use it all. Jonelle, she's not much inclined to put 'em up. And I always end up with more than I can give away, just like Daddy used to. Back then, his neighbors was grateful for 'em, but mine all run the other way when they see me comin'." He looks in the big cabinet under the counter. "But I don't reckon you remember that. Granddaddy used to kid him about it. Where's your big cookpot?"

Rita laughs and points to the big pot already steaming on the stove. Liam grins at her, gives her ponytail a playful yank. One by one he shucks the ears, pulls out the silks and hands them to Hildy to drop into the boiling water.

"Where did Jonelle grow up?" she asks him.

"Iowa. Farm country, just like us. You know the best way to cook this fresh, don't you?" He winks at Hildy, knowing she's heard the story before, but the kids are hanging onto his words, and he isn't about to let their attention go to waste. "You build you a fire out in the garden between the rows and when the pot's boilin', you bend the stalk over and . . . " He makes the motion of dunking into the pot.

Rita squints suspiciously. "Nuh-uh," Will insists.

Liam laughs. "Don't they teach you city kids anything?" They're not laughing. He tweaks Will's nose. "Just kiddin'." Finally, they smile.

Hildy goes on, "Well, I thought Jonelle was from a big city from how she talks." She sets a cube of butter in front of Will and hands a stack of paper napkins to Rita. "Hurry up, you two. Everything else is ready for the table as soon as this corn is done and I get the tomatoes cut up. Oh, and the biscuits."

Liam takes his usual chair back against the wall out of the way. "We can't be too hard on Jonelle. Some folks just have a harder time lookin' back on things than others do."

Hildy takes the pan of golden brown biscuits out of the oven. "Well, she's your wife, but if you ask me, she thinks she's better than you and me both."

The phone rings. Rita drops the napkins onto the table and races to answer it. "Mom, Judy wants to know if we can come over and watch television."

"No, you tell her you've got company tonight." Liam tries to signal that it's all right with him, but Hildy gives him a quick head-shake. She sets the platters of chicken and sliced tomatoes on the table, goes back for the biscuits.

"But Mom," Rita whines, "she already asked Aunt Peggy and she says we can. And she'll come get us."

Hildy takes a chair near Liam and motions to Will to bring the mashed potato bowl to the table. "Rita, tell Judy maybe you can come tomorrow night, and I'll drive you over. Now, you come on and eat."

Liam grins at Hildy. "Lord, these two are you and Little Will all over again." While they wait for Rita to hang up the phone, Hildy goes ahead and passes Liam the chicken plate. He helps himself to two pieces. "I still picture Little Will out by the smokehouse whittlin' on a piece of hickory. He was bigger'n me, but he seemed like such a little kid, kind of lost all the time, never fit. That war must've ate him whole."

He passes the chicken plate to Will, then thinks better of it and clears a place to put it down. "Too bad it couldn't've been . . . somebody else instead." Liam finishes up awkwardly, then wishes he hadn't said it. But he doesn't have to say any more. Hildy'll know who the *somebody else* is that he's talking about.

Rita comes to the table, sits down in a huff. Liam butters biscuits and places them one by one back onto the plate. "Yeah," he says, "These two are the spittin' image of you and Little Will."

Rita's pout disappears. "*Little* Will?" Will slouches down into his chair. She giggles. "Would you pass me a fork over here, Little Will?"

Will is up from his chair, punching at Rita's shoulder, and she squeals like a caught rabbit.

"Stop that, you two!" Hildy yells, and Will starts back to his chair, his teeth clenched.

"He gets mad because Aunt Peggy calls him 'Yum'," Rita says with a smug little giggle.

Will lunges at her again, but Liam catches the boy's arm before he can reach his sister.

"Mom, *she's* the one who starts it," he claims, pointing at Rita. "And then Judy and Rhonda keep doing it. Aunt Peggy doesn't even call me it anymore."

"I swear," Hildy says to Liam. She gets up from her chair and forces Rita to trade places with her to put more space between them. "Seems like boys get into bigger trouble, but with girls it's more like they're pokin' you to death with straight pins."

Liam hands Will a buttered biscuit.

Will gives him a begrudging smile and finds a small place for the biscuit on his already perfectly arranged plate. Liam starts to hand one to Rita, but she looks like she's studying something on the ceiling with an angelic look.

"Yeah," Liam says, "this pretty little gal is you all over. Feisty, this here one is."

"What's *feisty*?" Rita asks, grabbing a drumstick.

Hildy answers with only a frown, puts some sliced tomatoes on her own plate and some on Rita's, hands the plate to Liam.

"I don't know how you can say that. I was a homely little girl."

"What's *homely*?" Rita asks.

Liam passes the mashed potato bowl over to Hildy. "Why, Hildy, you was not, either. Where'd you get that idea?"

He turns to Rita: "When your mama was your age, she was little, like you."

Then back to Hildy: "I never would've imagined you'd ever be . . . uh . . . plump."

His forkful of mashed potatoes stops short of his mouth. "Uh-oh, I'm in trouble. You gals don't like people to notice that. Jonelle would have a fit if she was here to keep me in line. Uh, can I have the salt?"

Hildy says, "Lord knows Jonelle's told me enough times how she weighs ninety-nine pounds."

Liam grabs an ear of corn from the platter as it passes around, then when he sees there's no room on his heaping plate, he puts it on Will's plate.

"Jonelle wanted to come down today but she's tryin' to catch up from her night school and she hates to leave the cats all day. She's gettin' 'em ready for the state fair again. Sometimes I think it'd been better if we'd had kids. I'll bet them 'show cats' of hers do, too."

Hildy's face still has that pinched-up look and the more Liam talks, the more he feels like he's saying all the wrong things.

"Next week is Mom's birthday," Rita says. "Did you know that, Uncle Liam?"

"Why, no, I didn't." He looks at Hildy. "How old are you gonna be?" He whacks himself on the forehead, slides his hand down his face, over his glasses, to cover his mouth.

Hildy reaches for the pepper. "Twenty-nine." Well, damned if he's going to touch that one. Jonelle's been twenty-nine for several years now. "Uh . . . could you pass me that pepper . . . Chigger?"

Rita says, with a mouthful of biscuit, "What's *chigger*?"

"Never you mind," Hildy says, not looking up at either of them.

Liam waits until Hildy catches his eye, then winks at her. She ducks her head to cover her grin. Just like he knew she would. "It's a little bug," he says, "so little you don't know it's there 'til it gets under your skin. Kind of reminded our granddaddy of your mama."

"Finish your supper," Hildy says to nobody in particular.

Liam groans. "I think my eyes was way bigger'n my stomach."

"Well, I wasn't going to say anything to you about it," Hildy says, "but your waist could use a little watchin', too."

He rubs his belly, bulging over his belt. "Yeah, you and me, we was always more like Daddy. Who would've thought we'd either one ever . . . uh, never mind."

"Mom?" Rita shoves her plate away and leans on her elbows. "Do you remember him? Your father?" Before Hildy has a chance to answer, Rita turns to Liam. "Uncle Liam, how old were you when he died? Do you reemember him"

He decides he won't get into telling the whole story, not right now. "I was only about fourteen, so your Mama was what, ten or eleven?"

Hildy nods. "Ten or eleven. I don't even know when it was."

"Uncle Liam, how old were you when your mother died, then? Mom doesn't remember anything about her at all. Do you?"

Hildy's suddenly busy sopping the last of her gravy off her plate with a bite of biscuit.

Why, she's been tellin' these kids the same story I've been tellin' Jonelle all these years!

"Oh, now what's all this talk about dyin'?" Liam says. "I try not to think on things like that." He reaches for the last biscuit. He shouldn't let that last dab of gravy go to waste, after all. "I tend to let things lay instead of dwellin' on 'em too much," he says.

..... 1957 ..... President Eisenhower sends
1,000 troops to enforce integration at Little Rock's
Central High School ..... In a survey of 60,000
high school juniors and seniors, more than half
with an IQ of 130 or above will not attend college
because of lack of money or of goals for future
..... USSR stuns U.S. by launching first earth
satellite, Sputnik ..... Scornful parents look on as
Elvis Presley's fame skyrockets 1958
..... Dr. Linus Pauling says fallout already in the
air from exploded atomic bombs will cause
millions of cancer cases and defective births in
next 300 generations ..... 1959 .....
1st seven astronauts chosen from U.S. military test
pilots ..... Virginia and Arkansas
segregation laws ruled unconstitutional .....
Congress passes food stamp bill ..... U.S. satellites
Discovery 5 and 6 launched into orbit .....
Last Civil War veteran dies at age 117 .....

Two years later, October 1959
Sacramento, California

"There they are." Liam drops his rake and heads over to the driveway
where Hildy's car pulls up beside the jeep.

"Lee-um!" Jonelle calls from the front step, "I've asked you and
asked you to please not leave the tools on the lawn! And I told you to
park that heap of yours out back."

Before Liam can open the door, Hildy is already out of the car.
She stretches, pulls her hair up off the back of her neck. "Lordy, that's
a long hot drive. The car acted up halfway here, sounded like it was
hiccupin'."

"Let me take a look at it before you go back. Rita? Are you goin'
to sit in the car, or are you comin' on in? And where's Will?"

Rita drags herself out the passenger door and peers at them
over the top of the car. Hildy reaches back in for her purse. "He had
something at school. He wants to be on the junior football team this
year, whatever they call it."

"He gets to stay home just because he's in high school now," Rita complains from the other side of the car. "And just because he's a *boy!* Nobody cares if *I'm* almost thirteen!"

"Rita," Hildy says, smoothing down her wrinkled skirt, "You just turned twelve last week."

"Come on in now. Jonelle's been lookin' for you for dinner for more'n an hour. I told her 'about noon'—not like it's a fancy diner."

Jonelle appears at his elbow. The rake has disappeared from the middle of the lawn. "My, Hildy, you do look nice. I've always liked that dress." Jonelle's company voice is even thicker than usual, Liam thinks. No wonder Hildy thought she was from a big city.

"Do come on in," Jonelle says. "I'm afraid my salad greens may be a little wilted by now." She gives Liam a look that's obviously intended to wilt *him.* "I hope you'll excuse that horrible vehicle of my husband's. I asked him to move it around back." She waves toward the jeep, now hidden behind Hildy's twelve-year-old Chevy.

"Now, Jonelle," Liam says, "the kids always got a kick out of the jeep. And we don't have to try to impress Hildy."

"I wasn't trying to *impress* her, Liam. I just think it's so juvenile the way men want to hang onto things that remind us of the war. Don't you, Hildy?" She picks a tiny piece of lint off her gabardine capri pants. "It was such an awful time. All the *luxuries* we had to do without."

Luxuries. Liam is sure he never even heard that word before the war, much less owned any. And no matter how she sounds now, he doubts if Jonelle did either. He herds Rita and Hildy toward the house while Jonelle dashes on ahead. While Hildy and Rita take turns in the bathroom *freshening up,* as Jonelle insists, she sets the table with china salad plates and cloth napkins.

"Wow, this is really snazzy," Rita says, clearly forgetting her almost-teenage mope. "Mom, why can't we have fancy dishes like this?"

"This is our very favorite salad," Jonelle breaks in, bringing the huge salad bowl from the kitchen. "Well, it's mine, anyway. Liam prefers plainer food, I'm afraid." She pours dressing over the salad, tosses it with wooden salad tongs, then reaches for Hildy's dish. "Of course, I can't have it often. Avocados make me poof up big as a house—oh!" She sets the dish down with a thump and both hands fly to her mouth. "Oh, whatever was I thinking about, Hildy? I should never have served this, with you trying to reduce."

"I can pick 'em out," Hildy says. "I don't like avocados anyway."

Liam looks from one to the other of the women, feels relieved.

They don't look mad. But then with women it sometimes feels like they're saying more than just what he's hearing. "Uh, Jonelle?" He thought they were done, but he still feels like he's butting in. Now they're both looking at him, so he has to come up with something. "Uh, I'll bet Rita'd like to play with them new kittens of yours. Well, after din—uh, *lunch*, I mean."

Jonelle puffs up like an old hen. "Liam! The kittens are in the den because Miss Lucinda gets very agitated when she's disturbed. They're purebred and very high strung. They're not to be *played with*. I'm sure Rita understands."

"I'm too old for playing with kittens, anyway," Rita says. "Uncle Liam, I'm *almost* a teenager."

Well, now that he's managed to make all three of them mad at him, he thinks maybe he'd better just keep his mouth shut.

"Oh, no!" Jonelle smacks herself on the forehead. "I've done it again. I didn't think of these horribly fattening cashews either. You'll have to forgive me, Hildy I'm just not used to considering . . . "

Liam flinches. Surely Jonelle knows by now that Hildy's touchy on this subject. Why does she keep doing this?

"I wasn't heavy before I had babies," Hildy snaps.

Liam flinches again. Well, now, Hildy didn't have any way to know that's the subject that sticks in Jonelle's craw.

He can see Jonelle's neck cords tighten up, and he hurries to say, "We never had such fancy stuff when we was kids, did we? Remember when we used to tromp through the woods lookin' for hicker'nuts and haze'nuts, Chigger? Mammaw used to get after us for—"

"*Hickory* nuts and *hazel*nuts, Liam," Jonelle says in that honeyed voice of hers, but he swears her teeth are clenched behind it. "I've never been able to get Liam away from the country." She picks up the half-empty cracker basket and gets up. "And why you want to dwell on the past is beyond me."

"There was good things to remember, too, about back then."

"I can't imagine what they could be," she huffs as she disappears around the corner into the kitchen.

He tries to think of something new to talk about, something that would make Hildy feel better. "Chigger, I was wonderin', why don't you let your hair go back dark?"

As Jonelle comes back with the filled cracker basket he goes on, "I remember it bein' so pretty and dark and kind of curly, wasn't it? I'd sure like to see it like it was then."

"Nobody ever liked how I looked," Hildy says, her voice almost a whisper. "After a while, I just never tried."

"Well, I like it just like it is, Hildy," Jonelle says. "I confess I do have my hairdresser put a rinse on mine. She wanted to lighten it, but I was afraid it would kind of . . . cheapen it. Oh, but that was just mine. Yours looks just fine, bleached."

What's gotten into Jonelle, anyhow? Liam wonders. Her words sound like sugar, but her face is as brittle as ice on a pond in January. He studies Hildy, looking down at her untouched salad bowl. Her brooding face reminds him of the stubborn little sister he and Little Will always tried to keep out of trouble. He says, "Maybe it was just *you* that never liked how you looked, Chig. But I always thought you was a right pretty little girl."

Jonelle gets up from the table so abruptly she bumps the cut-glass water pitcher, grabs it before it spills. "Oh, Hildy, men don't know what they're talking about when it comes to fashion. You do whatever you want."

Now what did he say wrong? "Here, Chig," he offers. "Have some crackers. Uh, these are called crackers ain—aren't they Jonelle?"

After he's adjusted the carburetor on Hildy's car and they've waved goodbye, Liam locates the rake around at the side of the house and goes out to work at the few leaves that have fallen since noon. May as well try to make Jonelle happy. She comes out to the porch, picks at her geraniums in pots on each side of the steps.

"I thought you was takin' a nap," he says. He drops the rake, then grabs it back before she notices and drags it along with him.

"My headache is much better now, thank you." Her mouth still has that pinched-up look.

"Your flowers look real nice."

"Oh, they look *awful.* They're so dried out."

He leans on the rake handle, watches her pick the dry leaves from a red geranium, dropping them into a neat pile on the steps. "You know, I always hoped you two would get along," he says.

"Who?"

"You and Hildy."

"Whatever did you think we'd have in common?"

He shrugs. "You always said you wished you had a sister."

"I imagined one a little more *sophisticated,* who went to church, and had some . . . some *aspiration* for herself."

He decides to ignore Jonelle's big words this time. Whatever she means by them, he's sure they're not meant to flatter her sister-in-law. "I was thinkin' maybe we could teach her how to play canasta. We used to do that a lot."

"Honestly, Liam. *Nobody* plays canasta anymore. But then how could I expect *you* to know that? Honestly!"

He scoops up the geranium leaves, balls them up in his hand and lobs them out into the yard to rake up along with the sycamore leaves. "We don't go to church either," he says.

"Speak for yourself. I go to church!"

"Well, on Easter, and sometimes when you're, you know, mad at me." He grins at her, but she's already stomping into the house. Oh, well. Seems like all he does anymore is make her mad. He's pretty sure she'll be in church tomorrow.

Liam remembers back in the early years together, in the little stone house named Cecile, how he held her clumsily in the dark after she had another bad dream, and how she'd cling to him and cry her heart out. Now it seems like everything she wants to put behind her, he reminds her of just by being here. He picks up his rake and goes back to the sycamore leaves.

One thing, though. He suspects his sister and his wife are a lot more alike than he would get either one of them to admit.

. . . . . 1960 . . . . . New 50-star flag introduced, after Alaska and Hawaii admitted to union last year . . . . . Nobel Prize awarded for method of radioactive carbon dating . . . . . In spite of 1954 Supreme Court ruling, 94% of southern schools are still segregated . . . . . John F Kennedy defeats Richard M Nixon in presidential election, the closest in history . . . . . 1961 . . . . . JFK accepts full responsibility for failure of Bay of Pigs invasion of Cuba . . . . .

FCC chairman Newton Minow calls TV
a "vast wasteland"
. . . . . Alan Shepherd reaches suborbital flight
at beginning of
Mercury space mission . . . . .
Journal of American Medical Association
connects smoking with heart disease . . . .
Roger Maris breaks Babe Ruth's record of 60
home runs in a season
. . . . . Russian sector of Berlin is sealed off,
construction of a wall begun around city

1962 . . . . . Two U.S. military advisors killed
North of Saigon in southeast Asia
. . . . . Under U.N. supervision, soviet
missiles removed from Cuba after U.S.
blockades . . . . .
Violence erupts after
Governor Ross Barnett found in
contempt of U.S. Supreme Court of
Appeals order to cease interference in
integration of University of Mississippi
. . . . . Nobel prize to Drs. Watson and Crick
for discovery of DNA
double-helix structure . . . . .

Martin Luther King:
"I have a dream that one day
this nation will rise up and live out
the true meaning of its creed:
We hold these truths to be self-evident:
that all men are created equal."

. . . . . 1963 . . . . .
JFK assassinated in Dallas
Lyndon Baines Johnson sworn in
as 36th president on board Air Force One
. . . . . LBJ orders FBI search for 3 civil
rights workers missing in Mississippi . . . . .

1964 . . . . . Beatles arrive at Kennedy air-
port to screaming fans . . . . .
Sweeping Civil Rights act signed into law
. . . . .

PART FIVE

Four years later, July 1964
Richmond, California

Rita brings in a stack of mail, drops the bigger items on the kitchen counter, shuffles through the envelopes. Electric bill . . . water bill . . . bank statement. "Mom! Here's Mrs. Dalton's check. Can we go to the yardage store this afternoon?"

She and Mom have been waiting for payment for the twelve bridesmaid dresses they tailored for the Dalton wedding in June. Rita's share is earmarked for fabric for new clothes for college in the fall.

Mom puts down the dish she was wiping, wipes her hands on her apron and takes the envelope.

"Oh, and here's one from Will!" Rita rips open the envelope and a wallet-sized photograph falls out—Will in his smart new U.S. Marine uniform. "Geez, he looks so old. And mean!" She skims over the short letter and laughs. "He says they tell them to 'look tough, this is for your Mom!' "

She hands the letter to Mom and searches for a spot on the front of the fridge for the photo. "Can we take some of these old ones down?" Rita in her high school cap and gown in June. Rita, Rhonda, Judy and Betty at Fisherman's Wharf two years ago. Rita hates that one. "Geez, I definitely looked goofy with my hair short." Everybody else has cute Jackie flip hairdos or at least ponytails, but hers looks like a leftover Annette Funicello poodle.

Mom takes the picture of Will and holds it for a moment, frowns at the letter again. Rita can always tell when Mom's worried about something. She stares off out the nearest window like she was seeing all the way to the Golden Gate Bridge.

"Mom?" Rita touches her mother's arm, but the only response is a shiver, even though the kitchen is on the warm side of the house. "It's okay, Mom. It's not like there's a war or anything."

"But what do they do in the Marines if there's not any war?"

"Oh, you know Will, Mom. He likes all his things lined up in a row. And think of all the girls he can get with that cool uniform."

Mom is frowning at the photo again. "I never saw a picture of my brother in his uniform."

Rita eases the photo out of Mom's hand, takes advantage of this turn in conversation. "I wish we had one of our dad."

Mom doesn't say anything, but Rita can see her chest heave. Every time she mentions her father, Mom buckles on her armor. But some day Rita'd like some answers—some true ones for a change. "What about his family? Wouldn't they have some?"

Mom spreads the rest of the mail out on the counter and picks out a sale flyer from the hardware store, but Rita's pretty sure she's not looking at it, not really.

"Mom? What about—"

"I told you he didn't have any family."

Okay, okay. Geez.

Mom goes to the fridge and sets out a basket of boysenberries and a quart of milk. She puts the milk carton on the counter next to the Bisquick and sugar canisters, pours the berries into the colander in the sink. Then she digs into the cabinet under the counter and pulls out a shallow Pyrex pan.

Rita and Will used to fight over making Mom's berry pie, but it's not much fun anymore since Will got too big to care. Not really a pie, it starts out as a ghastly white purplish mixture that comes out of the oven toasty brown on the edges, soft and cakey and stained all through with purple berries inside.

Rita rummages through the second drawer for a measuring cup. "One cup? Two?"

"With just two of us, one ought to be enough, don't you think?"

Rita measures out the cup of sugar, cup of Bisquick, cup of milk, stirs it together and pours it into the pan. "Did your grandma Hilda let you make this when you were little?" Rita already knows the answer. But she noticed a long time ago that if she gets Mom started talking about her grandmother—her "Mammaw"—she'll come around to talking about other things. Sometimes.

Rita tries to see how long she can get her to talk before she clams up. Will always sees through her game. So what. Will's not here.

Mom rinses the boysenberries, sets the colander on the counter, dries the last of the dishes, putting the clean ones from the drainer into the cabinets above. "But Mammaw made it with blackberries. And her self-risin' flour didn't come in a fancy box. I think it was Martha White brand. They had a song on the radio . . . how many biscuits can you eat this mornin' . . . somethin'."

Rita pops a plump berry into her mouth while her mother's back is turned. "*Hilda* definitely sounds like a grandma name, but *Hildy* sounds, well, you know, kind of . . . younger." How embarrassing, for somebody overweight like Mom, to have such a little-girl name. "Too bad there's nothing in between, huh?"

She eats another fat berry, but this time Mom catches her, wags a finger at her. "The more you eat now . . . "

Rita laughs, wags a purple-stained finger back. " . . . the less you'll have in your pie."

"I always wondered why Mammaw said that when we picked 'em —there was worlds of them. I can see now she just wanted us to get done and not take all day about it."

Worlds of them. "Oh, Mom, you're so . . . provincial." Rita turns the oven on to 350 degrees. "So, they . . . your grandparents . . . they raised you, then, huh?" So far, so good. Mom's loosening up.

"I don't remember my granddaddy much. He was big and loud . . . sometimes it scared me the way he hollered and laughed."

Hollered and laughed. Rita mentally groans. She never dared ask anything when her friends were here from school. Except her best friend Betty. When Betty and Mom talked, both their accents got thicker and thicker. Rita misses Betty since she moved back home to Georgia after her dad retired from the Navy. Betty's drawl was kind of cute—the boys all loved it— but Mom just sounds . . . country.

Rita drops the berries one at a time into the thin layer of pasty-white batter; she eats one, then two more. Oh well, this time the "pie" will be more white than purple. She stirs the batter to spread the purple around. "So, what was your other grandmother's name?"

Mom takes off her apron, folds it and puts it in the bottom drawer, stuffs one end of the dishtowel through the refrigerator door handle. "I don't remember ever hearing what my daddy's mama was called. His folks never came over here. Maybe Liam knows."

"Probably something like Bridget. *Rita Bridget Rossi?*" She wrinkles her nose. "Well, it beats *Eppie*! Geez, where'd you get Eppie, anyway? None of my friends knew the whole thing all through school, but when they read it off at graduation"—her voice deepens to an official low—"*Rita Eppie Rossi*—geez, I nearly died."

She checks the oven, puts the pan in. "Only place I ever saw that was . . . well, you wouldn't know of it. It was a classic we read in junior English, *Silas Marner*."

"That's where I got it."

"No kidding?" Mom read *Silas Marner*? Rita can't imagine Mom reading anything but her magazines. "Well, at least you didn't name me . . . what was her real name? Hepzekiah or something, some religious something or other?"

"Hephzibah." Mom chuckles. "That's what I wanted to name you, but Peggy wouldn't let me."

Rita savors the chuckle. Mom can be almost fun, if she'd just relax a little. "Well, thank God for Aunt Peggy. I definitely owe her!" Through the oven's glass door she watches the pie beginning to puff around the edges.

She peeks sideways at Mom. "I would think you might have named me for your Mom, I mean, especially since she died when you were little. I mean, since it kind of runs in your family to do that. *Gerty*, now that sounds like somebody's grandmother."

Mom looks at her like she said a bad word. She hurries on, trying to sound casual. "Oh, not that I . . . well, I'm glad you didn't." She opens the oven door, grabs the oven mitt and turns the pan around.

"So . . . how come you named me after a movie star, and Heps whats-her-name, anyway?"

"I named you after a princess."

"But she wasn't a princess until after I was born. She was just a movie star."

Mom just shrugs and stoops to peer into the cabinet where she keeps the pots and pans. What was it Mom used to call them? *Cooking vessels.*

"Don't we have pictures of *any* of our grandparents *any*where?"

Rita's asked this a dozen times, but she always hopes she can somehow sneak up on Mom and get something new, different.

Mom visibly stiffens. "I told you, Rita. I don't remember there ever being any."

Along about now Will always appears out of nowhere, no matter what he was doing and hovers around between her and Mom, giving her that *knock-it-off-Rita* look. She almost expects him to walk in here in his Marine uniform, all the way from Camp Pendleton.

Well, Will's not here, and she has a right, doesn't she? It's Rita's family, isn't it? "I'll bet you always wondered what she looked like, then, huh? I mean, she died when you were . . . ?"

Mom rearranges the smaller pans, stacking, restacking, clanging the pans together.

Oka-a-a-ay. There's no easy way to sneak into the other subject. But Rita's gone this far, she may as well plunge on ahead. She makes a modest effort to tie it in, fingering the photo of Will on the front of the fridge, but it's wasted. Mom isn't looking. She's taking out pans and stacking them on the counter.

Rita tries to keep her words light, casual. "I've been wondering, exactly where was our father killed? I mean . . . " Before Mom can answer or refuse to, Rita hurries on. "I always thought he was killed in battle. In fact I thought that's what you said, but it must have been after. So where was he stationed after the war?"

Mom looks like she's on a full-scale kitchen reorganizing, taking out larger pans, replacing them with another stack of smaller pans.

Okay, you win. Let's back way way up, before you start ripping out the cabinets. Rita leans on her elbows on the countertop. "So, how did you happen to read *Silas Marner*?" Mom still doesn't turn to look at her, but her shoulders relax and she slows her frantic pan rearranging. "In high school," she says. "I read it in high school, just like you did. I've still got it someplace."

"Really? Where?"

"I think it's in the bottom of my chest of drawers." She sets the stack of Pyrex baking dishes carefully back into the cabinet and it looks like she might leave them there this time.

Rita scoots out of the kitchen and down the hall before Mom can object. She shivers at the thought of actually holding something from Mom's past, this past that she hangs onto so selfishly.

Sometimes she imagines Mom a spook who just materialized one day, who makes up a past as she goes along and only when she's forced to come up with it. She's probably in there wiggling her nose right now, conjuring up *Silas Marner* in the bottom dresser drawer.

Rita yanks out the bottom drawer, stuffed mostly with mementos of school years, hers and Will's. Her Brownie badges, his kindergarten handprints, over

THIS IS TO REMIND YOU, WHEN I AM VERY TALL . . . THAT ONCE I WAS QUITE LITTLE, AND MY HANDS WERE VERY SMALL

She puts the paper aside to torment her brother with next time he brings home a girl. At the bottom of the drawer, two books, a pageworn paperback Dr. Spock, and the ancient brown clothbound *Silas Marner* with Mahala School stamped on the top edges of the pages.

The book looks nothing like the paperback Rita struggled through in high school. But the flavor of the words is the same . . . **the fall of prices had not yet come to carry the race of small squires and yeomen down that road to ruin for which extravagant habits and bad husbandry were plentifully anointing their wheels** . . . the same old boring stuff. Geez, nobody cares about this stuff anymore, nobody but English teachers.

A small yellow envelope forces the book open to a page in the middle. And there it is on the open page: *Hephzibah.*

Oh, well. It could be worse. Mom could have read *The Hobbit.* She puts the envelope back in its rightful spot, then on second thought takes a closer look at the postmark. *Mahala, Kentucky. September 20, 1945.* "Geez!" She takes a furtive look back at the open bedroom door, then slips the folded yellow stationery out.

Dear Hildy,

Hon, I have worried so about you, not hearing from you since last winter. I wish you would have written us that your husband was lost at Okinawa.

Wait—wait a minute! Okinawa was one of those big battles near the end of the war. Something doesn't—wasn't it—she looks at the envelope. No mistake, not even blurred: *September, 1945.* Definitely a *5.* More than a year before Rita was born.

. . . your husband was lost at Okinawa.

No! This makes no sense!

. . . so sorry . . . Joe was a good boy . . . a shame he didn't live to see his baby boy.

The words are as unreal to her as for which extravagant habits and bad husbandry were plentifully anointing their wheels. Her breath catches in her throat and dams up in her chest. She looks at the envelope again. This must be some other Hildy, then. Some other baby, some other husband.

. . . Joe was a good boy . . .

Then it has to be some other Joe, too, that's all there is to it. Rita's mind is even willing to believe it's some other 1945. She skims the next paragraph twice, three times, tries to see different words other than the ones front of her face:

I'm glad you named him for Little Will. I know he will be a blessing to you in your grieving, Honey. And your granddaddy would have been proud too, for as you know your brother was named for him.

The rest of the words . . . unfamiliar names—*Naomi . . . Wayne . . . your mama same as always . . . Love, Aunt Emma*

—reach only to the back of her eyes and refuse to go any further.

Her hand presses itself against her mouth. She wants to close her eyes tightly but she darts from line to line, tries to rearrange the words into different truth . . .

1945 . . . Joe . . . Little Will . . . your grieving

but no new meaning forms.

She drops the letter into her lap. Her head won't stop shaking *. . . no . . . no . . . no!* as though by refusing them she can force the words to disappear. But deep inside her consciousness, her own identity has just been ripped out of the family album and torn to little pieces.

"Rita, what time did you put the pie—" Mom stops at the door. "What's wrong?"

Rita gets herself up from the floor, her head still reeling, her lunch turning sour in her stomach. She shoves the letter at her mother. "What does this mean? You have to tell me what this means!"

Mom stares at the letter and her face turns ashen. Before Rita can stop her, Mom grabs the letter and wads it in her hand.

"You have to tell me!" Rita demands. "Give me that back!"

"Nothing. No. It's . . . it's nothing."

Mom turns to leave, but Rita grabs her by the sleeve. "No! You're not going to lie to me any more. You owe me!"

She holds her mother's wrist, pries the letter from her hand, but instead of resisting, the hand goes limp and the wad of paper drops to the floor. Rita scoops it up.

Mom backs up against the wall and crosses her arms in front of her face. "I . . . I don't know . . . I don't remember. I . . . "

Words howl through Rita's mind. She must capture one after the other from the noise, form it in her mouth, hold it in with clenched teeth and release it only when she's sure it won't come out as a scream. "You're going to tell me the truth for once. You owe me that!"

Something that sounds like a whimper comes from behind Mom's hands. "I don't know."

Rita can feel the hysteria that rises, fills her chest until it feels like it's going to burst. "You owe me a father! You owe me grandparents! If you don't know, *who does?*"

The next day
Berkeley Hills, California

Rita paces between the piano and the bay window of the room that doubles as a library and what Aunt Peggy calls her "music room."

"So my father was the nothing husband of a Hollywood starlet." Rita wants to feel angry, but she's run out of anger since her big fight with Mom yesterday. "Geez, it's right out of The Guiding Light."

Aunt Peggy stands near the door, as though she's going to bolt any minute now. "Well, of course he wasn't the actress's husband then, but . . . later." She picks up a figurine from the end table, then replaces it an inch to the left. "They were killed in a car accident, both intoxicated. It was in all the movie magazines. I'm sorry, I just don't know what else to say."

"That's Mom for you. She always went for the drunks. So my father . . . whoever . . . is dead. Well, that slams one door that I don't have to bother with, anyway."

"Rita, please don't be this way."

Sarcastic comments buzz in Rita's mind, but by the time they reach her mouth, they've lost their edge. She just wants to run away from all of it, the whole soap opera. "So he was married to Mom *after* my . . . after Joe Rossi died, then."

"No," Aunt Peggy says, "No, he wasn't. He was never married to her, and I'm glad he wasn't. He didn't deserve her, and he didn't deserve you either. Rita, please. I know you're angry, but—"

"Oh great. So I'm a bastard, too."

Rita shrinks back, feels like she's going to be slapped. She wishes Aunt Peggy would scream at her. Rita's screamed enough. Her throat feels like a dried-out sponge. A rush of anger comes unannounced, disconnected. "And her own mother! She doesn't even know—or care—if her own mother was alive! The letter said 'your mother is the same as always'. I kinda doubt 'same as always' means 'still dead,' don't you?" She drops into the big leather overstuffed chair, dabs at her eyes with her fingers. "She always told me she didn't remember her mother. At. All."

Aunt Peggy stands at the window and peers out. "Rita, that part might not be a lie, exactly. I often see patients who can't remember things. Car accidents, shootings. Traumatic things. 'Can't remember' doesn't necessarily mean 'dead' either."

Aunt Peggy picks up a framed photograph from the shiny piano top. With her blouse sleeve she wipes nonexistent dust and puts the photograph back. "Anyway you can blame it on me. It was my idea for her to lie. To everybody, not just you. In fact, I wasn't even thinking far enough ahead to think of how it would affect you. It wasn't anybody's business what happened in the past, not Joe Rossi's or his mother's or anybody else's. Do you think I told Judy and Rhonda their daddy didn't come home from the war because he—"

"What? Wait a minute." Rita jumps to her feet. "You said Joe Rossi's *mother*? She always told me he didn't have any family."

Aunt Peggy sucks in a hard breath. "I'm sorry, Rita. I've said far too much. I have no right to say so much."

"And *what* was it that was 'nobody's business'?" A cold webby lump forms in Rita's stomach. "So what are you telling me—no, wait, don't tell me. Joe Rossi is a lie, too, right?"

"No, Joe Rossi is not a lie. I saw him. Once. And she was married to him when I met her."

Aunt Peggy hesitates. Rita waits.

Aunt Peggy picks at one of her manicured pink fingernails. "Look. Rita, I used to try to pry into your Mom's past and I realized over the years that she has some dark things that she can't look at back there. It's not your place or mine to try to make her look at them. It's in the past. Let it go, Rita, I beg of you."

"But this is *my* past we're talking about, too!"

"No, it's not. It doesn't matter one bit what's back there. *Now* is all that counts. You've got no right to try to take away a person's lie that she's paid dearly for and she needs so badly. She did a damn good job, the best she knew how. And that's all any mother owes her kids."

"It is not! She owes me a family! Sometimes I feel like our family is just a bunch of ghosts, even Mom. *Especially* Mom!"

"Listen to me, Rita. Your family are the ones who cared about you when not everyone did." Aunt Peggy chooses another photograph, one of a handsome gray-templed man in a tuxedo with Rhonda on his arm, her face demure and misty behind her tulle veil. "The man who left me without ever seeing Judy, do you think he's my girls' *real* father? No! Richard is their real father."

She pushes the photograph at Rita. "Look at him. He cried all the way down the aisle. And do you think anybody's going to be prouder of that baby next spring than he will? And here, see how the girls look at him? Do you think either one of them is whining, 'I wish my *real* father were here?'"

Rita turns away. "I don't need to look at the pictures. I was there. And I was so jealous of Rhonda that day, her with Uncle Richard, and me with Mom's assorted drunks, one after the other."

"Now you're just feeling sorry for yourself, Rita. It doesn't look very good on you." Aunt Peggy reaches to touch Rita's arm, but Rita pulls it back.

Aunt Peggy continues, "I wish Hildy had found herself a good man, too. I hope she still does find someone. But Rita, even if you had fancy pedigree papers saying you go back to Queen Victoria, what difference would it make? You're not those people back there."

She searches the bookcase, pulls out a tiny blue volume. "Here's something I read a long time ago that made me think about this kind of thing a lot." She opens the book to a page that's obviously been opened to many times before. "I have to go get dressed for work, but you take it. It doesn't answer any questions, but it kind of makes you ask . . . well, bigger questions." She aims Rita toward the leather recliner in the corner. "Sure, we all get stuff from our past, but it's not what you get or where from, but what we do with it. That's what I take it to mean."

Essays for Living, by B. J. McIntosh. Rita sits on the recliner's arm and begrudgingly reads the hand-lettered page Aunt Peggy pointed her to.

> Every family closeknit or distant
> has its share of hand-me-downs.
> Heirlooms, some . . . names and dates
> engraved in silver,
> pedigrees recorded in photo albums and Bibles,
> in diaries and letters,
> on certificates of marriage,
> death and military service,
> and on tombstones.
> Others invisible—rumors, legends, skeletons,
> genetic scars chiseled into family memory.
> For every child there is an inheritance,
> received at coming of age or
> inscribed on the newborn soul,
> suspended barely under the surface of awareness.
> Each child accepts into its innocence
> all of its heritage,
> polishes, catalogs,
> puts it away behind glass,
> paints it with the colors
> of its own dreams and delusions,
> and dutifully passes it on to its own children.
> Every so often,
> an heirloom is dropped
> or broken or burned.
> Or a child,
> from wisdom or from pain,
> by fortune or by chance,
> refuses to give birth to heirs.

Rita closes the book and replaces it in the bookcase. "Dreams and delusions . . . that part's right enough."

She wanders to the piano, picks up a photo of Uncle Richard and Rhonda dancing.

Another one, Uncle Richard dancing with Judy in her blue satin bridesmaid's dress. In the background, out of focus, an identical dress —Rita, dancing with Will.

With no warning, a sob breaks from her throat, then another. She sits down on the piano bench and releases the anger that has pressed tightly against her heart.

Aunt Peggy comes back, dressed in her nurse uniform, carrying her white shoes and stockings and her hat. She puts them down and sits on the piano bench next to Rita, pulls her into her arms.

"I'm so sorry, Hon."

Rita nods, can't bring herself yet to talk. Her throat hurts and her eyelids ache, but she returns the hug.

Aunt Peggy moves over to the ottoman and gathers one leg of her pantyhose over her thumbs, pulls it onto her foot. "These things are the greatest invention since pants pockets, huh?"

Rita manages a little smile, a nod. "Yeah." She looks around. Aunt Peggy points to a tissue box on the recliner's side table. Rita retrieves a tissue and blows her nose.

"So, Rita, what are you going to do now?"

Rita hasn't thought beyond today, but it comes to her exactly what she needs. "You remember Betty."

Aunt Peggy pins her cap onto her tastefully gray-streaked hair, adjusts it in the gold filigree-framed mirror. "Of course. The cute little blonde you girls ran around with in high school. Didn't she move back to the South a couple of years ago?"

"Yeah. Georgia, when her dad retired from the Navy. She's been after me to spend the summer with her. I think I will. Get away for a while before school starts. I've got money saved up."

"Which did you decide on for sure, Stanford or Cal Berkeley?"

"Cal, I think. Might as well stay close enough to live at home." Well, that seemed like a good idea last week.

"Good. Maybe you can get Judy to come home and join you. If last winter in Boston didn't convince her, maybe you can. It'd be nice to have at least you two close to home, with Rhonda so far away and Will off in the Marines."

Rita feels hot tears welling again. She grabs another tissue. "Geez, that makes him my *half* brother!"

Aunt Peggy turns from the mirror to look at her directly. "And does that make you feel any different about him?"

Rita begrudges an answer. Of course it doesn't. How could it?

"What if you found out, say, that Judy was really your sister? How would you feel about her?"

Rita can't help a wry little grin. "So are you going to tell me she is? Today I'd definitely believe anything. Geez, why not?"

Aunt Peggy's shoulders move in a silent chuckle. "As far as I'm concerned, Kiddo, she always has been."

She takes Rita gently by the shoulders. "Rita, you go ahead and do what you have to do for your own sake. It's not lost on me that Georgia is a hop and a skip from Kentucky. But whatever you find, you leave it there, okay? Your mom made choices you and I wouldn't make, but she has her reasons for them and her right to them. Will you promise me that?"

Rita can't promise, but she hopes the lack of an argument will do for now. "So, do you think all the ghosts are out? Am I getting any more surprises?"

Aunt Peggy looks at her for a long silent moment, runs her tongue along her top lip, finally lets out a long sigh, shakes her head. "Not that I know of, Kiddo."

Rita hopes what she just witnessed was a woman searching her memory and not another quickly thought-up lie.

Aunt Peggy digs into her purse, pulls out car keys. "I have to go to work now, Hon. You're welcome to use Judy's room as long as you want. Just let your mom know, okay?"

"Okay." At least she can promise that. She'll leave Mom a note when she stops by to pack some clothes tomorrow.

A week later
Sacramento, California

Hildy puts her hamburger down on its wrapper. "Are you sayin' I'm like her? Well, I'm not!"

Liam digs into the bag for another burger. He should have known she'd take it wrong.

"I was only sayin' that you and Jonelle both have a look about you, like there's something you're tryin' to get away from but you never can. Somethin' like Daddy always had."

Hildy tosses a french fry to a sparrow waiting on the umbrella-shaded table a few feet away. The bird pecks at it, picks it up and tries to fly away with it, but it falls apart and drops to the pavement. He comes back for a smaller piece.

"That's all I meant, Chig. Jonelle can't help it the way she is. That's why I don't let her bother me as much as she does you. She's got a lot of . . . well, she had somethin' done to her when she was fifteen. I don't need to tell you it all, but it left her so she couldn't have any kids. She wanted kids, but me, it was kind of a relief, not having any. But after bein' around Rita and Will, I'm kinda sorry now we didn't."

Hildy breaks a fry in half and tosses it to the bird, whose whole family has flown in to join him.

Liam takes a long drink of his root beer. "Jonelle and me, we didn't marry for love, exactly. She married me because she needed somebody, but I reckon I married her because she reminded me a little bit of you back then. And I felt bad I ran out on you."

"You couldn't help it," Hildy says.

"Daddy's leaving ate on me for years 'til I finally just had to let it be. He couldn't help himself neither, I don't reckon. You want this last hamburger? Half of it?"

She shakes her head, tosses another fry to the impatient birds. He goes on, "He used to tell me some about his folks, but there was somethin' else back there he never talked about but I could see it in his eyes. It helped me some, just watchin' Jonelle make herself into somebody she could live with. Can't say I'd have picked out that same somebody to live with, but I can't help thinkin' good of her for it."

He finishes off the last hamburger, chuckles at the sparrows that fight over bits of potato. He tosses the last bite of sesame-seeded bun to them and a dozen more birds swoop out of the nearby tree to join in the squabble for the pieces.

"You heard anything from Rita yet?"

Hildy doesn't answer out loud, but her mouth twitches. He waits, but she says nothing. She breaks the last french fry into several pieces, tosses them all at once.

Liam gets up. "I'm gonna get us another drink. Can you think of anything else you want?

"More napkins?" she suggests.

He gathers up the hamburger wrappers and wads them into a ball, drops it in a trash container on his way back up to the counter. When he comes back, balancing two paper cups and a fresh carton of french fries, he sits further under the umbrella this time. He takes a few fries for himself and hands the carton to her. "I brought some more, since you got all the sparrows in Sacramento waitin' here in line for 'em. They probably forgot how to find bugs for themself by now." He dips his fries all at once into the last of the catsup and eats them in one mouthful.

After he swallows them, he goes on. "I wish I could've talked to Rita before she left. I don't know what she'll find there. Mama might still be there, for all I know. Or Emma. That'll make a liar out of both of us. I feel real bad about that."

"Emma's not there," Hildy says. "Her whole family moved off to North Carolina. She used to write me before I came to California." She tosses the french fries one by one to the birds, then flings the rest to the ground near the other table, leans on her elbows on the table. "Liam, can you remember back when we were kids, what we did?" She wipes her hands on a napkin. "I dreamt about our old high school teacher, the one I liked so much? Now I couldn't even place her name."

"Miz Stanfill?"

She looks startled. "How did you remember that and I didn't?"

He shrugs.

"I dreamt this same dream before," she goes on, "about me playing down at the creek with a dollbaby. This time I was playin' in the water at Mahala Lake, down where the church had their baptizings. I wasn't with them. I was just playin' around in the water over where the trees were, by myself."

She absently gathers crumbs and herds them over the edge of the table. "That seems strange to me," she says. "You know how I've never liked the water. I still don't."

"Why, you did when you was little, Chig. We all did. Remember the big mud turtle that kept getting in our swimmin' hole down by the spring?"

Hildy looks puzzled, then goes on. "Anyway, I was just playin', mindin' my own business, and ol' Brother Earl . . . at least I think it was him . . . he was like a shadow. I could kind of see right through him. He came over to me and he took the dollbaby. In the dream it was an old one Rita had when she was a baby. I never had any when I was little."

Liam remembers a doll that Mammaw made her, one that Hildy dragged around with her for years, but he decides it's better if he doesn't interrupt her just now.

"Brother Earl, he came over and took the doll and tore it up," she goes on. "Tore its head off and its arms and legs, and I was beggin' him to stop it. The whole time he was tearin' it up, he was yellin' that it was a sinner, a black sinner. Then I looked down and all the pieces floatin' on the water were black, like he said, and they were bleedin' and the water was turnin' red. You know some people say they don't dream in colors? Well, I can still see that red water plain as day."

Even under the umbrella, it must be a hundred degrees out here, but Liam feels a chill around his shoulders. The sun has passed over and Hildy sits right in its heat, but she doesn't seem to notice.

"Then Aunt Emma, she came down the hill, ridin' on her old treadle sewin' machine like it was a horse. She kept reachin' for me, the whole time peddlin' it with her feet, but then it seemed like she got farther and farther away. Then she was Miz Stanfill and she was holdin' out that old book *Silas Marner* like she wanted me to grab hold of it, but she couldn't reach me." Hildy wipes her forehead with a napkin, squints up at the sun, moves over into the shade. "I woke up wringin' wet with sweat. Lord, I hope I'm not goin' through the change already."

The cold shiver starts at the back of Liam's neck, spreads to his shoulders. He studies the concrete table top, picks up sesame seeds one at a time and drops them in a little pile.

Hildy finishes her cola drink, takes off the lid and fishes out an ice cube. "Rita's always wantin' to know about things that I can't remember." She sucks the ice, then drops it back into her cup. "She's always askin' me about Mama. All I remember about Mama is her mouth. In the middle of the night I see a big slobbery mouth. It makes me think of the devil grinnin'."

"Yeah," Liam says. He hesitates, but thinks maybe it wouldn't hurt to add another face to Hildy's dream. "And I can't think of Bobby Ray without seein' his eyes. Talk about the devil. But I don't think I ever remember seein' Bobby Ray grin."

Hildy's face pales, and she sets her ice cup down with a thump. "It was *him*."

Liam sucks in a big breath, but determines to keep calm. "Who?"

"In the dream. It was *him* that was tearin' up the dollbaby. Bob— him. He was the one tearing up that doll."

Liam plays at finishing his root beer, not knowing how to start what he wants to say. "Chig, that dream, it makes me think of some things I've heard of before. Now don't get all riled up. I'm not sayin' you're like anybody else. But when we was first married, Jonelle used to have bad dreams and the army doctor that gave her some sleepin' pills told her that dreams *mean* something and maybe she ought to go see a psychiatrist and he could help find out—"

"You think I'm crazy?" Hildy starts to jump up, but Liam touches her arm; she sits back down. "Well, I'm not! It was just a silly dream."

"No, I don't think you're crazy, and I didn't think Jonelle was. But she said that same thing you just did . . . that she wasn't crazy . . . and she wouldn't go. Later on she told me what had happened to her, and I'm not any doctor, but *I* could even tell her dreams was about the same thing."

Hildy sits with her eyes toward the birds, but he knows she's lost interest in them. Finally she asks in a quiet voice, "What did happen to her?"

The sparrows mill around on the sidewalk and the empty table, waiting. They peck at the bare sidewalk, as though they're trying to give Hildy a hint of what it is they want. A teenage boy comes out with a broom and starts to sweep under the tables, and the sparrows scatter. "Let's go get in the car," Liam says, grateful that she's parked over in the shade.

He gets up, gathers the empty cups and wrappers. Hildy gets into the driver's seat, but Liam follows her in, nudges her to scoot over. He leaves the door open, hoping to cool the car down some. "I promised her I wouldn't ever tell anybody about this," he says.

Hildy looks relieved. "All right, then, you don't have to tell me."

"Yeah, I reckon I do, Chig." He leans his head on his arms folded across the steering wheel. "We was married five, six years before she could ever tell me about it. It was like she had put it out of her mind, but she remembered it when the doctor tried to find out why she wasn't having' any luck gettin' . . . why we wasn't havin' any kids. Hildy, when she was not but fifteen years old, her uncle, he forced himself on her." Liam watches Hildy out of the corner of his eye. She's staring out the windshield, but her shoulders move slightly. "Her folks had the doctor take the baby and say on his books it was appendicitis."

Hildy still stares at the windshield, but she blinks and he can see her swallowing hard. He goes on, "That's why as soon as she was able, she left home and ran with our gang."

Hildy's looking down at her hands, twisting a paper napkin.

Liam knows that sitting in the car in front of a hamburger stand in broad daylight is probably not the best place to look at all this, but he figures it's better than having Hildy seeing it in the middle of the night and waking up wringing with sweat, with nobody there to hold her and let her cry. "Chig," he starts, his voice husky and strained. "Is that what he . . . what *some*body . . . done to you?"

Rita always imagined mountains in Kentucky. On the bus all the way across from California, especially through the desert and the plains states, then down into the Southern states to Georgia, she'd looked forward to seeing the Kentucky mountains. But the western end of Kentucky where she found Mahala on the map, has only gently rolling hills. Definitely not mountains.

She thought she'd just hang around with Betty in Georgia for a couple of weeks, but Betty urged her to start her search right away. She even insisted that Rita take her new white Mustang convertible. Her dad could get her another one to use from his car dealership.

Rita politely suggested she wait until Betty could come along, after her summer school class was done, but by then summer would be just about gone. And who knows how long it would take to find Emma? She left behind the promise to tell Betty everything she found out— every delicious detail.

Out on the highway with her hair blowing free in the wind, Rita's glad to be alone. After all, she's almost eighteen now; she's not a little girl anymore. She doesn't need Betty to hold her hand.

She turns off the highway and drives down past a gas station and into Mahala, a little nervous about talking to someone, although she's sure they will have all noticed her by now. The main street of town turns quickly into a quiet, shady avenue lined with homes. She waves to a middleaged lady who sits on her porch, then to an old man sitting on the steps of the next porch. Some houses are prim little dollhouses with white fences, gardens out at the side. Some look worn and old, badly needing paint. But they all have those swings on the porch. Most of the swings have somebody sitting in them, and she's sure those somebodies are all watching her.

And the trees! Almost every house, no matter how humble, backs up to a forest. Some of the nicer brick houses that sit back from the road have trees—lots of them—in their front yards too.

Soon the houses are fewer, with grassy pastures and planted fields in between. She feels jealous of the cows that stand motionless on the gentle hillside in the shade of—what kind of trees are they? Dark green ones with deep gray shade. She tries to remember trees at home. Are there any trees at all in Richmond? How odd. She can't remember.

She turns into the next driveway she comes to, more like a gravel road that leads to a farmhouse, where children stop their playing to watch her. A woman comes out onto the front porch, taking off her apron as she starts down the steps. Rita backs the car out onto the road and turns around.

On the street that looks the most like "downtown," she grabs her candy bar—the only breakfast she took time to buy—and pulls over into the shade next to a tiny park. A bronze soldier stands in the center, with a greenish plaque at his feet. "They Gave Their Lives in Honor and Glory," it reads. Then "The War Between the States," with four names following; "The Great War," with three names. "World War II," it says, with seven names. Then "Korean War," and two names in newer, smaller letters, as if somebody realized the six inches of empty space might not be enough for all the wars to come.

World War II. The very first name is William Carmody. Somehow she'd expected to see "Little Will." So there he is, the uncle that her brother—her *half* brother—is named for, followed by Larry Arthur Hargis . . . Lewis Raymond Hite, Jr. . . . . Willard Fred Hite . . . Dwight Suggs, Jr. . . . . Sanford Lee Teague . . . Harlan Whitehouse . . .

Rita shades her eyes and looks down the short street, takes a bite of the chocolate that is already getting soft and squishy in the warm, humid morning.

She has the oddest feeling that these relatives of Larry and Lewis and Willard and Dwight and Sanford and Harlan are peeking at her from behind curtains, wondering why a stranger is standing in the middle of their town eating a candy bar.

"Lookin' for somebody, Ma'am?"

Rita sucks in her breath so quickly that the chocolate catches in her throat. "Oh! You scared me!"

"I didn't aim to, Ma'am . . . uh, Miss." He smiles, and it wrinkles up his whole face. "I ain't seen you around here before." He looks over at the convertible. "You all by yourself?"

"I'm just visiting. Actually, I'm looking for my aunt . . . my great aunt, Emma Hartley. Does she live around here?"

"Oh, you ain't about to find her around here. She moved, 'way back yonder, after the war. Not Korea, but the Big One, not long after that son of hers come back crippled up. She lived right down yonder, ran her sewin' business across from my place. The Luthers live there now. He's a good man. He's a veteran, wounded at Guada Canal, but not so's you can tell it now, raised three boys after the war. My wife

Loretta, she passed on last year, she liked Miz Hartley, hated to see her go. They left after the war—not Korear, the Big One. They sold the sawmill and the house to Sam Luther; he was wounded at—"

"Guadalcanal."

Malcolm's face lights up. "Oh, you know Sam Luther?"

"Kind of. But about Emma? Where did she go, do you know?"

"They took the family to North Caroliny, Asheville, I reckon it was—or was it Charlotte? No it was Asheville. It was the Pleasants that moved to Charlotte. Charlie Pleasant, he farmed out on Hanson Mill Road."

Rita's hopes sag. Now what? *Do I go all the way to Charlotte . . . uh, Asheville?* "Thank you, Mr., uh . . . "

"Malcolm."

"Well, thank you, Mr. Malcolm."

The old man laughs. "Naw, just Malcolm. Malcolm Brown. Loretta Brown, she was my wife, passed away last winter. November twelfth, it was. She really liked Miz Hartley."

As Rita eases her way back over to the car, Malcolm follows her.

"Well, thank you, Mr. Brown."

"Malcolm." He grins another broad grin, friendly and full of deep weathered creases. She gets into the Mustang. The air is getting hot and sticky, just the kind of day a convertible was made for, but only if it's moving. Malcolm leans on the passenger side door.

Rita turns the key in the ignition. "I'll be on my way now," she says. "It was Asheville, you're sure?"

"Yeah. Asheville. Loretta's cousin moved over to Raleigh, but Emma, she moved to Asheville. She talked about it just a week or two ago when she was here. One of the Luther boys, he thought she said Nashville and he wanted to know if she knew the Carter Sisters and Mother Maybelle."

He grins at the joke, then goes on, "She comes over here ever' so often. Her grandson brings her to see her sister." Malcolm takes his hands off the car, backs away. "Yeah, I reckon was just a week or two ago they was over here. Too bad you didn't come then."

Rita eases the car out onto the street, her thoughts as scattered as Malcolm's roadmap. Oh, well. She may as well give up and— *what?*

From the jumble of the old man's talk, one word suddenly stands out like a neon light. She stomps on the brake, shifts into reverse, backs up to where Malcolm still stands, grinning his wrinkly grin, almost as though he expected that she'd be back.

"Her . . . *sister?*" Is there another aunt Mom never told her about?

"Why yes. Her sister. Do you know her, too?" He slaps the car door and laughs. "Well lordamercy, a 'course you'd be kin to her if you're kin to Miz Hartley. Sister Carmody's 'bout the same as always. They's some of the sisters from the church that look after her for Emma. Ol' Brother Earl Spivey, he used to—"

"Omigosh! Carmody? You don't—you can't mean . . . *Gerty?*"

Malcolm frowns, looks puzzled. "Why, yes, Emma's sister."

Rita's sense of time has just tied itself into a knot. Did she drive Betty's Mustang into the Twilight Zone? "Where is she?" she asks, louder and more bluntly than she meant to.

He points out away from town. "She lives out yonder past the sawmill about a mile and a half. Other side of the hill, the on'y place before you get to the new school house."

"Thank you!" Rita starts the car with a roar, and the old man jumps back. She pulls out into the street, remembers to turn and wave to him.

Just before the small hill that Malcolm pointed out, she pulls the car over into the shade of a big tree to catch her breath and try to slow her heart that feels like a bass drum. It was a shock to find out from the old letter that her grandmother was still alive in 1945. But still alive now, almost twenty years later? She looks into the rearview mirror, pulls her fingers through her wind-tangled hair. "I can't see my grandmother like this," she says to herself in the mirror. "She'll think I'm crazy!"

I'm gonna see my grandmother! She imagines the ancient, delicate lady sitting on a porch, rocking, knitting, with a white picket fence surrounding the house, the yard full of flowers. Like Betty's Nana . . . fluffy silver-white hair, a pale lavender dress with teeny flowers and maybe a crocheted lace collar. Rocking . . . telling stories of the old days, back when Mom was little.

But oh, no, what if she's more like Granny Clampett? Like Jed Clampett and Uncle Liam always say, "feisty"?

Rita decides she prefers to picture herself kneeling beside the rocker, face-to-face with the frail little lady in the lavender dress.

"Good morning. I'm your granddaughter."

"Grandmother, I'm Rita, Hildy's daughter."

But then Granny Clampett might be fun . . . *feisty.* "Hello. Are you Gerty Carmody, my feisty grandmother?" *Geez.* Her excitement stirs together with the leftover anger from last week. Her almost-empty stomach bubbles up chocolate-tinged acid. "Hi! I'm your long-lost granddaughter, Rita. You know, the one from another planet? Do you know any more about me than I know about you? And why not?" She wonders if this lavender-silver-white grandmother with the lace collar will be as angry as she is for having been cheated out of all this.

She takes a deep breath, then another. "Okay, calm down. People go see their grandmothers every day." She starts the car and carefully pulls away from the shade.

On the other side of the hill she passes one worndown house, but her eyes veto it. No picket fence. No flowers. She rounds a sweeping curve in the road, comes to a new-looking brick building, turns the car into the empty parking lot. *Mahala Elementary School* is carved into the concrete above the wide door. She backs slowly onto the road, looking both ways, then realizes the silliness of it. Since the school is deserted, obviously closed for summer, there isn't anybody here to watch out for. She eases the car back toward town, watches more carefully for another house, one that must be hidden from sight by all these lovely trees. Yes, it must be. As the road starts up the low hill, there it is, the same house. The only house there is. Wasn't that what the wrinkly old man said?

"Oh, well. I didn't really expect her to be rich, did I?" The anger that sits in one corner of her stomach rises again. How could Mom not care that her mother is poor? That other people take care of her? She wipes her eyes hard with the palms of her hands.

She turns up into the empty space by the front of the house. No driveway or fence of any kind, no flower garden, not even a lawn, not anything that could be called a "front yard." Somebody has cut down a bunch of weeds at the side of the house recently and left them to dry on the ground. She gets out of the car, resists the urge to jump back in and rush over the hill to find—what was his name? Malcolm.

There's a slight movement up on the porch. Someone's sitting in the porch swing, half hidden by some sort of vines that grow up the posts and onto the roof. How could Rita have missed her? The woman must weigh 400 pounds. Well. So much for feisty.

It would be awkward to leave now. The old woman has surely seen her. Rita makes her way up to the porch steps. One step looks like it's been replaced recently, and the rest look questionable. "Hello?"

The old woman is staring out toward what looks like it used to be a small garden, but Rita can't picture this huge woman stooping to weed a garden or to pick vegetables. "Hello? Excuse me, are you Gerty Carmody?"

Every nerve in her body hopes the answer is *no*. The old woman doesn't answer or even look Rita's direction. She just smiles a weird smile that looks like nobody's home behind it.

Rita wipes her sweaty hands on her jeans. "I'm Rita, your grand-daughter, and I came to find out more about my family." *Geez, Rita, you're not making a speech here.* "My Mom . . . your daughter Hildy and I, we live in California. Maybe you know that already? And my brother Will? He's named for your son Will? Your son Little Will?" *Geez, why do I sound like a five-year-old, with question marks at the end of every sentence?* This isn't going at all like Rita imagined. Maybe there's been a mistake. No, a joke! Old Malcolm is sitting back there on the park bench laughing at the silly girl from out of town.

"I've got a brother Will, too," she says when she can't think of anything else to say. But she's already said that, she's sure. So what. She's trying to make conversation with a person she didn't know for certain existed until an hour ago, and she's still not too sure.

The woman's face comes alive. "Little Will, he went to the war."

"Yes! Mom's twin brother Will. My brother is named for him."

The woman's head bobs up and down and she smiles. "Little Will wrote letters for his Mama."

"Did he send any pictures? Mom never had any of herself either. Is that true, there are no pictures of my mother?"

The odd smile is still there, but the face has gone blank behind it, as though it had said what it meant to say, and is now finished.

"Are there any pictures of my . . . of Hildy? Hildy . . . Will . . . her twin brother Will? The one who went to the war?" She looks around at the porch, scattered with old bits of clothing, papers, a pork-and-beans can. The photo she imagined— twins, wearing matching outfits, sitting in one of those twin strollers, maybe—is completely out of place here.

At first she can't tell if the woman's face is still and quiet because she's digging around in her memories for a place to start, or if she just didn't hear Rita at all.

Well, she certainly isn't very . . . friendly. Not for someone who's supposed to be her own flesh and blood. Rita shudders. No, surely she must have the wrong house, the wrong grandmother. Surely this huge

mound of a woman must be somebody *else's* flesh and blood. But
she has to try. She's come so far. "What about my grandfather? Well,
of course he really didn't have any chance to be a grandfather, since
he died before we were born." She feels stupid for saying that. "My
grandfather? Your husband?" One more try: "Daniel?"

With this there is a stirring in the woman's face. "Daniel," she
parrots, as though her mouth has not formed the word in fifty years.

"Geez, I should have waited for my psych degree for this." Rita
knows she should be embarrassed for saying it aloud, but she gets the
feeling she'd get the same response if she recited the Preamble to the
Constitution, or sang "I Want to Hold Your Hand."

The woman shifts her weight in the swing, rummages in the
pocket of her faded gingham apron, pulls out a little round tin. She
opens it, tucks a pinch of dark powder behind her bottom lip. Rita's
eyes watch, fascinated, but at the same time her mouth tries to ignore
the picture.

She looks at her watch. The morning's gone, so she may as well
go on. "Is there a family cemetery? Would that be where Daniel is
buried?" She glances quickly around the yard, then feels foolish. Is she
expecting tombstones to pop up right here in the yard or something?
Well, lately anything's possible.

The old woman looks disturbed. "Daniel," she repeats. Dark
brown liquid runs down from the corner of her mouth. She leans and
stretches down over the chair arm, struggles to reach the pork-and-
beans can on the floor. She spits black-brown juice, returns the can to
a spot on the middle rung of the porch railing, wipes her mouth with
an apron corner that has obviously been used for the same thing many
times before.

Rita winces, feels the chocolate stirring in her stomach. She may
never eat chocolate again.

"Who are you?" the old woman blurts out, as if she just woke up
and noticed Rita for the first time.

"I'm Rita, your . . . granddaughter," she says, even though she's
less and less sure of it. But the woman—whoever she is—she did
know about Little Will, didn't she?

The woman becomes animated again, as if somebody had wound
up a big key in the middle of her back. She removes herself from the
swing by climbing her hands up the chain until she is almost upright
and the swing slips out from under her.

Rita, startled that the huge mass is moving, scrambles to move away, down the steps.

Without a word the old woman lumbers past her and goes inside, lets the ragged screendoor flap against the broadest backside Rita has ever seen.

Rita isn't tempted to follow, not that she's been invited. "I guess I'll come back later," she halfway promises the screendoor, but she's not at all sure she'll have the nerve.

She'll ask around, maybe at the post office. Wouldn't it be a good joke if she finds out she's been at the wrong house, bugging somebody else's grandmother? Betty would get a big laugh out of that.

That same afternoon

The screendoor slaps shut and Gerty makes her way down to the end of the porch, where she nudges the orange cat from the oversized rocker. Her bones creak in unison with the chair frame as she lowers her bulk between the paintbare wooden arms. She rocks steadily. The *squeak squeak squeak* of the rocker comforts her. Her glance wanders again in the direction of the road, out beyond the railing where a cat tucks back into her disrupted sleep. Gerty dreads what she might see out there, and yet she's drawn to it, waits for it. Was it this morning that the strange girl came? Yesterday?

She hugs her fleshy arms to her bosom and her shiver deepens to an uneasy chill. The girl's face haunts her . . . she has seen it before. The image stirs Gerty's recollection like the lyesoap kettle of the old days, and now the contents refuse to settle to the bottom.

On the railing, the cat yawns himself to its full length, spreading his claws. Beyond him, the white car—that strange white car with no top on it—pulls up from the road onto the bare dirt near the house.

The cat jumps down from the railing to meet the girl as she walks slowly up to the porch and stands at the bottom of the steps. "Hello there," the girl says to the cat. "Hello, uh, Grandmother," the girl says. "What's her name? What's the cat's name?"

Gerty frowns. *Such foolishness. It's just an old cat.*

The girl keeps talking, but her voice irritates Gerty. She tries to brush it away from in front of her eyes. *Pictures,* the girl keeps saying. Pictures, blurring pictures, all blend into one that focuses sharper in Gerty's mind. She gets up from the old rocker. The girl backs away, and the cat runs up under the porch.

Gerty goes inside and rummages through the pile on her bed,

finds her Bible, thumbs through it until a tattered, faded photograph falls out, a picture of a baby in a polka-dot gown.

On the radio, the country music is playing and that means next it will be time for Bobby Ray.

Gerty goes back out. The girl is standing on the bottom porch step. Gerty shoves the photograph toward her. It flutters to the ground. The girl stoops to pick it up, shakes it, turns it over.

"Pitcher!" Gerty says. *Fool girl, she don't even know what it is.*

"Who is this? Is this . . . there's no name on it."

Gerty wrinkles her face. The name. The girl wants the name. Gerty tries to remember. She knew a name a few minutes ago, but now it has escaped again. She searches for it in the void of her memory.

"Please try to remember? Please," the girl says again, turning the photograph over one more time.

Gerty looks around inside the vacuum of her mind and picks up a name recently dropped there. "Daniel," she says, proud that she has settled on a name for an answer. She nods. "Daniel."

The girl's eyes get big. "This is my grandfather?"

Try to remember. There. Now Gerty has remembered, and she is done. She has something else important to remember. The country music is on the radio. "My Bobby Ray is comin' on the radio."

The girl is still staring at the picture. "Huh? What did you say?"

Gerty squints, peers at the girl. Foolish girl. "My Bobby Ray is on the radio!" she shouts. "You better listen to him!"

The girl backs away a few feet. Gerty stares directly into her eyes, squints, turns her head a little to the side. A name . . . yes, the girl has a name . . . she knows it . . . what is it? A lump rises to just behind her collarbone as images churn to the surface. Odessa! But no. Odessa has on her bonnet. Mama put it on her this morning. And where are her long plaits? This girl is not Odessa. Foolish girl. She thinks she's Odessa. "You're not Odessa," Gerty yells. "No you're not! You won't get her! You can't have her!"

The girl turns and runs to the car.

Satisfied with herself, Gerty shuts the girl out of her mind. She goes inside to the voice on the radio. It's her boy, her preacher man— her Bobby Ray, telling the sinners to go to hell and damnation. But he's not talking about Gerty. She's his mama. And Bobby Ray loves his mama. He brought her a radio, didn't he?

"Come on in the house, Sweetie. Mama wants you to help her." But what was it she wanted Bobby Ray to do? She can't remember.

Later that afternoon
Nortonville, Kentucky

Rita tries to shove the door of the booth closed, but it is dirt-welded into a permanent V-fold. Just as well. She can't see a thing through the dirty gray-brown glass, and she doesn't dare let Betty's Mustang out of her sight, especially after a VW van pulls up to the lone DX gas pump in front of the roadside grocery store, not twenty feet from the phone booth. The booth has a distinct odor of—"Oh, geez, its pee! It smells like old pee in here!" A dirt drift in the corner of the booth is obviously dried mud, and a shiny spot near the corner could be a coin, but she isn't about to investigate. She thumbs two nickels into the middle coin slot and dials Betty's number, stretches the phone cord as far out the door as it will go. It's no use, the odor follows her like a finger of invisible steam, blending with the exhaust that coughs from the tailpipe of the van.

"Geez, Betty, answer the phone, will you?"

The teenage boy refilling a Pennzoil display just outside the station door gives Rita a puzzled squint, yells something over to the driver, who is squatting at the back of the van, inspecting the engine.

Rita can barely make out the familiar yellow-on-black of the van's dusty California plate. "Figures. With that hair, he can't be from around here," she mutters.

The ringing is interrupted by a honeysuckle voice all but drowned out by the van.

"What?" Rita yells into the receiver. "Betty? I can't hear—Betty? Is Betty—"

"Deposit one dollar and ten cents for the first three minutes, please."

From her collection of coins on the wooden shelf, she jams in the three quarters, the dimes and a nickel, leaving one lone nickel next to the reminder scratched into the wooden shelf: JESUS SAVES.

Three more boys about Rita's age pour out of the van and swarm around the Mustang parked on the sparse patch of dead grass over by the store. She feels their grubby hands caressing the convertible's hood, its doors, as surely as if they were touching her own skin.

"Rita, Hon, is that you? Are you all right? Lord, you've not got in a wreck have you?"

"Betty? Can you hear me?" Rita presses her palm tighter against her free ear, which makes her sound like she's yelling into a bucket.

"Look, kid, I'm coming back. I'll be into Macon tonight late."

One of the boys from the van has obviously seen the Mustang's Georgia license plates. He elbows one of the others, grins, points over at Rita.

The van's engine cuts off and in the instant silence Rita's voice bounces off the grimy, spiderwebbed walls. She glares at the boys and they laugh, pushing, shoving one another, waving. The redhaired one puts his fingers to his mouth and lets out one shriek of a whistle. "Hey, Honeychile, is this your little ol' car?"

Rita hunches over the receiver, blinks back the tears that film her eyes. She is determined not to cry.

"Hon, you're not givin' up so soon, are you?" Betty asks.

Rita sneaks a look at the Mustang. The boys are still there. "Hey, Honey, come on over here and take me for a ride!" the one with blond hair yells.

"Idiots! Immature beatnik idiots," she mutters. "Geez!"

"What?" Betty's voice pulls at her from the earpiece, "But, you knew it might take all summer to find Emma."

"No, that's not it. I found her! Not Emma . . . I found my *grandmother!* I've actually *seen* her. Twice. It's just no use. It was awful! She's . . . she's weird, Betty. She's totally out of it."

"Deposit ninety cents, please, for the next three minutes."

"Geez, it's been three minutes already? Just a minute . . . " She rummages into the purse again, hoping. "I'm sorry, I don't . . . I've got to go." One last dig produces two fuzzy Certs, which she tosses out the door.

"Here, Hon, let me. Operator, would you please reverse the charge on this call?"

"I'm sorry Ma'am, I can't do that. The calling party will have to place the call again collect."

"Listen, I'll just go—"

"No, you call me right back!" Betty is gone. Rita wishes she could start this whole miserable day over again.

She slowly hangs up the receiver. "Geez, can't I just get away from here?" Then she grabs it back. "Operator?" Only a dial tone answers. "Geez, now Betty'll stand there by the phone and wait. Well, I'm not going in that store, no matter what."

The only other choice is the coin on the floor. With a slightly used tissue from her purse, she picks the coin—a dime—from the floor and quickly drops it on the wooden shelf. "Oh. Sorry, Jesus."

Once Betty comes back on the line, her questions roll over each other. "So you talked to her, no kiddin'? What did she say? Did she seem like . . . then how come . . . Hon, are you all right? Are you cryin'? You sound like you're cryin'."

Tears have rushed up into Rita's eyes, and she can't hold them back any longer. "I just want to get away from here, okay?"

At least the boys from the van have gone on into the store.

"I'm sorry," she says. "Look, I'll tell you about it tonight. That is, if that's okay with your folks."

"Now don't you be silly. To hear Mama tellin' it, you're her long-lost movie star daughter from Hollywood. Are you sure, Hon? I mean, don't you want to just stay there and—"

"Oh, Betty she was dirty and disgusting, and she weighed maybe 400 hundred pounds, and . . . and . . . she *yelled* at me! Listen, Kid, let's talk about it later, okay? I've got to go. I'm getting a headache."

"But wait . . . where are you now?"

"I'm on . . . just a minute." She leans out the door of the phone booth, stretches to see the sign out on the highway past the gas pump. The boy with the oil cans points at himself with a hopeful *Me?* written on his face. Rita waves him away. The heat that shimmers from the blacktop warps the road sign. She squeezes her eyes shut but the shimmers are still there. "Oh, geez, I'm getting a migraine, I just know it. Okay, I'm on Highway 41, someplace called Northville or something. Listen, this is running up your folks' bill."

"Oh, they don't give a hoot about that. I'll wait up for you—now, you've got to tell me just everything. I can't believe it, you actually found your grandma!"

"It's not like you think at all, Betty." Rita's throat tightens, and it feels like something is trying to choke her. She can't hold in this horrible day's dammed-up strain any longer.

"Betty, she didn't know anything! She acted like she never even heard of Mom . . . or any of us. I felt so weird, like I was invisible, like she didn't even hear me talking to her. And listen to this . . . she just went on in the house and left me on the porch, said her son was on the radio. And she yelled at me like a crazy woman!"

"Oh my."

It takes a lot to quiet Betty for more than a moment. "Betty? Are you there?"

"But . . . what about Emma, then?"

"Oh, She's moved off to North Carolina someplace. But she's probably the same way. I don't even care any more! I just want to leave, right now! I can't—"

"You at least took snapshots, didn't you?"

"No, I forgot. But she gave me this one baby picture of my grandfather. I can't wait to show it to Mom. I mean, her own father and all."

"Maybe that'll help patch up y'all's fight, don't you reckon?"

"Listen, I gotta go, Kid. I'll never get there if I don't get going. Bye now." Rita fishes the Ford keys from her jeans pocket and heads on out to the convertible. A loud chorus of laughter bursts from the screendoor of the store.

She scrambles into the car and starts the engine, but the red-haired boy rushes up to the passenger side. "Hey, Miz Scarlett? Why don't you give little ol' me a ride in your car?"

Another day she probably would have flirted with him, or with the one who looks a little like Paul McCartney. And she would have laughed in their red faces when they found out their phony drawls were wasted on her, that she's from California, too.

But today she's had all her nerves can stand. She wants to get out of here, to go home. She yells over the roar of the engine, "Get your hands off this car, or I'll call the cops!"

The redhead jumps back, laughing, his hands in the air. "Yes, *Ma'am!*"

Three, four miles south of Nashville, where the highway curves into a stand of tall sycamores, the concrete is grayed and cooled, shaded from the dogdays heat. Rita slows the Mustang, pulls off the highway at a wide gravel area where three mailboxes stand guard over a private road that plunges into the deep woods and disappears.

She unsnaps the front pocket of her purse and pulls out the tiny photograph, touches the face in the oval, resists turning it over to check one more time for writing on the back.

Her eyes want to follow the baby's gaze to the right, somber, so very familiar. Whatever is he looking at? Then it hits her. "It looks like *me!* Like my little birthday face, the one on Mom's dresser!" The baby grandfather's face blurs in front of her eyes. "Oh, geez," she whispers. *Oh, geez.*

She tucks the photograph into the clip on the sunvisor, and it stares toward the passenger seat, eye level with Rita. "So, Grandpa, I guess it's not just you I'm looking for after all, is it?"

Rita backs the Mustang into the crunch of the gravel driveway, wipes her eyes hard with the back of her hand. She spreads her roadmap on the seat beside her and studies it for a few minutes, then pulls out onto the road back to Nashville to catch Highway 40 east to North Carolina.

The next afternoon
Asheville, North Carolina

Maybe she should have waited until Betty could come along with her. On the phone last night, Betty sounded kind of sorry she didn't.
It was creepy, checking in at the Travelodge in Knoxville, pretending it was no big thing that Rita was by herself. She knew everybody wondered what a seventeen-year-old girl with a California drivers license and Georgia plates was doing out on the road alone late at night. Definitely creepy.

But this morning, driving seventy miles an hour down a highway lined with about forty billion trees . . . and nobody knowing for sure where she is . . . well, after all, she *is* almost eighteen. She doesn't need Betty tagging along on the first grown-up thing she's ever done.

She turns onto the main street of Asheville, a street that looks like it could belong back home in Richmond or Sacramento, much bigger than Mahala. She'll have to remember that here, "Richmond" means the Robert E. Lee one, not the San Francisco Bay one.

The nice Information operator assured her there were indeed two Hartleys—one of them a furniture store, neither of them Emma—listed in Asheville. And there were none in Charlotte. She asked about Charlotte, just to be sure. But what if there's nobody here? What if they've all recently moved away—to where? She runs her fingers through her sticky hair. In this humidity her hair is curlier, tighter, glued to the back of her neck. She passes a Mode O'Day store . . . J.C. Penney's . . .

Sure, she thought of calling ahead, to save herself the trip if some neighbor named Malcolm told her that Emma was sent off to a mental hospital last week, it runs in the family, didn't she know? Or what if Emma had answered the phone? Then she couldn't have changed her mind and backed out.

A bookstore . . . a coffee shop . . . Woolworth's . . . The baby grandfather in the photo on the visor has stared at the passenger window, unblinking, for ten hours across Tennessee. "Geez, it didn't look that far on the map, did it, Kid?"

She could still turn around and go back, even now. Relief settles around her shoulders at the thought. Yes. She could turn at this next corner, go around, get right back on the highway, take the direct road to Macon and be there before dinner. But if Betty were here, she wouldn't let her give up that easily.

The baby stares. Was that teeny frown on his face before? Is he disappointed? She can't disappoint him and Betty both, can she?

She looks for a phone booth, passes a drugstore . . . another coffee shop . . . a furniture store . . . *Hartley & what?* She pulls sharply to the curb and hears the squeal of tires, honking horns behind her. People stop on the sidewalk to look. Faces appear at the windows above the stores. *Geez, how embarrassing!* She gets out of the car, grabs her purse, stops to catch the breath that is stuck in her chest.

A young man runs out of the furniture store and insists on helping her to a bench under the awning of the coffee shop. He sits down beside her, eases his arm protectively onto the bench behind her, waves the bystanders on. "I'm Marc Hartley. Are you all right?"

He has a cute smile and his voice is calm and pleasant, kind of eager, but not in an obnoxious way. And not nearly as formal as his tie and white dress shirt would have her to believe.

"*That* Hartley?" She ducks to peek under the awning, pointing at the sign above the furniture store. "Then I'm looking for you!"

"Oh thank you Lord my prayers are answered," he says, with a wide grin. "Well, unless you're the FBI or something."

Geez, he's cute! Definitely glad Betty's not here. Definitely.

"Well, you're a start, I mean . . . I'm actually looking for . . . "

His grin fades. "Oh."

"What I mean is . . . wait! Marc? Is it Marc-with-a-c?" She digs into her purse, for the folded stationery, points to the bottom of the page that she's read at least fifty times. "Then, are you this Marcus?"

He takes the letter, skims quickly over it, laughs, nods. "Emma's my grandmother, and Wayne and Naomi, they're my folks. But let me guess. You're not this Hildy, right?"

"No, that's my mom." She laughs, too, then tries to remember if she brushed her teeth before she left the motel this morning.

He hands the letter back. "So, then, we're some kind of cousins, the once-removed kind or something." He leans back, arms folded across his chest. "What fantastic luck, huh."

"I think that would make us second cousins—but you'd be once-removed to my mom. And me to yours. Oh, yeah. Lucky us, huh?"

He stands up, shoves his hands into his slacks pockets. "Well, so, does this mean our date's off, then?"

She gets up, brushes off her jeans. "Our date?"

"Yeah." He grins. "The one I was just goin' to ask you for, just as soon as you told me your name, and right after I made a big fuss over your car." His grin is back, not quite as big as before. "And before we found out that golly-gee-whoopee we're cousins."

What cute charmers these southern boys are! Definitely no Betty, or anybody else, needed or wanted.

"But you know what?" he continues. "I don't reckon North Carolina has any laws against second cousins eatin' together. I mean, if we sit across the table."

"Well, I'm Rita," she says, laughing, "and if they do, can't we just go to another state? I've been in lots of 'em lately."

"Well, depends. How old are you?"

He has the crinkly kind of eyes that almost wink when he smiles. He offers his hand, and she slips hers into it as comfortably as if she'd grown up with him. They can think about this cousin thing later. "But I reckon we'd better make that date supper with my folks. Grandma—Emma—she lives with us. Or we live with her, I never did figure out which. Listen—" He stops in the middle of the sidewalk, wiggles the knot of his tie loose and drops her hand long enough to pull out the free end of the tie and unbutton his top shirt button, then grabs her hand again.

"Come on. I've got to go back in and sign myself out of the store. But I'm not lettin' you out of my sight, now, you hear?"

She smiles. Not a chance.

Early that evening

The voices at the front door pull Emma from her embroidery. She puts it down and peeks around into the living room.

"You should have called us, Marc," Naomi chastises. She brushes her hair out of her face "We're glad to have you for supper, Rita, if you don't mind it's just potluck. Wayne? Emma? Come here and meet Marc's friend!"

Emma waits at the parlor door. The girl with Marc looks haunt-ingly familiar. A granddaughter of one of her club friends? No, Emma puzzles. Something stirs from a long time ago, much longer ago than the Asheville Rose Garden Club.

Marc gathers the pretty girl by the waist and brings her over. "And this is my Grandma Emma. Grandma, Rita came a long way to meet you." His eyes are mischievous. What is this boy up to now? Emma stares at the girl as only a seventy-year-old can get away with.

The girl smiles and offers her hand. "My mom is your niece, Hildy."

Emma's hand goes automatically to her throat. "Oh my Lord."

Naomi comes over, smoothing down her apron. "Marc, you're a rascal." She pats Emma's arm and chuckles. "He was tellin' us this was his new girlfriend."

Wayne clumps into the room with his unwieldy crutch. Naomi rushes to help him, but he swats her away and makes his way over to the girl. Naomi follows after him, tugging at his sleeve. "Wayne," she says, "that's Rita, Hildy's girl."

Wayne brushes Naomi's hand from his arm, never taking his eyes off Rita. "I know it," he says. His voice is softer than Emma's noticed it in a long time, and she swears his eyes are misty. "I knew that the minute I laid eyes on her," he says. "Honey, is she—is your Mama all right?" He offers his left hand, nods toward the crutch in his right. "Oh, now don't you mind that. I was wounded in the war. They made me a wooden leg, but the blame thing never did fit right."

"Wayne!" Naomi smacks him on his shoulder. "I'm sure she isn't interested in all that."

Emma starts to speak, but no words come to her. Rita looks a little flustered with all the attention. *Poor girl*, Emma thinks. *She looks like a rabbit caught in a trap. Lord, that look is so familiar.*

"I've got a picture of my brother," Rita says, pulling it from her jeans pocket. "He's Will number three I guess. He's in the Marines."

The photograph of Will goes quickly from hand to hand, and Wayne's eyes light up. "Now me, I was in the Navy, a signalman on the *USS Bunker Hill.*"

"Uh-oh," Marc says, "Now you got Daddy started."

"Marc here was named for my commander, Marcus Mitscher. You ever hear of the Great Turkey Shoot?"

"Now, Daddy," Marc says, "I don't reckon Rita wants to hear all about that."

Marc tries to lead Rita over to the couch. "The fool Navy, they sent him home after one of his legs got cut off when a plane crashed right next to him on the deck. Reckon they didn't notice he had *two* legs to give for his country."

"Oh, hush up!" Wayne mutters, taking his seat in the big rocker by the fireplace. "You younguns don't know anything about nothing." He flings a little embroidered pillow at Marc. Marc ducks, catches it.

"At least Billy Wayne's in the Navy," Wayne goes on, "He's gettin' himself some education and seein' the world."

Marc tucks the little pillow behind Rita. "Yeah, Bill's carryin' on Daddy's military hero tradition. Me, I'm stuck here carryin' on the legacy of sellin' dinette sets." He grins. "But you watch out, next he'll be tellin' you about the ship that did nothing but make ice cream."

"You still think I'm lyin', don't you?" Wayne starts to get up, but Naomi steps in and pushes him back down into the chair.

"You'll have to forgive these children of mine, Rita," Naomi says. She gives Rita a friendly pat, hands the photo back to her. "I'm goin' to go in and get you some iced tea. You look like you could use it."

"Thanks." Rita accepts a seat on the couch, and Marc takes the couch arm, sitting protectively over her. "It's so overwhelming," she mumbles, "all at once, so much more family than I ever knew about."

"Well," Wayne calls over from the rocking chair, "if you came back here to find out all the mysteries of your family, you've got a lot to work on. I'd start out with that brother of your mama's. He's a mean one, liked to've knocked my head off once. I've still got the scar right here"—he points to his forehead—"to prove it. I always said he had something to do with his—his and your mama's—daddy disappearin'. I wouldn't put it past him. And he shot that boy that time, then tried to claim Aunt Gerty did it, as if she'd've known one end of a .22 from the other."

With that, Emma finds her voice at last. "Wayne, you hush! Good Lord, you've got no call to dump all that onto this poor girl. Look at her, she looks like she's ready to bolt out the door!" Emma sits on the other side of Rita, takes her hand. It's as cold as ice. "You don't pay any attention to him, Honey. He's losin' his mind faster than I am." She slips an arm around the girl's waist and can feel her whole body shivering.

Rita's still staring at Wayne. Her eyes look like they're going to pop out of her head.

"What's the matter, Hon?"

"Uncle . . . *Liam* . . . did that?"

"Oh no," Marc says. "The other one, the big radio preacher, *Robert Ray*," he says with a sneer.

Rita still looks stunned. Why, Emma realizes, the girl's never heard of Bobby Ray! But then that surely isn't a surprise. Hildy never would have exactly bragged about him.

"The radio?" Rita says, "Then wait . . . maybe . . . maybe that's what she was talking about . . . Bobby somebody?"

Emma pulls Rita up from the couch and steers her toward the parlor. "You sit down in here, Honey. Marc, go see what happened to that iced tea." She can hear Naomi's voice in the kitchen on the phone.

"But I want to show Rita around outside, Grandma."

"No, you've hogged her long enough. I'm takin' her in the front room and havin' her all to myself for a while. The poor girl can use a little rest from the likes of you two."

Marc laughs, rolls his eyes at Rita. "Well, see if I ever bring home any more pretty kissin' cousins."

Emma sits Rita down on the loveseat and perches herself right beside her, taking her hands. "Honey, have you got a picture of your Mama? Not that I need one . . . I'm lookin' at her right now. Last time I saw your mama, she was your age and looked just like you, except her hair was a little darker, and not as curly. There's not a day goes by that I don't think of her. But I always picture her just like that."

Rita relaxes a little, smiles. "She's changed some. For one thing I can't imagine her hair dark. She's bleached it for just about as long as I can remember."

"Well, she'll soon be sorry of *that*." Emma laughs, pats her own silver hair, pulled back in a neat bun. "One of these days the Lord will peroxide it for her, like He did mine."

Naomi brings two tall glasses of iced tea, sets them down on the coffee table. "We'll keep supper a little longer, if you can hold out. Rose and Sissy . . . my girls . . . they're lookin' forward to meetin' you, Rita."

Rita smiles, but her chest heaves with a visible sigh. Emma holds onto her hand, gives it a squeeze. She thinks this poor girl's surely had all the family she can handle.

"Don't worry, Hon, the worst the girls'll dump on you is my three great-grandkids. 'Course any one of them is enough to make you forget all about what you came here for. I've always said I wouldn't take ten million dollars for 'em, but I wouldn't give ten cents for another bunch just like 'em!"

Emma laughs at her own favorite comment, one she's made at least a hundred times before. Obviously Rita has more on her mind.

"I can't believe it," Rita says. "Mom has a brother I've never even heard of."

"Well, Bobby Ray is nothing to brag about, especially for your mama." Emma stirs her tea with a long silver teaspoon. "I doubt if she left much of anything behind she would want to be reminded of, but especially not of him."

"I didn't know her mother was alive, either." Rita's face pinches up into a pout, but it softens when Marc pokes his head in the door.

"Grandma, can I—"

"Marc, before I forget, you go up in the attic and find that old radio to give to Rita, so she can take it to her mama." She pats Rita's knee. "Now, that's something good she might like to remember."

Rita's eyes follow Marc, then she takes a long drink of iced tea and settles back into the loveseat with another big sigh. Emma can't help smiling. It looks like Marc's not the only smitten one here. She sips her tea. Naomi's made it too sweet again, sweeter than she likes.

"You saw Gerty, did you?" she asks. When the trapped-deer look comes over Rita's face again, Emma decides to save this to talk about later.

She picks up the photograph of Will that Rita has dropped on the coffee table. "Well, he surely does look like the Will he's named after. But then I guess you've heard that before. Let's see . . . he'd be Marc's age, or a little younger."

"Marc and I were talking about that. Actually, Will is about three months older."

No . . . no . . . this doesn't ring true, Emma thinks. "He wasn't born in the fall? For some reason I thought her boy was born in the fall." But surely Rita knows her own brother's birthday.

"Nope. In May." Rita sips her iced tea. "This is so good. I've never been much of a tea drinker before."

Something far back in Emma's mind screams for attention, something she can't quite place, but something.

Rita drains the tea glass and puts it back on the table, blows out a long breath. There's a bustle of noise from the front door, little kids' voices.

Marc pops in again. "Mama says come on and eat. I got the radio down for you." He reaches for Rita's hand. "Come on, Cousin! I at least get to sit by my date, don't I?"

Naomi herds everybody into the kitchen, introducing them on the way. Emma catches Wayne by the shoulder. "Wayne?"

"Yeah, Mama?"

"How long was it after you were wounded that you got home?"

"Five months. I was on the hospital ship two months, then three months at Pearl before they got me home. But before that—"

"I didn't ask you before that, Wayne. I just wanted to know when you got home." She heads on into the kitchen.

"Well, why on earth do you want to know that, Mama?" he calls after her.

"Oh, nothing. Nothing. Come on in here and eat."

Late that night

In the quiet of her own room at the back of the house, Emma takes out her hairpins, pulls her long hair around to the front where she can reach it to brush her nightly hundred strokes.

She can hear the young people's voices out in the living room. Let Rita laugh and have fun tonight. There'll be plenty of time for the tears tomorrow, the tears that anybody can see are right under the surface, needing to come out.

At supper they all fussed at Rita for eating like a bird, as though the poor girl had a chance to take more than a bite before she had to answer yet another question.

No, Rita isn't really worried about earthquakes. She's never even felt one in her life. *Yes,* her mother still sews—well, that question was Emma's. In fact, Hildy has quite a business going, sewing fancy dresses for San Francisco society weddings. And Rita helps. Emma smiles at herself in the mirror for that, as she plaits her hair into a long braid.

And the whole time, Marc stuck close by Rita's side, waiting on her, offering her more food while she nibbled at the full plate. Emma's never seen him so taken with a girl since that little redheaded girl in grade school. It brings back a picture of Wayne, six or seven years old, fussing over Hildy when she was little.

After the little kids were settled into corners of the couch and in the armchairs, curled up with their great-grandma's crocheted afghans, and after she got Rita's promise to stay in Asheville a few days, Emma begged off early and left the young people to themselves. She was tired, she insisted. Lordy, why is it the kids get all that energy when it's the old folks who need it most? Another of her favorite things to say.

Rita obviously has plenty that needs talking about, but tomorrow is soon enough. Before then, Emma has her own pondering to do.

She changes into her long plisse nightgown, but she doesn't expect she'll go to sleep for a while yet. She crawls under the eyelet coverlet and pulls its comforting softness up around her face, but her mind is too busy to even think of sleep.

All right, she'd be telling the truth if she said she didn't know Hildy was expecting when she left Mahala. The easiest thing would be to say the boyfriend died in the war. But no, there's been way too much lying already. And Rita wouldn't let it go, now that she's come across the country to find her answers. She'll insist on names. If Emma doesn't give her one, well, there's the plaque right in the middle of Mahala with all the boys' names on it. Rita would hunt *all* of their families down.

She has to tell the girl something, just for that reason—so she'll stop hunting. And it has to be the truth. But does it have to be the whole, awful truth? Does Emma have a right to hold anything back? It's just a suspicion anyway isn't it? She counts on mental fingers, over and over, as though her mind doesn't want to accept the obvious, simple arithmetic.

Already she hears her own voice in her mind, stepping carefully, trying to find the most acceptable words for what she can't deny any longer. What a stupid old fool she's been!

She rolls over, turns her pillow to its cool side, punches it to fit this side of her face. She doesn't sleep so well any more like she used to after a long day of sewing. Many nights she lies awake thinking of all the foolish things she's done in her life, kicking herself that there's not a blamed thing she can do about them now.

Most nights she reads until she's sure she'll sleep all night and not wake up in the wee hours to start her self-chastising all over again. She always heard that you see your whole life go before your eyes like a movie just as you're dying. Well, with Emma the Lord won't need to bother with the movie. He can take her straight on up to heaven.

And now she has a new, worse thing that ought to keep her awake the rest of her life if she lives to be a hundred. She owes Hildy so much, and yet what about this young girl, this copy of Hildy? What does Emma owe her? No, she won't tell Rita any lies, no matter how much easier that might be. She's not sure what she will tell Rita, but her mind is made up. It'll be the highest truth she can find. Or at least the best she can bring herself to say outloud.

Later still, that same night

Emma hesitates, then taps gently on the door to the bedroom her granddaughters grew up in. She first opens it a crack, then steps in, closes it behind her. "I was walkin' around out in my roses and saw the light on up here. I go out there at night sometimes when I can't sleep."

Rita sits at the window seat. She looks ten years old in her baby-doll pajamas that scarcely skim the bare feet tucked up under her hips. "I saw you out there. I'm sorry . . . I hope we didn't keep you awake. But I'm sure we did. Uncle Wayne got after us a couple of times."

Emma takes the old rocker, the one she rocked Sissy and Rose in many a time in this room. "Oh, I heard y'all, but it tickled me that you were havin' such a good time with the kids. I 'spect you're goin' to have to beat Marc off with a stick when it comes time to leave."

"Oh, I thought I'd just tuck him into my suitcase and take him with me," Rita teases. She turns to the open window. "It's so warm here all night. At home it gets cool at night even when it's hot during the day."

"Then I 'spect you must freeze your fanny off in a little nightie like that one." Emma's surprised at how easy it is to tease this girl that she's known not even a whole day yet. So like Hildy—but what is it that's so different too? The quick smile, of course, the easy laugh.

Rita hops up from the window seat, retrieves a pile of pale blue chenille from the bed and holds it up. "See? In case of fire." She tosses the robe aside and arranges her tan legs Indian-style on the bed.

Again the shadows of the girl's slender face, backlighted from the soft bedside lamp, bring back an image from a long time ago.

Rita traces her finger around the sunbonnet of the little girl in one of the many squares of the quilt folded at the foot of the bed. "This is so beautiful," she says. She unfolds the quilt partway, drapes it over her knees, looking at the little appliquéd girls. "They're no two that match, are there? They're all different."

"That was always Rose's favorite pattern, Sunbonnet Sue. The dresses and bonnets are pieced from scraps of dresses I made her and Sissy." She never made Hildy a quilt, not even for a wedding present, she realizes. "Were you havin' trouble gettin' to sleep too, Hon? Oh, but then it's way earlier in California, isn't it?"

Rita yawns, pulls a pillow down from the head of the bed and curls around it. "I'm sleepy, but there's just so much to think about."

They sit in the still house, each in her own thoughts. So much Emma wants to ask, to say, but there's no natural way to start. Each question is rejected and fades away before it becomes a whole idea.

Finally a feeble beginning, but a beginning, at least. She tries to keep her voice casual and natural. "Hon, how is it that you decided to try to find everybody just now?" Rita is so quiet for a moment that Emma wonders if she has dozed off.

Then without a word, Rita pushes the quilt aside, swings her long legs over the side of the bed. She retrieves her purse from the dresser and comes back, sits on the rug close to the rocker. "Mom and I had a big fight before I left, because I found this." She pulls the wrinkled yellow paper from the purse and holds it out.

Emma gingerly takes it. "Oh, my word." Her own younger, steadier handwriting from the past leaps off the stationery. "My writin' was so much better then, what with my arthritis now."

She holds the paper at arm's length, but in the dim light the words are still fuzzy. "I don't have my readin' specs, Hon. Would you read it to me?"

Rita reads over the words quickly as though she can't afford to hesitate on any one of them. As she ends the letter, she looks like she's going to cry and her voice is tiny. "Before this, I always thought . . . she always let me think Joe Rossi was my father too."

"Oh, Honey!" Emma reaches over the chair arm to run her fingers through the girl's soft curly hair. Rita pulls back, digs into the purse for a used tissue.

"So, then, Hildy remarried . . . " Emma starts. Rita shakes her head, not really answering the question, Emma notices. She decides to let this go by, that she already knows more than is her right to know.

"My father is dead," Rita goes on. "I found that out, so there's no sense digging any further into that. I thought at least I could find out about my . . . our . . . grandparents. I didn't know my grandmother was still alive then"—she points to the letter—"much less that she was now. But there's so much, and none of it so far is anything like I imagined it would be."

And Lord, Lord, Honey, I'm afraid there's still a whole lot more. In this middle-of-the-night quiet, Emma tries to summon up the least hurtful words she can find to talk about the delicate subject. Finally she says, "Honey, what are you goin' to do with what all you find out?"

Rita looks away, shaking her head.

Emma takes in a deep breath and begins, even though she doesn't have any idea what she will say from one sentence to the next. "I've been puzzlin' things out all night. Honey, don't be too hard on your mama. If she lied to you, I'm sure it was because it was the only thing she knew to do."

"But why? What right does she have to lie to me?"

"Didn't you ever lie to your mama?"

"Well, sure, little stuff." Rita gets up and sits on the bed, tucks her feet under her. "Like the time I threw away the school paper for my diphtheria shot and I told her I never got one. But that's different."

"But why did you lie about it?"

"Well, you know. I was embarrassed to tell her what I did."

Emma eases herself up from the rocker, goes over and sits at the head of the bed, leans back against the headboard and pats the pillow at the other side, motioning for Rita to join her. Rita turns around and leans on her elbow facing Emma, her face crumpled into a frown.

"So Rita, Honey, do you reckon if you'd done something a whole lot worse, you might've been even more ashamed?"

Rita doesn't answer. She looks like she's staring at the Sunbonnet Sue in the yellow gingham dress, but Emma doubts if she's seeing it.

Emma keeps her voice as quiet and calm as she can, even though the words inside are building up to what she fears will be a scream. "And what if it was worse . . . a whole lot worse . . . but it was done *to* you?"

Rita's head jerks up and her eyes are wide awake. "What are you trying to say?"

Now Emma's the one who turns away. She reaches over and switches off the bedside lamp, and the room turns black, then pales to silver in the moonlight from the window. She hears her own heavy breathing in the darkness, and she wills her speech to continue even though every nerve in her body is pleading with her to stop.

"Rita, your mama left Mahala with Joe Rossi and married him the day she met him. In October, as close as I can work things out. Seven months before your brother was born."

Rita's body shifts on the bed and Emma can see her silhouette, can see her sitting up. "So that's all? She was pregnant when she got married? Geez, how many people does that happen to?"

Emma reaches out in the dark and puts a hand on Rita's shoulder, and Rita lies back down, but she keeps talking. "She got married and got pregnant, not in that order, and not the same guy. So what? Did people crucify you for that back then?"

"Well, it wasn't accepted too well, no." Emma gets up and goes over to the window, closes it, comes back and sits at the foot of the bed. "I've pondered and pondered about tellin' you this, whether I've got a right to. But the reason I'm goin' to is to make you see that you've got to let this go, for everybody's sake, especially for your mama's."

"Well, geez, so she didn't marry her boyfriend. She found a ticket out of town instead. I still don't see anything so wrong with that."

Emma takes a deep breath and it catches somewhere in her chest as a sob, but she closes her eyes and holds her words as steady as she can. "Rita, she didn't have a boyfriend. I would've known if she did. She came to live with me two months before she left because I made her do it. Two months, Rita. I made her because her brother . . . not Little Will or Liam . . . they were both . . . gone, by then . . . "

Her voice tightens in her throat and when she speaks it is barely more than a whisper. "I made her come live with me after her brother *beat* her the worst he ever had. I threatened to kill him. I still to this day wish I had. I don't doubt that I would have, whatever it took, if I'd even imagined . . . anything more."

Please, Rita, please hear what I'm saying. Don't make me say this ugly thing. There are words that Emma has never said out loud, some thoughts that nice girls in her day weren't supposed to even *think*, and she's having a hard time bringing herself to start now.

Rita's silhouette is as still as a rock, and Emma can't even hear a breath. Then Rita's up and off the bed, backing away toward the window. "Oh. My. God." Her legs hit the window seat behind her and she sits with a thump. The moon scoots behind a cloud, and both women sit soundless in the stifling darkness.

Emma waits until she's sure she can go on, but her throat feels so dry that her voice cracks. "That poor little girl. She wasn't any more than your age, but she seemed like a lot younger." She chokes on a sob, and the tears she's been trying to hold in brim over.

Rita comes over and sits on the edge of the bed. Emma realizes Rita is crying too and she pulls her close.

"This doesn't really happen, not really, does it?" Rita starts, then stops, then starts again, "I mean . . . people write about it . . . but, you know . . . Faulkner . . . and . . . and . . . my God, Peyton Place . . . "

"I know, I know," Emma says. She holds Rita for a few moments, then brings herself to whisper, "I honestly could . . . after all this long . . . I honestly could still kill him with my bare hands right now."

"I feel awful," Rita's muffled voice says. "I said some mean things to her. I don't know what to say to her now, but I have to—how do I tell her this, that I know? God, she'll be so embarrassed."

"Rita, that's the hardest part . . . that's the burden I'm layin' on you. You can't tell her you know, or you'll hurt her a whole lot worse than what's happened to her already."

Emma holds her great-niece in her arms and feels her deep breaths that come out bumpy, irregular. Finally Rita pulls back and sits up sniffling. "I've always imagined some deep dark thing like this."

"Well, if you did, you were smarter than me. I never gave it a minute's thought. It never entered my mind until you said how old Will is, and when he was born. I feel like such an old fool."

Rita reaches over and turns on the bedside lamp on her side. "But . . . isn't he some kind of minister or something, now?"

Emma squints at the light, pulls her robe tight around her, wishes she could pull it up over her face. She gets up and takes her place back in the rocker. "He was then, too. I never saw anything good in the religion Bobby Ray followed then, and he's done nothing better since. None of us claims any kin to him."

Rita paces over to the window, then back to the bed. "Omigosh! What is Will gonna say? You don't know Will . . . he'll be mad. He'll be ready to go kill him himself."

"Honey, don't you see? You can't tell your brother either. Anything he did would hurt your mama. And what good could it possibly do? It's a burden I've dumped on you, and maybe I shouldn't have. I'm already thinkin' I shouldn't have."

Rita retrieves her purse from the floor next to the rocker and pulls out the photograph of Will. Without a word she hands it to Emma. She doesn't want to look at the picture, but her eyes are drawn to it. One quick glance at it, and she looks away. As if she can read Emma's thoughts, Rita says "He doesn't always look that mean. It's, you know, for the Marines." She laughs a nervous little laugh. "Honest, he laughs a lot and he's a really neat guy." Her laugh turns to a sob that rises without warning. "I don't know how I'm going to do this! First my grandmother, now this!" She sits on the rug by the rocker.

Emma reaches over and takes her hand. "Rita," she says when she can find her voice again. "I wish I could have told you about

Gerty first, before you went. I can just imagine how it must have been, without you being ready for it. You don't even have to tell me. When I was over there just this last time, I just didn't have the patience for it. She's my sister, and I know I should do more, but . . . " Aunt Emma looks away.

"Well, one good thing. She gave me a picture. I left it out in the car . . . a picture of my grandfather. He's turning out to be the biggest mystery of all, the way everybody talks. And Uncle Wayne said—"

"A picture of Daniel?" Emma interrupts, sitting up straight in the rocker. "Wherever did she get one? What does it look like?"

Rita looks puzzled, startled at Emma's words. "It's a baby picture in a little oval. It looks kind of like my baby pictures, I thought."

Emma dwells on this for a long moment, then remembers . . . yes, there was a picture like that, but—"Oh, Honey, if that's the one I think it is, it's not Daniel. It's your Uncle Liam. Now where in the world did Gerty get that?"

"Oh." Rita gets up and wanders back to the bed. "So then I don't have anything of him, either." She sits on the bed, dejected.

Emma goes over and sits beside her. She pulls Rita's chin up so that their eyes meet. "Rita, you have something of him every time you look in the mirror."

Rita's chin quivers. "What was he like, my grandfather?"

What a strange thought . . . Daniel, the grandfather of this young girl. Emma has no trouble seeing herself as the matriarch of her own family of four grandchildren and three great-grandchildren, but Daniel remains forever young in her mind, what little part of her mind holds a picture of him at all.

She struggles to find a place to start, so long that Rita says, "I'm sorry. Did I say something wrong?"

Emma shakes her head. "He was a good sweet man, Rita. He tried hard, but he was no match for Gerty and her . . . her problems. Wayne could be right that Bobby Ray helped drive him off, but I don't reckon it would've taken much. I think whatever happened, he left just because he couldn't bear his life anymore." She hesitates and a truth comes to her, all at once and clear as day—why, she didn't know Daniel at all! Not the thoughts that drove him from day to day, not the wishes he had for himself or his children, or the memories that haunted him. What in the world has she been thinking all those years?

She sighs and goes on. After all, Rita is waiting. "It was the longest time that I couldn't believe he wasn't comin' back." Lord, what was she holding onto? "I made him a promise—well, I made it to myself, but for him, that I'd take care of your mama. I've lived out all these years knowin' I didn't do right by her, by that promise. And now . . . " her voice breaks. "How could I not have known what happened? I'm such an ignorant old fool!"

Rita puts an arm awkwardly around Emma. "I guess we don't really know for sure. It's not exactly something anybody'd tell you. Mom sure didn't." The two of them sit in the dim light, hoping there's some truth to that, hoping for words that will make them both feel better. Emma remembers something. "Wait right here a minute. I do have something of your granddaddy's to give you!"

She goes downstairs to her bedroom, digs into the desk drawer for the small wooden box, then on the way out she picks up a little blue book from her night table. She doesn't bother tiptoeing back up the upstairs. The family is used to her night wanderings.

"You'll need to ask Liam about it," she says, dropping the watch into Rita's cupped hands. "His daddy gave it to him, but maybe he'll pass it along to you," she says, sitting back in the rocker. "Liam didn't know it, but I kept it for him." A little smile plays at the corners of her lips. "He'll be surprised, I expect."

"You've kept this watch all these years?" Rita's eyes twinkle in a way that Daniel's or Hildy's never did. Rita's eyes sparkle with life, even when they're shiny with recent tears.

"Aunt Emma, it sounds to me like you definitely had a crush on my grandfather." Emma feels the color rise from her neck to her face. She wonders if anybody else saw this over the years? But then . . . it doesn't matter anymore. It all seems like a story she read somewhere a long time ago.

Why, she must have, a long time ago and without even noticing, she must have laid to rest whatever jealousy she had of Gerty and the fuzzy memories she has of a husband named Daniel. "What an old fool I've been!" She smiles, and so does Rita.

Rita's face turns wistful. "It sounds to me like you've had more of him than anybody else. At least you have some memories. I don't think she—my grandmother—I don't think she has any at all."

"Why, Honey, I never would have thought of it that way."

Rita takes her place on the rug by the rocker. "I do wish I had more, a picture of him, something. Would you do something for me? When you have the time, would you write down everything you remember about him?"

Yes, Emma thinks, and this would be good for her too. With that last, she could give Daniel back to his own. "I will," she promises, "but every time you look in the mirror, you think of him, all right? Pictures don't tell much of the truth anyway, just like your picture of Liam. What they show is just what you make of them, I think. I thought of this little book last night. I want you to have it. It's like poems, but they don't rhyme or anything." She hands Rita the little blue book.

"I have this already! Well, my Aunt Peggy does. But I'm afraid I wasn't in much of a mood to appreciate it."

"Here's the part I was thinkin' of," Emma says, flipping the pages toward the back as Rita holds the book open. "Would you read it out loud?"

> A photograph does not lie, or so they tell us.
> Perhaps, then, its sin is not of dishonesty
> but of barely skimming the truth—
> the posed stance, the counterfeit smile, the coerced
> touching of one who abhors being touched.
> The truth becomes any truth seen by the beholder.
> A name may be scrawled in pencil on the back, but
> from the front peers a fading ghost, with no hint of
> a mind inhabited by fantasy, or dream or delusion,
> no suggestion of faith—its existence or lack of it,
> or in which gods.

"I 'spect memories are just the same," Emma says. "They're only what we each one of us makes of them. Maybe we ought to look more to all our family instead of to separate ones. Kind of like a quilt—we can look at the whole pretty pattern from the top, instead of lookin' for every little knot on the bottom."

"Dreams or delusions," Rita says. "Funny, the part about what we inherit from our families said that too."

"Mmm-hmm, I imagine it does. I could name a few delusions of my own family's, real easy." Wayne, hanging on to his navy ship and the war all this time. Naomi and her dreams of watered silk ball gowns and hoop skirts. Emma closes her eyes, rubs the place between her eyebrows. And yes, her own foolishness all those years over Daniel.

The window has turned to a pale pink-gray rectangle as the early morning begins to light the eastern sky. As Rita thumbs through the book, Emma goes over and opens the window, letting in a wisp of breeze that puffs the white sheer curtains. "Maybe you could go to Ireland some day and find where your people came from, and find your grandfather that way."

"You want to go with me?" Rita says, with that charming smile that her mother, bless her heart, might have had, if she'd had more reason to.

Emma feels the warmth creeping up from her neck again. "No, I reckon this old fool better stay here and sort out her own business. Why don't you take your Mama—and your Uncle Liam?"

She reties the sash of her bathrobe and starts for the door. "Now I reckon you'd best get an hour or two of sleep before that grandson of mine is up and ready to show you off around town. Oh, and Rita . . . in your day you call it what? A *crush*? In my day, we said you were *sweet on* each other. And don't think I haven't noticed a whole lot of 'sweet' going on. So I'll be checkin' that suitcase when you leave." With a mischievous grin, she slips out the door and pulls it closed behind her.

Several days later
Macon, Georgia

After a late supper, Rita and Betty escape to the swing on the back veranda out of earshot of the rest of the house. Rita yawns, sleepy, full. "Geez, I'll gain fifty pounds if I stay around here!"

Huge suppers and this humidity apparently don't slow Betty down at all. "I can't get over that picture of Will," she says. "In high school he was such a big gawky teddy bear."

"He still asks about you sometimes," Rita says, not bothering to cover the yawn that escapes in the middle of her sentence.

"Do you think he had a crush on me?"

"Geez, Betty. You were the first one to get boobs. *All* the boys had a crush on you! And you knew it!"

Betty giggles, puts her hands behind her head and thrusts her chest out, flutters her eyelashes. "Are you all referin' to my little ol' feminine charms?" She exaggerates more as she goes along. "Sugah, Ah have struck dumb my share of Southenuhs and Yankees alike with these risin' beauties of mine."

"Yeah," Rita says, laughing. "And you won't believe the big party us girls had after you left. It was months before the boys started looking at the rest of us. Of course, it helped that we all got boobs, too." She pushes out her own chest with much less impressive results.

With her own affected drawl, she looks down and says, "Why, Ah do declare, she can hold hers in fu'ther than Ah can stick mine out!"

"Shhh!" Betty jumps up and peers through the window "Okay, the colored girl's finished up and left, so Mama'll be goin' up to tend to her bookkeepin' pretty soon. Now come on, you have to tell me everything—just everything! You promised!"

Rita stops the swing and gets up. How odd that Betty calls the housekeeper a *girl*. She must be at least as old as Betty's mom.

"What's her name?"

Betty is studying her fingernails. "Who?"

"The, uh . . . *colored* . . . uh . . . woman."

"Oh, I don't know. They don't stay around very long. Mama got spoiled bein' an officer's wife. Everywhere we lived she had somebody assigned to wait on her. She can't find any help around here that satisfies her." Betty stretches her shapely legs out in front of her and wiggles her toes in her sandals.

Rita walks over to the railing, stretches, tries to relax. She didn't realize her shoulders felt so tight. "Does she live around here? I didn't see any car."

"Around here? Oh landsake no. They have their own part of town. She walks down to the bus stop, I think. It's just a mile or so."

Rita leans on the corner post and runs her finger along the railing. Sure, scary things have been on the news this year about how things are in the South, but Rita always thought of Betty's southernness as just her cute accent and her peaches-and-cream complexion.

Of course, Betty hasn't said anything *wrong*, exactly. She didn't mean anything by it, really, did she? And didn't they just pass some new laws to fix all those problems?

Betty's mom comes to the screendoor. "I've goin' upstairs now, girls. Y'all come on in pretty soon out of that night air." She smiles at Rita. "I've told her and told her the night air's not good for you, but do you think she listens to me?"

"Yes ma'am," Betty calls to her mother's back, then whispers to Rita, "Shoot, if she knew how many boys I've smooched with out here 'til after midnight!"

Rita leans against the porch post, sniffs the flowery air. "I can't get used to how it stays so warm at night here. Look!" A tiny light flashes out in the magnolia trees. Betty's soft laugh fills the whole porch. "And I can't get used to how you Californians take on so over lightnin' bugs! Betty goes down the porch steps and out into the yard, comes back with her two hands together, little flashes lighting up the cracks between her fingers. She opens her hand and grabs one of the bugs. When its light flashes on, she smears the back half of the bug down the leg of Rita's jeans, leaving a florescent streak on the denim.

"Eeeeewwwwww!" Rita shrieks, waving her hands. "Betteeee! Eeeeeeeewwwwww!"

Betty laughs. "When we were kids, we used to come in lookin' like somethin' from Mars."

Rita stares at the streak on her pants, her nose wrinkled. "Eew."

Betty takes her place back in the swing, pats the spot beside her. "Now, come on and sit down here. I'm just dyin' to know what the big mystery is. You've stalled long enough now."

Rita hesitates, takes her time arranging herself in a way that she won't accidentally touch what's left of the bug. Eew.

"So? Tell me!"

Rita's almost sorry she hinted that there was more to tell. Just finding out that preacher was related would have kept Betty and her mom buzzing for days, definitely. Weeks, maybe. "Eeew," she says to the memory of the bug one last time and her shoulders shiver a little.

"Go on!" Betty waits with her eyes bright, reflecting the soft light from the wide window.

"Aunt Emma said I wasn't to tell anyone this," she stalls. Well, that's not completely true. Aunt Emma said she wasn't to tell Mom or Will. So why does she feel so uneasy about telling Betty?

"Now Rita, you quit teasin' me. Go on."

"I don't know . . . it seems so . . . gossipy."

Betty smacks Rita's arm. "Well, like they always say, it's wrong to spread gossip, but what else can you do with it?"

Betty's soft laughter sounds like music—flutes, piccolos. Yeah, it was more than just the boobs that enchanted the whole football team at Richmond High.

Rita tucks her feet up under her, still trying to avoid touching *that* side of her jeans.

It's no use. She has to tell somebody or she'll explode, and Betty's the safest—and definitely the closest—one. "Well, Aunt Emma thinks . . . well, she's not sure, but she figured out the timing and all—"

"Rita, you're drivin' me crazy! What?"

Rita takes a deep breath. "Aunt Emma . . . thinks my mom's brother—the preacher one—she thinks he . . . " She licks her lips that have gone suddenly dry. "She thinks he's Will's father."

The minute the last word is out, Rita is absolutely sure she should never have told. Ever.

And she's definitely never seen Betty speechless before.

"Oh my Lord," Betty's mouth forms the words, but no sounds come out. Her hand goes to her mouth and she sits there motionless for a long time, her eyes blazing.

Rita looks off into the yard, where there are now dozens of fireflies. They blink on and off in the bushes and trees, reminding her of the time Aunt Peggy took them all to Disneyland.

Betty finally finds her voice. "Lord, you hear about things like that. My mama has a younger brother that looks just like one of my daddy's older brothers and there's always been gossip . . . but your mama? I can't believe she'd do that with her own brother. Shoot, I can't imagine her doin' it with anybody! But especially him. I still can't believe you didn't even know who he was. Why, he's always in our newspapers for some wicked thing or another, and two wives divorced him. We figure y'all hear about our jerks in your newspapers, but I reckon California has jerks of its own to read about."

Rita stares at her. Betty was always like this—if she stops talking for one minute, it dams up inside her and all floods out at once.

"Oh my Lord," Betty says again. "He's exactly the kind who would do that, and she . . . she . . . well, that'd be a darn good reason why she never told you about him, wouldn't it? She didn't do it *with* him! I bet he did it *to* her!" Her hand flies to her mouth again.

Rita can only bite her lip. In the pit of her stomach she was trying to deny that it could be true. But speaking the words aloud somehow makes it more believable. She wishes now she could have held onto the doubt. And as much as she likes Betty, deep in her gut she is sure she's going to be sorry someday for telling her.

Somewhere inside the house, a telephone rings.

"Don't you ever tell anybody, Betty. You have to swear to God."

Betty's mom opens the screendoor slightly. "Rita, Honey, there's a long distance call for you. It's your Uncle."

Betty's eyes are big. "Him? Speak of the devil!"

Rita smacks her on the knee and mouths *No, Silly*, to Betty but her stomach feels like it just flipped upside-down. Of course not. He doesn't know Rita's here . . . he doesn't know she *exists*. Does he?

She follows Betty's mother into the house, takes the phone in the front parlor.

"Uncle Liam? Is that you?" It is, isn't it?

"Rita, Aunt Emma called me." Uncle Liam's voice sounds formal and stiff, but at least it is him. "Mama . . . your grandma . . . has died. I'm goin' to drive back, but I can't leave 'til Monday. I thought I ought to go see what I can do about the property and all. Aunt Emma tells me you saw Mama, but she didn't know if you'd want to go back up there or not."

Rita wonders if Aunt Emma told him anything else. But then maybe he already knew. Oh, of course, he probably did!

Then Uncle Liam's words hit her. Her grandmother—the crazy old woman—her grandmother who has been dead to her all these years, now really is dead.

"Rita? You there?" He's waiting for her to answer, and she doesn't know what to say. But she definitely doesn't want to go back there alone.

She opens her mouth to tell him she'll wait for him, but instead she blurts out: "Why didn't you and Mom tell me she was alive?"

The last day of July 1964
Mahala, Kentucky

The Greyhound bus turns off the highway and pulls over on the side of the road at the DX station. Rita's the only passenger standing to get off, and there doesn't appear to be anyone waiting on the roadside to get on the bus.

"You need some help with that, Ma'am?" the driver asks.

"Oh, no thanks." Rita insisted on hanging onto the old radio all the way from Nashville, where it had to give up its seat to a real passenger. She can carry it another few feet. The driver follows her off the bus, opens the luggage compartment and pulls out her suitcase.

"Somebody here to meet you?"

"Uh huh." She's relieved to see Uncle Liam's jeep parked over on the other side of the gas pump. He comes out of the little store with two pop bottles, waves to her, hops into the jeep. The jeep disappears around the front of the bus, then pulls up from behind her, stopping short a few feet from where she stands. "I've been watchin' for this bus for half an hour," Uncle Liam says, "then the very minute I turned my back, there it was!" He grins at the driver.

"Well, then." The driver sets her suitcase down and climbs back onto the bus. "Bye now."

"Thanks!" Rita can't wave, but she includes him in her smile.

Uncle Liam gives the driver a smile, too. He takes the radio from her. "Where'd you get this old thing?"

"Aunt Emma said it belongs to Mom. She said I should take it home to her."

"Why, I believe that's the one Mammaw and Granddaddy had. That sure does bring back some old memories." He unsnaps the worn gray canvas at the back of the jeep and sets the radio inside, then grabs her suitcase and stashes it next to his.

She takes the two R.C. Colas from where they're propped in the passenger seat, hands one to him, and climbs into the jeep. "Just *good* old memories, I hope."

She's answering him, but her mind is wandering back to the fun times she's had in this jeep over the years. She gives the windshield a little pat. Funny, she's never thought about the old jeep this way before. Everything seems to be touching emotions that are hanging just under her thoughts today.

The familiar jeep has been a part of her childhood as far back as she can remember. Here, it seems suddenly strange, set down into the jumble of feelings that have washed over her—almost drowned her— this past two weeks. It seems like months since she's been home.

She drinks down half the cola. "Thanks. That really hits the spot. It must already be ninety degrees out here." She pulls her hair up off the back of her neck, wishes she had a rubber band. "I can't believe I took a bath before I left this morning."

Uncle Liam pulls the jeep out onto the road. "I'd clean forgot how sticky it gets here."

She takes off her sandals and slides down into the seat until she can prop her bare feet up near the windshield. "It's so weird to see you here!" Something pokes her in the middle of her back; it feels like a sharp rock. She digs it out from the seat behind her and before she can toss it out onto the ground she notices that it's a fat little chicken carved from wood. "What's this?"

"Little Will used to always whittle things. I found it out in the barn yesterday. I was goin' to take it to your Mama."

She cradles the little chicken in her hand as if it were made of glass and tries to swallow the lump that has crept up into the back of her throat. All these years she's pestered her mom for the past and now it's coming at her from all kinds of unexpected directions. Uncle Liam is staring straight ahead, not talking. Rita's sure he must be feeling the same thing.

They pass by the little park in the middle of town. "It seems like a year ago that I was here," she finally manages to say. "It must seem like a hundred to you."

Old Malcolm sits on the bench next to the statue. She waves at him, but he's shading his eyes, squinting into the sun and probably can't tell who she is. Uncle Liam waves, too. "That's Malcolm Brown," he says. "I talked to him a good while yesterday."

"So now you know all about Whats-his-name who was wounded at Guada Canal."

Uncle Liam wags his finger at Rita. "Yeah, but not so's you could tell it now!"

Rita finishes off her R.C. "He's the one who told me where . . . where she lives. Lived."

The jeep starts up the little hill by the sawmill. "I helped my granddaddy at that sawmill many a time," Uncle Liam says. "Well, I don't know how much help I was. I hung around in the way a lot, anyhow."

As they pass, Rita looks into the lumberyard where two men—an older one and one about her age—load a board onto a truck. Funny, she didn't see it last time.

"That's Sam Luther and one of his boys," Uncle Liam says.

Rita laughs. "Reckon its one of them passel of boys he raised after the war? Not Korear, the Big One?"

"Could be, could be!"

Over the hill, just where the road levels out, Uncle Liam slows and drives into the clear space beside the house—right where Rita parked the Mustang less than two weeks ago.

Still no picket fence or flowers. And now no grandmother on the porch, either. Rita stares at the empty porch swing. Her feelings push and shove one another. Sure, the old woman was crazy, but she was the only grandmother Rita had. She didn't have time to get used to having one, any one at all, and now that one is gone.

Uncle Liam gets out, stares down at the ground. "Rita," he says finally. "Like I told you on the telephone, me and your mama should never have lied to you. We didn't mean it to hurt you kids."

She tries to hold in the tears that threaten to fill her whole face. "I know." And she does, a little bit, but her heart is feeling something different right now.

She slips her sandals on, jumps down from the jeep. Uncle Liam leads the way up the porch steps, holds the screendoor open for her.

At first she just peeks in, then steps carefully into the small front room ahead of him. The walls are covered with a thick faded kind of wallpaper that used to have a flower pattern, she thinks. There is a little fireplace, a high bed in one corner, a dresser heaped with clothes.

Coats and dresses hang on metal hangers from two nails on the wall. "Aren't there any closets in here?" she asks, but Uncle Liam has already gone into the next room. She takes another quick look around, shivers, and tries to walk calmly through the door.

She's surprised to see that this room also has a bed, and one of the little fireplaces built into the wall back-to-back with the one in the other room.

"This here is where us kids slept," Uncle Liam says. "It seems like it was a whole lot bigger than this. But then I reckon I was just a whole lot smaller back then."

Rita tries to imagine her mother a little kid, dressing in front of that tiny fireplace, standing on her tiptoes to hang her dresses on that nail on the wall.

"All the coal and kindlin' I carried in here . . . " Uncle Liam says.

Rita gets the feeling he's talking to himself more than to her. She peeks into the next room. There's a huge kitchen table covered with an assortment of pots and dishes, and chairs pushed back against the wall, holding cardboard boxes half-filled with kitchen things.

"I took everything down and tried to sort some of it out here," Uncle Liam says. "I don't know if anything's worth keepin'."

Rita is drawn to the tablecloth, starkly new compared to everything else. She runs her fingers over the slick material with yellow flowers printed on it.

On the wall by the door hangs a rectangle that says

Judgment is mine
sayeth the Lord

in what must have been silvery letters on a dark blue background when it was new. She pokes a shiny spot with her fingernail and chips of silver glitter fall off. "How long has this been here, do you think?"

"What?" Uncle Liam says from where he's gazing out the back door. He comes over to see. He shrugs. "Way too long, I'd say." He rips it down, drops it on the floor.

Rita pokes around the big iron stove, shivers. The whole house feels like something . . . spoiled. Something . . . old. Something dead. Spooky. When she realizes Uncle Liam has stepped out onto the little back porch, she hurries to the door, feeling suddenly smothery. He leans on the porch post, his body still. She strains to see what he's looking at, but there's nothing out there except the trees.

"I went out to the cemetery yesterday," he says, still looking out at the trees. "We could go back out there if you want to. They put Mama out there with my Mammaw and Granddaddy. They told me they had to hurry and bury her the same day, since they figure she must've died in her sleep, and nobody knew it for a couple of days.

"If they called you right after I left Aunt Emma's, she must have died while I was still there, just a couple of days after I saw her."

"Yeah, I reckon. Aunt Emma thought she'd wait to come, since she was just here a little bit ago and it's a long trip for her. They'll have some kind of a service then. If we'd known that, we could've waited too, you and me."

That's okay, Rita thinks. It's still hard to attach the family she found in Asheville with the experience she had here in Mahala. She'd just as soon keep it that way for now.

She can think of lots of questions—did they really have a coffin big enough? How did they—wouldn't they have to—but she decides maybe she doesn't really want to know the details. Instead, she says, "Everybody says my grandfather left . . . that he was driven away. Does that mean he isn't there, at the cemetery? Is he buried someplace else? Does anybody know?"

Uncle Liam turns and looks at her a moment, then sits down on the top step, motioning for her come sit with him. "I need to tell you some more about that too."

What next? Rita wonders. She had hoped she'd heard all the secrets there were to hear.

After she sits, he starts, "Nobody knows when Daddy died, or where. He just walked off one day and never came back. The last time I saw him, he stepped into the woods over yonder." He points to the area he was looking at before.

"Didn't anybody try to, you know, find him? Try to find out where he went?"

"I wanted to try. I wanted him to take me with him, but he said no, he couldn't. I wanted to run after him anyway but he told me to take care of the kids. I didn't do a very good job of it, 'cause I left, myself, a few months later. I just couldn't take it anymore, with Daddy gone and with Bobby Ray the way—" He sits up straighter and shakes his head, as though something had just smacked him in the face.

"What? What?"

He leans on his elbows on his knees, runs his fingers through his sparse hair. "Bobby Ray was standin' right there . . . that night . . . right there where you're sittin' . . . he was watchin' Daddy too."

Rita shivers. This is getting too spooky. She gets up, looking back at where she was sitting, brushes off her jeans. Uncle Liam stands up too and goes down the steps and out toward the barn. "I don't know why I just saw that, in my mind," he mumbles, without even looking back at her.

Once again Rita's not sure if he's really talking to her. Maybe she should leave him alone for a while. But he turns around quickly as though he'd just remembered her. "Have you got some other shoes in your stuff? Go get 'em on and let me show you somethin'."

She goes to the jeep and opens her suitcase, pulls out her Keds and a pair of socks. She sits on the back bumper and puts them on, runs to catch up with him out past the barn where there's the start of a wide swath of low tree stumps and cleared brush.

"They've cut a place out there for the gas company to walk their lines," he says. "I walked it a couple of miles yesterday. Took me 'way back, it did. I always used to love the woods. I kept lookin' down at myself to see if I'd turned back into a little kid." He grins, and Rita is glad to see the Uncle Liam she recognizes.

"I'm jealous," she says. "I'd love to have all these woods in our back yard."

They hike on for at least a mile, with Uncle Liam pointing out cedars and hickories. At one place he stops so abruptly she almost bumps into him. "Listen!" He starts off into the trees and motions for her to follow. Not ten feet from the clearing, a tiny stream of water pours over a huge flat rock, drops to a pool five or six feet below.

"That's a lot of noise for such a little bit of runnin' water," he says. "I used to love to find places like this. I reckon this creek runs all the way to the lake, but it's pretty dry right now. I'm not sure where the property line is back here."

Rita would love to dabble her fingers in the cool water, but there's no easy way to reach it. She timidly steps into the brush to get closer but Uncle Liam warns, "This time of year there's probably poison oak in there. And snakes."

"Snakes?" She scrambles back to the clear space and grabs his arm. "Snakes?"

"Aw, they're more afraid of you than you are of them."

"I doubt it," she says. Her heart still thumps so hard she's pretty sure he can hear it. "Not unless they've proved that snakes wet their pants!"

He heads back out to the clearing and she follows as closely behind as she can, stepping into his footprints as soon as he leaves them. She breathes freely only when her feet crunch on the stobs of cleared brush.

Maybe she doesn't really want a woods in her back yard after all.

"Listen!" This time there's no gurgling water. "Thunder off to the west, yonder," he says. "We don't want to get caught in the woods in a lightnin' storm."

They start back, Rita watching her every step. For a half mile or so she tries to reason with herself: *snakes wouldn't come out here in the open, would they? We didn't see any on the way, did we?* Out loud, she asks, "Are you glad you came back?"

Uncle Liam walks on for several moments and Rita wonders if he's even heard her. Then, he says, "Yeah, I reckon. I didn't know I needed to, but maybe it'll help me let it all go." He picks up his pace and Rita hurries after him, trying not to think of snakes.

She should say something about Robert Ray. But what? Does Uncle Liam know about it—about him? Would Mom have told him? She stops and pulls at the stickers in her socks. "Uncle Liam?"

He turns around, comes back to her.

"You and Mom never told me about your . . . the other brother, either." She didn't mean for it to come out as an accusation.

He looks quickly away. "We better get back," he says. "We've got a quarter of a mile to go yet." He starts off in a brisk walk, then slows to let her catch up. They walk side-by-side for a moment. "He was the one I meant back on the porch, the one who was watching Daddy."

"Yeah," Rita says. "I know."

Thunder rolls off in the west, louder, closer. Walking as fast as they can across the stubble and the flat-to-the-ground tree stumps, they manage to reach the barn and pull the door open just as the first big drops pelt the dust.

Rita pulls off her shoes and tries again to pick the stickers off her socks, but she finally gives up and stuffs the socks into the shoes.

Uncle Liam tries the rickety wooden ladder up to the loft, but says, "I'd best fix that before somebody breaks their neck climbin' it."

A striped yellow cat pokes her head out from behind a rusted milk can. "Well, look who's here," Rita says. "Do you remember me?"

She picks the cat up and tries to snuggle it closer to her, but obviously it's not a snuggley kind of cat. It squirms, hisses, tries to get down. "Look at you," Rita says. "Somebody's keeping you fed, huh?"

Uncle Liam calls over from the barn door. "Naw, nobody feeds country cats. I imagine she finds all the mice she wants around here."

"Ewwww!" She drops the cat, and it hisses at her again before retreating behind a loose board.

Uncle Liam laughs. "This farm livin' don't suit you much at all, does it?" He points to a big hole high in the roof. "Let's run for the front porch before it comes down heavy. I doubt if it'll stay very dry in here."

Rita picks up her shoes and they make a dash for the front porch, as a whoosh of wind splatters drops into the dust, sending up little poofs of dirt. The sky has turned dark and threatening. Lightning flashes over beyond the barn and thunder crashes almost immediately after it.

"Whooooweee! That was close!" Uncle Liam says. He joins Rita in the big porch swing. She can't help noticing how they both fit easily where one person sat barely ten days ago.

"Do you suppose my showing up here upset her and . . . "

He pats her arm. "Now I don't reckon you need to worry about that. To tell you the truth, it seems like to me that everybody—even Aunt Emma—was more relieved than anything."

He pushes against the porch floor and the swing moves; the chain on the hooks above them screeches. "Anyways," he goes on. "If it hadn't been for you comin' back here, there's no telling when we'd ever heard about it. Took us a while to track you down, but—"

"But what would that have mattered to you and Mom?" She didn't mean for that to sound rude. But what *would* it have mattered, really? She's been dead to them for how long?

"Rita, like I said, I'm sorry we—"

"I know, I know. I guess somewhere inside I'm still mad that my fairytale grandmother didn't show up. Not at you, though. Sorry."

Uncle Liam stares off into the trees, and Rita notices a line of ants coming up through the porch floor, playing follow the leader along the window sill and up into a crack above the window.

"Did you see anything here you wanted to keep?" he asks her.

She looks around, thinks of going back into the house, but she shivers at the thought. "No, I guess not. What about you? Are you going to take anything of hers back with you? Do you think Mom will want anything?" She already knows the answer to that. Why did she bother to ask?

The swing moves slightly as Uncle Liam shifts his weight. "Rita," he says, adjusting his glasses, then taking them off and wiping them on the tail of his shirt. His eyes look so vulnerable without them. She has the uncomfortable feeling that she's looking at him naked.

"I shouldn't speak bad of the dead," he goes on, "but you might as well know this. Mama was a hateful woman, to me and to Hil— to your mama . . . and to our Daddy too." He turns his head away from her. "I imagine we both . . . me and your mama . . . I reckon we both carry more stuff of hers already than we can ever get rid of."

Rita swallows hard, her eyes tear up. "I'm sorry. Nobody ever told me that before, either. But I guess I should have figured it out."

He reaches over and pats her hand. "Makes you wonder what folks are thinkin', tryin' to hang onto stuff from the past, don't it?"

"I'm surprised you came back then," she says. "Why did you?"

He pushes his feet against the floor and the chain squawks in complaint but he doesn't seem to notice. "I reckon I did it for Daddy. When I run off from here, I left everything about him here too, little as there was. Not *stuff* so much as feelin's. I was hopin' I could find some of it, but . . . " He shrugs.

Rita listens to the *squeak, squawk* of the swing, then suddenly remembers: "I have something!" She jumps up and dashes down the steps to the jeep, reaches under the canvas and grabs her purse. She makes it back to the top step just as thunder rumbles out past the barn and a sudden gush of wind picks up dry leaves, swirls them around the corner of the house.

She offers him her closed hand. He looks at it, then up at her, puzzled. "This is yours, I believe?" She smiles and drops the watch into his open palm.

His face is blank for a minute, then a knowing look comes over it. He chuckles. "Well, I'll be damned."

"What? What?"

"Oh, nothin'," he says with a smile, but his eyes glisten. "Just the good Lord takin' care of innocent people. I'll have to thank Emma proper one of these days." He takes off his glasses and wipes his eyes on his sleeve.

"While I'm at it," Rita says, "I guess this is yours, too." She pulls out the photograph and hands it to him. "I thought it was your father—my grandfather, but now I know it's you."

He grins. "See? That shows you you can't be sure of anything, no matter what you thought it was, no matter what it looks like."

She takes her spot in the swing. "Aunt Emma said she'd write down all she can remember about my grandfather. Would you do that for me too?"

He's quiet for a moment, then says, "Well, I don't write so well, but I'd like that, yeah, I think I would. Maybe your mama might like to read it too. She claims she don't remember anything of him."

"What about Malcolm? He's way older than you. He'd probably remember something about him, wouldn't he?"

"Yeah, him and Russ Gamblin. Russ was the sheriff way back then.I talked to them both, but they both say the same thing, that Daddy wasn't a man you could get to know, kept to himself. They gave up a long time ago wonderin' what happened to him."

Rita knows she should say something else to Uncle Liam, something about his brother, the preacher. "I want you to know," she starts, taking quick glances at his face. "I promised Aunt Emma that wouldn't say anything to Mom about . . . anything. About anything that I . . . that she told me." Uncle Liam's face doesn't move, but his eyes aren't meeting hers or grinning anymore.

He gets up abruptly from the swing, goes to the end of the porch. She walks over and stands next to him. He puts his arm awkwardly around her shoulders. "I'm glad to know that, Rita. Your mama'll look at all that in her own time. We can't make her. I know I tried."

She slips her arm around his waist. "I read something that said we all inherit stuff and some people give it to their kids and some people don't. It even said some people don't *have* kids sort of on purpose so they can break the pattern, and that part kind of made me think of you. I want to have kids someday but I want to be one of the ones who don't pass it on."

"I expect you will, Rita." He pulls a handkerchief out of his back pocket and blows his nose. "Yeah, I expect you will."

Lightning flashes directly overhead and instantly thunder booms so loudly they both jump back from the railing. "Geez!" Rita says. She wanders back to the swing, but Uncle Liam shoves the front door open and peers inside.

"So, what's going to happen to all this?" she wants to know.

He scratches his head. "I've been thinkin' about that a whole lot since yesterday. You know, I always talked about buying me a little piece of property in California, maybe out in Dixon or Rio Vista.

But you know, I'm thinkin' my daddy and my granddaddy would've been proud to have one of us come back to clear off this land and farm it. Then you kids would have a place to bring your younguns of a summer. And who knows, maybe their grandma would come with you."

"*Younguns?*" Rita laughs. "You sound more like old Malcolm by the minute, you know that? You always used to do that when you told us kids about your *Mammaw* and your *Granddaddy*. Mama does it too."

His eyes twinkle and a big smile spreads across his face.

"What? What?"

"*Mama?* You called her *Mama.*"

"Well . . . " She can feel the warmth rising from her neck and she knows she's blushing.

He chuckles. "Aw, sometime I reckon I hold onto it just to get Jonelle's goat."

"What?" she says with as serious a face as she can, "Jonelle has a *goat?* Is it a *show* goat?" They both chuckle and return to their separate musings. She looks around at the scattered rags and junk on the porch.

"I can't imagine Jonelle living here," she says, her voice turning serious for real this time. The angry dark clouds continue to rumble overhead, and the fat drops of rain splatter the dusty ground in earnest, turning it quickly to mud.

"No," he says, "I 'spect she'll be happier stayin' in Sacramento. She's got her cats and her new bookkeepin' job at the auto parts store, and the house is paid for. It'd probably be a relief for her not to have to work so hard at citifyin' me anymore."

"You wouldn't want to live . . . *here,* would you?" Rita points to the big window next to the swing. She shivers a little despite the warm damp air.

He rubs his chin, leans to peer into the old window with the crack running across one corner. He pulls out his pocket knife and digs the blade into the window frame. "Wood's pretty rotten."

He looks up at the sky now dissolving into slate as the rain batters the porch roof.

"Lot of these old houses burn out," he goes on. "Lightnin' . . . them old coal grates. Never surprises anybody." He closes his eyes and takes in deep breaths. "I always enjoyed it when it stormed of a summer afternoon. Nice warm rain, washin' everything clean."

Over at the corner of the porch, water runs noisily from the roof and into a barrel. Rita thinks of home, where rain is always cool, even the summer. And there's never any rain in the summer anyway. "Yeah, it's a shame," Uncle Liam goes on. "Everything goes up in smoke. People start all over, forget about it in a year or two." She senses that he's waiting for her to look around, but when she does, he isn't watching her after all. "Why don't you go ahead and get in the jeep," he says. He nods toward the jeep again.

She gathers up shoes and purse and makes a run for the jeep across the slick mud that clings to her bare feet, leaving dry footprints that quickly fill in with more mud. Only after she manages to climb into the seat and hold her feet out, letting the rain wash off most of the mud, does she look back toward the house.

Uncle Liam walks calmly toward the jeep, stops to turn slowly, his hands outstretched, looking up into the rain, letting it flood his face and drench his clothes.

Her eyes catch a slight movement on the porch. Behind the sheets of runoff from the roof, behind the empty swing, the window turns to a curtain of bright flickering orange against the gray of the house and the sky.

Uncle Liam climbs into the driver's seat, ignoring his soaking wet clothes. He takes off his glasses and wipes the water from them.

"Wha— but—how—" Rita points at the house, shakes her head, but her mouth can't quite put two words together.

"I reckon we'd best be gettin' this jeep on down the road," Uncle Liam says. "When we stop for dinner we'll find a telephone and give your mama a call long-distance, tell her we're on our way home. Should be there by Sunday evenin', with two of us drivin'." He glances at her stuff behind the seat, her suitcase and the old ghost of a radio, and he grins. "You *was* plannin' on goin' back with me, wasn't you?"

"Uh ... sure ... but ... " Her finger is still jabbing at the air in the direction of the house. Smoke billows from the window and through the open front door.

Uncle Liam turns his face lazily toward the house, scratches the back of his head. "Well, I'll be danged. Somebody must've knocked over a coal oil lamp in there." He starts the jeep engine. "Well."

"Oh, yeah," he goes on, pulling the wet photograph out of his shirt pocket and handing it to Rita. "You take this home with you. It belongs to your mama. I gave it to her once before. You tell her to hang onto it this time and don't lose it. It's family."

ॐ

Joy is a Kentucky native who lives in Northern California with her teacher /photographer husband, Tom. Her genealogy search takes her back to visit her Kentucky cousins often. Joy and Tom plan to retire there as soon as they can convince children and grandchildren to tag along.

Other than making dry mudprints, eating snowcream, picking blackberries and enjoying peach juice running down her arm on a warm summer's day, Joy swears nothing in this work of fiction actually happened to her. Really. But she's sure it has happened in *some* family tree, to *some*one, *some*time, *some*where. Maybe even hers. Maybe yours.